"I have no choice but to help Grelun and his people," Zweller said. "And all I ask is that you keep an open mind."

They came to a stop before a partially demolished wall. The squat ruin offered them some small respite from the raging winds. Zweller watched as Riker's boyish face changed, settling into hard planes and angles. An aurora crackled far overhead, like an electrical arc jumping between the uprights of an old-fashioned Jacob's ladder.

Zweller handed the tricorder to Riker, who immediately began scanning the wall and the surrounding terrain. The dour-eyed guards stood by quietly while Riker pored over the readouts.

The wall bore a small humanoid silhouette. A child's shadow, rendered in a micrometer-thin layer of carbon atoms. Several other nearby structures bore similar marks.

Riker's mouth was moving. Lip-reading, Zweller thought he made out a "My God."

Zweller shouted into the wind. "Chiarosan weaponry isn't all ceremonial flatware, Commander. Especially among Ruardh's people."

Zweller paused, smiling mirthlessly before continuing. "Sometimes those folks use disruptors."

STAR TREK
THE NEXT GENERATION®

SECTION 31™

ROGUE

ANDY MANGELS
and
MICHAEL A. MARTIN

Based upon STAR TREK:
THE NEXT GENERATION®
created by Gene Roddenberry

POCKET BOOKS
New York   London   Toronto   Sydney   Singapore

This book is a work of fiction. Names, characters, places and incidents are products of the author's imagination or are used fictitiously. Any resemblance to actual events or locales or persons, living or dead, is entirely coincidental.

An *Original* Publication of POCKET BOOKS

POCKET BOOKS, a division of Simon & Schuster, Inc.
1230 Avenue of the Americas, New York, NY 10020

STAR TREK is a Registered Trademark of Paramount Pictures.

A VIACOM COMPANY

This book is published by Pocket Books, a division of Simon & Schuster, Inc., under exclusive license from Paramount Pictures.

ISBN: 0-671-77477-8

First Pocket Books printing June 2001

10 9 8 7 6 5 4 3 2 1

POCKET and colophon are registered trademarks of Simon & Schuster, Inc.

Printed in the U.S.A.

For the late Kimberly Yale. In a time when few editors in the comic world would work with an openly gay writer, she gave me my first *Star Trek* assignment. She is missed.

A.M.

To Jessie M. Martin (1924–1999). She had been looking forward to reading this book, but left us too soon.

M.A.M.

Everything that deceives may be said to enchant.

—Plato, *The Republik*, 329.

PROLOGUE

Stardate 50907.2

Population approximately nine billion . . . all Borg.

Picard's breath fogged the large window on his cabin wall, the moisture momentarily making the view of his homeworld indistinct and devoid of color. Even now, five days after they'd been uttered, Data's words reverberated through his mind as he once again relived that terrible moment on the bridge. On the main viewscreen had been an Earth altered beyond belief, its continents transformed into a bleak technological sprawl, its oceans dark, its atmosphere thin and gray. Caught in the temporal wake of a Borg sphere, Picard and his crew had seen with their own horrified eyes what the Borg had wrought by fleeing into Earth's past.

But the *Enterprise* had pursued them, and in so doing, stopped the Borg from assimilating Earth, and ensured the completion of humanity's historic first warp flight.

Picard closed his eyes and straightened his posture, moving his forehead off the back of his hand. His breath evaporated, and Earth was restored to its tranquil blue and white.

And now we're back in the present, Picard thought somberly. *Earth is as it was, at least as far as we know . . . although who really knows what effect our presence in the past—however carefully controlled and covered up—has had on* this *timeline?* He had told his crew that they were going back to repair whatever damage the Borg had done, but how much change had his own actions in the past had upon the present?

Picard didn't like thinking about the issues inherent in the temporal tampering, though the analytical portions of his mind had wandered there all too often in the last few days. If the *Enterprise* crew aided Zefram Cochrane's 21st-century voyage, hadn't they always been there in the mists of history, however unrecorded? And if the Borg had conquered Earth and had then been beaten back, hadn't that *always* occurred? Following Data's own theoretical ruminations on the topic, Picard had been forced to tell him to keep the subject to himself; he was tired of thinking about it.

Better than thinking about the alternative, the voice in the back of his head would tell him. Picard and his crew were already dealing with the direct consequences of their journey, and even though they had saved the future of mankind, the reward of that knowledge seemed to pale when stacked against the costs. It had taken La Forge and his engineers a couple of days to create a makeshift replacement for their lost navigational array, one capable of reproducing the effect that had allowed them to journey to the past in the first place. During that time, Will Riker and Worf had been busy rounding up the ASRV lifeboats that were jettisoned when Picard had initiated the *Enterprise's* autodestruct sequence.

Once that danger and Borg threat had been stopped, retrieving the nearly 200 escape pods had proven more challenging than his officers had expected; some had made it to Earth, some had lingered in orbit. Although about three-quarters of them had made it to the rendezvous point on Gravett Island in the South Pacific, crewmembers from some of the other autonomous survival and recovery vehicles had been grounded elsewhere—mostly due to Borg-related system glitches. Many of those had dispersed into the regions they landed in, some taking refuge in the wilderness in case of Borg pursuit, others trying their best to blend in with the ragged factions of postapocalypse humanity they encountered.

Most of the repairs to the *Enterprise* had to wait until the ship got to McKinley Station, where they were now docked. Most of the crew were still in the long queues for the starbase's massive medical complex; they had to be quarantined, scanned, and decontaminated, not only for any possible Borg infection, but for any viral or bacterial pathogens they may have picked up while in the past. It wouldn't do to release a 21st-century virus, whether natural or bioengineered, into the 24th century.

After being given clean bills of health, the crew would have some time off. How much time was unknown at this point. Engineering crews—all wearing biohazard containment suits—were scouring the ship, removing the self-replicating Borg technology from corridors and circuit panels and Jefferies tubes. Many of the ship's main systems would have to be repaired as well. Panels were off the walls, and circuitry was spread across the deckplates. *Only a year out in the* Enterprise-E *and we're already in need of a major overhaul,* thought Picard, his ruminations still dark.

Picard's own cabin was untouched, and, except for the occasionally malfunctioning environmental controls, it offered him a place of rest and solitude. He knew that the repair crews hadn't touched his ready room yet. He suspected that Riker had told them not to. It too had not been violated by the Borg or their technology, but the display case which had held models of the previous *Starships Enterprise* was still half-destroyed, smashed by the phaser rifle Picard had swung at the case during his fit of pique. *You broke your little ships,* the woman from the past had said. Lily Sloane had known that the battle against the Borg was too personal for him. But it wasn't until afterward, when he saw the wrecked models, that Picard had seen it too.

He heard a knock, and the door of his quarters swished halfway open before grinding to a halt. "Captain?" a voice questioned. Two strong hands pushed the door the rest of the way into its wall recess, and Picard turned, seeing a familiar face. Like the captain, Riker had hardly slept the last several days, and the bags under his eyes showed it.

"Rather a mess out there, wouldn't you say, Number One?" Picard asked, gesturing out the door, where work crews could be seen removing Borg conduit hoses from a ceiling duct.

"Yes, sir. From the reports I'm hearing, the Borg circuitry got farther into our systems than we realized. We're lucky we made it back in one piece," Riker said. He didn't need to add the words "this time."

Picard sat on his couch, gesturing for his first officer to sit opposite him. It was late, but until the Borg matter was completely concluded, Picard didn't mind Riker interrupting his all-too-rare quiet time. The padd his first officer carried hadn't escaped the captain's notice, and as much as Picard might not wish to face the duty it represented, he knew that he must. He owed it to them.

But not just yet.

"How is everyone coping?" he asked.

"Medically, most of the crew appears to be fine. Dr. Crusher and Nurse Ogawa were cleared very quickly, and they've been helping in the sickbays on McKinley. So far everyone's been in the clear. They're trying to process our people through the rest of the tests as quickly as possible. They've even got a dozen or so EMH programs running. I'm glad we aren't forced to use one of those on *our* ship very often. They don't quite have Beverly's bedside manner."

Picard crossed over and sat behind his desk, sinking into his chair. Riker continued. "Worf has to depart for Deep Space 9 as soon as possible, perhaps first thing in the morning. Things are getting very tense with the Dominion, and they need him back there. Chief O'Brien's going to have his hands full finishing the repairs on the *Defiant* that the McKinley techs started. Data's eye and skin have been repaired. And, understandably, Deanna's been especially busy since we returned; she's coping well with the workload . . . though she swears she'll never touch a drop of tequila again."

"Pardon?"

Riker grinned for perhaps the first time in days. "She got a little drunk down there with Cochrane, sir. But I can assure you it was purely in the line of duty."

"What was it like?" Picard asked suddenly, leaning forward. Riker looked at him quizzically. "The *Phoenix.* What was it like? I got to . . . I *touched* it, but you . . . you *rode* in it! You and Geordi were *part* of it. Mankind's first warp flight!"

Riker's demeanor loosened a bit, and he focused his eyes on the windows, out into space. "I don't know if I can describe it. I've never felt anything so unsettling since flight training at the Academy, and this was even worse. I wasn't sure that we weren't going to blow apart at any second, that the ship wasn't going to scatter me through space nearly three hundred years before I was even born. The whole time this song was playing, ear-splittingly loud, and my teeth were vibrating. And we saw the *Enterprise* out of the window and . . ."

Riker paused, as though collecting his thoughts. "We take it for granted, Jean-Luc." He rarely called the captain by his first name, but at this moment it seemed to come naturally. "We move among the stars every day at high warp, surrounded by all the comforts of a posh hotel. But being there, jammed into that little cockpit, with my teeth chattering and my ears ringing as we just barely made warp one . . . It was the fastest I've ever moved in my life."

The two officers sat in silence then, Riker staring into the darkness of space, Picard closing his eyes and clasping his hands together.

After a brief time, Riker sniffed, and wiped at his nose. Picard opened his eyes again, as Riker cleared his throat. "Geordi is working with the McKinley crews on cleanup, but I'm going to have to order him to take some down time. Barclay is . . . well, I think Barclay may be asking for a transfer off the ship. He seems ill-at-ease with everything that's happened. You know how he is with people, anyhow. I think he may just want to take on a less exciting atmosphere for a while."

Picard's mouth pursed into a grim smile. "There are times when I think that might be the best choice myself."

Riker hesitated, then handed the padd to his captain. He didn't seem to want to acknowledge its contents; neither did Picard. "This is the final casualty report. We lost seventeen back on Earth from the ASRV landings. One hundred and forty-eight crewpersons were assimilated by the Borg. All of them are now dead. Those that weren't killed in combat—or as a consequence of the plasma coolant that flooded engineering—apparently couldn't survive the death of the queen."

Picard nodded without speaking, remembering the malfunctioning drones who fell around him and the hideous sight of the mottle-skinned woman dissolving before his eyes.

"Do you think we've seen the last of the Borg? Now that their queen is dead?"

Picard sighed heavily. "We can always hope. But I don't think so, Number One."

Riker continued his oral report. "The bodies of those who were assimilated have been quarantined to the Borg Sciences unit for study. Finally, twenty-five people were killed in combat against Borg drones. Total loss: one hundred-ninety crewmembers."

Picard looked down at the padd in his hand, frowning. The names scrolled by slowly, in no particular order. *Carter, Lynch, Batson, Nelson, Eiger, M'Rvyn, Tret, Kewlan, Rixa, Porter* . . . all of them dead. Not just dead, but assimilated, *then* dead. They couldn't even be properly buried until they had been taken apart by Starfleet scientists. And given some of the secrets which he knew some subsections of Starfleet were capable of holding, Picard wasn't even sure that the crewmembers' families would *ever* receive their kin's remains.

As if to underscore this thought, the padd scrolled down to another name. *Hawk, Sean Liam (Lieutenant).* He, too, knew about some of Starfleet's darkest secrets. Or rather *had* known.

"Were we able to recover Lieutenant Hawk's body?" Picard asked, almost too softly for Riker to hear.

"No, sir. We're assuming that it stayed in low Earth orbit for some time after we left 2063. Data thinks that atmospheric drag would have brought it down eventually. It . . . would have burned up then."

Picard shut his eyes tightly, remembering the scene. He, Worf, and Hawk had all been in their environmental suits, their magnetized boots allowing them to traverse the ventral side of the *Enterprise*'s hull. They had just about freed the maglock servo clamps for the particle emitter dish—in their attempt to stop the Borg from using it as an interplexing beacon to summon other Borg cubes—when Hawk was caught by a Borg drone. Shortly thereafter, with Borg nanoprobes creeping through his bloodstream, controlling him and necrotizing his flesh, Hawk had tried to stop Picard from completing the command sequence to free the final clamp. Worf had then blasted Hawk with his phaser rifle, sending the young lieutenant tumbling away into the void of space.

Picard remembered the look on Hawk's face, as the last vestiges of his humanity fought against the Borg nanoprobes coursing through him.

Even if Hawk had burned up in the atmosphere, Picard doubted that that was what had ended his life. Assuming that Worf's phaser blast hadn't killed him, the lieutenant had most likely suffocated in his environment suit, frightened and alone as his humanity was torn from him. Picard shuddered. He knew what it was like to have his consciousness subsumed within the hive mind of the collective. After the Borg queen had been destroyed, what then? What had Hawk thought in the last few hours of his life, separated from both humanity and the collective?

"Damn," said Picard softly, putting the padd down on the table. Riker stood and leaned forward, momentarily putting a supportive hand on his captain's shoulder, and then exited the room without a word.

The padd blinked. *Hawk, Sean Liam (Lieutenant). Hawk, Sean Liam (Lieutenant).*

Such a loss. So enthusiastic and passionate. So much promise . . .

Hawk had been on the ship slightly less than a year, transferring with a group of others onto the newly commissioned *Enterprise-E.* It didn't take long for him to be assigned to the conn during alpha watch. He was bright and fast, and well-liked by all. He had said how pleased he was to serve aboard Starfleet's flagship, which he considered a special honor since he was only a few years out of the Academy. But that time had been long enough for Hawk to forge a personal relationship with a man whom he loved, long enough for him to rise in the ranks, long enough for him to reach his own personal crossroad.

Everyone eventually reaches a crossroad, if he lives long enough. Six months ago, Lieutenant Hawk had reached his.

Chapter One

Stardate 50368.0

The coffee cup suffused Captain Karen Blaylock's hands with a cheery warmth as she strode purposefully onto the bridge of her ship, the *Excelsior*-class starship *Slayton*. Though the alpha watch wasn't due to begin for another ten minutes, she wasn't at all surprised to see several key bridge officers already hard at work at their consoles, which hummed and beeped agreeably.

Commander Ernst Roget, her executive officer, turned toward her in the command chair and favored her with a reserved smile. "Captain on the bridge," he said, vacating the seat for her.

Heads turned toward Blaylock, distracted momentarily from their vigilance. These were good officers, science and engineering specialists all, and she hated allowing command protocol to interfere with their work, even momentarily. She often envied them their single-minded dedication to discovery. How ironic, she

thought, to have allowed her command responsibilities
to come between her and the very thing that had brought
her out to the galactic hinterlands in the first place: the
pursuit of pure knowledge.

Blaylock nodded a silent *as you were,* and each
crewmember quickly returned to the work at hand. She
took her seat and sipped her coffee.

Commander Cortin Zweller approached Blaylock
from the science station on the bridge's starboard side.
His thick shock of white hair was belied by the boyish
twinkle in his eye. During the nearly four months he had
served as chief science officer, he had proven to be a
valuable member of the *Slayton* team. Though by no
means a brilliant researcher, Zweller was well-liked by
the other science specialists, an administrator apparently
gifted with the good sense not to step on the toes of his
better-trained subordinates—unless absolutely necessary.

"The anomaly still seems to be hiding from us,"
Zweller said. "So far, at least."

Blaylock sighed, disappointed. The *Slayton* had last
made long-range sensor contact with the subspace anomaly eight days previously, but had turned up nothing
since. Several weeks before that, the Federation's Argus
Array subspace observatory had detected intermittent but
extremely powerful waves of subspace distortion that
seemed to be coming from the region of space for which
the *Slayton* was now headed. Unfortunately, the phenomenon had neither lasted long enough—nor repeated
itself regularly enough—to reveal much else.

How wonderful it would have been, Blaylock reflected, to have discovered an entirely new physical
phenomenon while en route to a dreary diplomatic appointment on gods-forsaken Chiaros IV. But Blaylock
knew it would be just her luck for the anomaly to re-

turn briefly—and then vanish forever—while she and her crew were preoccupied with the tedium of galactic politics.

The captain turned toward Lieutenant Glebuk, the Antedean helmsman. In the year since Glebuk had come aboard, Blaylock had assiduously avoided asking the galley replicators to create sushi, one of her favorite foods. Glebuk, who was essentially a two-meter-tall humanoid fish, was notably edgy about such things.

Like most of her kind, Glebuk would have found the rigors of interstellar travel intolerable but for the effects of the cortical stimulator she wore on her neck. Its constant output of vertigo-nullifying neural impulses kept her from lapsing into a self-protective catatonic state during long space voyages. Despite this handicap—or perhaps because of it—Glebuk was one of the best helm officers Blaylock had ever worked with.

"What's our present ETA at the Chiaros system?" Blaylock asked Glebuk.

The helmsman fixed an unblinking, monocular gaze on the captain and whispered into the tiny universal translator mounted in the collar of her hydration suit, "The *Slayton* will reach the precise center of the Gulf in approximately fifty-three minutes. We will arrive at the fringes of the Chiaros system some six minutes later."

Blaylock nodded. *Almost the precise center of the Geminus Gulf,* she thought with a tinge of awe. *Three wide, nearly empty sectors. Sixty light-years across, all together. Nearly two weeks travel time at maximum warp.* Even after a decade of starship command, she found it hard to wrap her mind around such enormous distances.

During the long voyage into the Gulf, Blaylock had had plenty of time to familiarize herself with the region. More than enough time, actually, since so little was actually known about it, other than its size, location, and strategic significance—or rather its lack thereof. It *was* well-known, however, that most of its sparse stellar population were not of the spectral types associated with habitable worlds. In the Geminus Gulf, young supergiant "O" type stars predominated—the sort of suns whose huge mass blows them apart only a few hundred million years into their lifespans—rather than the cooler, more stable variety, such as the "G" type star that sired Earth and its immediate planetary neighbors.

But the Geminus Gulf was important in at least one respect; it lay just outside the boundaries of both the Federation and the Romulan Star Empire, and it had yet to come formally into the sphere of influence of either power. Nearly smack in the center of the Gulf's unexplored vastness lay one inhabited world, the fourth planet of the politically nonaligned Chiaros system. Under recently negotiated agreements, neither the Federation nor the Romulans could establish a permanent presence in the Gulf until invited to do so by a spacefaring civilization native to the Gulf. Blaylock was only too aware that her job was to do everything the Prime Directive would allow to obtain that invitation from the Chiarosans, who comprised the only warp-capable culture yet known in the Gulf, and thus were the key to the entire region, and to whatever awaited discovery within its confines.

Never mind that there isn't any there *there,* Blaylock thought, absurdly reminded of the 20th-century human writer Gertrude Stein's often-mischaracterized description of an empty region on Earth.

Settling back into her chair, Blaylock smiled to herself. She had already reviewed the Chiarosan government's preliminary application for Federation membership. Less than two weeks from now, the planet's general population would formally vote on whether to invite in the Romulans or the Federation. Fortunately, since the pro-Federation position was being staunchly backed by the planet's extremely popular ruling regime, it seemed to Blaylock that her mission was already all but accomplished.

Blaylock therefore felt amply justified in allowing her thoughts to return to the matter of the mysterious subspace distortions—and their possible causes. Now that they had piqued her curiosity, she couldn't bear the thought of leaving the bridge for a diplomatic conference whose results were already foreordained.

"Just how important is the captain's presence at this conference?" Blaylock said, turning toward Roget.

Seated in the chair beside Blaylock's, Roget leaned forward, his mahogany-colored brow wrinkled in evident confusion. "It's crucial, Captain. The natives of Chiaros IV are a warrior people. If you're not there, they're likely to take offense."

Her exec's discomfiture brought a small smile to her lips. "Don't panic, Ernie. I'm not planning on going AWOL. What I mean is, how important is it that the captain be present with the first away team?"

Roget appeared to relax at that. Stroking his jaw, he said, "It's not critical, I suppose. You have to remember, though, that the Chiarosans are very hierarchical and protocol-conscious."

"So I noticed," Blaylock said. "They've planned just about every minute of our itinerary while we're on their planet. And we won't even meet First Protector Ruardh until our third day on the planet. It's all just lower-level functionaries until then."

" 'When in Rome,' Captain," Roget said.

"I agree. Therefore I've decided I'm staying aboard

the *Slayton* until you finish up the preliminary business with the first away team. That'll give me at least another full day here on the bridge before I have to join you down on the planet."

Roget smiled knowingly. "You want to keep looking for those subspace distortions yourself."

Blaylock didn't smile back. Roget needed to know that she was deadly serious. "There's more at stake here than my scientific curiosity. We already know that the Romulans will have a delegation on Chiaros."

"That's unavoidable, unfortunately, under the treaties." Roget, too, was no longer smiling.

"Wherever you find Romulan diplomats, you'll probably also find a cloaked Romulan ship nearby—*certainly* up to no good."

Roget regarded her with a silent scowl. He was giving her *the look* again. She knew that he had to be thinking, *a cloaked Romulan ship that causes intermittent subspace distortions that can be picked up five sectors away?* Fortunately, Roget was not one to question her orders in front of the crew.

Until I find out the answer, she told herself, *I'll be damned if I'm off this ship one second longer than I absolutely have to be.*

At that moment, Zweller rose from his station and faced Blaylock, an eager expression on his face. Though he was in his sixties, his unbridled enthusiasm made him appear much younger.

"Captain?"

"Yes, Mr. Zweller?"

"If it's all right with you and Commander Roget, I'd like to be part of the first away team. From what I've read about Chiaros IV, the place could keep a dozen science officers busy for years."

16

Blaylock looked toward her exec, who nodded his approval. She turned the matter over in her mind for a moment, then rose from her chair and regarded Zweller approvingly. She liked officers who weren't afraid to show a little initiative.

"All right, Mr. Zweller. Assemble a few of the department heads in the shuttlebay at 0800 tomorrow. You and Commander Roget will oversee the opening diplomatic ceremonies."

Zweller thanked Blaylock, then returned to his station to contact his key subordinates. She had no doubt that Chiaros IV would more than justify his scientific curiosity. For a moment, she regretted her decision not to lead the first away team.

But she had a mystery to solve, and a ship to worry about. *Needs must,* Blaylock thought, *when the devil drives. Or the Romulans.*

Sitting beside Roget in the cockpit of the shuttlecraft *Archimedes,* Zweller finished his portion of the preflight systems checks in less than five minutes. The eight-person craft was ready for takeoff even as the heads of the biomedical science, planetary studies, xenoanthropology, and engineering departments took their seats.

At Roget's command, the triple-layered duranium hangar doors opened, accentuating the faint blue glow of the shuttlebay's atmospheric forcefield. The shuttle rose on its antigravs, moved gently forward, and accelerated into the frigid vastness of space.

The perpetually sunward side of Chiaros IV suddenly loomed above the *Archimedes,* presenting a dazzling vista of ochers and browns. Gray, vaguely menacing clouds surged over the equatorial mountain ranges. High above the terminator separating eternal night from unending day, Zweller could see the glint of sunlight on metal—Chiaros IV's off-planet communications relay, tethered to the planet's narrow habitable zone by a network of impossibly slender-looking cables. Zweller noticed that the portion of the tether that plunged into the roiling atmosphere was surrounded by transitory flashes of light.

Lightning? he wondered, then looked more closely. *No, it's thruster fire. If the Chiarosans didn't compensate somehow for the motions of their turbulent atmosphere, that orbital tether wouldn't last ten minutes.*

Zweller took in this vista—the untamable planet as well as the tenacious efforts of the Chiarosans to subdue it—with unfeigned delight.

"Hail the Chiarosans, Mr. Zweller," Roget said, interrupting his reverie. Zweller complied, immediately all business once again. His hail was answered by a voice as deep as a canyon, which cleared the shuttlecraft to begin its descent into the churning atmosphere. The computer received the landing coordinates and projected a neat, elliptical course onto the central navigational display.

"A pity we can't just beam straight down to the capital," Roget said as the *Slayton* receded into the distance.

Andreas Hearn, the *Slayton*'s chief engineer, spoke up from directly behind Zweller. "Between the radiation output of the Chiarosan sun, the planet's intense magnetosphere, and the clash of hot and cold air masses down there, we can't even get a subspace signal down to the surface—at least not without the orbital tether relay. I wouldn't recommend trying to transport anyone directly through all that atmospheric hash."

"Oh, enough technical talk," said Gomp, the Tellarite chief medical officer, who was seated in the cabin's aftmost section. "I want to know what these people are really like. The only things I've seen so far are their official reports to the Federation. Medically speaking, all I can really say about them is that they're supposed to be triple-jointed and faster than Regulan eel-birds."

"Then I wouldn't recommend challenging them on the hoverball court," Hearn said with a chuckle.

The *Archimedes* entered the upper atmosphere. On the cockpit viewer, Zweller watched as an aurora reached across the planet's south pole with multicolored, phosphorescent fingers. Lightning split the clouds in the higher latitudes. Atmospheric friction increased, and an ionized plasma envelope began forming around the shuttle's hull.

"Gomp makes a good point," said xenoanthropologist Liz Kurlan, as though this didn't happen very often. "All we know about these people so far is what they *want* us to know."

"So we'll start filling in those gaps in our knowledge today," Roget said with a good-natured shrug. "That's why we're all here, isn't it?"

Sitting in silence, he moved his fingers with deliberate precision over the controls. Then the shuttle hastened its descent toward the rapidly approaching terminator, the demarcation line between the planet's endless frigid night and its ever-agitated, superheated sunward side.

On the *Slayton*'s bridge, Blaylock heard an uncharacteristic urgency enter Glebuk's voice. "Captain! The anomaly has reappeared!"

The bridge crew suddenly began moving in doubletime. Blaylock was on her feet in an instant. "Location!"

"Scanning," Glebuk said.

Ensign Burdick, the young man at the forward science station, beat the Antedean to the answer. "A massive subspace distortion wave-front has appeared . . . four-point-eight astronomical units south of the planet's orbital plane."

"Speed?"

"One-tenth light-speed in all directions. Speed is constant."

"Transfer the coordinates to the helm," Blaylock said.

"Coordinates received," acknowledged Glebuk.

"That's our heading, helmsman. Engage at warp factor two. Take us half an AU from the wave-front, then full stop. Close, but not too close. On my mark, get the hell away at maximum warp."

"Aye," Glebuk said, altering the ship's speed and direction. Blaylock could feel the slight telltale vibration in the deckplates.

"Ensign Burdick, record everything you can about those subspace distortions," Blaylock barked, then whirled toward the tall, dark-tressed woman who was working the aft communications station. "Lieutenant Harding, try to raise the *Archimedes*."

Precisely sixteen seconds later, the *Slayton* had come to a full stop at a safe distance from the slowly-expanding subspace effect. On the forward viewer, the starfield rippled slightly, as though attached to a curtain being blown by a strong wind.

"No contact with the *Archimedes*, Captain," Harding said. "They must have already entered Chiaros IV's atmosphere."

"Captain!" Burdick suddenly cried out from the science station, getting Blaylock's full attention. "The wave-front's speed has just increased almost a hundredfold!"

How can that be? Blaylock thought in the space of a heartbeat. *Unless the phenomenon has begun dropping in and out of normal space, gaining velocity from subspace . . .*

She wasted no time. "Raise shields!" she shouted. "Glebuk, get us out of—"

The wave-front struck at that moment, instantly overwhelming the *Slayton*'s inertial dampers. The bridge went dark and the deck lurched sideways, throwing Blaylock from her feet. Her body slammed hard into a railing, which she grabbed with both arms. She felt at least one of her ribs give way under the impact. A portside panel exploded in a bright shower of sparks, leaving tracers of light behind her eyelids. She heard a sharp scream cut through the alarm klaxons, then cease.

The emergency lighting kicked in, casting an eerie, blood-colored pall across the bridge. The deck leveled itself. Smoke billowed from a burning panel. Bodies lay sprawled everywhere, some moving, some not. The bridge viewer was dead. Blaylock noticed that Glebuk had been hurled forward over the helm console and onto the deck. The Antedean lay still, water seeping from a tear in her hydration suit, her neck bent into an impossible question-mark shape. Fighting down a surge of horror, Blaylock sat behind the helm console.

The controls resolutely refused to respond. What the hell was she dealing with here?

Blaylock spun her chair toward Burdick, whom Harding was helping back into his seat. Blood surged into the ensign's eyes from a gash on his forehead.

"Status report!" Blaylock snapped.

Harding, the more experienced officer, began consulting a nearby undamaged instrument panel. "The shields are down. We've got hull breaches all over the place and we're down to battery power."

"I need to see what's out there. Can you get that screen working, Lieutenant?"

"I'm on it." Harding tapped a console at a furious pace.

The bridge lights dimmed. "Try not to lose the mood lighting, Zaena," Blaylock said. Harding smiled weakly in response.

The viewer came to life in a brief burst of static. Stars shone whitely, no longer distorted by the subspace phenomenon. And something else was there as well. A shape . . .

"Can you increase the magnification?" Blaylock said.

Harding nodded. The lights dimmed further and the half-seen shape resolved itself into lines of hard metal. It was a large, toroid-shaped ship—or perhaps it was a space station—circled by dozens, or perhaps hundreds, of much smaller objects. Buoys? Service modules of some sort?

"Why didn't we notice all of this when we entered the system?" Blaylock said, turning toward Burdick and Harding.

Blaylock saw that Burdick's eyes were glued to the screen. Pointing a shaking finger, he said, "Maybe because *they* didn't want us to?"

Blaylock was unsurprised to see the ominous, double-bladed shape of a Romulan warbird rippling into existence on the viewer. *I hate being right all the time,* she thought mirthlessly.

The *Slayton* had to be well within the range of the de-cloaking warship's weapons. The Romulan vessel was more than twice the *Slayton*'s size, and her disruptor ports glowed with menace. And the *Slayton* was dead in space.

But Blaylock told herself that the warbird's captain wouldn't harbor any hostile intent. With so little really known about the Geminus Gulf, why would the Romulans want to risk starting a war over it?

Then the warbird fired.

The *Slayton* lurched again, and the lights failed once

more. Blaylock wondered how long it would take for the warp core to lose antimatter containment. And just what it was the Romulans knew about this place that she didn't.

The bridge flared into cerulean brilliance a moment later, followed immediately by more blackness. This time, the dark was absolute and eternal.

The *Archimedes* continued its descent through Chiaros IV's storm-tossed Dayside atmosphere. Zweller ignored the low conversational murmurs passing between the department heads and concentrated on his piloting chores. Though the inertial dampers succeeded in canceling out most of the turbulence, Zweller could still feel the deck shimmying slightly beneath his boots. And the structural integrity field was being taxed far more than usual.

Adjusting the viewer to compensate for the ball of white-hot plasma that now completely surrounded the shuttle's hull, Zweller quietly admired the savage beauty of the landscape quickly scrolling by below. It was a place of immiscible contrasts, irresistible forces in perpetual stalemate. It was a place he could understand.

As the *Archimedes* entered the nightward terminator, Zweller reduced the craft's velocity, lowering the hull temperature and making the plasma fires gutter out. He brought the shuttle down toward a range of cheerless brown mountains and arced into a northeasterly heading. In seconds, the craft cleared the peaks, and the relentlessly baked Dayside gave way to a fog-shrouded valley. Auroral flashes arced repeatedly across the sky, leaping the planet's everlasting twilight belt, momentarily linking day with night. The vapor dispersed as the ground grew nearer and unveiled a quiltwork of hardscrabble farmland and narrow roads. Small settlements and isolated dwellings hove into view and just as quickly passed away. A great cityscape glittered in the haze, barely perceptible on the northern horizon. It appeared to fade toward a tumble of dry hills and barren escarpments that extended into the planet's dark side as far as Zweller could see. Lights twinkled across the city's remote nightward periphery.

"Looks like we've found the planet's single worthwhile piece of real estate," Gomp said with a porcine chortle.

Finishing a long countdown in his head, Zweller thought: *It's time.*

An alarm light suddenly flashed on Zweller's console, and a klaxon brayed a warning. The tactical display at Zweller's left side came to life.

"What is it?" Roget said, sounding cautious, though not particularly alarmed.

"I think we're about to have some company," said Zweller.

"A Chiarosan honor guard?" Hearn ventured.

Zweller felt his jaw clenching involuntarily. "I . . . I don't think so."

"Shields up!" Roget shouted. "Red alert!"

Something struck the shuttle at that moment, making the hull reverberate like an enormous bell. The engineer and the doctor fell into a heap atop Liz Kurlan. Tim Tuohy, the head of planetary studies, helped Gomp get his hooves beneath him. Everyone scrambled back into their seats and activated the crash harnesses.

The shuttle rocked again, more violently than before, as though punched by a giant. His harness kept Zweller from being spilled from his seat. Though partly obscured by static, the tactical display showed a fast-approaching trio of small, aggressively contoured vessels. They appeared to be fighter craft of an unusual configuration. Zweller recognized them as Chiarosan.

"Status!" Roget shouted, trying to compete with the rumbling of the hull.

"Shields and weapons are off-line," Zweller said. "I can't keep anything working with all this atmospheric ionization."

A static-swept male voice, deep and harsh, emanated from the comm system. "Federation shuttle: You will follow our lead vessel's navigation beam into Nightside. Consider yourselves our prisoners."

Roget spat a nearly inaudible curse before replying. "We are here on a diplomatic mission at the invitation of First Protector Ruardh, the head of this world's duly elected government. On whose authority have you attacked us?"

"Had we *attacked* you, you would be dead," came the reply. "You are in the custody of the Army of Light. If you attempt to resist or flee, we will not hesitate to destroy your vessel."

Roget made a slashing gesture, and Zweller responded by temporarily interrupting the audio.

"Make best speed for the capital, Mr. Zweller," Roget said. "There are bound to be official patrols there who can drive these characters off."

Zweller shook his head emphatically. "They're right on top of us, sir. We'll never make it."

The shuttle lurched again and the hull braces groaned. Zweller watched the structural integrity telltale dip into the red. *A near-miss,* Zweller thought; a direct hit probably would have breached the hull and blown everyone out of the shuttle. The lights flickered as the battery-powered backup life-support system kicked in.

Roget's frown could have curdled milk. "You don't seem to be trying very goddamned hard, mister."

Raising an eyebrow, Zweller ignored the comment. "I

don't think our welcoming committee enjoys being kept waiting, sir."

After pausing to glare at Zweller, Roget tapped a command into the console, relinquishing control of the shuttle's navigational computer to their captors. He turned toward the somber group in the seats behind him.

"Looks like we're taking an unscheduled detour, folks."

"Never a cop around when you need one," Gomp muttered. Nobody laughed.

The *Archimedes* abruptly banked and descended even farther. The shuttle barely cleared the hills beyond the sprawling city's nightward side as she continued into utter blackness, flanked by her "escorts."

Chiaros IV had no natural satellites and possessed a thick cloud canopy, conditions that made Nightside quite dark, except when the clouds were riven by lightning and auroral fireworks. The *Archimedes'* trajectory, however, stayed mostly within the swirls of the clouds blown in from Dayside, cover that made the auroras—and therefore the ground—difficult to see from the shuttle's windows. The few flashes of light that did enter the cabin merely served to prevent the crew's eyes from adjusting to the darkness. To the hapless occupants of the *Archimedes*, Nightside appeared more tenebrous than the inside of any tomb.

After crossing the terminator into night, the *Archimedes* flew for more than an hour, changing directions sharply several times, banking and spiraling. Whether because of atmospheric effects or damage sustained in the attack, the onboard instruments couldn't determine the shuttle's location or even its altitude. Sitting behind his useless control panel, Zweller realized that he might as well have been blindfolded.

Roget and the department heads somberly discussed their options, including whether or not they ought to open the weapons locker and put up some real resistance after landing. Though Gomp was the loudest proponent of the "stand-and-fight" notion, Zweller suspected that it was all rhetoric; he'd never met a Tellarite who didn't prefer a loud, abusive argument to actual combat. After everyone had spoken his piece, Roget announced that they were to forget about fighting their way out of this situation; after all, they had come to conduct diplomacy, not warfare.

They received a hail, and the crew cabin fell silent. "Prepare to land," said the harsh voice of their captor over the background of static.

A pattern of lights appeared on the ground, perhaps a quarter of a kilometer below the shuttle. Roget tried to turn the landing over to the computer, but it again failed to respond. Zweller tripped the manual override and began bringing the craft down, aiming for the center of the landing pattern.

A moment after the shuttle came to rest, the ground itself began to sink. Enormous mechanisms groaned as the surface beneath the shuttle lowered into a dimly illuminated subterranean chamber. Zweller watched on the viewer as a metal roof quickly rolled into place about eight meters overhead, shutting out what could be seen of the obsidian sky.

"I'll bet this place is completely invisible from the air," Gomp said, sounding impressed. "Very neat."

A bank of bright lights flared to life along the chamber's ceiling, revealing its enormous size. Several small fighter craft of the same type as their attackers were parked nearby. Perhaps twenty large, armed humanoids were taking up positions surrounding the *Archimedes*.

Kurlan and Tuohy both gazed significantly at the weapons locker, and then back at Roget, as if to say, *This is our last chance.*

"No phasers," Roget reiterated, and the rest of the human officers nodded their assent. Gomp spat a monosyllabic Tellarite curse.

Roget fixed a steely gaze on Zweller, but Zweller met it unblinkingly. "Commander Zweller and I will go out first," Roget said. "Unarmed."

Hearn opened the shuttle's hatch manually, then stepped aside. Roget walked through it to meet their captors. Zweller followed, the planet's slightly higher-than-Earth-normal gravity making his feet feel leaden.

From what Zweller knew of Chiarosans, the soldiers of the Army of Light were fairly typical representatives of the species. A robust people, none of them were shorter than two meters. Zweller was immediately struck by the strangeness of their eyes, which were the color of iridescent cobalt, and had an almost crystalline appearance. Though broad in the shoulders, the Chiarosans were whipcord lean, their bare arms striated with muscles like steel cables, and half-covered with a fine, brown fur. The hairless portions of their skins resembled burnished copper, and shined almost as brightly as the long, curved blades that hung from the sashes of their gray uniforms. Their obvious strength was complemented by a fluid grace of motion, as though their musculoskeletal systems were capable of an impossibly wide range of motion.

If one of these guys had helped us against those Nausicaans back in '27, old Johnny Picard never would have needed that artificial heart.

The troops wasted no time escorting everyone off of the shuttle. After taking the Starfleet officers' combadges and searching them for weapons—as well as confiscating the phasers they had left aboard the *Archimedes*—the Chiarosans manacled the wrists of each of their six captives. The soldiers then frog-marched them out of the hangar complex, down a lengthy, narrow corridor, and then into a second large chamber. Several slim ceiling-mounted illumination panels bathed the room in a dull white light. Zweller's gaze took in the room's bare stone walls and floor, which were adorned with edged weapons, as well as paintings and sculptures depicting what must have been important battles and revered war heroes from the annals of Chiarosan history.

A pair of bare-chested Chiarosan males faced one another in the center of the room, neither of them acknowledging the presence of the Starfleet prisoners. The larger and more striking of the pair was yellow-haired; the smaller, darker Chiarosan appeared no less formidable, however. Both of them held long, curved blades in each of their hands, and were in the midst of sparring, their graceful, triple-jointed movements reminding Zweller of Japanese *kata*. Their limbs moved with unbelievable control and precision, almost faster than the eye could follow. Though their weapons clanged together forcefully, often striking sparks, both men obviously were exerting tremendous discipline over both blade and sinew. It occurred to Zweller that the trio of guards standing behind them were largely superfluous, present only to provide additional intimidation.

Stepping inside the guard of the darker, smaller swordsman, the yellow-haired fighter suddenly trapped his opponent's thick neck between his blades. Though both men abruptly froze in place, Zweller half-expected the victor to snip the other man's head off, like a gardener trimming a shrub. Instead, the winner sheathed his blades after a moment, and the other man followed suit. The fighters bowed to one another.

Shaking perspiration from his abundant hair, the winner of the contest turned toward the Starfleet contingent. The Chiarosan's head made the motion first, turning almost 180 degrees before the rest of his body followed. He greeted his "guests" with a smile made eerie by his preternaturally wide mouth and his razor-sharp, silver-hued teeth.

"Clear water and rich soil to you, my guests," he said in heavily accented but intelligible Federation Standard. "Please allow me to thank you for coming among us."

"You didn't give us a great deal of choice in the matter," Roget said, his face an impassive mask.

The blond Chiarosan chuckled. His sparring partner merely stared belligerently at the captured officers.

"My name is Falhain, and I command the Army of Light," the yellow-haired Chiarosan said. "Allow me to introduce Grelun, my Good Right Hand."

Zweller heard Gomp muttering behind him. "And here I am without my dress uniform."

"Shut the hell up, Gomp," Tuohy hissed. Sullenly, Gomp complied.

Fortunately, Falhain appeared to be ignoring everyone except for Zweller and Roget, perhaps sensing from their body language that they were the senior officers present. Or maybe, Zweller thought, the Chiarosan rebels are familiar with Starfleet rank insignia.

"As you may have gathered," Falhain said, "my people are having . . . difficulty accepting our government's plan to enter the Federation."

Zweller opened his mouth to reply, but Roget beat him to it. "Sir, abducting Federation citizens is hardly a constructive way to air your grievances."

"Desperate times prescribe desperate tactics," Grelun said, his eyes narrowing to slits.

Falhain nodded toward his lieutenant, then locked a humorless gaze upon Roget. "I will cut straight to the heart of our 'grievances,' as you so trivially characterize them: Ruardh, our world's 'duly elected leader,' leads a government of murderers."

Zweller tensed. His superiors had not included that information in his mission briefing.

"What are you talking about?" he said.

"I'm talking about unanimity, my honored guests," Falhain said. "The kind of unanimity that earns a planet Federation membership. My people are paying the price for that unanimity. With their lives."

"I'm afraid I don't understand," Roget said, shaking his head.

"I speak for many of the outlying tribes and clans—a tiny minority of this planet's population, to be sure—but a people who prize their tradition of independence. That independence is unpopular in the capital, where we are seen as little better than vermin who compete with the cities for water and arable land, which our world gives to no one in abundance."

"The Federation can help you resolve those problems, if you let us," Roget said. "Besides, your alternative is far worse. The Romulan Empire isn't likely to respect your people's independence."

Falhain laughed mirthlessly. "The Romulans have never frightened us. Nor have they ever tried to conquer us."

"We have nothing that they want," Grelun said.

"Maybe Ruardh and her ministers don't believe that,"

Zweller said. *After all, the Romulans always want* something.

"Perhaps," Falhain said. "But none of that matters.
What *does* matter is that the Federation has allied itself
with an ender-of-bloodlines."

His eyes as cold as a Nightside storm, Grelun addressed
Zweller. "For the past six years, Ruardh's people have been
trying to extinguish the clans, to increase the cities' share
of our scarce subsistence resources. At last count, this has
cost my people over 600,000 lives. Only a small fraction of
that number survive, to fight on and avenge the murdered."

"What is your word for it, human?" Falhain said to
Roget, who was blanching visibly. " 'Genocide?' "

Zweller swallowed hard, taking in the enormity of
Falhain's charges. If they were true, then how much
worse could Romulan rule actually be for these people?

"So now you're abducting noncombatants?" Roget said.

Falhain bared his teeth, making Zweller think of a
cornered animal. "Unlike Ruardh, we have at least confined our targets to those wearing uniforms. And as long
as the Army of Light answers to me, we will continue to
strike only at the guilty."

"We are even prepared to listen to Ruardh's honeyed
words of peace," Grelun said with a sneer, his anthracite-
hard gaze engaging Falhain's. "Even though doing so
may well be an exercise in futility."

Moving too quickly to see, Falhain's hands flew to the
hafts of his blades, making plain his intended response
to any further challenge to his authority. Grelun remained as still as a statue for several protracted heartbeats, then backed slowly away. But Zweller could see
that fire still burned in the dark-haired warrior's eyes.

*Falhain won't be able to keep that Good Right Hand
of his tied behind his back forever.*

The rebel chieftain relaxed his posture and turned his cold gaze once again upon Roget and Zweller. "My people are not bandits, humans. But we *are* determined. We *will* achieve peace, either at the talking table . . . or with the sword."

Then Falhain brought his impossibly limber elbows quickly together, a motion that produced an alarmingly loud noise which was half whistle and half sandpaper rasp. Responding immediately, the guards hustled the sextet of Starfleet officers out of the room.

Zweller was the first to be separated from the others. Almost an hour after the meeting with Falhain had concluded, one of the guards escorted Zweller from a rock-walled holding cell and ushered him into a small, darkened office. A pneumatic door hissed shut behind him. Zweller was now unguarded, though still manacled. He approached the door through which he had entered. It remained solidly closed. Zweller guessed that the guard had locked it from the outside.

He heard a footfall behind him, and turned quickly toward the noise. "Lights," said an aristocratic male voice, and the chamber's illumination immediately rose to a faint twilight level.

A tall, ramrod-straight figure stepped into view from the shadows of an alcove. He had straight raven-black hair, combed forward, and the tips of his ears came to graceful points. His upswept eyebrows lent an air of expectation to his expression, as though he were a man accustomed to receiving satisfactory answers to his every question. He wore a gray-and-black Romulan military uniform, which was unadorned except for the emblem on his collar. The stylized sigil conjured for Zweller a mental image of a voracious, predatory bird.

Commander Cortin Zweller stood facing Koval, the chairman of the Tal Shiar, the Romulan Star Empire's much-feared intelligence bureau—an agency which even members of the Romulan Senate crossed only at their peril.

Zweller held his shackled hands up. Koval spoke a terse command to the computer on his desk. The manacles dropped to the floor and Zweller gently rubbed his wrists to restore their circulation.

"Mnek'nra brhon, Orrha," Zweller said, a phrase that meant "Good morning, Mr. Chairman," in the other man's language. Sometimes it was a good idea to remind an adversary that his secrets might not be as safe as he thinks—especially an adversary with whom one expects to do business.

Koval raised an eyebrow slightly, then replied in perfect Federation Standard. "Morning? An odd choice of words, Commander Zweller, considering where we are. But I must compliment you. Your accent is virtually undetectable. Section 31 trains its operatives well indeed." He bowed his head almost imperceptibly.

Zweller failed to suppress a wry smile. *Conversational Romulan 101,* he thought. Aloud, he offered, "All part of the service. And likewise, I'm sure."

"Then let us avoid any further irrelevancies and proceed directly to the business at hand."

"A moment, please," Zweller said, carefully holding the Romulan's gaze. "About my colleagues—"

Koval looked impatient for a fleeting moment. "Falhain is having each of them interrogated. They are being held separately. And as far as any of them know, you are receiving precisely the same treatment."

Zweller was relieved to learn that his cover wasn't blown, though he knew he would still have to mend his fences with Commander Roget. But even though Zweller appreciated Koval's professional courtesy, he knew it was never wise to mince words with a Romulan. Especially *this* Romulan.

"Thank you," Zweller said. "May I also presume I have your guarantee that they won't be injured or harmed in any way?"

Koval paused for a moment before responding. "You have my word. None of the officers we captured will suffer any injury while they are here." Though his eyes were dilithium-hard, the Romulan spymaster's expression was otherwise unreadable.

Then Koval moved on to other matters. "Now let us discuss our transaction. I am prepared to keep my part of that bargain. Are you?"

The list, Zweller thought. Who knew how many lives Section 31 would save by acquiring a list of Tal Shiar agents operating covertly not only within Starfleet, but also in civilian institutions across the Federation?

Zweller nodded. "Of course. With my help, Falhain and his troops will nudge the coming planetary vote on Federation membership to the side of the minority pro-Romulan factions. Then the Chiaros system will become a Romulan protectorate."

Koval nodded impassively. "I'm certain that my . . . indigenous clients will be delighted to accept your assistance."

Zweller kept thinking about the spy list. It would constitute a substantial countermeasure against Romulan espionage, even though the list would almost certainly be incomplete. Koval was no fool, after all. Still, the only cost to Section 31 would be the Geminus Gulf—a few worthless, backwater sectors of trackless interstellar desert. Zweller agreed with Section 31's higher echelons that they had struck a good bargain.

But still . . .

"I have to ask you, Mr. Chairman . . . Why do you *really* want this system?"

Koval seemed more annoyed by the question than surprised. Zweller doubted whether much of anything surprised him. "Simple survival, Commander. When a state's boundaries remain static, it will eventually die. Is that not reason enough?"

"If I may say so, the Geminus Gulf hardly seems worth the effort."

"I could reverse the question, Commander. After all, under our agreements, either *we* expand into the Gulf—or *you* do. Why should your benevolent Federation begrudge our expansion into an admittedly resource-poor region? A region which you yourself have called worthless?"

Koval's eyes flashed with a preacher's fervor as he continued. "Allow me to speak plainly, Commander. Whether you accept it or not, your Federation is as bent on conquest and assimilation as the Borg collective. Oh, you are quiet about it. You shroud your acquisitiveness behind lofty-sounding ideals: the vaunted civil rights of your citizens; your renowned respect and tolerance of other cultures; your so-called 'Prime Directive.'

"But your Federation has expanded greatly in every direction over the past century. One hundred and fifty worlds. Eight thousand light-years from border to border. And still you want more. What you cannot conquer with starships you take by subversion. You subtly change the cultures you encounter to suit yourselves. Your alliance with the Klingon Empire is a shining example, Commander. You've remade them in your own image." Koval allowed himself a brief smile. "Why, thanks to the Federation, the Klingons are practically *housebroken*."

Zweller chuckled, shaking his head. "I had no idea

you were such a political hard-liner, Mr. Chairman. I had hoped that you'd agreed to cooperate with us because you wished the Federation well."

Koval's only response was the small, fleeting smile that played at the corners of his mouth. Then he touched the emblem on his collar, activating a tiny communications unit. "Please inform Falhain that his presence is requested for a high-level briefing to be conducted with one of our . . . guests." A deep voice tersely acknowledged Koval's transmission.

Then, folding his hands behind his back, Koval spoke again to Zweller. "A wise man knows when it is best to allow his adversaries to speculate about his motivations."

And so does a good spy, Zweller thought.

As a single guard entered the room, no doubt to conduct him to the briefing, Zweller knew with certainty that he had just made a deal with the devil. He only hoped that, unlike Faust, he'd still have his soul after the bargain was complete.

Chapter Two

Captain's log, stardate 50390.8. Starfleet Command has dispatched the Enterprise *to Chiaros IV, the only known inhabited planet in the entirety of the Geminus Gulf—and a world whose future is now uncertain in the extreme. As the Chiarosan electorate prepares to vote on whether to pursue Federation membership or a formal alliance with the Romulan Empire, pro-Romulan guerrilla groups are attacking the planet's governmental institutions and civil infrastructure in order to further their cause. This volatile situation could lead to a bloody planetary civil war, disqualifying the Chiarosans for Federation membership—and thereby giving the Romulans control of the Geminus Gulf.*

My primary mission therefore is to assist the Chiarosan leader, First Protector Ruardh, in maintaining order and ensuring that the referendum on Federation membership proceeds freely and fairly.

While in the system, my crew will also make a thor-
ough search for the Federation starship Slayton,
which vanished near Chiaros IV a week ago on the
eve of its diplomatic mission there. I agree—

The ready room's door chime sounded, momentarily interrupting Jean-Luc Picard's train of thought. "Computer, pause log entry," he said. Shifting in his chair,
Picard addressed his visitor. "Come."

The doors parted with a pneumatic hiss, and a smiling
Will Riker entered the room. Picard gestured to one of
the chairs in front of the desk. "Have a seat, Number
One. I'll be finished updating my log in a moment."

As Riker sat, Picard resumed his dictation: "I agree
wholeheartedly with Starfleet's assessment that the only
way to assuage the unrest on Chiaros IV is to arrange a
negotiated settlement between the government and the
dissidents. However, because of my renowned lack of
experience in such matters, Starfleet Command is sending us a 'professional' diplomat—"

Picard paused again when he saw Riker's smile expand into an ear-to-ear grin. The captain responded with
a wry smile of his own. "Computer, pause log entry." To
his second-in-command, he said, "You're quite right,
Number One. That won't do at all."

"Computer, delete the last sentence."

The computer acknowledged, and Picard continued:
"To this end, Starfleet has given overall command of the
Chiarosan mission to . . . an expert in the field of inter-
stellar diplomacy.

"Computer, end entry."

Picard rose from his chair and straightened his tunic.
Riker got to his feet as well, his smile persisting. "We're
about to rendezvous with the *Thunderchild* to pick up

our 'expert diplomat,' Captain. Has Starfleet Command said yet who they're sending?"

"No," Picard said, frankly annoyed at that fact. "But it isn't the first time a starship captain has been left out of the loop."

Then he strode toward the door, which parted and admitted him onto the bridge.

"Activate viewer, Lieutenant Hawk," Picard said, settling into the center seat as Riker took up a position behind the duty station at his right. "Let's have a look at her."

Hawk's fingers sped nimbly across the helm console, his enthusiasm for his job apparent. The dark-haired young man reminded Picard of a decade-younger version of his first officer.

Counselor Troi was already seated at Picard's left. Her dark eyes were fixed on the sleek, catamaran-like image that had just taken shape on the viewer.

"The *U.S.S. Thunderchild,*" Picard said. "The new *Akira* class. One of Starfleet's latest designs."

"*Thunderchild,*" Troi repeated. "What a peculiar name."

Standing beside one of the starboard science consoles, Lieutenant Commander Data watched the approaching ship with evident appreciation. "Actually, the starship's nomenclature is an allusion to the imaginative literature of Earth's late nineteenth century. In *The War of the Worlds* by H. G. Wells, the *H.M.S. Thunderchild* was one of the vessels the British navy sent to fend off an invasion by hostile Martians."

Picard heard Hawk's quiet chuckle. He recalled then that Hawk had grown up on Mars.

"And how did the *Thunderchild*'s crew fare against these . . . Martians?" Troi asked Data, her eyes brimming with restrained amusement.

"They were . . . not entirely successful. However, the

literary genre in question was often prone to unfounded speculation, well into the twenty-first century. Many of these works contain an abundance of factual inaccuracies."

"Such as the existence of bloodthirsty, tentacled Martians," Riker deadpanned.

Data nodded. "Precisely, Commander."

Picard remembered *The War of the Worlds* well, having savored the Victorian tale of alien invasion several times during his boyhood in Labarre, France. He had reread it during his Starfleet Academy days, and again years later aboard the *Stargazer.* He could only hope that this latter-day *Thunderchild* would never face a crisis like the one that had beset her literary namesake.

"We are now within transporter range," Data said.

A tall, slender Skorr female, whose golden-feathered wings were closed unobtrusively behind her, swiveled from behind a communications console toward the bridge's center. "They're hailing us, Captain," the avian said.

"Thank you, Ensign Rixa," Picard said, rising to his feet. *"Thunderchild,* this is Captain Jean-Luc Picard of the *Enterprise."*

The image on the viewer shifted, displaying the *Thunderchild*'s bridge, where a half-dozen Starfleet officers busied themselves at various tasks. A uniformed human female, fiftyish, occupied the captain's chair. To her right sat a male humanoid of robust middle age, dressed in a high-collared, gray civilian suit. Picard could not recall ever having seen him before. Sitting at the captain's other side was a slightly built, silver-haired human woman, wearing Starfleet regalia and an admiral's pips.

Picard recognized her instantly. Had his heart not been artificial, it might have skipped a beat. He suddenly became aware of Troi watching him, her eyebrows slightly raised in an unspoken question.

"Captain Picard," the *Thunderchild*'s commander said. "I am Captain Evelyn Hoffman. Please allow me to introduce the Federation's special envoy, Ambassador Aubin Tabor."

The civilian beside Hoffman smiled and nodded in Picard's direction. He projected an air of authority that was just short of arrogance. When he spoke, his words were crisp and precisely measured.

"I am looking forward to working with you and your crew, Captain Picard."

Picard noticed the gray mottling at the man's temples, markings that identified him as a member of the telepathic Ullian species. He could now see a good reason for putting aside his initial umbrage at not having been selected to head up the Chiarosan diplomatic mission; having a true telepath in the thick of things might be a real boon to the coming negotiations.

"Likewise, Mr. Tabor," Picard said, bowing his head slightly.

"And this is Vice-Admiral Marta Batanides," Hoffman said as the silver-haired woman smiled and rose to her feet. Picard was struck by how little she had changed during the forty-odd years since they had exchanged their farewells at Starbase Earhart. Certainly, her hair color was different, her rank had advanced, and many small lines now framed her eyes. But those eyes and that winsome smile took him straight back to his hell-for-leather Academy days.

"Captain," she said simply. Though her tone was businesslike, her smile struck him as mischievous.

Picard's throat suddenly felt as dry as the desert on Lambda Paz. "Admiral. We'll beam you and the ambassador aboard as soon as you're ready."

"We are ready *now*, Captain," Tabor said, rising and

taking a step toward one of the turbolifts. "The sooner we get under way the better. And I would appreciate it if you would organize a briefing so that I can bring your senior staff up to speed on some of the difficulties we'll be facing. Say in thirty minutes?"

"Absolutely, Ambassador. In the meantime, my first officer will see that you are issued appropriate quarters."

Apparently satisfied, Tabor dismissed Picard with a nod, then strode toward the *Thunderchild*'s turbolift, with the admiral in tow. Captain Hoffman signed off, and the viewer once again displayed the other vessel. "I'll meet them in transporter room three," Riker said, then excused himself from the bridge as several beta-watch officers entered, their shifts about to begin.

Picard faced the helm. "Mr. Hawk, make best speed to Chiaros IV as soon as our guests are aboard."

"Aye, sir. ETA in approximately twenty-three hours."

"Mr. Data, you have the conn," Picard said as he walked back toward his ready room.

Marta, Picard thought. *Whatever have you been up to all these years?*

Even after the ready-room doors had closed behind him, he thought he could feel Troi's inquisitive gaze burning holes into the back of his head.

Awash in memories, Picard ran a finger along the model *Stargazer*'s warp nacelles when the ready-room door chime sounded once again.

"Come," Picard said, facing the door and straightening his uniform tunic with a quick tug. The doors hissed open and Vice-Admiral Marta Batanides entered.

The doors closed behind her. They were alone together. She smiled broadly. "Johnny. It's been a long time."

"Indeed it has, Marta," was all he could think of to say.

The admiral took a step toward him and extended her arms. "Don't tell me you can't spare a hug for an old friend."

He paused to look at her face. Even after all these years, she still had the same elfin, graceful quality he had found so endearing during their Academy days. But overlying that was a subtle toughness that only years of experience could bring. Somewhat awkwardly, he allowed himself to be drawn into a firm but chaste embrace.

They separated to arm's length moments later, and continued regarding one another in companionable silence. Like Picard, Batanides had graduated from the Academy class of '27, and despite the intensity of his subsequent experiences over the intervening decades, his thoughts often drifted back to those heady yet relatively carefree times, when cadets Jean-Luc Picard, Marta Batanides, and Cortin Zweller had been an inseparable team. Picard suspected that those days had left an equally strong imprint on Batanides. And although they had never been more than close friends, Picard knew that he would always wonder what he and Marta might have shared together had they both been less caught up in the exigencies of their duties.

And less afraid, he thought wistfully. *But that ship sailed long ago.*

"Would you like something to drink?" Picard said finally, breaking the long silence.

She grinned. "I'll have whatever you're having."

He rose, chuckling as he walked toward the replicator niche. "I'm afraid my tastes have become somewhat . . . tamer since we last saw one another. Computer, tea, Earl Grey, hot. Two cups." The replicator hummed as the beverages materialized.

Batanides seated herself in front of his desk as he set

44

down a pair of steaming cups. She accepted one and took a tentative sip.

Picard settled into his chair, holding his cup while its contents slowly cooled. "I couldn't help but notice that you've beaten me to the rank of admiral."

She laughed briefly, a pleasant, liquid sound. "It's not nearly as much fun as it looks, Jean-Luc. My advice? Don't be in too much of a hurry to get promoted."

"Believe me, I'm not," he said, tasting his tea. "I'm perfectly happy right here."

"You have a right to be," she said over the edge of her cup. "I've followed your career since we went our separate ways. You've made quite a mark for yourself. Rescuing that ambassador on Milika III. Your years aboard the *Stargazer.* And then commanding two Federation flagships after that. Pretty impressive."

He felt a surge of embarrassment. "I'm afraid I have a confession to make, Marta. I don't think I can encapsulate *your* career quite so readily."

Setting her cup down on the desk, she said, "Don't blame yourself for that, Johnny. When you work for Starfleet Intelligence, you try to keep a low profile."

Picard tried to hide his surprise, evidently without complete success. He could see that she noticed his reaction.

"Johnny?"

After a considered pause, he said, "Forgive me for saying so, Marta, but I'm not terribly enthusiastic about Starfleet Intelligence."

"Care to elaborate?"

"Three years ago, I became aware that your department had covered up an illegal cloaking device test. That incident nearly cost me the best first officer I ever had."

She nodded contritely. "The *Pegasus* affair. It came to light shortly before I made admiral. 'Ranar's folly,' we called it. It was a blot on the bureau's reputation, and won't be repeated. At least not as long as I'm wearing all these pips."

Though he knew he was unlikely ever to forget or forgive the *Pegasus* incident, Picard allowed his anger to subside. But he still had unanswered questions about the bureau and its agenda.

"Marta, I'd wager that your presence is proof that Starfleet Intelligence is more than a little interested in the Chiarosan situation. I have to wonder what they know that I don't. Perhaps the Geminus Gulf isn't so strategically worthless as the official reports seem to indicate?"

"That would make this whole business a lot simpler, wouldn't it?" she said, smiling ruefully. "But as far as Intelligence knows, you can take the Geminus Gulf at face value. It consists of one barely habitable inhabited planet, dozens of lifeless star systems, some fluky subspace readings that are probably just instrumentation errors, and about sixty-six thousand cubic parsecs of otherwise extraordinarily uninteresting space."

Picard wasn't quite satisfied with that. "Space in which the Romulans have nevertheless shown a distinct interest."

"For reasons which probably have more to do with Romulan misdirection than the Gulf's intrinsic value," she said with a shrug.

Picard mulled her words over for a moment. If she valued their mutual Academy days as much as he did—and as much as she appeared to—then he could assume that she was telling him the unvarnished truth. He decided to proceed from that assumption.

"Fair enough, Marta. You've eliminated the simple-but-incorrect answer. But what's the complicated-but-correct one?"

She cast a backward glance over her shoulder, as

though concerned that someone might overhear, then looked him straight in the eye. "We have reason to believe that the Chiarosan rebels are using Starfleet weapons. Weapons they may have obtained from the missing starship, the *Slayton*. And that may mean the ship met with foul play."

That took Picard aback for a moment. If the rebels really were using Starfleet matériel to carry out their guerrilla campaign, then the Federation could be inadvertently responsible for starting a planetary civil war. Such a development would surely warrant the attention of the highest echelons of Starfleet Intelligence.

But why would the bureau risk such an important officer by sending her into such a volatile situation?

"Forgive me for saying so, Marta," Picard said carefully. "But I still don't think you've told me everything."

She smiled a poker player's smile. "You're right. And I'm not at liberty to do that, as I'm sure you're well aware. But I can tell you this: Corey Zweller was the *Slayton*'s science officer."

Picard felt as though he'd been kicked in the stomach. He set his cup on the desk with an audible *clink* and struggled for calm. After collecting his thoughts for a moment, he said, "Marta, are you entirely certain that your interest in this matter isn't . . . personal?"

She stood slowly, her movements calm, her face impassive. But her eyes blazed with an inner fire. "You're damned right it's personal, Johnny. But fortunately, rank hath its privileges. That's why Aubin and I are on *your* ship and not someone else's."

Picard was mildly surprised to discover that Batanides was on a first-name basis with the ambassador. The man had struck him as rather aloof.

"I assure you, Marta," he said, meeting her gaze unflinchingly, "I will do everything possible to get to the truth about what's been happening on Chiaros IV. *And* to recover Corey, if he's still alive. He'd do no less for me."

Her expression softened, and her smile returned. "Thank you, Jean-Luc. I knew I could count on you. I'll see you at the mission briefing." Then she turned and left the room.

What are friends for? he thought, his gaze drifting to the viewing port and the changeless stars beyond.

As Commander Will Riker exited his quarters, carrying with him a padd, he spied Data turning the corner down the hall. Data called out to him. "Commander, may I walk with you to the briefing?"

Riker turned and grinned good-naturedly. "Sure, Data." He waited for the android to catch up to him before resuming on his way. "How are things going?"

By now, Data seemed so at ease with the nonspecific ways in which his human counterparts questioned him, that he barely raised an eyebrow. "By 'things,' I assume you mean how the elements of my day are fitting together, rather than the status of the ship or its crew? Things are going well. Prior to going on duty this morning, I reread the first half of the complete works of twentieth-century horror writer Stephen King, in an attempt to better understand the concept of fear. While I was sitting in my chair, I was suddenly surprised by Spot, who chose a particularly odd moment to decide that my hair needed to be rearranged. I was, for a moment, more frightened by the cat's actions than I was by the passage I had been reading."

Riker chuckled, picturing Data wrestling with the feline furball atop his head. "Yes, well, animals have a strange way of behaving sometimes. It's hard to tell why they do the things they do."

Data looked befuddled for a moment. "I am sure that animals have a motivation for their actions, just as do all sentient creatures. Whether they are aware of that motive or not is a question perhaps worthy of further study."

As they walked, Riker spied two men coming toward them in the corridor. The shorter one was Lieutenant Sean Hawk, whom Riker had grown fond of during the short time he had been on the *Enterprise*. Hawk had amazingly fast reflexes, making him perhaps the best conn officer—other than Data—with whom Riker had ever worked. He also had an astonishing memory, and was a good conversationalist as well.

The man with him was Lieutenant Commander Ranul Keru, the head of the ship's stellar cartography department. He was a giant of a man, broad-shouldered and good-humored. He was bearded, like Riker, but sported an old-fashioned bushy mustache. Keru's distinctive Trill facial markings were very visible due to his receding hairline. Riker hadn't spent much time with the man, though he had played against him a few times in games of velocity.

"Good afternoon, Commander. Lieutenant," Data greeted them warmly.

"Commander Data, Commander Riker, good to see you," said Keru.

"Hello, sir," Hawk nodded to Riker, then added, "Hello, Commander Data."

"Where are you two off to?" Riker said.

"Well, we finally got our shift schedules pretty compatible, so we're going for a drink in the crew lounge, and then thought we'd take in a holodeck adventure," Hawk said, grinning a little sheepishly.

"Something with pirates?" said Riker. When Hawk looked surprised, the Commander gestured toward Keru, smiling. "Ranul told me about your *Captain Blood* scenarios during one of our velocity matches. They sound like a lot of fun."

Keru looked down at Riker, a twinkle in his eye. "I understand that you and the captain sometimes run a holographic program involving an old sailing vessel known as the *Enterprise*? Someone once mentioned to me that Lieutenant Commander Worf received his last promotion there."

Riker laughed, remembering the double-dunking of Worf and Dr. Crusher that had occurred shortly before the *Enterprise-D* had been dispatched on its final mission. "We'll have to revive that program if—*when*— Sean gets lieutenant commander's pips of his own."

Data spoke up then. "I believe the two of you have a different kind of celebration coming up soon. Your second anniversary is next week, as I recall?"

Riker shot the pair a questioning look. Keru grinned under his mustache, and put his arm around the shoulders of the shorter Hawk, pulling him in just a bit. "That's right. Two years since that fateful day on Risa."

"I was spelunking in the crystal caves and lost my footing," said Hawk. "I fell over the side of an outcropping, and landed wrong. Luckily, Ranul was exploring the same caves, and he rappelled down to help me."

"He had broken his leg," said Keru. "So, I hoisted him over my shoulder like a sack of Andorian *curm'esh,* and climbed up to safety and a medic."

"He waited for me to get out of the medic lounge, took me to dinner, and we've been together ever since," said Hawk. "We were even both able to arrange transfers onto the *Enterprise-E* before its launch."

"And we're all the better for it," said Riker. He clapped a hand on top of Keru's—which was still on Hawk's shoulder—and nodded past them. "We have to get to a briefing. But if you're up for it, I'll buy you a celebratory drink next week for your anniversary."

"Thank you, Commander. That would be nice," said Keru.

"Good-bye, gentlemen," said Data.

As the two men headed for the crew lounge, Riker and Data went to catch the turbolift to their meeting.

Dr. Beverly Crusher had come to the ready room to deliver the crew medical evaluation report, and minutes later Picard found himself sharing the quick turbolift ride to deck three with her and Counselor Troi.

"Have either of you met the ambassador yet?" Picard said.

"Very briefly," Troi said. "After Commander Riker had shown him and the admiral to their quarters."

"And what was your impression of him?"

She shook her head. "Ullian minds are opaque even to full-blooded Betazoid telepaths, so my vantage point is no better than yours, Captain. But I did sense that Admiral Batanides was trying to conceal something."

Intelligence operatives, Picard thought. He couldn't help but wonder what secrets she might still be withholding from him, despite the nostalgic bond between them.

"What do you suppose it is that she's hiding?" Crusher said.

A thoughtful look crossed Troi's countenance. "For one thing, she doesn't seem to want anyone to discover that she and Ambassador Tabor are romantically involved."

"What?" Picard said. He realized too late that he had spoken much more loudly than he had intended.

A sly smile blossomed across Crusher's face. "Isn't the admiral an old friend of yours, Jean-Luc?"

"Yes, Doctor. But that's *all* we were. And that was a very, very long time ago."

The chief medical officer spread her hands in an exaggerated gesture of peace. "Sorry, Captain." Stage-whispering to Troi, she said, "Deanna, I think you'd better schedule a counseling session."

"Thank you, Doctor," Picard said, trying not to smile. Troi's face flushed with barely bridled mirth.

At least now I know why Marta calls the ambassador by his first name, Picard thought. He assumed that she never mentioned the relationship for professional reasons.

The turbolift stopped. The three entered an empty corridor and headed toward the fore part of the deck. Just before they entered the main forward observation lounge, Picard overheard Crusher tell Troi that *she* had figured out that the admiral and the ambassador were an item when she noticed that Will had assigned them both to the same VIP stateroom.

Inside the lounge, Picard saw that all the rest of the ship's senior officers were already taking their seats around the conference table. Aubin Tabor looked professorial, his hands behind his back as he stood before the star-flecked observation windows. Picard was impressed that Tabor was greeting everyone by name, without even once consulting a padd.

Or is he simply plucking whatever information he needs from each person's mind?

As soon as everyone was settled, Tabor called the briefing to order.

"To understand the people we seek to bring into the Federation," Tabor said, "we must understand the world that produced them."

Raising a small remote-control device before him, he summoned a holographic representation of a planet, which began slowly turning above the conference table. Half of the planet was engulfed in inky, impenetrable darkness. The other hemisphere was brightly lit, colored with a pallet of inhospitable rust reds and sulfuric yellows. It reminded Picard of something out of Milton.

"Ladies and gentlemen, I give you Chiaros IV," Tabor continued. "Because its rotational period precisely matches its sidereal year, this planet presents the same face to its sun at all times. In other words, half the planet exists in perpetual, broiling daylight. The opposite side is consigned to an endless night. This leaves only a narrow swath of habitable area—the so-called 'twilight meridian'—girdling the planet from pole to pole and back again. As you can see, Chiaros IV is a place of remarkable contrasts."

"Remarkable indeed," Troi said. "The very existence of this planet seems to defy all the odds."

"Actually," Data said, "such orbital configurations are not uncommon. For example, Earth has a single natural satellite that orbits in exactly the same fashion."

Smiling indulgently at the android, Tabor said, "Actually, Mr. Data, I believe the counselor's words were quite well-chosen." He then resumed addressing the rest of the room: "Besides the ferocious weather systems caused by the planet's tide-locked orbit, one must consider the Chiarosan star's prodigious output of hard radiation. Without the protection of the planet's immense magnetic field, no life of any sort could exist here. The solar bombardment long ago boiled away most of Dayside's surface water, leaving the Chiarosans with the unenviable options of either pumping it out from dozens of kilometers beneath the nutrient-poor ground, or collecting Nightside ice—the latter alternative being extraordinarily difficult and risky, given the permanently frozen conditions there. On Chiaros IV, life itself is very much against the odds, let alone the Chiarosans' warp-capable civilization. But the Chiarosans are inveterate survivors; they are a people long accustomed to 'beating the odds.' "

"It's hard to understand," Crusher said with a slight shake of her head, "how a warp-capable society can have so much trouble just keeping its people fed."

"Not really, Doctor," Batanides said. "These people don't have any trading partners within ten parsecs in any direction. On top of that, they only discovered faster-than-light travel about a generation ago. Zefram Cochrane's first warp experiments didn't bring us asteroid mines and food replicators overnight. Until the start of the twenty-second century, after the first Oort cloud resource-extraction operations had gotten under way, Earth was still in pretty rough shape economically."

Tabor nodded toward the admiral before continuing. "As I'm sure you're all aware by now, the Chiarosans are about to make a choice that could be as critical as their discovery of superluminal travel. In a little less than five days, they will decide whether to become a provisional member of the Federation, or yet another vassal of the Romulan Star Empire."

"And if the Chiarosans enter a pact with the Romulans," Batanides said, "then they also gain effective control of the entire Geminus Gulf."

Picard looked at the impassive faces of each of his senior officers, none of whom looked overly impressed by the point Batanides had just made. Lieutenant Commander Geordi La Forge, the *Enterprise*'s chief engineer, was the first to give voice to what they all must have been thinking.

"I've seen the reports about what's in the Gulf. Or rather about what's *not* there, at least in terms of resources. To put it delicately . . . why are we so concerned about whether or not the Romulans annex the place?"

"Other than simple altruism," Riker said, "the best reason I can think of is because the Romulans seem to be very concerned about whether or not *we* annex the place."

Tabor nodded. "And because First Protector Ruardh's planetary government has officially invited the Federation in, pending ratification of its decision by a popular vote."

"There's also the matter of the *Slayton* to consider," Batanides said. "The Chiarosan government claims that the *Slayton* launched a diplomatic shuttle toward the planet shortly before the starship mysteriously disappeared. But the *Slayton*'s diplomatic team never made it to the Chiarosan capital. We need access to the planet and the surrounding space to mount a proper search for the crew. But if the Romulans force the Federation out of the Geminus Gulf, then we can forget about ever getting at the truth."

Or finding Corey, Picard thought. Aloud, he said, "Admiral, are you saying that you believe the Romulans had something to do with the *Slayton*'s disappearance?"

"I can't prove it," she said. "But I wouldn't put it past them."

Picard was skeptical. He tried to word his objection as diplomatically as possible. "Admiral, to risk war with the Federation over three sectors of essentially empty space would not appear to make a great deal of sense."

"Granted," Batanides said. "But it's hard to evaluate the Romulans' logic when we have so little hard intelligence about their agenda here."

Crusher spoke up then, her brow creased in thought. "Putting aside the Romulans for the moment, how difficult can our mission to Chiaros be? The planet's government was duly elected by the Chiarosan people, wasn't it?"

"Of course," Tabor said, raising an eyebrow. "We would not be considering them for Federation membership were it otherwise."

"Exactly," Crusher said. "So if the duly-constituted Powers That Be on Chiaros IV want us in and the Romulans out, then it seems to me that we'd have to work pretty hard to fail."

Tabor smiled his indulgent smile once again. "I'm afraid it isn't quite as simple as that, Doctor. Despite their proven ability to unite themselves behind a single government, the Chiarosan social order remains a patchwork of clans and families, some of whom harbor ancient rivalries. It is a fragile coalition, and it can be broken by resource disputes . . . or by outside alliances made by Chiarosan clan leaders.

"A pro-Romulan dissident faction—run by a man named Falhain—has been launching guerrilla attacks on government infrastructure. It is the opinion of Ruardh's government that the rebels are using Federation weapons seized from the *Slayton* to carry out these raids. Needless to say, the citizenry is talking. Whether or not these charges are true, the prospect of Federation weapons getting into rebel hands has made even Ruardh's supporters question the wisdom of siding with us."

"Making the Romulans look more and more like the better alternative," Picard said grimly, his eyes on the slowly turning holographic globe.

"And making us responsible for cleaning up the mess our own weapons may have created," Riker added.

"Precisely, Commander. Captain, my mission—and therefore *your* mission—is to help Ruardh and Falhain put their ancient enmities aside and reach an accord, so that Chiaros IV will at least have a chance of taking its place alongside the other members of the Federation." With that, he lifted the remote and the holographic image of Chiaros IV winked into oblivion. No one else spoke for several long seconds afterward, as the import of his words sank in.

Batanides stood, signaling that the briefing had come to a close. "The *Enterprise* will arrive at the Chiaros system in approximately twenty-two hours. Captain Picard will assemble a team to accompany Ambassador Tabor to the Chiarosan capital for the initial peace summit between Ruardh and Falhain."

And to make certain that everyone gets out of the proceedings alive, Picard thought.

Picard lingered in the observation lounge after his officers had left. Besides himself, only Batanides and Tabor remained.

Tabor took one of Batanides's hands between his own. "I'll be in our quarters, my dear. I have a great deal of reading and preparation to do before tomorrow." He turned toward Picard. "Captain, I understand that you and Marta are old friends. Friendship is something we Ullians value very highly. Why don't the two of you take advantage of my preoccupation and spend some time catching up on—how do you humans say it—'old times'?"

Batanides tilted her head to the side as though weighing her options. Then she favored Picard with a slightly mischievous smile.

Picard felt awkward in the extreme. "Marta, I completely understand if you're too busy—"

Tabor interrupted him. "Please, Captain. I insist." Then he walked to the door and was gone. Picard and Batanides stood alone together, looking out onto a stunning vista of stars.

"I think I can spare a few hours of my time," she said brightly. "Let's see if you still know how to show a girl a good time, Johnny. How about a holographic jaunt to the Bonestell Recreation Facility and a few quick games of dom-jot before dinner?"

He smiled sheepishly, then said, "All right. But let's ask the maître d' to hold the Nausicaans this time, shall we?"

She grinned and took his arm.

Whatever am I going to tell Beverly tomorrow morning at breakfast? he thought, as they exited the lounge together.

Chapter Three

Aubin Tabor stepped into the quarters to which he and Marta had been assigned. As the door hissed closed behind him, he spoke into the air. "Computer. Dim lights. Blue illumination."

As the computer adjusted the room's lights, Tabor moved to a sleek case lying on a side table. Opening it, he removed a small sculpture, a representation of two entwined water nymphs, sea foam gathered at their ankles. The nymphs were facing away from each other, though their arms were interlinked behind them; each a part of the other, but watching vigilantly to either side. He had bought it for Marta on a trip to Crete a few years ago, when they were still newly discovering each other. So many secrets were shared in those early days, so much revealed. Marta had recently broken up from another relationship, and her mind was guarded. Aubin had promised her from the start that he would not use his telepathic powers on her—that he would *never* use them on her—and it had helped to forge the bond that had grown between them since then.

Still, each of them hid secrets from the other. *All couples do.* Tabor knew that. When he wanted to, he could *see* their secrets. It had aided him as a diplomat, and elsewhere. Marta kept secrets from him that usually had to do with cases being investigated by Starfleet Intelligence, but he also knew about her occasional indulgences with Andeluvian chocolate, and of her secret love for a distractingly loud form of 22nd-century Earth music known as "splitter." *Aptly named.*

And he knew that Marta still harbored feelings for Jean-Luc Picard, the captain of this starship. She hadn't spoken of him more than twice in the time she had been Tabor's lover, but he knew—long before she had told him—that she had intentionally chosen the *Enterprise* as the ship to transport them to Chiaros IV. He didn't begrudge her these feelings. In fact, they made his tasks easier. So much to prepare.

He pulled the communicator from his sleeve pocket, pressing his thumb into a recess on its underside. It began to vibrate, almost imperceptibly. He wedged it in between the backs of the two nymphs that made up the statue. It clicked into place smoothly, and the sculpture emitted three short light-bursts. Those flashes signified that the circuitry that had been specially built into the communicator and the sculpture—neither of which could work without the other—was active now. Tabor's quarters were now completely shielded from all sensor scans and computer surveillance. No matter what he did within these rooms, no one would be able to track him.

The shield was most useful whenever he had to access protected Starfleet records. It was one of the many devices that made Aubin Tabor's covert work with Section 31 easier.

Half an hour later, Tabor had narrowed his choices down to three potentials. Their personnel dossiers were all open on a computer screen in front of him. He punched a few more codes into a padd, accessing data files that Starfleet security only used in the most extreme of circumstances. He was an invisible entity in the database, his codes wrapping and doubling back on themselves, disguising his movements from any of the seventy-three concurrently running automatic programs that sought out potential intruders.

He brought up the complete dossiers on the trio of *Enterprise* crewmembers, his eyes scanning over the files quickly. He processed the information almost as quickly as the files scrolled upward. Here were the details on every movement of the three crewmembers since they had entered Starfleet Academy; their grades and performance scores, teachers they had favored, or who had favored them, links to any personal logs that had been kept on Academy computers, travel itineraries for every trip they had ever taken. Here too were the complete records of their actions post-graduation, through whatever ships they had been assigned to prior to the *Enterprise*. Any mention of them in crew logs was flagged, and all duty and personal logs were catalogued. If he wanted to, Tabor could even find out what the crewmembers in question had eaten each day from the replicator, how often they used the sonic showers, and the intimate details of their personal holodeck programs.

Tabor had noted that some of his human counterparts in Section 31 were less than enthusiastic about poking into their subjects' histories in such depth, especially if those subjects were Starfleet personnel. Invasive, they generally called it. But it was one of the reasons that

Tabor made a good recruiter; as a Ullian, he was used to sifting through the clutter within people's minds—memories of which they were not even consciously aware. He was not "invasive"; he was merely utilizing the abilities he had been born with. Because of their reticence, few human operatives could do what he did. One man, Luther Sloan, was among the handful of human Section 31 agents whose scruples were, like his, completely subjugated to his duties.

Tabor's superiors had recently made the decision to recruit a new operative aboard the *Enterprise*. Given the crew's illustrious history, and Captain Picard's penchant for becoming involved in politically sensitive interstellar issues, having an operative here was an obvious choice. And while Section 31 could easily have transferred an officer onto the ship—they did that all the time, most recently on the *Slayton*—it seemed like a better idea to recruit from the existing crew. Trust was already established.

One of Tabor's three choices was Lieutenant j.g. Kehvan Zydhek, a Balduk who worked in engineering, alongside his brother, Waltere. The Zydheks had entered Starfleet Academy upon completing their training as warriors on their homeworld. They were brilliant technicians, whose work on ships' systems kept them close to Lieutenant Commander Geordi La Forge. The fact that they knew the *Enterprise* and its computers so intimately made them good prospects as agents, but Tabor felt that Kehvan held the stronger potential for Section 31 work because of disciplinary incidents in his past. Still, the odds of one brother not telling his sibling about his covert affiliations were slim; in cases of close familial contact, Tabor had learned to err on the side of caution.

Another choice was Jyme Soule, one of the barbers. A jocular older Bajoran, Jyme was well-liked by the command crew of the *Enterprise*—as was his colleague, the Bolian Mr. Mot. Jyme's in-shop patter with the officers and crew while cutting or styling their hair meant that he knew a lot about what was going on aboard the ship. And his loose schedule—as well as his civilian status on the ship—would allow him to accomplish many types of covert missions more easily than could a crewmember who was constrained by Starfleet regulations and protocols. However, that same civilian status would mean that Jyme would require a great deal of training to keep abreast of Starfleet operations, which was a negative toward choosing him, as was the fact that he would not have clearance to access all areas of the ship.

Which left Tabor with his final choice, Lieutenant Sean Liam Hawk. The officer's records showed exemplary service in Starfleet, with a quick rise in rank following his first assignment, to the *U.S.S. Yorktown.* He was particularly adept at the conn, with reflexes faster than most of his fellow officers. He was athletic, personable, and well-liked by his superiors. Tabor noted twenty-three separate commendations in the files, and seventy-nine other instances in which the *Yorktown*'s Andorian Captain Kentrav, or the *Enterprise*'s Picard, had favorably mentioned him in their reports.

Searching the files, Tabor probed further into Hawk's past. He was born on Mars, the third son of Rhyst and Camille Hawk. Rhyst was a horticulturist whose work on the hydroponic gardens on Mars had gained him considerable renown in his field, while Camille was a popular novelist who specialized in period adventure stories set in Earth's 17th and 18th centuries. Sean's eldest brother, Darey, was the primary mining supervisor on Janus VI, while middle brother Jason was an archaeologist who had gone on a few digs in the Gamma Quadrant.

Sean had entered Starfleet Academy as soon as he was old enough, noting his desires to "explore space" on his application. He had performed extraordinarily well in his classes, leading experts to theorize that he possessed an eidetic memory. Tabor would have to test that theory when he met with the young man. A few simple mind probes should suffice. If he did indeed possess an eidetic memory, it would heighten his value to Section 31 immensely.

Tabor noted that Hawk was in a relationship with another male Starfleet officer, and that it was only his second major relationship. The first, with a classmate at the Academy, had broken up after a year; the man had later been killed in a battle against the Cardassians. His current partner was an unjoined Trill, who apparently had no desire to become joined with a symbiont. According to holodeck logs, Hawk and his partner spent much of their time in adventure scenarios, no doubt inspired by Hawk's mother's writings. A quick check of content showed, among other settings, seafaring pirate scenarios and programs set during the 19th-century's war between the North and South of Earth's United States.

Times and settings filled with moral ambiguities.

He's the one.

Tabor meditated for a moment, storing as much of the information in his own prodigious memory as possible, before backing out of the hidden files. His computer screen flared for an instant as it disconnected, the recursive Section 31 algorithms covering his exit, and then he was done.

Tabor stood and cleared his throat softly. He extracted his communicator from its resting place in the statue, repinning it to his lapel. He spoke then, his voice cutting the silence. "Computer, please locate Lieutenant Sean Hawk."

"Lieutenant Hawk is in the Botanical Arboretum."

* * *

As Tabor had surmised, Hawk was in the section of the arboretum that housed a dazzling array of Martian flora; Sean's father had bred most of the variations seen here. Tabor circled the area, to make sure that there were no other crew members nearby, and he took the precaution of setting up a personal perimeter device in his chronometer; should another person get within seven meters of them— even someone telepathically shielded—he would be alerted. He was pleased to note that Hawk was sitting near a small waterfall, where the sound of the water would muffle their conversation.

Hawk turned smoothly as Tabor approached him. He seemed to regard Tabor for an instant, as if ready to spring to his feet if he were a ranking officer. In a blink, his shoulders relaxed slightly, and he offered a smile.

"Ambassador Tabor. May I be of some assistance?"

"Perhaps. May I sit?"

"Certainly." Hawk grinned, gesturing toward a stone set near the one on which he sat. The waterfall raised a fine mist in the air, while large purplish fronds from one of the trees provided shade from the hydroponic lamps set high above.

"It's a beautiful setting here. These are all Martian plants, aren't they?"

"Yes, sir," Hawk said. He paused, then added, "My father bred several of these plants."

"Ah, yes. The famed Rhyst Hawk." Tabor watched Hawk closely, gauging the slight look of surprise in his eyes. "I know of him. I was involved for a few years with a botanist from Telfas Prime. She used to go on and on about her love of your father's work. That would make you the son of Camille Hawk as well then? I've read some of her books. Quite . . . vivacious."

"Yes, sir. Dad says she's to blame for my yen for adventure."

"Oh, you don't need to call me 'sir,'" Tabor said, holding up his hand as if to push the honorific aside. "I'm Aubin. And if it's all right, I'll call you Sean."

Hawk grinned. Tabor pushed slightly into his mind, seeing that he was unused to the informality, especially from someone older and more traveled. Tabor didn't give him time to ponder his friendliness, but pressed on. "So, is that 'yen for adventure' why you joined Starfleet?"

"I guess so, yes. When you've grown up reading about warriors and spies and pirates, I guess a typical job behind a desk seems . . . I don't know, *boring*. I had to escape the Martian suburbs somehow, and Starfleet seemed like a good way out. And it *has* been interesting. I've met scores of people from different civilizations and cultures. There are so many things out there beyond what we know about back home." Tabor raised his eyebrow slightly, as if shocked, and Hawk looked sheepish for a moment. "Oh, I hope I didn't offend you. I don't mean to imply that being an ambassador would be—"

"It's quite all right, young man. But I guarantee you that for every day I've spent behind a desk or in chambers somewhere mediating a treaty, I've also had more than my share of . . . adventures. Not all missions of peace end with olive branches, as your own captain can probably tell you. These upcoming talks on Chiaros IV could be quite difficult."

"What do you mean?" Hawk asked. Tabor knew that he hadn't been told much about the mission.

"Chiaros is beset by two factions fighting against each other in a civil war. One of the groups is led by the elected First Protector, but the opposing group feels that her rule is corrupt. Each side is claiming atrocities have been committed against them, and neither seems willing to stand down. They are a warrior race, and reportedly as tough and unyielding as Klingons. How true are either of their grievances? Which side, if any, is in the right? I don't yet know.

"That's part of the reason I became a diplomat," Tabor said with a friendly grin. "Learning about cultures such as the Chiarosans' fascinates me, but in practicing diplomacy, I have to see those cultures from many different sides. I must foresee all the ways in which any *one act* can be interpreted, positively or negatively. I have yet to find a situation in which everything is black-and-white and crystal clear. Life is all about color, about variations, not about absolutes."

Tabor could read Hawk's mind, hearing his own words as they were processed through his memory. It created an odd echo effect. *He's right,* Tabor heard Hawk think, just before the young man said out loud, "I'm learning that. Watching Captain Picard and Commander Riker on the bridge has been an invaluable education for me."

Although Tabor had initially planned to cite a few of Picard's and Riker's more unorthodox decisions—to demonstrate that even high-ranking officers don't always follow approved procedures—he could see in Hawk's mind that the young man idolized his superiors. The ambassador altered his strategy slightly, saving those examples for later. "They certainly are among the best, even if Starfleet doesn't always recognize it. But we both know that Starfleet makes mistakes every now and then, don't we?" He paused for a moment, his telepathic power spearing into Hawk's memories, seeing exactly which memories this evoked. Grasping them, he spoke again. "After all, look at all the mistakes that have been made in strategizing the battles in the demilitarized zone between Federation and Cardassian space. A lot of good men and women have died there. Good Starfleet officers. And good *ex*-Starfleet officers as well."

Hawk looked away for a moment, and Tabor could feel him remembering his loss at hearing the news that his first lover—and several Academy classmates—had been killed in a battle against the Cardassians. He finally turned back toward Tabor. "Yes. I've lost several friends . . . out there."

"I sympathize. On several occasions, as an ambassador, I've even argued to the Federation Council that it has badly mishandled the entire Cardassian Demilitarized Zone–Maquis situation," said Tabor. "That surprises you, doesn't it?" He knew that it did. He could feel it in Hawk's mind. "And I disagree with the Council *now*, regarding the situation on Chiaros IV."

"But you're going there as a Federation representative." It was both a statement and a question.

"Yes, because that is my job. The First Protector has asked for Federation intervention, promising to ally her people with us if we aid in ending the conflict and thereby help keep her in power. The other side has made overtures to the Romulans, and doesn't want the Federation involved."

"The Romulans?" Hawk's eyes were wide with surprise.

"That's one of the reasons why the *Enterprise* is here," Tabor said, lowering his voice. He knew that in doing so, he was making Hawk feel as though he were being entrusted with privileged information. Which, in a subtly expanding way, he was. "Starfleet's flagship is a symbol of its military might. The Romulans dare not try anything untoward with Picard around."

"So what does that mean for the peace summit?"

"It means that an already unstable—and morally ques-

tionable—situation has become more *aggravated*, Sean.
I argued to my superiors against the alliance with Protector Ruardh's side, but they didn't concede my point. The advantages to having Chiaros join the Federation are few, and the ethical implications are shady at best. And there are advantages to letting the Romulans have the Chiaros system, even though doing so would give them control of the entire Geminus Gulf. I can't tell you what those advantages are, but they would strengthen both the Federation and Starfleet."

Tabor sensed Hawk's confusion before he spoke. "Surely you can't be saying that you plan to defy the Federation Council's agenda," the younger man said. "You can't just act on your own initiative."

"My own initiative? No, not entirely. But I do have a certain autonomy once the negotiations start. As a diplomat, the specific direction of the talks is often mine to choose." Tabor felt Hawk inwardly wince, and quickly added, "As much as I care about galactic peace and interstellar amity, I feel just as strongly that the Federation must be protected, *at all costs*. Sometimes, that goal can only be achieved in unorthodox ways. Why, your very own captain has bent the rules of the Prime Directive more than once to achieve a greater good."

"I'm not sure I know what you mean, sir . . . Aubin."

"Haven't *you* ever felt that the people making the rules sometimes make mistakes?"

"You aren't suggesting that Starfleet Command is—"

Tabor leaned in closer to Hawk, conspiratorially. "I'm not suggesting that Starfleet Command is incompetent. But Starfleet is a gargantuan organization. Surely you can understand how some things might slip through the cracks? How mistakes can be made? How poor policies can be implemented and perpetuated?" Tabor probed again, and heard Hawk's mind whisper *Maquis*, as if validating the ambassador's words. He was relieved that Hawk was not prejudging him. He was, in fact, wanting to understand Tabor better.

"I will let you in on a secret, Sean. Starfleet *knows* that mistakes can be made. *Are* made. They've known it since the beginning. It's why the founders of Starfleet created a secret bureau, an elite group whose job is to provide for the organization's best interests."

"You mean Starfleet Intelligence? They're hardly a secret."

"No, not S.I." Tabor paused for a moment, knowing that what he was about to say marked the turning point in their conversation. "The group I'm talking about is known as Section 31."

"I've never heard of it," Hawk said. Tabor could feel the hunger for more information within the young man.

"Most people haven't. I doubt even your Captain Picard, as wise and as knowledgeable as he is, is aware of the group, even though it was a part of Starfleet's original charter two hundred years ago. Section 31 exists to identify anything that might threaten the Federation—and then deals with it, efficiently and quietly."

"Has Starfleet really been all that bad at indentifying and handling threats?" Hawk said. Tabor could feel the lieutenant's mind—his very conscience—struggling to wrap themselves around the ideas they were receiving.

Tabor smiled. "I didn't mean to imply that, Sean. But the laws and principles that Starfleet's officers of the line are sworn to uphold can hamstring them in certain . . . ethically gray situations. Section 31 has no such encumbrances. And that autonomy protects the ethical integrity of Starfleet's mainline officers and the Federation's leaders. Its agents answer to internal superiors, who, in turn, implement the decisions that other Federation operatives cannot."

Tabor could tell that Hawk was truly becoming conflicted; he had begun to question not only modern-day Starfleet's decisions, but also the schoolboy assumptions about history that most Federation citizens rarely called into question.

And yet, the lieutenant still could go either way. Tabor knew he had no choice but to press on.

"Sean, Section 31 also exists to make sure that mistakes that *are* made can be *corrected*. That the dangers which threaten the Federation's existence—and those who are naive enough to expose the Federation to those dangers—are neutralized. Sometimes the agents have to step outside the rules to help keep the Federation's true best interests in the forefront."

Hawk rocked back on his seat, his brow furrowed. His voice was soft, almost a hiss. "Are you saying Starfleet has something like the Cardassian Obsidian Order or the Romulan Tal Shiar? That they *sanction* those sorts of operations?"

Tabor put on a wounded expression, and prepared to take the next step—confirming that he *was* a part of Section 31. He could read in Hawk's mind that the young man had guessed it anyhow.

"We're not assassins, son. The steps those groups will take to accomplish their ends are much more . . . proactive than ours. However, we value the survival of our way of life every bit as much as our adversaries do theirs. 'Necessity knows no law except to prevail.' One of Earth's philosophers said that."

"Publilius Syrus," Hawk said quickly. "But he also said,

'Pardon one offense, and you encourage the commission of many.' It seems as if this group is above the law."

"Not above it. Beneath it, perhaps. You might think of the bureau as the bulwark that makes the Federation's ideals possible in the first place. The only reason freedom exists at all, Sean, is because of those who stand vigil outside on the ramparts. Section 31 *upholds* the Federation's principles. Just as Picard has done on those occasions when he has bent the rules. Even in your short time on the *Enterprise,* I'm sure you can think of more than a few instances wherein he, or Commander Riker, have made decisions based more upon conscience than on the rule book."

Tabor could feel Hawk's thoughts swirling, but one question rose to the forefront more quickly than any other. "You're wondering why I'm telling you this, aren't you?" Tabor asked.

"Yes," Hawk said, simply.

"It's because Section 31 has need of new agents. Strong, reliable, honest men and women who are *committed* to the dreams of the Federation." Tabor looked him directly in the eyes. "I believe you to be one of those men, Mister Hawk."

"Me? I'm not—"

"You embody *all* of the qualities of the best Starfleet officers. Additionally, I believe that you may have an eidetic memory, a valuable tool for an agent."

"I've always had a near-photographic memory, but . . ." Hawk shook his head, then asked, "Why now?"

"Because I fear that Section 31 may have lost an agent who was aboard the *Slayton.* Commander Cortin Zweller. He was on an important mission to Chiaros IV—a mission that would have altered the outcome of the peace talks in a way that would ultimately have benefited the Federation."

"You mean . . . he was there to make sure the Romulans gain control of Chiaros IV."

Tabor nodded slowly. "As you've no doubt surmised, I've decided to make sure that his mission succeeds. Especially if that mission has cost him his life."

If Cortin died trying to trade the Geminus Gulf for that list of Romulan spies, Tabor thought, *then I'll be damned if I'm going to let his death be in vain. There's too much history between us for that.*

"I may need your aid in this matter, especially if something *has* happened to the *Slayton* and its crew. And beyond that . . . I would like to call upon you from time to time to help Section 31 in defending the Federation."

Tabor felt Hawk's apprehension and fascination grappling like opposing storm fronts. *There's trepidation there, yes, and confusion,* Tabor thought. *But the lad does indeed love a good adventure.*

"Are you asking me to leave the *Enterprise*?" Hawk said.

"Not necessarily. This *is* the Federation's flagship, after all. Section 31 could certainly use some alert eyes and ears here."

Hawk's crystal-blue eyes were wide as he considered everything Tabor had just said. Tabor could feel that he had punched all the right buttons for the young officer; now, the lieutenant just had to make the right decisions.

"I'm not sure about this, Ambassador. Covert operations, spying . . ." Hawk trailed off.

"Sounds like something out of one of your mother's books," Tabor said, almost lightheartedly. "There are many instances in history where selfless people have had to stand alone or work in secret for the benefit of all." He let his words hang in the air for a moment. Tabor could sense that it was time to ease up and disengage. Gently, he said, "I understand, Sean. Really, I do. And I appreciate the gravity with which you are approaching my offer. It speaks highly of your personal ethics."

He paused, then added, "But I would ask you to keep our conversation confidential, even from your partner. I am not exaggerating when I tell you that the very safety of the Federation depends upon Section 31's continued secrecy. And I'm trusting *you* with an *enormous* secret." Tabor stood, and offered his hand to the young man.

"I understand, sir," Hawk said, standing as well. He gripped the ambassador's hand firmly and shook it. "I just need some time to think." Probing gently, Tabor noted with relief that Hawk had made no plans as yet to inform his superiors of this meeting.

"Certainly. But I hope you can decide soon. I believe that something may have gone terribly wrong in the Chiaros system. We could discover things there that we didn't anticipate. And such surprises could jeopardize not only the bureau's Chiarosan mission, but also the Federation's vital interests elsewhere. If you truly care about the Federation's security as much as I think you do . . . well, I hope we'll be talking again soon."

Aubin Tabor turned and walked away, his eyes and nose taking in the lovely sights and smells of the arboretum, while his mind drank in the thoughts of a very conflicted Lieutenant Hawk.

As the bridge turbolift doors hissed open, Captain Picard saw Commander Will Riker stand abruptly from the captain's chair, tugging at his tunic. With Admiral Batanides at his side, the scowling Picard strode toward the center of the bridge, looking at the viewscreen.

"Is that what I think it is, Number One?"

"Yes, sir. It's wreckage from the *Slayton*. It seems to

be scattered throughout this region of space. It might have been spread out by radiation pressure, or maybe by a spatial distortion wave of some sort."

Data, already at his post, looked down at the computer panels upon which information scrolled. "These specific pieces are hull plating from the starboard side. Scans show a distinct pattern of disruptor weaponry. The type is indeterminate. I am attempting a more complete scan to match any residual disruptor particles with—"

"Data, are there any survivors?" Picard asked, interrupting.

"Unknown, sir. The dispersal of the wreckage over such a wide volume of space has made it impossible for us to tell if any escape pods were jettisoned." Data turned, looking over his shoulder toward Picard. "If there are any survivors, it is likely that they would have traveled to Chiaros IV."

Batanides spoke up. "Have you been able to trace any combadge signals?"

"The planet's atmosphere appears to be impenetrable to combadge signals and disrupts most other subspace traffic as well, including transporters and sensors," Data said. "Ship-to-ground communication is possible only through the Chiarosan government's orbiting communications tether."

"Have the Chiarosan authorities made any progress searching for survivors?"

"They have been conducting searches ever since the delegation from the *Slayton* failed to arrive in the capital city. However, the authorities report that no Starfleet personnel have been located anywhere on the planet's surface, either on the Dayside or the Nightside."

"We can't give up on them, Mr. Data," said Picard. "Continue searching for survivors any way you can."

A voice came from behind them. "There are other concerns, Captain." Picard turned to see Ambassador Tabor, standing just outside one of the turbolifts. He had not heard the doors open, nor did he know how long the ambassador had been standing there.

"With all due respect, Ambassador, the Chiarosan negotiations can—"

"Captain, was not your *primary* mission to this system a diplomatic one?"

Picard seethed inwardly, resenting the ambassador's intrusion. "Yes, it is. But there are missing Starfleet personnel who may be *alive* in an extremely hostile environment." He pointed to the aurora-swept surface of the planet on the viewscreen, the backdrop to the floating debris from the *Slayton.*

"I'm well aware of that, Captain. One of those missing is an old friend of yours, and of Vice-Admiral Batanides. But since there seems to be little you can do at the moment to expedite the search, the preparations for my mediation between First Protector Ruardh's government and Falhain's dissident faction should take precedence. It's entirely possible that the *Slayton*'s survivors are safe and sound in the company of the Chiarosan rebels."

Such a development didn't quite fit with Picard's notion of "safe and sound." His eyes narrowed slightly as he considered the ambassador's words. He turned, addressing Riker.

"Number One, prepare a shuttlecraft. We'll depart for the planet just as soon as it's ready. We'll be arriving a little early for the peace talks, but we can spend the extra time searching for survivors."

"Here's hoping we'll find out what happened to the *Slayton* by talking to her crew," Riker said, as he left for the shuttlebay.

"Amen to that, Number One," Picard said quietly to Riker's back. He turned again toward Tabor. "I trust this will be acceptable to you, Ambassador?"

"Certainly, Captain," Tabor said, smiling graciously. "It seems you have devised a *wonderful* solution."

"I'll be in my ready room," Picard announced curtly, and exited the bridge.

Chapter Four

The search had proved fruitless, with not a single trace of wreckage from the *Archimedes*—nor any combadge signals—showing up on the sensors, even once the *Enterprise* shuttlecraft *Brahe* had gone below the worst of the roiling atmospheric storms. As Picard and his away team traveled to the Chiarosan capital, sensors had picked up faint traces of energy signatures which *could* have belonged to Starfleet weaponry, but the ion-charged air had dispersed the particles so much that nothing conclusive could be found. Still, Picard was wary, remembering Marta Batanides's assertions that the rebel factions were using stolen Starfleet weapons.

The shuttle had been joined by a Chiarosan escort as it neared the capital city, Hagraté, a glittering collection of low-built monolithic towers and spires. The ships had threaded their way between the buildings, flying just above the tallest of them; since the winds buffeted the shuttle even at this low altitude, Picard understood why no building stood higher.

The tallest of them appeared to be religious temples or churches; when the captain had mentioned this, Tabor confirmed that the Chiarosans worshiped multiple deities, and that the more affluent were seen as blessed by the gods. *Religious classism,* Picard thought, glad that Earth's society had long ago evolved beyond such artificial stratification.

Throughout the city was a vast tangle of pipes and aqueducts, which Picard guessed carried water from whatever processing stations or reservoirs existed. He suspected, given the planet's known shortage of agricultural resources, that the most heavily guarded buildings they had passed on the outskirts of Hagraté might be the water-pumping stations, vapor-extraction facilities, and soil-enhancement plants.

Upon landing, Picard's team—Commander Riker, Data, Counselor Troi, and Ambassador Tabor—disembarked from the *Brahe,* and were greeted by an armed escort, each carrying bladed weapons hung from ornate sashes. Picard tugged at his formal dress-uniform tunic, straightening it, as a female Chiarosan stepped forward, from behind several of the guards. "I am Senator Curince. Welcome to Chiaros IV."

Picard smiled slightly, gesturing to his companions. "I'm Captain Jean-Luc Picard, of the *U.S.S. Enterprise.* This is my first officer, Commander Will Riker, and two other members of my senior staff, Lieutenant Commander Data, and Counselor Deanna Troi. And this gentleman is Federation Ambassador Aubin Tabor."

Tabor stepped forward and performed a complex series of movements with his hands before bowing almost imperceptibly, his formal robes shimmering slightly as the light caught their metallic threadwork patterns. "I apologize that I cannot greet you with the grace of your people," said Tabor, "but my joints have never been as limber as yours, Madam Senator."

Senator Curince evinced a sharp-toothed grin, obviously impressed. "Your greeting is appreciated nonetheless, Ambassador." Her gaze took him in for a moment more, then she turned her head slightly toward Picard, ignoring his other officers completely. "Were your ship's instruments able to find any trace of the missing diplomatic shuttle?"

"No, Madam Senator," Picard said. "I'm afraid the atmospheric turbulence of your world limits the full range of our sensors."

Curince raised an eyebrow, and said, "Our planet is a harsh and unforgiving one. You are among the first members of any . . . *weaker* species to ever visit its surface."

Picard offered a wan smile, unsure whether to feel insulted or not. His eyes shifted over to Tabor, who was smiling calmly.

A Chiarosan assistant approached and handed Curince a large electronic tablet, mounted on which were a display screen and a number of blinking buttons. She looked at it briefly, then held it out to Picard. "This device contains all the data we have on your missing shuttle, and on the apparent use of Starfleet weaponry against our defense troops. Our comm tellers transmitted the files to you previously, but given the effect that recent storms have had on our communications relay, it was decided that an uncorrupted transmission recording might aid you in your search." As Picard prepared to take the device, she added, "If you need one of our people to help you interpret the use of the recorder, we can provide a technician."

Picard gave another polite smile. *This woman is really taxing my patience.* "Thank you, Senator. We have excellent technicians on our ship. As generous as your offer is, I'm sure we will be able to decode the files ourselves." He turned and handed the machine to Data, almost imperceptibly rolling his eyes. Only his crew saw the gesture.

Curince spoke again. "I also apologize that we are not meeting in the capitol building. The rebels refused to negotiate in a place that was completely under the rightful government's control. We will, instead, be meeting in a private arena, whose location is being decided upon as we speak."

"Will both First Protector Ruardh and Grand General Falhain be present at these negotiations, as planned?" asked Tabor.

"Yes. As will the Romulan diplomatic delegation. Their own ship arrived a few hours ago."

"Ah," said Tabor, bobbing his head agreeably. "I trust that they have sent their best diplomats?"

"The leader of their group is a woman named T'Alik. I do not bother to remember those of her subordinates."

"T'Alik can be very persuasive," Tabor said soberly.

"I think she will not persuade our First Protector much," Curince said. "The Romulan presence is tolerated only because they have not struck against us. They claim neutrality, but Falhain's minions—the so-called 'Army of Light'—have allied themselves politically with the Romulans. We feel that taints the Star Empire, showing them as the enemy of the duly proper government of our world."

One of the Chiarosan escorts let out a discreet clicking sound, holding up a smaller version of the padd-like device Curince had given Picard. The senator looked at it briefly, then back to the landing party. "The location has been announced. Security will be minimal, so it is our fervent hope that Falhain's people will act honorably in this matter." She paused for a moment, before looking pointedly at Tabor and Picard. "I am hopeful that the presence of an outside arbiter at this meeting—and that of the Federation—will allow for a sense of security, and begin a closure of this difficult rift among our people."

Tabor smiled warmly. "Madam Senator, I believe I can promise you that the détente that we are about to inaugurate today will change the future of Chiaros IV—for the better . . . and forever."

Picard stared at Tabor for a moment. He hadn't liked the ambassador much, but he had to admit that the man had both charm and a persuasive demeanor. Perhaps he *could* help to bring an end to the Chiarosan political struggle.

As they stepped forward, Tabor leaned in toward Picard and whispered. "Senator Curince is telling the truth about the *Archimedes*. At least as far as she knows." Picard did not need to question how the Ullian ambassador was aware of what Curince knew or did not know. He also knew that Ullian telepathy tended to be more intrusive than one of Troi's empathic scans.

Picard wondered: *If the man would enter the senator's mind with so little compunction, then what else might he be capable of?*

Curince didn't explain what their meeting place had once been used for, and neither Picard nor Tabor asked. The circular arena had many columns and benches in the main part, with shadowed recesses and rows of stadium seating rising up on every side. Although it seemed almost like a sporting or gladiatorial arena, Picard was under the impression that it might actually have been used for lectures or debates of some sort. Given the visible dust, it had not been used in quite some time.

Standing in the well-lit center of the arena was First Protector Ruardh and her bodyguards, while the perimeter of the room was ringed with a dozen or more soldiers. A stately matron, Ruardh was wearing an auburn dress that complimented the long plaited braid of brown-blond hair that curled down her shoulders. The dress was split in the center, wrapping around each leg, allowing for more ease of movement.

Senator Curince introduced Tabor to Ruardh, and the ambassador performed the elaborate hand greeting again. Picard stepped forward as his own name was called, bowing slightly to the Chiarosan leader. "I'm sorry that I cannot greet you in the manner of your people, First Protector," he said, echoing Tabor's earlier comment. He also knew better than to introduce his "subordinates" this time.

"No slight is taken, Captain. And your very presence here suggests to me that you will be much more . . . successful than the previous delegation the Federation sent."

"Captain Picard is often successful, First Protector," said a strong voice. A robed Romulan woman stepped toward the group from a side entrance, three other Romulan functionaries at her sides. "He commands Starfleet's finest warcraft, the vaunted *U.S.S. Enterprise.* He brings you a honey-tongued diplomat in a vessel that could level your city if he commanded it. Small wonder you would choose to ally yourself with the Federation; but can you truly trust a people who are so weak that they lose ships and weapons one day, then arrive in a battleship the next?"

"I know that I cannot trust the Romulans, Ambassador T'Alik," Ruardh said, her head swiveling to the side. "You have chosen to ally yourself with those who oppose me."

"We have not chosen either side, Protector. It is not *our* weaponry that your opposition has used against you," T'Alik said, her haughty gaze moving toward Picard and his crew. "We have offered the rulers of Chiaros IV the protection of the Romulan Star Empire. It is *you* who have chosen to side with the Federation. You might, upon further consideration, choose to ally yourself with us. That is *our* hope."

Picard looked to Tabor to see if the man was going to respond, but Tabor's gaze told him to let the matter alone. As if cued by T'Alik's speech, the rebel Chiarosans melted out of the shadows in the arena, their triple-jointed forms moving lithely and almost soundlessly. Ruardh and her men did not seem surprised—and the Romulans' preternatural calm implied that they expected the intrusion—but the Starfleet officers didn't disguise their own jumpiness quite as well. With the rebels now ringing the outer perimeter of the arena, Picard felt like prey—even more so, given that both the rebels and the bodyguards were all heavily armed.

A few of the rebels parted, allowing a tall, blond-haired Chiarosan to stride forward, a shorter dark-haired man trailing him. "Ruardh!" the blond snarled. "I half-expected you to renege on our meeting."

The matronly Chiarosan leader stared impassively at the light-haired rebel. "And I had expected you to attack rather than to negotiate, Falhain."

Aubin Tabor stepped forward, holding his hands out, palms facing upward. "It seems that both sides have come in good faith, despite any preconceptions either had held toward the other. Shall we proceed? There is precious little time remaining—three days, in fact—before the Chiarosan referendum begins."

Falhain turned his head, his crystalline eyes narrowed and steely. "You must be the Federation ambassador, come to convince us of the rightness of Ruardh's cause."

Tabor bowed his head slightly, and again performed the complex series of hand-gestures that Picard had seen twice earlier. "I am Aubin Tabor, Grand General Falhain. But I am not here to champion Protector Ruardh's cause, only to find a pathway to peace between your faction and hers."

The darker rebel by Falhain's side spoke up then, his voice challenging. "As far as we know, your Federation's laws forbid you to interfere with indigenous cultures. Why do you meddle with ours?" The man looked briefly at T'Alik and her contingent, who stood to the side, passive.

Tabor smiled benignly, his voice not rising at all. "You speak of the Prime Directive. A wise and wonderful rule, but it is not the *only* thing that governs us, just as one law is not all that governs you. And because we have been *asked* to intervene on behalf of the legal government of Chiaros—"

"*Legal?*" Falhain shouted then, taking a menacing step forward. Picard gave a quick glance over to Riker, who had taken a defensive stance. Riker stood down after Picard's gaze traveled to the face of Deanna Troi. Her dark eyes were intent on Tabor and the two Chiarosans as she appraised their intentions. The captain was relieved to note that the counselor seemed to find the natives' emotions more accessible than those of the ambassador. Seeing no immediate alarm on Troi's face, Picard relaxed a bit.

"Does the Federation know how the 'legal' Protector keeps hold of her throne?" Falhain continued. "Are they aware of the thousands of Chiarosans she has ordered slaughtered, the villages she has commanded to be burned, the children she has willed to be eviscerated? The dry riverbeds of Chiaros now run gray with her victims' lifeblood."

Ruardh looked appalled. "You exaggerate, Falhain, as always. You were the one who left my service, just as those who follow you made their choice to embrace political dissidence." She turned her back on Falhain, though her head swiveled to remain looking at him as she walked behind one of the desk-style platforms nearby. "You paint me as a monster, and yet where is the proof of my alleged atrocities?"

Tabor stepped forward, his voice soothing. "Protector, General, we need to focus on the matters at—"

"You think that this is *not* the matter at hand?" Falhain reared back, and Picard realized that his full height was more imposing than he had originally imagined. His brows furrowed, and his sharp teeth glistened as he spat his interruption. "The government that the Federation has allied itself with has been practicing *genocide*. It is not enough that their raiding parties remove our precious soil and water, leaving the outland villages to choke on dust—they also murder any who have the courage to gainsay their greed, whether armed or not. Our fight is not about politics. We struggle for our very *survival!*"

The dark-haired aide to Falhain reached behind his back, his arms swiveling impossibly in his shoulder sockets. As the Chiarosan bodyguards defensively unsheathed their weapons, he removed a device from a satchel he wore on his back and displayed it in front of him. It was less than half a meter tall, with three short legs at its base, and a circular lens at its top.

"You ask for proof, Ruardh?" Falhain swiveled his head toward Picard and his officers. "No doubt your Starfleet allies are equally suspicious of *my* motives, having heard only *your* arguments to the Federation. Here then are the records of your monstrous deeds. Grelun?"

Responding to Falhain's command, the dark-haired warrior touched a recessed space on the device, which he had placed on the floor. A flickering light shot up into the air, before coalescing into a three-dimensional, full-motion image of a village. Homes were burning, as their inhabitants tried to put them out. Chiarosan troops, in military garb, were attacking the villagers, killing many of them. Picard winced to see that many of the victims were women and children.

Data leaned toward Picard and Riker, his voice carefully modulated so that it was not heard by the others. "It appears to be a holographic projection, sir."

"That I can figure out for myself, Data," Picard whispered. "What I need to know is whether or not these images are genuine."

"Understood, sir."

The first image dissolved into another image, this time of the Chiarosan soldiers leading villagers down a road. Their captives—people of all ages—were bound, with half meter tethers holding each of them together from neck to neck. That hologram changed to another, this one showing a soldier bayoneting an older man in the back as he stood at the edge of a long trench dug into the soil. Lying in the trench were the bodies of many others, their gray blood oozing from wounds in their backs or sides, or from slit throats. Thick clouds of insects buzzed above the corpses.

Data leaned in again. "While it is possible to forge any scene with holographic technology, I believe these images are taken from real events. The slight focus problems and partial blockage in these images implies that the person or persons recording them were in concealment."

But a clever forger could fake that as well, Picard thought. Still, it did seem real enough to raise his concern.

Picard stepped forward, tugging at the bottom of his tunic. "General Falhain, I believe we have seen enough for the moment. Despite your conviction that we are siding wholeheartedly with Protector Ruardh, it seems that some doubt has been raised about the manner in which she governs her people. None of these images, nor this information, were *ever* presented to the Federation Council—"

"There's a good reason for that, *Captain*," Ruardh said, imperiously spitting out the final word as though it left a bad taste in her mouth. "The reason is that these images are partially a fabrication, and partially the work of Falhain himself. As you are aware, Falhain used to lead my royal troops, and many of the regiments are still faithful to him. He commanded his men to commit these crimes, then accused me of giving the orders."

"You *dare* imply that this is *my* work?" Falhain bellowed. "You are known by the people as the 'Ashen Ruler,' for the blood that creeps up the trains of your gowns. I left your service after your political mandates began afflicting the outlanders with *further* hardships— where goods could be sold, how the clans could support each other, where we could live, and how many of us could continue to eat and drink. Your parliamentary decisions filled the prisons with the desperately poor and the infirm. I have opposed you in the streets and in the shadows ever since these injustices began. But I have never, *never* killed an innocent!"

Tabor stepped forward, his voice louder, but still soothing. Picard could tell that he was trying to exert some calm control over the situation, which was quickly deteriorating. "General Falhain, Protector Ruardh, *please*. This wall of recrimination and accusation cannot stem the tide of unrest amongst the Chiarosans. The referendum begins in three days, and it is the people who will decide then whether your planet becomes a part of the Federation, or falls under the control of the Romulan Star Empire."

"And who will vote in an election that threatens their lives and families?" asked Falhain. "The rebels are not allowed to vote or they will be incarcerated or executed.

And are you truly so naive as to believe that a ruler who so oppresses her people would allow for a true and just election?"

Falhain gestured over toward T'Alik and her contingent. "And as for the Romulans, they do not appear overly interested in any struggle of Chiarosan against Chiarosan."

Picard shot a quick glance at Troi, who shrugged slightly. *She can't tell whether that's true or not,* he thought.

"Then why do you suppose they want this system?" Picard said to Falhain. "In my experience, the Romulans never do anything just because it helps someone else. They are conquerors. What makes you so sure that they will not enslave your entire society if the Chiarosans choose not to ally themselves with the Federation?"

Falhain looked to Picard again, one eyebrow raised. "Your question is rather pointless, is it not, Captain? If the Romulans were going to conquer us, why have they not done so *before now?*" He paused for a moment, seemingly for the question to sink in, then continued. "I am not a blind man, Picard, nor one who is easily convinced in any argument. The Romulans have neither hindered nor aided us in our battles. My belief is that their chief concern in whether or not Ruardh continues to rule is that they wish to expand the boundaries of the worlds that are a part of their empire, and to stop the creeping expansion and domination of your people. If the referendum moves to Ruardh's wishes—toward acceptance of Federation membership—the Empire will ultimately lose. If the *people's will* wins out, and we *reject* the Federation, then we will be able to continue to chart our own destiny, free of an oppressive outside structure which would support a government that kills its own children!"

Tabor held up his hands to call for order, and Picard broke his eyes away from his steady gaze into Falhain's.

Behind him, and to his side, he saw Deanna Troi's expression change dramatically, from one of concern to one of pain and shock. Suddenly, she leaped forward, pushing Picard to the ground. A sizzling beam of energy sliced through the air where he had been standing seconds before.

And then all hell broke loose. From the top of the arena, disruptor fire rained down upon the Chiarosan leaders, the Romulans, and the Starfleet personnel. The second blast struck one of Falhain's rebels in the chest, leaving a smoking crater in his furred skin as he toppled backward. In moments, the Chiarosans—on both sides of the political spectrum—had drawn their scimitar-like swords, or other bladed weapons, and a melee erupted.

As Troi dove toward a bench, a disruptor blast searing the marble floor by her feet, Picard rolled to one side. A Chiarosan rebel turned and saw him, and raised one scimitar above his head to strike a killing blow. Picard kicked his foot up between the warrior's legs, and the impact had the desired effect. Picard rolled again as the rebel's now-unsteady swing missed its mark. A sharp whistling sound went over the captain's head, as a nearby Chiarosan used his own blade to chop off the sword arm of the attacker, burying the metal into his foe's chest. The severed Chiarosan arm flopped down on top of Picard, still clutching its curved weapon.

The captain quickly wrested the scimitar from the hand's grasp and stood in a defensive crouch. In his mind, Picard cursed the rules of Federation diplomacy that forbade weapons, leaving himself and his officers the only ones unprotected in the fight. He searched for his friends in the melee, but couldn't spot them. Nor could he see Tabor.

The fighting was loud and brutal, and inhumanly fast. The soldiers and the rebels were interlocked in savagery, their guttural yowls and clanging steel blades creating an awesome din. Picard spotted a soldier advancing on two of the Romulans, holding his weapons in both hands. The captain launched himself at the warrior with a yell, but one of the Romulans was killed before he could cover the distance.

The Chiarosan swung one sword high, and the other low, but Picard ducked and brought his own blade to parry the lower blow. Picard kept the blades in contact and forced both to swing to one side. Before the warrior could recover, Picard brought his weapon down again. It connected with his opponent's wrist, and the lightly furred hand was cleanly separated from his arm.

The attacker howled, and slashed at Picard with his remaining scythe. Although his aim was unsteady, he still managed to connect, the tip of his weapon slicing through Picard's tunic and slitting his upper chest. Suddenly, the Chiarosan howled and crumpled forward, a saber wound bleeding at the base of his spine. Behind him was one of Ruardh's bodyguards, who gave Picard a brief glance of respect before turning to fight another of the rebels.

Picard sensed a presence behind him and turned, his blade at the ready. He relaxed only slightly when he saw that it was Data, now holding a Chiarosan sword himself. He had no doubt that the android's reflexes allowed him to fight valiantly, but as he put a hand up to his own bleeding chest, engaging in more battle was not on his mind.

"Data, access the shuttle's onboard computer and beam us out." Data used his free hand to punch several buttons on his tricorder, while Picard scanned the arena to see if he could spot Riker or Troi or Tabor; he still couldn't see them through the fighting hordes. Picard tapped his combadge, and yelled to Riker, but the din was too intense for him to hear if there was a reply.

"I've got it, sir." As Picard looked toward Data, two Chiarosans toppled toward them, caught in a mutual death grip, each skewered on the other's blades. "Energizing."

And in a moment, Picard was back aboard the shuttle-craft. He tumbled off the transporter pad, still flinching from the two warriors who had been falling toward him. Data squatted on a nearby pad.

"Where are Will and Deanna? And Tabor?"

Data scrambled over to the transporter console, and punched a few buttons, moving his fingers downward in a swift motion on the touchpad. "Attempting retransport now, Captain."

The familiar sparkle of the transporter shimmered on three pads, but what materialized wasn't Picard's first of-ficer and counselor. Instead, their combadges clattered to the floor. On the third pad was Tabor, his back to them as he stood, hunched over. He turned toward them, stum-bling, his right hand holding his throat, his left hand at his chest.

Tabor's legs could no longer hold him, and he fell for-ward, his left hand moving forward to break his fall. Pi-card heard a chilling sound when the ambassador hit the floor, as the point of a Chiarosan dagger pushed up through Tabor's spine. Data and Picard turned Tabor over, only to discover purplish-crimson liquid spilling from between the diplomat's fingers.

"We've got to get him to the *Enterprise*," Picard said. "Data, get us out of here."

As the android moved to the shuttle's flight controls, Picard tried to apply firmer pressure to Tabor's neck wound, holding his head upward. The knife still jutted from his chest, but Picard knew better than to try to remove it before getting him back to the *Enterprise*. Crusher could save him, if anyone could. He silently cursed the fact that shuttles did not come equipped with Emergency Medical Holograms, and vowed to bring that up with Starfleet Command in his next report.

Entering the stormy atmosphere, the shuttle lurched from side to side. Picard braced himself with one hand, trying not to let Tabor move too much. Tabor's left hand grabbed weakly at Picard's tunic, pulling him down. The ambassador was trying to say something, though the sounds coming from his mouth made Picard's skin crawl. He leaned in closely, listening.

"Fal ... Falhain ... is ... dead."

What had seemed a heated debate less than ten minutes ago had just ended more horribly than Picard could ever have imagined. Falhain, the leader of the rebels, was now a martyr. Ambassador Tabor lay dying in his arms. Riker and Troi were missing, and possibly killed as well. The Chiarosan government—however corrupt—might soon fall to the Romulan Empire. And there was still no sign of survivors from the *Slayton*.

These are the times that try men's souls, he thought ruefully as the shuttle sped into orbit.

Chapter Five

Hawk sat in the darkened quarters, the soothing voices of a Celtic choir washing over him from the computer speakers. Sometimes it felt odd to him, hearing the ancient songs and melodies of his pre-Martian forebears—the bohdran and the oud and the harps—reverberating in the pristine starship environment. He did feel, however, that the juxtaposition of his life now, traveling the stars with the lives of his ancestors, the nomadic Celts who explored ancient Europe, created a comfortable overlap. Exploration was in his blood.

But is espionage?

Following his meeting with Ambassador Tabor in the arboretum, Hawk had eaten a meal—alone in a storage bay—and then wandered the corridors of the ship. He purposely avoided walking anywhere near work stations of crewmembers he was friendly with; he didn't really want to talk to anyone. Ranul hadn't contacted him on his combadge, but he knew that eventually, he would.

Hawk had finally returned to their quarters to further

ruminate about what he'd been told. The ambassador's words replayed in his mind almost exactly. His memory was—as always—crystal clear. *An eidetic memory.* That's what Tabor had called it. But what good were Tabor's words, laid out in his mind like a map, if he wasn't sure whether he could trust the intent behind them?

It made sense, really, that Starfleet would have a secret intelligence branch. Every other major power in the quadrant had its own intelligence communities. Still, it felt at odds with the stated purpose of Starfleet to engage in the kind of surveillance and skulduggery that Earth's inhabitants had left behind after making first contact.

At the same time, he knew that Starfleet wasn't infallible. During his time as a junior officer and serving on the *Enterprise*—*especially,* perhaps, while serving on the *Enterprise*—he had seen many of his superior officers make decisions that ran counter to the tenets he had been taught at the Academy. Although those choices were always made with the best intentions, he saw that the rules were made to flex and bend to fit the situations. The Prime Directive was clearly *not* the end-all of solutions.

Although the music drowned out the sound of the opening doors, the sliver of light that came into the room signaled to Hawk that Keru had returned. He looked up and gave his partner a half-smile, then resumed his downward gaze. He knew that Keru would sense that something was wrong; he just didn't know how he could talk to him about the subject without breaking the secrecy Tabor had requested of him.

"Computer, lower music," Keru said, as he crouched down in front of Hawk. He looked to him, his eyes showing concern. "What's wrong, Sean?"

"Nothing I can talk about."

"What? Did I do something?" Keru looked crestfallen for a moment, and Hawk knew that he was steeling his nerves for whatever was to come next.

Hawk quickly amended his statement. "It's not about *us*," he said, reassuringly. "It's . . . it's something classified."

The Trill looked up, relief showing on his face. He moved up and sat next to Hawk, putting a hand on his shoulder. "I understand. Is it something about this Chiarosan situation?"

Hawk hated being evasive, especially with the man he loved. "Yes and no. I can't talk about it."

"Is the ship in danger? The Romulans?"

"I *said* I can't talk about it," Hawk said edgily. He stood, and paced over to the wall.

"They found the wreckage of the *Slayton* a few hours ago," Keru said, getting up and moving to the replicator. "No survivors. Still no sign of the *Archimedes,* though." He ordered a dark ale, and it shimmered into solidity on the replicator pad.

"I hadn't heard." Hawk's hand reflexively clenched. *Tabor was right. Something* did *happen to the ship. To that other agent's mission. Commander Zweller.*

Keru took a sip of his ale. "Oh. I thought *that* might be what this *mood* is about."

Hawk sighed heavily. "No, it's not, Ranul. And I'm not in a 'mood,' I just have some important things to think about."

Keru sat down on the couch, spreading one hand wide as if sweeping the air. "And here I thought that after two years together I could recognize your moods. Dark room, Celtic music, avoiding the topic—"

"I *told* you it was classified," Hawk said sharply.

"Fine, whatever." Keru took another sip of his ale and

sat in silence for a moment. "Do you want to get something to eat?"

"I already ate."

Keru put his glass down on a table next to the couch and stood up, wiping a bit of foam from his mustache. "Well, I guess I'll go eat *alone,* then. Let you continue your nonmood." He moved toward the door and hesitated, looking over at Hawk.

"I'm sorry," Hawk said quietly.

The door whisked open in front of Keru, and the sound of raised voices and running came from down the outside hallway.

"Something's wrong," Keru said, peering down the corridor. Hawk moved over swiftly to join him, in time to see the turbolift doors close in front of a very distraught-looking Vice-Admiral Batanides and two security officers.

Hawk looked down the corridor, and spotted another pair of security officers. He recognized one of them as Lieutenant Sallee Huber, and called out to her. "Lieutenant Huber. What's happening?"

The older of the two stopped and turned toward the two men. "It's all hit the fan, Hawk. There was a massacre down on Chiaros IV. Commander Riker and Counselor Troi are missing, and Ambassador Tabor's been badly wounded. They've just beamed him to sickbay!"

The color drained from Hawk's face as he turned toward Keru. Standing next to him, his partner appeared equally surprised by the news, his mouth hanging open.

First had come Commander Zweller's disappearance, then the discovery of wreckage from the *Slayton.* Now Tabor had been attacked. If Hawk needed another sign that he needed to act, then perhaps this was it. Something was seriously wrong, and Hawk knew that he would do whatever it took to help find a solution. And if that meant working with Section 31, then so be it.

"I'm going up to the bridge. They might need me." Hawk gave his partner a quick kiss on the cheek, and stalked into the hallway, tugging at the bottom of his tunic.

"Marta, please!" Picard grabbed the admiral by the shoulders, more forcefully than he had intended. Ambassador Tabor had died fifteen minutes ago on the operating table, despite Dr. Crusher's best efforts. Since then, once the scimitar gash to his own chest had been sealed, Picard had tried to comfort Marta Batanides. At first, she had resisted being taken from sickbay, until Crusher had made it a medical order. Picard had brought her to his quarters; her own would have been a painful reminder of Tabor.

Picard had just slipped into a new tunic in the other room—he had discarded his blood-splattered outer garments in sickbay—when he heard a crash. He emerged to find that Batanides had thrown a glass vase across the room and into a wall. Now, as he grabbed her, she moved into his open arms, sobbing.

He found himself simultaneously uneasy and comfortable as he held her. Her hair was falling down in strands from the back of the intricate braided bun she wore, tickling his hands. He felt the years melt away, recalling their friendship at the Academy, the romance that could have been but had never blossomed. And he now felt like her protector; she may have outranked him, but for the moment, she was a friend in pain, and he was doing what he could to shield her, to comfort her.

Batanides stopped crying, and sniffed. He felt her hand unclench near his clavicle and wipe at her eyes. And then, she backed away from him, turning slightly as she wiped her cheek.

"Marta, I'm so sorry."

She straightened slightly, closing her eyes and breathing in deeply through her nose. And then she finally spoke, the tremors still evident in her voice, but the commanding presence of mind returning to her once again. "Yes, thank you, Jean-Luc. I know you did everything you could to help him."

"It wasn't nearly enough," Picard said, resignedly.

"No, I don't blame you. From what you've said, nothing could have prevented what happened . . . except perhaps a little restraint on the rebels' part."

"We don't know for certain who initiated the fighting. In fact, the first one I saw killed by disruptor fire was a rebel soldier."

Batanides looked him steadily in the eye, once more the cool senior Starfleet officer. "Regardless, from what you've already told me, the rebels were definitely firing on your away team, the government delegation, and the Romulans as well. This Army of Light seems willing to resort to any level of violence to thwart Ruardh's diplomatic efforts, and to bring the legitimate government down."

"Marta, there is more to this situation than the Federation has been told. Falhain's people have made grievous charges against the government. I saw evidence implicating Ruardh in military strikes against civilian dissidents—and even 'ethnic cleansing.' I'm no longer so firmly convinced that we're supporting the right side in this matter."

She frowned. "Are you saying that we should throw our support behind Falhain's followers instead? Allow Chiaros IV to fall into the hands of the Romulans?"

"No. What I'm saying is that—"

"Wait." The admiral held up her hand, her face expressing surprise. "Why didn't we look at this before?

Could the *Romulans* have been behind this attack, even at the risk of their own diplomats? They're already our prime suspects in the *Slayton* affair, whether or not we can prove it."

Picard nodded, weighing her words. "It could be that the Romulans' plans for the Geminus Gulf are related to the *Slayton*'s destruction."

"Maybe the rebels didn't touch off the chaos in Hagraté after all, Johnny. Maybe the real culprits were a few well-placed Romulan *agents provocateurs.*"

"Unfortunately, Commander Data's analysis doesn't quite bear that out. None of the energy signatures he detected were Romulan in origin. But some of them actually appear to belong to Starfleet weapons."

"So the finger of blame points back toward the rebels after all," she said, looking satisfied.

"No, not necessarily," Picard said. "You said that Starfleet Intelligence had been given reports that the rebels were using stolen weapons, but that could have been deliberate disinformation intended to muddy the local politics even further. You could have been strung along, given false information. . . . It certainly seems possible, given that the alleged atrocities of Ruardh's regime have been kept secret until now."

For a long moment, Picard's eyes locked with Batanides's. Behind her intense stare, he knew that her mind was racing, trying to overcome her grief using cold, hard logic. But the situation on Chiaros IV was too complex, too unstable, to be explained by simple dialectic reasoning. Too many elements were wild, or just plain unknown.

How can we be sure of anything when every corner seems to hide someone's secret agenda?

Picard's combadge chirped, and Beverly Crusher's

voice dispelled the silence of the room. "Captain, I've found something."

"The admiral and I will meet you in my ready room," Picard said crisply.

"What?" Batanides looked incredulous.

Beverly Crusher stood her ground. Picard knew that as a doctor, she had become used to delivering bad news; it didn't make it easier just because she had done it before, but it had made her emotional hide thicker, so that she didn't take the reactions personally. Crusher placed a small vial down on the ready-room table, slowly and deliberately.

"I'm not sure what it is, Admiral. But I found this implant in your . . . in Ambassador Tabor's brain."

Picard picked up the vial and studied the small item inside it. It was a microchip of some sort, with multiple hair-thin cables extruding from its interface, looking like so many ganglia. "Do you have any idea what its purpose might be?"

Crusher sighed. "I'm not sure. It could be medical, but it's not a piece of technology that I'm familiar with. It might also be something unique to the Ullian species." She turned slightly toward Batanides. "Did the ambassador ever mention having suffered a brain trauma or neurological disorder in the past?"

"No. He was always in perfect health," the admiral replied. "But I suppose it could date back to before we met."

The doors hissed open, and Lieutenant Commanders Data and Geordi La Forge stepped into the ready room, each of them snapping to a more formal posture than normal due to Batanides's presence.

"Good timing," said Picard, handing his chief engineer the vial. "Geordi, Data, I want you to analyze this component and determine its purpose."

"Yes, sir," La Forge said, and moved to a corner of the ready room with the vial. He scrutinized its contents closely while Data began scanning it with his tricorder. They spoke to each other in low tones.

Batanides turned toward the doctor. "Did you find any other . . . abnormalities during the autopsy, Dr. Crusher?"

"No, Admiral. A full scan showed that his health was as good as you've said. His death was entirely the result of the internal and external trauma caused by the Chiarosan weapons."

"Killed by a dagger and a sword. Not even a disruptor." Batanides shook her head. "And we don't even know who did it. Or *why*." The admiral stepped over to the window, looking out at the stars. "Every calamity that's happened on that world, every disaster that's hit this region . . . and it's all due to the hidden agendas of rebels and rogues."

A heavy silence hung in the air. Picard exchanged glances with Crusher, but neither of them seemed inclined to speak just yet.

La Forge cleared his throat, ending the awkward moment.

Picard turned toward Geordi and Data, and immediately noticed the android's satisfied smile. "Did you find something already?"

"Yes, sir. Our scans have identified the likely source of this chip. Its technology has, however, been greatly modified."

"Modified from what, Data?" Crusher asked.

"From a Cardassian cranial implant," said La Forge.

Picard looked stunned. "Cardassian?"

"The chip is similar to a highly classified biotechnological implant that has been used in the past by operatives of the Obsidian Order," Data said. "The original implants were designed to stimulate endorphins, thus allowing operatives to withstand great amounts of pain, and even torture. Starfleet Command first learned of these devices more than two years ago, thanks to a report filed by Deep Space 9's chief medical officer, Dr. Julian Bashir."

"What are you talking about?" asked Batanides. "Why would Aubin have a *Cardassian* chip inside his head?"

"The chip merely appears to employ Cardassian technological principles," Data said, addressing the admiral. "However, it was not necessarily *built* on Cardassia, or by Cardassians."

Picard nodded. "What is its function, Mr. Data?"

"The original version stimulated the pleasure centers of the brain to make agents of the Obsidian Order resistant to torture. It appears that this new implant has been greatly modified to act as some kind of emotion-amplification device. As we know, Ambassador Tabor had Ullian telepathic abilities. Our theory is that this device enabled the ambassador to amplify his innate abilities—in effect, to broadcast his own emotions simultaneously to entire groups of people rather than to specific individuals."

"Which would certainly be a help with his diplomatic missions," said La Forge.

Batanides raised an eyebrow, her gaze intent on La Forge. "Are you suggesting that the ambassador was using implanted thoughts to force negotiating parties to act against their will?"

"No, sir. Even if he had wanted to do something like that, this device just doesn't have enough bandwidth for that. But if you wanted to convey general emotional states to another mind, rather than specific thoughts, I think this chip could do it." La Forge hesitated for a moment. "You probably couldn't change another person's thoughts radically, but I think you could 'nudge' somebody farther in the direction they were already heading. If you were negotiating with somebody who was calm, you could soothe that person even more during a delicate negotiation. Like having quiet music in the background."

Picard stared pointedly at La Forge and Data. "Are you both sure about this?"

"It is only a theory at present, sir," Data said. "We will have to study the chip further to ascertain if this is indeed the case. Nevertheless, I should note that at the time of the ambassador's death, the chip's active isolinear circuitry recorded not a state of calm, but rather one of intense rage."

"That's not surprising in the least, Commander," Batanides spoke quietly, her manner stiff, her eyes betraying nothing. "A Chiarosan rebel had just stuck a dagger into him."

Rage? Picard thought. *Shouldn't there have been fear of imminent death there as well?*

But there was no time to dwell on the thought. Picard knew he had to diffuse the tension created by Data's last statement. "Thank you, Mr. Data. I want you and Mr. La Forge to continue your study of this chip, and give me a full report."

"That is not all I had to report, sir," Data said.

"Go ahead."

"We have identified trace protein residues on Commander Riker's and Counselor Troi's combadges. It appears that Commander Cortin Zweller was the last person to handle them."

The silence in the room was palpable. Data couldn't have shocked his superiors more if he had suddenly broken out into a soft-shoe song-and-dance routine.

"Are you telling me that Zweller is *alive?*" asked Picard.

"I cannot confirm that, Captain. But his DNA was found on both the front and rear surfaces of both combadges. It would seem likely that it was he who removed them."

Batanides's hand dropped to her side heavily. "Incredible!"

"Have any of the crew been able to track life signs from Zweller or any of the other *Slayton* crewmembers?" asked Picard.

"No, sir," Data responded. "The atmospheric disturbances are continuing to block all orbital scans."

"We *have* to find him. Keep trying, Data. Geordi, do whatever you can to penetrate the Chiarosan storms with our sensors. If we can find Zweller, we may find Riker and Troi as well. And the rebels."

Data and La Forge exited the ready room, leaving Picard standing alone with Crusher and Batanides.

"I don't know what to think about this, Jean-Luc," said Crusher. "This is getting more Byzantine by the minute. The loss of the *Slayton*, the death of the ambassador, the Romulans, the rebels, this chip, and now Commander Zweller's involvement . . . Can either of you make any sense out of this?"

Picard looked over at Batanides, who shook her head. He was sure that these new revelations about Tabor and Zweller had added to his old friend's pain—they had certainly rocked *him*—but he also knew that she was more than strong enough to soldier on.

"Marta, I know this is difficult for you on a personal level, but it appears that there are a number of hidden agendas at work here. Ambassador Tabor didn't strike me as enraged when we beamed him aboard the shuttle. I'd characterize him more as . . . frightened and grief-stricken—"

"I think that shows that your android got things wrong," Batanides said coolly, interrupting. "If the implant has been modified as much as he says, how can he be certain *what* its purpose was? Or what emotion Aubin was feeling? And how do we know that Corey isn't being framed as a rebel collaborator?"

"You're right, Marta," Picard said calmly, lowering his voice. "We don't have all the facts. And I'm not accusing either Corey or Ambassador Tabor of anything."

She nodded, stone-faced. "I'm delighted to hear that. Treason is a serious charge to lob at a senior ambassador of the Federation. Or at one of your two oldest friends, for that matter."

"I never said anything about treason, Admiral," Picard said crisply.

"So what *are* you saying?"

Picard paused for a moment to gather his thoughts before speaking. "It certainly seems likely that Cortin Zweller is alive. And we can't dismiss the possibility that he may be involved with Falhain's Army of Light, willingly or otherwise. Especially given the apparent presence of illicit Federation weapons down th—"

Picard didn't have time to finish the thought. The *Enterprise* lurched suddenly to one side, throwing him against a bulkhead, shoulder-first. Batanides and Crusher stumbled as well, catching themselves on the desk.

"What the hell?" Picard spat out as the ship stabilized itself. He quickly made his way to the ready-room door that connected to the bridge, Crusher and Batanides following.

"Status, Mr. Hawk?" Picard asked, heading for the captain's chair.

Hawk spoke without taking his eyes off the conn panel. "Captain, we appear to have been caught in a massive subspace interstitial slippage. It came out of nowhere. Our instruments haven't been able to track its source."

Picard turned to his second officer, who stood at one of the science stations. "Data, could this phenomenon be related to the *Slayton*'s destruction?"

"It is possible, sir. If the slippage had been 3.47827 percent stronger, it would have caused severe damage to our warp core, as well as possible structural collapse of our nacelle struts."

"Captain, sensors also showed an anomalous subspace distortion just south of Chiaros IV's orbital plane," said Hawk

"Can you track it?"

"Not precisely, sir. It was intermittent, and now appears to be gone. Should I set a course to investigate?"

Picard's eyes narrowed as he looked at the viewscreen, which displayed a portion of Chiaros IV's eastern Dayside limb in its lower corner. "No, Mr. Hawk. Hold position. At the moment, we have a few too many mysteries, and not enough sleuths."

He turned to the tall blond officer standing behind one of the ops stations on the upper bridge and spoke: "Mr. Daniels, I want all scientific and engineering personnel on duty. I want to know what's out there in Chiarosan space. I want this ship fortified against any more subspace slippages. And I want a way to get our sensors through that atmosphere."

"Yes, sir."

"I'll be in the observation lounge, with Admiral Batanides," Picard said. He noticed that Lieutenant Hawk was watching him, his eyes narrowed slightly, as if deeply troubled. The younger man seemed to have the weight of the world on his shoulders.

"Was there something you wanted to say, Mr. Hawk?"

The helmsman blushed slightly and turned back to the control panels. "No, sir."

Picard nodded curtly, then spun on his heel and headed toward the exit, with Batanides and Crusher following him.

Chapter Six

Bundling up in the special thermal clothing Grelun's quartermaster had issued him, Zweller ventured a short distance outside the Army of Light's compound—and into the permanent night of Chiaros IV's dark side. To ensure that Ruardh's forces couldn't find them, Grelun's troops had relieved him of his combadge, though Zweller knew it probably wasn't detectable through the planet's heavily ionized atmosphere anyway. But he knew also that outlaws could ill afford to scrimp on caution.

Zweller felt the thin rime of hoarfrost crunching beneath his boots as he walked across a featureless, rock-strewn plain. The air smelled of ozone, giving it a burned quality that belied its bitter chill. Despite the layers of clothing separating him from the elements, the wind bit into his flesh with innumerable small razor teeth, numbing his nose and ears. The cold seemed to aggravate the lassitude caused by the planet's intense gravity. He jammed his gloved hands deeply into his jacket pockets in a vain effort to warm them.

About fifty meters before him sat a squat, frost-encrusted structure, about the size of a Starfleet photon torpedo tube. The apparatus gave off a faint blue glow, which Zweller assumed wasn't visible from the air; he recognized it as a Romulan cloaking device, probably merely one of many. Doubtless the machine was here courtesy of Koval, and its presence helped explain how the rebels had evaded capture for so long. Though Grelun evidently hadn't seen fit to conceal the cloaking device from him, Zweller was certain that the blue light surrounding it was a protective forcefield of some kind. He probably wouldn't be able to damage it even if he wanted to.

Zweller looked upward. The sky was utterly dark, except where small gaps in the omnipresent Nightside haze revealed momentary, random patterns of multicolored light every few seconds. It was an atmospheric conflagration that would have put Earth's Northern Lights to shame. Zweller tried to guess the rebel base's exact position—information that Grelun, the Army of Light's new leader, had yet to divulge to him—but quickly gave up the effort. The atmospheric pyrotechnics gave him no clue; the highly energetic interactions between the solar wind and the planet's magnetic field made such auroral displays visible from any point on the globe, and would be visible even in the brilliance of Dayside. The rebel compound could be anywhere from just nightward of Chiaros IV's habitable twilight meridian to one of the poles to the frigid, windswept reaches of the Nightside equator.

A flash of illumination unlike any of the others drew his attention; it resolved quickly into a small point of light that moved almost directly overhead. At first he thought he'd sighted one of the outer Chiarosan planets until he realized that the luminous speck was moving far too rapidly. He followed the light with his eyes for several minutes, until it vanished into the haze on the horizon.

A government patrol ship, Zweller thought. *It was right on top of us, but it couldn't pierce the cloak.*

The crackle of a footfall directly behind Zweller interrupted his ruminations. He instantly turned to face the sound, backing away to give himself room to maneuver. A colorful flash from the sky allowed Zweller to recognize Grelun's dark visage, just a few meters away. *For such huge people, these Chiarosans are remarkably stealthy,* he thought.

Apparently contemptuous of the elements, Grelun wore only a light jacket over his gray duty uniform. Zweller tried to suppress a shiver and failed.

"You really shouldn't sneak up on a trained Starfleet officer like that," Zweller said, pitching his voice only a little louder than the chill winds.

"Do not worry, human," Grelun said with an inscrutable smile. "You could not have hurt me."

Anger flared within Zweller's chest, momentarily banishing the cold. "Let's hope we never have a reason to test that hypothesis." For reasons Zweller still couldn't fathom, Grelun was even more distrustful and xenophobic than his late predecessor, Falhain.

The Chiarosan chuckled dismissively, then glanced skyward. "I see that you are still brooding about your silent ship."

It was useless to deny it. But it was just as useless to give up hope entirely. "Maybe your subspace receiver isn't functioning properly," Zweller said, trying to sound upbeat. "It can't possibly work as well as the government's orbital comm system. Maybe Captain Blaylock has been trying to raise me for the past week but can't cut through all the atmospheric static."

Grelun nodded soberly. "This may be so," he said, and took a single long stride back toward the compound. "Nevertheless, my communications sentinels will continue listening to the sky."

Grelun's tone held little hope. The rebels did possess a fairly sensitive subspace radio transceiver, after all. Despite its being located at the bottom of Chiaros IV's turbulent atmosphere, it should have picked up *some* trace of the *Slayton* by now. But the starship apparently had been silent ever since Koval had arranged for the shuttle *Archimedes* to be diverted here more than a week ago. And the security-minded Grelun had given strict orders that no subspace signals be transmitted until after the planetary referendum. Zweller could make no attempt to contact his crewmates until Grelun had finished carrying out Falhain's plan to evict the Federation from Chiaros IV.

But Zweller had another, even more fundamental reason to worry about the *Slayton*'s fate. He knew it was useless to dwell on it, but he found the matter impossible to ignore completely. He still couldn't resolve one simple, nagging question to his satisfaction: If the *Slayton* and her crew were safe, then why had the Federation dispatched a second starship to the ill-fated conference in Hagraté? Grelun hadn't seen fit to divulge which starship the two captured Starfleet officers had come from—if he even knew or cared about that piece of information—but Zweller was certain that he had never seen either of the unconscious captives before the rebels had made their escape from the battle in the Chiarosan capital.

Grelun interrupted his gloomy reverie. Taking a single long stride back toward the compound, he said, "Freezing to death will not make your silent comrades speak to you. And I have need of your services."

Zweller's teeth were beginning to chatter. "What do you want me to do?"

"Our two newest . . . guests have at last regained consciousness." Grelun reached into his jacket and produced a Starfleet-issue tricorder, one of the devices his troops had confiscated from the crew of the *Archimedes*. He tossed it to Zweller, who caught it clumsily between his cold-numbed hands.

"I wish for our guests to see what I have already shown to you," Grelun said. "But *you* must be the one to show *them,* if they are to be persuaded that our cause is just."

"I can do that," Zweller said without hesitation. Stowing the tricorder on his belt, he fell into step beside Grelun.

He felt he had every reason to cooperate with Grelun's request. Despite the complications created by Falhain's unforeseen demise at the Hagraté peace conference—it was unfortunate that Zweller had not had a chance to confer with Tabor prior to the ambassador's arrival on Chiaros IV, or to discuss the aftermath of the melee with him—Zweller was satisfied that he had already achieved Section 31's desired objective: He had set the vast wheels of Chiarosan internal politics into motion, and once started they couldn't be stopped. The outcome of the referendum on Federation membership—to be held in a mere three days—was now all but certain to go in favor of Romulus, thanks to Starfleet's 'catastrophic failure to maintain order' in Hagraté. And assuming that Koval was as good as his word, Zweller would soon return to Federation space with ample compensation for this favor—a list of the Romulan intelligence operatives working within the Federation.

Zweller could see no serious downside to his decision

to help Grelun end the genocidal war being carried out by Ruardh's armies. This sort of meddling would almost certainly get him cashiered out of Starfleet, but he had been thinking about retiring soon anyway.

He felt certain he would still have a home within Section 31 after the conclusion of the Chiaros affair. After all, his assisting Grelun couldn't affect the outcome of this mission. And, even more important, it *felt* like the right thing to do.

The time had finally come to bring the horrible truth about Chiaros IV to light.

Flanked by a pair of silent Chiarosan warriors, Zweller and Grelun made their way along a corridor adjacent to—but not directly visible from—the solitary-confinement cells in which Commander Roget and the other *Slayton* captives were still being held pending the referendum. After continuing for several meters, they stopped before a small, doorless chamber, where a single guard stood at attention, his back to the slightly orange-tinged forcefield that rippled across the room's entrance.

Inside the detention cell, a man and a woman sat side by side on a low-slung cot, the room's only piece of furniture. Both prisoners were attired in somewhat distressed-looking Starfleet dress uniforms, the man wearing red, the woman in blue. Though their combadges were missing, each officer's collar bore a trio of shiny brass pips, indicating that both held the rank of commander.

I guess I won't be pulling rank on anyone here. Have to rely on the old Corey Zweller charm instead.

The man rose to his feet first. Tall and vigorous-looking, he had rumpled brown hair that made an incongruous counterpoint to his neatly trimmed beard. His manner was calm, belying the outrage behind his blue eyes.

"I am Grelun, who now guides the Army of Light," the dark-haired Chiarosan said to the male prisoner before the officer could speak. Then the Chiarosan angled an impossibly limber elbow in Zweller's direction. "I present to you your countryman, Commander Cortin Zweller." Grelun then made a courtly, triple-jointed bow toward the prisoners. Zweller interpreted the gesture as ironic, a Chiarosan sign of contempt.

Barely acknowledging Grelun, Riker trained his piercing gaze on Zweller. "Would you mind explaining exactly what is going on here, Commander?"

Abruptly returning to an upright posture, Grelun overrode Zweller before he could respond. "Please accept my apologies, Commander Riker, Commander Troi. I regret that you were handled so roughly. I assure you, we were as gentle with you as the circumstances would permit."

Zweller noticed that the woman's eyes were unusually dark. He decided that she probably wasn't human after all, at least not completely. Perhaps she had some Betazoid ancestry. That could pose a problem. Zweller used the disciplines he'd learned during his training as an agent and quickly erected a barrier around his thoughts and emotions.

"Then can I infer that you intend to return us to the *Enterprise?*" Troi asked.

The Enterprise? Zweller struggled to conceal his surprise from the Betazoid. *Johnny.* He hoped his old friend wouldn't get himself swept up in this dangerous situation. But he remembered the brashness of his old Academy classmate all too well; if Jean-Luc Picard was here, then he would soon be in the thick of things. And an already complex and dangerous situation would undoubtedly become even more so.

"In a short time, yes, we will send you back to your ship," Grelun told Troi.

Riker glanced at Troi. "Deanna?"

The Betazoid scrutinized Grelun for a long moment before speaking. "He's not lying, Will. Though he harbors a great deal of hostility toward us, he's sincere about his intention to release us later. But I sense there's something important he wants to accomplish first."

Grelun bared the points of his teeth, evidently displeased that one of his prisoners could find him so transparent.

Looking as though he'd just solved a puzzle, Riker addressed Grelun, ignoring Zweller for the moment. "I think I understand now. We'll be free to go. But only *after* the Romulans have finished . . . influencing the planetary referendum."

"Once my people formally acknowledge the Federation's inability to make good on its promises of security and order," Grelun said coolly. "Only then will you be free to leave us."

"If your faction wins in the vote," Riker said, "we won't have a lot of other options."

"Exactly so. Your Federation's own laws will force your withdrawal from our world. And with the Federation gone, our independence from *all* degenerate outworlders will be assured."

"That is until the Romulans take your world from you by force," Troi said placidly.

Grelun's hands twirled for a moment in a complex, eye-blurring pattern, as though he were cleansing the very air of her words. "This they could have tried to do long, long ago. Because they have not, we will speak no more of it."

Zweller noticed that Riker had begun looking at him appraisingly. "Commander Cortin Zweller," Riker said, a calculating look in his eyes. "Captain Picard has told me a great deal about you. Including the fact that we might find you among the *Slayton*'s survivors."

Survivors?

Zweller's heart leaped into his throat. He took a deep, calming breath before speaking, pausing to make certain that his mental shields were still intact.

"What are you saying?"

"I'm saying that the *Slayton* was blown to pieces several days ago," Riker said.

"By whom?" Zweller said, swallowing hard. He had grown quite close to many members of the *Slayton*'s crew. For the past several days, he'd been trying hard to avoid facing the possibility that, except for the few who had accompanied him to Chiaros IV, they were all dead.

"When we left the *Enterprise* for the peace conference," Riker said, "we were still trying to determine exactly what happened."

Zweller wondered if Koval might be involved. But what did the Tal Shiar chairman have to gain from the *Slayton*'s destruction? It made no sense; the Romulans had already all but won the Geminus Gulf. The region simply didn't have enough value to justify the commission of an overt act of war.

"We recovered some wreckage," Troi said, "shortly before we escorted Ambassador Tabor to the peace conference."

Taking care not to let the Betazoid sense just how well he knew Aubin Tabor, Zweller said, "How is the ambassador?"

Riker shook his head. "I don't know for sure. The last time I saw him, he'd just been run through with a rebel dagger. One of your friends here evidently tried to assassinate him."

Zweller suddenly felt as though there wasn't enough air in the room. So many friends and colleagues gone, so quickly. It was too much to digest all at once.

"You call us assassins?" Grelun barked, his voice tinged with murder. He made a quick hand signal to the holding-cell guard, who immediately dropped the force-field. Then a wicked-looking dagger appeared in Grelun's hand, as though conjured out of thin air. The rebel leader took a single menacing step toward Riker.

Riker made no move to back away, nor did Troi.

"Speak that lie again, human, and I will cut out your tongue! Your 'ambassador' was caught drawing a weapon on Falhain."

"That's not how it looked from where I was standing," Riker said. His muscles were tensed, but he didn't budge. He neither advanced nor gave ground.

Zweller knew that to show fear before a roused Chiarosan warrior was to provoke a lightning-swift, lethal attack. But he also knew he had to disperse some of the tension in the air, or else Riker was sure to be crippled or killed. Concealing his apprehension behind a stern expression, Zweller stepped between the two men and spread his hands in a placating gesture.

"Falhain would not have wanted this, Noble Grelun," Zweller said, struggling to back his words with the correct blend of authority and deference. "Too much blood has already been spilled. Instead, I ask you: Let me show them what you've shown me."

A long moment passed, during which time Zweller wondered if Grelun weren't seriously considering killing them all. Then the rebel leader sheathed his blade as quickly as he had drawn it. He stared at Riker and Troi, his eyes still as cold and hard as the farthest reaches of frozen Nightside.

Grelun's gaze remained fixed on them even as his body swiveled toward his guards, to whom he said, "Manacle them and bring them to the vehicle pool." He then stalked away down the corridor and was gone.

Riker emerged from the cell, followed by Troi. The presence of the three armed guards seemed to persuade them both that any attempt at escape would be ill-advised. The pair stood impassively while the guards bound their hands before them.

"I don't see any handcuffs on *you*, Commander," Riker said to Zweller. "Am I correct in assuming that you've decided to cooperate with these people?"

Zweller sought the proper words to answer Riker's pointed question, but they refused to come. What came instead was a surge of guilt for having deprived Riker and Troi of their combadges after they'd been dragged unconscious into the catacombs beneath the Hagraté auditorium; there, a pair of Falhain's most vigilant guards had kept Zweller "supervised," and out of the fray for the duration of the peace conference. Zweller knew that by taking the combadges—which the Chiarosan guardsmen had promptly confiscated—he may have prevented Riker and Troi from being beamed to the relative safety of their own shuttle.

But he was also well aware that brief captivity could be a powerful instrument of persuasion. And it was terribly important that he persuade them.

"I have no choice but to help Grelun and his people," Zweller said finally. "And all I ask is that you keep an open mind."

Then he led Riker, Troi, and the guards down the corridor toward one of the hangars.

The antigrav-propelled transport's hull was painted a dull, unobtrusive black. The passenger cabin was wide, windowless, and unadorned, everything in its interior the same monotonous gunmetal blue. Zweller shifted in a vain effort to get comfortable in his too-hard, too-straight seat. Clearly, human ergonomic considerations had not been uppermost in the minds of this vehicle's designers.

A pair of surly-countenanced warriors, a male and a female, sat facing the still-manacled Riker and Troi, who passed the fifteen-minute trip in silence. Seated between the guards, Zweller let his thoughts wander behind the safety of his mental shields. Though he found the transport's gentle shudders and vibrations oddly comforting, he knew he didn't dare relax his guard in the Betazoid's presence.

Zweller found himself desperately hoping that Tabor had somehow managed to survive whatever injuries he'd suffered in the Chiarosan capital. Zweller had always regarded Tabor as both a friend and a mentor, the man who had given his life and career a clarity of purpose that even Starfleet Academy had not been able to do. Tabor had saved him from the consequences of his youthful impetuousness decades ago, on more than one occasion. Had Tabor not warned him away from the beautiful young woman Zweller had taken up with during a shore leave back in '29—a woman who turned out to be a Tzenkethi saboteur—Zweller would likely have returned to the *Ajax* in a body bag, to say nothing of compromising the safety of the ship and her crew. Just two years later, during his second tour of duty with Captain Narth aboard the *Ajax,* a female Vulcan agent had recruited Zweller into Section 31, where he had come under Tabor's direct supervision and sponsorship. A universe of opportunities, none of which ever seemed to come fast enough for him as an ordinary Starfleet officer, had opened up for him then. And he had never looked back.

And now Tabor might well be dead. Swept away, just like Captain Blaylock and the crew of the *Slayton*.

Zweller found coincidences hard to accept. His mind returned to his earlier query: Had Koval been responsible for the attack on Tabor as well as the deaths of his shipmates? Perhaps the Romulan had never intended to surrender the spy list. Maybe he was already back on Romulus, confident that Zweller would never survive his sojourn on Chiaros IV. Regardless, it was abundantly clear to him now that Koval had another agenda besides his deal with Section 31.

But what is it?

The vehicle ceased its shuddering, touching down with a light thump. A moment later, the guards perfunctorily removed Riker's and Troi's manacles and handed them thermal blankets, which the captives wrapped about their shoulders on their way to the vehicle's rear hatchway. Still wearing his jacket, Zweller declined a blanket of his own. Then, his tricorder at the ready, he led the way outside the transport.

Because this near-Nightside region did not have the benefit of the mountains and canyons that shielded much of Chiaros IV's habitable meridian, the howling wind struck them brutally. They had to lean into it as they walked in order to make any forward progress at all. The charcoal sky scattered the wan almost-twilight, revealing the tumble of indistinct shapes that lay ahead. As they trudged closer, those shapes resolved themselves into ruined stone walls, the remnants of dwellings, and the fossil-dry pieces of a shattered water-extraction machine. Chunks of burned, shattered masonry lay about in random heaps, like toys discarded by some colossal, tantrum-prone child. The exposed bedrock, wind-scoured for countless ages, bore scorches and craters of obviously much more recent origin. Jagged flashes of ionospheric brilliance leaped across the sky, casting fleeting, irregular shadows in every direction across the detritus of unnumbered destroyed and uprooted lives.

As they walked, Riker shouted to be heard over the keening of the wind. "Is this the same village from the hologram Falhain showed us in Hagraté?"

Zweller hadn't seen Falhain's presentation at the peace conference. But the rebels had made him well-acquainted with those particular—and extremely persuasive—holographic images.

"I'm not sure, Commander," Zweller shouted back. "But does it really matter when there are hundreds more just like it?"

They came to a stop before a partially demolished wall, which appeared once to have been part of a village well. The squat ruin offered them some small respite from the raging winds. Zweller watched as Riker's boyish face changed, settling into hard planes and angles. Troi looked physically ill. An aurora crackled far overhead, like an electrical arc jumping between the uprights of an old-fashioned Jacob's ladder.

Zweller handed the tricorder to Riker, who immediately began scanning the wall and the surrounding terrain. The dour-eyed guards stood by quietly while Riker pored over the readouts.

The wall bore a small humanoid silhouette. A child's shadow, rendered in a micrometer-thin layer of carbon atoms. Several other nearby structures bore similar marks.

Ashes, ashes, we all fall down, Zweller thought without a scintilla of humor.

Riker's mouth was moving. Lip-reading, Zweller thought he made out a "My God."

Zweller shouted into the wind. "Chiarosan weaponry

isn't all ceremonial flatware, Commander. Especially among Ruardh's people."

Zweller paused, smiling mirthlessly before continuing. "Sometimes those folks use disruptors."

Zweller could still feel the bone-deep chill even as the antigrav vehicle returned them to the rebel compound nearly an hour later. Nobody spoke until after the guards had escorted Riker and Troi back to their holding cell.

Standing beside the guard outside the cell's forcefield, Zweller was the first to break the grim silence. "*Now* do you understand why I've decided to assist Grelun's movement?"

Nodding, Riker said, "I understand that you see them as the local underdog. I probably would myself, in your place. But how do we know you showed us the whole story?"

"Commander, I hope you're not implying," Zweller said with a scowl, "that there's any way to justify the slaughter you just saw."

Riker shook his head. "Of course not. But how do you know the rebels aren't the ones actually responsible for the killing? They could have staged the massacre themselves simply to discredit Ruardh's government."

Outside the cell, one of the guards growled and spat on the floor. "I don't believe that, Commander," Zweller said. "And I don't think you do either."

"I sense no such duplicity among these people, Will," Troi said. "They follow such a strict code of warrior ethics that I don't think they have the capacity to mount and maintain a deception of that sort." She paused to look at one of the guards who stood in the corridor, and a look of surprise lit up her face before she spoke again. "In fact, Grelun's warriors seem every bit as bound by honor as Klingons."

Riker appeared to mull the facts over for a moment,

then sighed and looked at Zweller. "All right. Maybe we ought to take this story at face value. When did all this begin?"

"Over a decade ago," Zweller said, "when Ruardh and her council decided that the tribal ethnic minorities were too much of a drain on the planet's extremely limited natural resources. The government started forcing the tribes farther and farther from the prime habitable zone. That should have been a death sentence. But these people were just too tough and ornery to die.

"More recently, Ruardh started worrying that the exiled tribes might complicate her initiative for Federation membership. So she ordered them liquidated, town by town, village by village. There are new massacres every few weeks, but Ruardh has managed to keep a lid on things so far by jamming whatever long-range subspace communications capabilities the rebels may have. And since her people control the orbiting transmitter, the Federation knows only what Ruardh wants us to know. If the Federation wins the referendum—and Ruardh hangs onto power—these people can't hope to hold out for much more than another year or two. Not without help, anyway."

Riker stroked his beard calmly, giving Zweller the impression of a man about to place a bid in a friendly game of poker. "Commander, the sooner we get back to the *Enterprise,* the sooner we might be able to provide that help."

"Grelun has promised to release all of us after the referendum," Zweller said. "That includes the three of us and my shuttle crew."

Troi shook her head. "Even if the vote goes the way Grelun wants it to, we'd all still be stuck here for the next three days, unable to help *anybody.* And if what we saw in the village is any indication, a lot more people could die during that time."

Excellent point, Zweller thought, taking care to keep his mind opaque to Troi's empathic senses. He wondered how many more Chiarosan children might have to pay with their lives for his adherence to prearranged mission timetables. After all, if they were all to escape to the *Enterprise* sooner rather than later, there might be time to expose Ruardh's crimes to the general populace—and to the Federation Council—before the planet-wide referendum.

Zweller assumed that the vote would, in any event, still go against the Federation because of its earlier failure to broker peace between Ruardh and Falhain. But that also meant, as Zweller reasoned it, that an early departure could not disrupt the bargain he'd made with Koval on behalf of Section 31. Therefore, his mission objective would still be accomplished even if he and the other prisoners were to leave *right now.*

Turning away from the guard, Zweller whispered, "Let me see what I can do."

After the visit to the destroyed village, no one had thought to relieve Zweller of the tricorder Grelun had returned to him. Zweller had maintained possession of it by leaving it attached to his belt, right out in the open. He had, in effect, hidden it in plain sight. The rebels apparently didn't see the point of confiscating something that he was clearly making no effort whatsoever to conceal.

While Grelun hadn't exactly given Zweller the run of the Army of Light compound, the rebel leader *had* allowed him considerable freedom of movement in exchange for his tactical advice. That, and for helping the Chiarosans use the replicator salvaged from the

Archimedes to create weapons and spare components for the freedom fighters' dozen or so battered fighter craft. Zweller thought of his surviving *Slayton* crewmates, reflecting that Roget would be extremely upset if he ever discovered just how badly maintained the ships that captured the *Archimedes* had been; the Starfleet shuttle could easily have held its own against them.

During the eight days or so he had spent among the Chiarosan rebels so far—it was awkward expressing time in terms of days on a world without sunrises and sunsets—Zweller had come to feel that these grim warriors had become at least tolerant of his presence. Many of them now genuinely seemed to like him, and were no doubt grateful for his help.

Thus Zweller was unsupervised when, less than ten minutes after parting company with Riker and Troi, he entered an empty alcove. Here he opened a wall-mounted panel through which part of the compound's optical data network ran. Having been designed for Chiarosans, the panel was quite high, forcing him to stand on tiptoe, his arms stretched uncomfortably above his head. Alert for the sound of approaching Chiarosans, he worked as quickly as possible, patching the tricorder into the microminiaturized ODN terminal node he had installed four days previously; he'd left it there while ostensibly helping one of the rebel engineers run a diagnostic on the base's communications system. Forcing contemporary Starfleet hardware to work reliably alongside the Chiarosans' systems—most of which appeared to be analogous to Federation technology from the late twenty-second century—had been a bit of a challenge, despite his extensive training in obsolete technologies. But core technological principles rarely changed much, even after two centuries.

Using the tricorder's input pads, Zweller navigated through a complicated series of hierarchical icons. This complex command sequence was intended to surreptitiously isolate this particular comm terminal from the rest of the base's computer system. At the same time, it would attempt to seize control of a portion of the backup comm system using every possible clearance code, running the code sequences at nearly a billion cycles per second. After each attempt, the program in the tricorder would erase all evidence that it had ever tried to jimmy its way inside the facility's systems.

A tense minute elapsed while the small display on Zweller's tricorder repeatedly flashed a single word: WORKING. Two minutes passed. A bead of cold sweat crept down the small of his back, chilling him. Three minutes.

Then the display gave way to a cheerful green: COMMUNICATIONS ARRAY: ACCESS APPROVED.

Yes!

Zweller's hands were now becoming slick with sweat from the effort of holding his body in such an unnatural posture. As carefully as he could, he entered the next sequence of icons, a grouping even more complex than the previous one. The idea behind this particular command set was to get inside the base's security grid. Were he actually to try to use the base's transmitter before doing that, he would more than likely trigger a security alarm.

It would take only a few moments to send the *Enterprise* a burst of data containing a set of detailed instructions, including the coordinates of each of the holding cells relative to the location of the rebels' subspace transmitter. Assuming that the transmitter could pierce the local static, Johnny and his crew would trace the signal to its source, establish its location, and then apply his coordinate correction data to calculate the positions of each of the imprisoned Starfleet officers. While Zweller was well aware that the transporters aboard the *Enterprise* could not beam anyone directly off the planet— there was far too much atmospheric ionization to permit that—he was reasonably certain that a low-flying shuttlecraft could pull it off, with a little luck.

He decided that he would preprogram the holding cells' forcefields to come down in six hours. Six hours would give Picard ample time to get a shuttle close enough to the compound to beam every Starfleet captive to safety. And because even the Chiarosan government probably couldn't intercept such a brief, tightly focused subspace transmission, the rebel compound's location would remain beyond the reach of Ruardh's military machine.

It was a win–win scenario. Zweller grinned at his own cleverness.

WORKING, flashed the tricorder as it continued trying countless security-grid access codes. Another crimson-blinking minute passed. Then two.

Three minutes. More sweat flowed, this time stinging his eyes. He brushed it away with his palm, stifling a curse.

Four minutes. Why the hell was this taking so long?

He heard the deliberate clip-clop of a soldier's boots. The sound approached, then withdrew, then ceased entirely.

His hands had begun to shake. *I'm getting too old for this.*

Then, in green: SECURITY GRID: ACCESS APPROVED. The muscles in his calves and shoulders were aching from his awkward, upward-reaching stance. His fingers had become slippery with sweat and his arms were growing numb. Not wanting to risk revealing his presence by using the tricorder's voice interface, he began scrolling and entering the icons that would transmit his data-burst to the *Enterprise*.

The tricorder's display flashed an interrogative icon. Then he saw what he had done. He had inadvertently mistaken one icon hierarchy for another. It was the equivalent of making a typographical error on a computer equipped with an old-style keyboard interface.

He began scrolling and entering commands again, more slowly this time. The shaking of his hands intensified. Muscle fatigue was making his right leg begin to shimmy. He entered the final icon in the command sequence.

TRANSMITTING.

He never heard the footfalls of the stealthy Chiarosan guard whose rough hands seized his shoulder half a second later.

Will Riker was surprised when a pair of very angry, very large Chiarosan warriors suddenly marched him and Troi from their cell, only to escort them into another similar one located a fair distance away.

He was even more surprised to see Commander Cortin Zweller awaiting them there, already confined in the cell. Zweller appeared to have lost his favored guest status; his tricorder was missing and his face bore several bruises that hadn't been there when they had parted company some twenty minutes earlier.

Riker found it difficult to suppress a wry smile. So, evidently, did Deanna.

"I take it that Grelun has declined your request for our early release," Riker said blandly.

Zweller responded with a humorless chuckle. "Vehemently. I suppose he moved all the other prisoners, too, once he suspected that I'd transmitted their transporter coordinates to the *Enterprise*."

A surge of hope swelled within Riker's chest. He made certain his back was to the guard standing on the other side of the forcefield before he responded. "And did you?"

Zweller shrugged, then spoke in a barely audible whisper. "I think so, but there's no way to be sure. But I am certain about one thing—I managed to sabotage the security grid before I got caught. I don't think they'll discover it until after it's too late."

"And what will that accomplish?" Troi wanted to know.

Zweller absently touched a bruise on his forehead and winced. "The detention-cell forcefields should come down in a little less than six hours. I tried to send a burst-message asking the *Enterprise* to send a shuttle for us then. If they can get to within a few kilometers of us, they should be able to beam us all out of here, even through all the atmospheric interference."

"If your message got through, then the captain will get us that shuttle," Riker said quietly. He needed to buoy his spirits. This was a slim hope, but it was *something*.

"Fat lot of good it'll do us if Grelun's moved everybody around," Zweller said. "The shuttle crew won't know where to try for a transporter lock. And they won't have a lot of time to run scans if Grelun scrambles his fighter craft to intercept them."

"I'm afraid I have more bad news," Troi said, her eyes closing.

"I don't see how things can get much worse now," Riker said.

"I do. I'm picking up extremely strong emotions from Grelun. He no longer has any intention of releasing us." Her eyes came open then, twin pools of apprehension. "He's furious, Will. If the referendum doesn't go the way he wants it to, Grelun intends to declare total war on his opponents. He'll probably start by executing all of his prisoners, and then . . ." she trailed off.

"And then?" Zweller prompted.

"The rebels have left Chiarosan civilians out of the conflict so far, but—"

Riker finished the thought for her. "—but the gloves will be off if the pro-Federation side wins."

"Judging from the ugly state of Grelun's emotions," Troi said, "you can expect a bloodbath. A long, drawn-out planetary civil war."

Zweller smiled. "You're overlooking an important detail, Commander Troi. The pro-Federation side doesn't stand a snowball's chance on Vulcan of winning the referendum."

Riker shot a grave look at Zweller. "I might be inclined to agree with you, Commander. Except for the one thing that *you* seem to have overlooked."

"Which is?"

Riker pointed toward the stone ceiling. "Which is that the man commanding the *Enterprise* is Jean-Luc Picard. The man who served as Klingon Chancellor Gowron's Arbiter of Succession. Thanks to the captain's diplomacy, the Klingon civil war lasted for months instead of years."

Zweller's smile faltered then. "Diplomacy wasn't his strong suit when I knew him, Commander."

"It's never a good idea to underestimate Captain Picard," Troi said.

Zweller looked up at them both. "Then for everyone's sake, you'd both better hope he fails in a big way this time."

Never during the nine years he had so far spent serving alongside Captain Picard had Will Riker thought he would find himself agreeing with such a sentiment.

Now, he had no other option.

Chapter Seven

"Launching probe, Captain," said Data, his hands gliding over an ops panel.

Hawk watched as Picard leaned forward in his seat, staring at the forward bridge viewscreen as the small probe sped off into the starry blackness. The captain's eyes narrowed, as if by squinting he could see more clearly what the probe saw.

Data turned. "Would you like me to activate visual telemetry, sir? It would be more effective."

Hawk stared at Data. The android's directness always amazed him. Coming from anyone else, Data's question might have seemed an insult, but Hawk—and everyone who had ever served on the bridge—knew better.

"Yes, Data," Picard said, settling back into his chair.

The image on the viewscreen changed only slightly, though digital counters and coordinate graphics appeared around the edges, showing the data that the probe was recording as it sped through space.

While they had been supervising the technicians who had worked on the probe, Data, Hawk, and La Forge had analyzed the sector maps, using the residual radiation traces found on the *Slayton*'s wreckage—as well the starship's velocity and trajectory—to pinpoint the probable site where the vessel was destroyed. Not surprisingly, this location was very close to the volume of space that Hawk's sketchy sensor data labeled as the likeliest source of the first subspace slippage, as well as the probable epicenter of the half-dozen or so lesser spatial disturbances that had followed.

A quick visit to the stellar cartography labs had provided Hawk and Data with further scientific background of the Geminus Gulf. Hawk was somewhat surprised to discover just how little there was to go on. According to the few pertinent records that Keru had managed to retrieve—which had come, thanks to the barrenness of the Gulf, mostly from some of the more obscure stellar cartographical journals, as well as from his correspondences with colleagues serving aboard other Federation starships—the random subspace fluctuations in the vicinity had intensified substantially over the past two years. Prior to that, even the most patient and long-suffering researchers hadn't seen fit to spend much time taking readings in the Gulf; one science-vessel commander had characterized the entire region as a kind of "interstellar *tabula rasa*."

Hawk was back at his post, mentally reviewing the dates, locations, and intensities of all known subspace fluctuations in the Geminus Gulf when the turbolift opened. Batanides strode out, dressed impeccably in her admiral's uniform, her face once again composed. Hawk knew she must be holding in an enormous amount of emotional strain following the death of her lover. What he *didn't* know was whether or not *she* had been aware of the ambassador's involvement with Section 31. Had Tabor managed to keep his association with the bureau a secret from her as well?

His eyes tracked her as she went to sit at Picard's right-hand side, in the chair usually occupied by Will Riker. She gave Hawk a brief glance—and in that look he saw not the slightest glimmer of recognition. At that instant, the lieutenant became relatively certain that even if she *did* know about Tabor's activities, she remained unaware of the ambassador's efforts to recruit him.

Hawk's mind raced as he turned back to the conn and the viewer, while behind him, Picard and Batanides conversed in low tones.

A few minutes later, Data interrupted them, his eyes steady on the screen while his fingers slid across his console. "Captain, I believe the probe has encountered something."

"What specifically, Mr. Data?" Picard looked at the screen intently, though the starfield looked no different now than it had moments before.

"Impossible to tell for certain, sir. There is definitely an energy field being generated at coordinates 294 by 025 by minus 121. It appears to be a cloaking field of some kind, though its size is larger than anything our computers have ever mapped."

"Is it natural?"

"Unknown. It *could* be a natural phenomenon, but the readings I am seeing are inconclusive. It is also possible that the field is technological in origin."

"Which doesn't tell us much," Picard said. "Data, approximately how large would you estimate this field to be?"

The android cocked his head slightly, a move that Hawk recognized as a sign that Data's curiosity had been piqued. "The probe is moving along the outskirts of the field now. It appears that the cloak may cover a volume of space roughly the size of a large gas giant planet."

"What?" Batanides leaned forward in Riker's chair, a surprised look on her face. "Are you saying there's a cloaked planet in this system?"

"Not necessarily, sir. We do not know *what* is cloaked, nor if anything is indeed 'cloaked' in the traditional sense of the word."

Picard spoke up, pointing at the screen. "Data, what happens to the signals that the probe is sending toward the field?"

"They disappear, sir. They are not reflected, nor deflected. All trace of them is gone."

Hawk fidgeted slightly at his console. Before he realized he was doing it, the captain evidently noticed it. "Is there something you want to contribute, Mr. Hawk?"

"Captain, may I suggest that we attempt to send the probe into the field itself?" Hawk asked, relieved. "At worst, we get one of our probes destroyed."

"Yes, perhaps you're right," Picard said agreeably. "We might be able to get some valuable telemetry readings from a probe, even if the field does destroy it. I think the *Enterprise* is sufficiently far from the . . . anomaly to prevent whatever happened to the *Slayton* from happening to us. Still, we can't be too careful." Picard then raised the volume of his voice, though everyone on the bridge was clearly already listening. "Yellow alert. Shields at maximum."

Then, the captain nodded toward the young helmsman. "Go ahead, Mr. Hawk." The lieutenant moved his fingers over the console swiftly, while to his left, Data stared attentively at the numbers and pictographs displayed on the screen.

The silence on the bridge was palpable, and all eyes were on the viewer. Suddenly, the blackness of space began slowly wavering, as if the starfield were a curtain being moved aside. For an instant, the viewer showed the infinite emptiness behind that curtain, and then in a burst of static it was gone.

"All signals from the probe have stopped, captain," said Data. He tapped at his console, then turned his head toward Picard. "I cannot restore contact."

"What did we just see?" Picard asked as he rose to his feet.

"Whatever it was, it lasted precisely .763 seconds."

"Interesting. If I had blinked at the wrong moment I would have missed it. Replay and freeze the image."

"Yes, sir." Once again, the viewscreen displayed the hazy picture, suspending it in time. The effect was like looking into a warped funhouse mirror, with space itself showing odd distortions, and reflections of the probe broken up throughout the image. The only tangible-looking object visible in the immediate foreground appeared to be an artificial satellite of some sort; the numerical telemetry overlays, which Data displayed on the viewer, showed that the device was no larger than a Starfleet shuttlepod.

"Enlarge that object."

As Data did so, the satellite came into view somewhat more clearly. It was nondescript, a smooth metal ovoid with no markings, nor any visible means of propulsion.

"Curious," Picard said, frowning slightly and tugging at his tunic. "Enlarge the initial image further and scan it in sections for any other incongruities in the local visible and subspace fields."

Data studied the screen as enlarged portions of the image sped by, almost too quickly for the human eye to follow. After almost a minute, the android spoke. "I have detected numerous other similar concentrations of matter, as well as an apparent central point-source of sub-space distortion. Displaying now."

The screen returned to a wide-angle display of the main image, with four square sections highlighted in red. Data touched the face of his console, isolating and then magnifying images of four separate objects. "I have displayed the device we initially observed beside magnified images of two more distant, but apparently identical, objects. Interestingly, these three artifacts seem to be arranged in an equidistant formation. Nearby sensor shadows would seem to indicate that many more similar objects exist within the field."

Picard pointed toward the screen's upper right corner. "What is that fourth object?"

Data touched his console again, and the fourth section of the screen moved forward, magnified to its fullest potential. Though the image was tremendously clouded and distorted, the object clearly wasn't of the same construction as the satellites.

Without waiting to be prompted, Hawk input a command that enhanced the image further, editing out the empty space surrounding it.

A double-bladed, emerald-hued vessel hung in the viewscreen's center. Picard was hardly surprised. "A Romulan warbird."

Hawk's mind raced, scrambling to sift through details he'd studied about the crew's previous missions. Within moments, he seized on the proper memory. "Captain, I've got a theory that might explain some of this."

Batanides looked over at Hawk, one eyebrow raised as if to question his impertinence.

"Go ahead, Mr. Hawk," Picard said.

"About four years ago, you discovered a Dyson Sphere. I believe we may have stumbled onto something similar here. What if this trio of satellites we've spotted—and the other subspace distortions—are part of a network of thousands of buoys, each one equipped with a Romulan cloaking device—"

"Yes, I see," Picard interrupted. "With a network like that, the Romulans could enclose and cloak an enormous volume of space. *Without* having to build a solid structure around it."

"That *is* theoretically possible," said Data. His hands flew over the controls. "I am linking the identifiable point-sources together." A new image appeared on the screen, this time showing a spherical gridwork of lines with hundreds of intersections, each of which presumably represented an object like the first device the probe had detected. Although the pattern contained gaps—which Hawk attributed to imperfect telemetry readings—the visual effect was similar to the latitude and longitude lines on a planetary map, or a complex spider's web bent into a globular shape. And the warbird was stationed near the inside northern edge of the hypothetical web.

"Incredible," Batanides said, leaning back in her chair. "They *could* be hiding a planet the size of Jupiter for all we can tell."

"It is also possible that this network is shielded in a manner that would disrupt the operation of approaching ships or probes," Data said. "That would be consistent with the loss of our probe's telemetry."

"But Romulan ships would have to be able to pass freely through the field," Hawk said.

Data nodded. "Any vessel authorized to enter the cloaked zone would probably gain admittance by emitting a particular cloaking-field resonance frequency."

Picard said, "But anyone else trying to get across might find their systems completely shut down."

"Making them defenseless against an attack," said Batanides. "Maybe now we know what happened to the *Slayton*. And why they never sent a distress signal or launched a log buoy."

"If something inside that cloak is so important to the Romulans that they would destroy a Federation starship to keep it a secret, then it's got to be bigger than our Chiarosan diplomatic problem," Picard said grimly.

"Maybe the two are interrelated, sir," said Hawk.

"No doubt, Lieutenant. They've gone to great pains to conceal something from us. But they risk starting an interstellar war. What could possibly justify such recklessness?"

Hawk watched in silence as Picard stared at the Romulan warbird's blurred image, and asked himself the very same question.

"Protector Ruardh, you must understand my situation. We came here to help mediate your conflict, not to aggravate it." Picard was exasperated, but he tried not to show it as he stood still behind his desk in the ready room. Chiaros IV's orbiting communications array was finally working again—for the moment—allowing the *Enterprise* to make contact with the Chiarosan capital. He was uncomfortably aware that the signal strength this broadcast required meant that any ship within the system, visible or cloaked, could easily intercept his conversation with the Chiarosan leader.

On the desktop screen, Ruardh was not so sanguine; she was visibly angry as she paced in front of the screen in her palace. "You saw for yourself what these traitors are capable of, Picard! You very nearly lost your life, and your ambassador *did* make that final transition. What more proof do you need that this Army of Light is wreaking destruction upon our society?"

Crusher sat on the low sofa, just out of the screen's line of sight; Batanides stood beside her. Picard noticed that the admiral had stiffened slightly at the mention of Tabor's death. "Madame Protector," the admiral said coolly, "the political situation on your planet is far more volatile than we had understood when you first requested Federation mediators. In this matter, we must remain as neutral as possible. Our Prime Directive—"

The incensed Chiarosan stepped hard on Batanides's words. "Don't speak to me as if we are some species with whom you have just made first contact! We are a people who have petitioned for membership in the Federation, and you are refusing to aid us against our enemies! Have we chosen the wrong power to side with? Should we have chosen the Romulan Star Empire as our *Dhaekav* all along?"

Batanides took a deep breath before responding. "Your government has indeed petitioned for membership. But it appears that your government does not enjoy the full support of your people, Protector. It is my understanding that the upcoming referendum will decide whether your citizenry wish to join with us or not." The admiral's next words were delivered with a deadly calm. "If they decide in favor, we will be much better able to help you defend against any . . . insurgent attacks."

Picard interjected before Ruardh could speak again. "As for the Romulans, we have reason to believe that their empire has more of a stake in this region of space than we had previously considered. This makes the situation even more volatile. We cannot risk igniting a war with—"

"Risk? What you are risking are my *people,* Captain! And *your* people as well. Or have you forgotten that two of your own command crew are still in rebel hands?"

The picture on the viewscreen flickered, Ruardh's image and words splitting into fragments.

Picard tapped his combadge. "Geordi, we're losing the signal. Can you boost it?"

The engineer's voice piped through the small transceiver. "Sorry, Captain. The problem seems to be on the Chiarosans' end."

Picard leaned in toward the small viewscreen. "Protector Ruardh, I'm afraid that we cannot maintain subspace contact for much longer. But I promise you that we will try to find a way to help *all* of your people and—" The signal suddenly blinked out, and Ruardh was gone, replaced by a silver-white Starfleet insignia superimposed over a dark background.

Picard sighed heavily and leaned against the desk, tapping his fingertips on its gleaming top. "*That* certainly went well," he said sardonically, gazing first at the admiral, then toward Crusher.

The doctor, still seated on a low sofa in a far corner of the room, finally broke her silence. "It went as well as could be expected, Jean-Luc. This . . . situation . . . is difficult, to say the least."

Batanides put a supportive hand on his shoulder. "At least you won't have to make any precipitous decisions without a higher-up on board. Whatever we decide to do, *I'll* be the one who has to answer to Starfleet Command."

Picard looked over at her, and saw a wan smile on her lips. Through her cool exterior, he could sense her grief. He searched for something to say in reply, when his combadge chirped, followed by Data's voice. "Captain, we've just received another transmission from Chiaros IV."

"Ruardh?"

"No, sir. It came on a Starfleet frequency. And it appears to be from Commander Cortin Zweller."

Picard, Batanides, and Dr. Crusher entered the bridge quickly. Hawk was busy at the conn station, while Data stood before one of the science consoles, working alongside the Vulcan technician, K'rs'lasel. The Vulcan spoke first, facing the captain. "Sir, I intercepted a subspace signal moments ago. It was very brief, but I believe it was intended for us. The signal contained a Starfleet identification code belonging to Commander Zweller."

"The subspace burst was weak, but we have managed to salvage most of it over the past three minutes," Data added. "It appears to contain several adjacent sets of coordinates located on the Nightside of Chiaros IV. It also contained a garbled message about security-grid forcefields, the significance of which I have yet to ascertain. In addition, the transmission mentioned the word 'prisoners' very prominently, as well as a stardate which will occur five hours, fifty-seven minutes from now."

Picard smiled broadly as hope welled up within his chest. "He's telling us that he's their prisoner," he said to Batanides. "And that he needs our help."

"Captain, the message *could* be a ruse," Batanides said, her voice pitched low enough so that only Picard, Data, and K'rs'lasel could have heard it. "They may have tortured Zweller to gain access to his command codes."

Picard looked at Batanides, then at Crusher. He shook his head. "Somehow, I don't believe that the rebels would do that. And if Troi were here, I think she would concur."

"The Chiarosan rebels might not be the ones doing the torturing, Captain," Crusher said. She didn't need to finish that thought for him to know exactly what she meant.

Picard weighed the options in his mind. Zweller might indeed be a prisoner, and might have found the means— somehow—to send that signal. On the other hand, the message may have originated either from the Chiarosan rebels *or* from the Romulans. Even Ruardh's people could have sent the signal, as a catalyst to force Picard's hand.

And yet, Corey is still down on the planet. And so are Riker, Troi, and heaven only knows how many survivors from the Slayton.

Then Picard made his decision, and it felt right, somehow inevitable. His jaw set in determination, he began giving orders. "Mr. Data, I want you to pinpoint as close as you can the coordinates that signal gave us." He turned to address the blond officer who was monitoring a sensor display near the rear of the bridge. "Mr. Daniels, prepare the shuttlecraft *Kepler* for passage through the planet's atmosphere. I'll need the shields operating at maximum efficiency, and I want as much firepower on board as possible." He sincerely hoped he would not be called upon to use it.

"Aye, sir," Daniels said, then strode purposefully into the starboard turbolift.

"Sounds like you're planning a rescue operation, Johnny," Batanides said, smiling.

Picard gestured toward Crusher. "Nothing overly aggressive, Admiral. Just myself and the doctor. There may be wounded at those Nightside coordinates who will require her attention."

"There'll be three of us in that shuttle," Batanides said, her tone and posture brooking no argument.

Picard nodded, knowing that there were some battles he couldn't hope to win. "All right," he said. "But we must leave quickly. The message's time reference could mean that we have less than a six-hour window."

Data spoke in a manner reminiscent of the Sherlock Holmes persona he enjoyed playing on the holodeck. "At which time it may be possible to penetrate the detention grid mentioned in the message, then extract whoever is being held at the specified coordinates."

"My thoughts exactly," Picard said. "Mr. Data, you'll be in command until I return." The android nodded soberly, and Picard stepped toward the port turbolift, preceded by the doctor and the admiral. The doors whooshed open and the two women entered ahead of him.

"Captain," said a voice from the front of the bridge. Crusher held the door as Picard stopped and turned toward the man who had spoken.

"Mr. Hawk," Picard said. The lieutenant had risen from his seat behind the conn station.

"Sir, I need to speak with you. Privately."

Though he wasn't pleased about the interruption, Picard managed to keep the exasperation out of his voice. "Lieutenant, we have very little time."

"I know, sir," Hawk said quickly. "And that's exactly why we need to talk."

Picard knew that this forward behavior was very unlike Hawk. The lieutenant's gaze was locked with his, his expression unreadable.

Something truly dire must be on the young man's mind. He turned toward Crusher and the admiral and asked them to wait for him in the main shuttlebay.

After the turbolift doors had closed he turned back toward Hawk and appraised him. "You have two minutes, Lieutenant. In my ready room. Now."

Hawk was deep in thought as he followed Picard into the ready room. *Strange that I'm not feeling more . . . fear.* He recalled telling Tabor that watching Picard had been a valuable education for him. The ambassador had reminded him that sometimes the captain bent the rules to achieve the correct aims. This was most certainly one of those times.

More important, Tabor had told Hawk that Zweller was particularly significant in whatever secret agendas were unfolding in this sector. It seemed vitally important to Hawk that he do everything possible to ensure the commander's rescue. Zweller, after all, just might be the key to the mysteries of Chiaros IV and the rest of the Geminus Gulf.

Hawk wondered if he should tell Picard about Tabor's overtures, and about Zweller and his connection to Section 31. But the ambassador had been so clear on the need for utter secrecy regarding the organization that Hawk hadn't even told Keru about it, or about his discussions with Tabor. Despite the ambassador's death—or perhaps because of it—it seemed wrong to betray this confidence now.

Hawk suddenly became aware that the captain was speaking to him. "Have a seat, Lieutenant," he said from the chair behind his desk. Hawk wondered when the captain had sat down, and cursed himself for woolgathering.

"Thank you, sir," Hawk said, swallowing convulsively as he took the proffered chair.

"What's on your mind, Mr. Hawk?"

Hawk gathered up his courage, then spoke his mind. "I'd like to go along with you on the rescue mission, sir."

Picard said nothing at first, an indecipherable look in his eye. Finally, he broke the silence. "I appreciate your enthusiasm, Lieutenant, but I don't think your presence on this mission will be necessary."

Hawk shifted awkwardly in his seat, but calmed himself by recalling the best advice his partner had ever given him when dealing with Starfleet matters: *Trust your instincts.*

"Sir, may I have permission to speak freely?"

"Of course, Lieutenant."

"Sir, with respect, I think my presence *is* necessary. Your shuttle has three command officers, one of whom is a doctor. You are about to attempt to navigate treacherous atmospheric storms, approach a hostile military base—which may or may not be a trap—and rescue an unknown number of Starfleet personnel from either the Chiarosans or the Romulans."

Picard leaned back in his chair, one eyebrow cocked, as Hawk continued. "No matter how good a pilot *you* are, sir, your attention needs to be focused on getting everyone back to the shuttle safely. Admiral Batanides will be of some help, but what happens to the shuttle while you're rescuing the prisoners? Do you leave Dr. Crusher behind to face a possible attack? Or do you leave the admiral on board?"

He paused for a moment to let his words sink in, then resumed his plea. "I understand why you aren't taking a large security contingent along; there's no room in the shuttle, especially if you hope to bring our people back. But there *is* room for an excellent pilot and navigator. You're familiar with my record, sir. You know that I'm one of the best pilots serving on the *Enterprise*. So I think it's in *everyone's* best interest for you to have me come along."

Picard sat in silence for a long moment, his eyes boring into Hawk's. The lieutenant's heart raced as he forced himself not to break the captain's basilisk gaze. He hoped he hadn't pushed him too hard.

Finally, Picard spoke, a slight smile tugging at the corners of his mouth. "We'll be under way in twenty minutes or less, Mr. Hawk. I'd suggest you get your best driving gloves on. Dismissed."

Hawk grinned, and rose to exit. "Thank you, sir."

As he moved out onto the bridge, Hawk's heart beat strongly in his chest. One way or another, he was now on a collision course with Zweller, Section 31, and possibly every secret the Geminus Gulf held.

He couldn't be sure whether his racing circulation came from trepidation or exhilaration.

Probably both.

Chapter Eight

The shuttlecraft *Kepler* descended swiftly through the turbulent Dayside atmosphere, its passage creating plumes of superheated plasma that clutched at the hull like the fingers of some angry god. The cockpit rattled and jerked. Picard stole a backward glance at the admiral, who was sitting beside Crusher in the crew cabin. He could only imagine the hell she had endured, having first lost Tabor and then having discovered the ambassador's possible malfeasance on Chiaros IV. He noticed then that her skin had taken on an almost greenish tinge; space-sickness, adding insult to injury.

"Will someone please explain again just why the Federation is so interested in this place?" Crusher said as she scanned the admiral with a medical tricorder.

Batanides smiled weakly. "I *could* tell you. But then I'd have to kill you."

"Excuse me?" Crusher said, looking startled as she deactivated the tricorder.

"Sorry, Doctor. A very old intelligence operative's joke." The cabin shuddered again, and the motion appeared to intensify the admiral's nausea. "I just had an even better idea, Doctor: Why don't *you* kill *me?*"

Smiling, Crusher touched a hypospray to Batanides's neck. "You'll start feeling better in a minute or so, Admiral."

Lieutenant Hawk occupied the control station to Picard's right. "The plasma discharges are still affecting the inertial damping system, Captain," he said.

"Continue compensating manually, Lieutenant."

"Aye, sir." Hawk's fingers moved nimbly, almost too quickly for the eye to follow. Picard was reminded for a moment of Data's ultrafast motions at the ops console.

"Ship's status, Mr. Hawk?" Picard said.

Hawk continued manipulating the controls as he spoke: "As predicted, sir, our sensors are at less than half efficiency, thanks to these atmospheric effects. And even our enhanced subspace transmitter can't make contact with anything as small as a combadge, if any of the survivors still have one. Shields won't function at all in the lower atmospheric layers, but the phasers are operational. The transporter is on-line, but I wouldn't recommend trying to exceed a two-kilometer radius with it."

"Grand," Picard said wryly. He was grimly aware that without shields, a single hostile phaser blast could finish them all in the space of a heartbeat. Fortunately, that problem cut both ways; most of the rebel compound would be accessible via the *Kepler*'s transporter, even if the base's detention-area forcefields were to remain intact.

Though the sensor display was still obscured, the forward viewer showed the planet's rapidly approaching terminator. Seconds later, a nightward mountain range rolled past and a shroud of darkness enveloped the little ship. To avoid detection, Hawk brought the ship low, hugging the planet's dim curvature, maintaining an altitude of no more than sixty meters. The topographic map Batanides had obtained from Ruardh's Intelligence Ministry was helping to keep the half-blinded shuttle clear of hills and rock outcroppings.

Hawk tapped several controls on the navigation console, and the shuttle responded by banking gently onto a southeasterly heading. The craft's forward velocity began to diminish, as did the buffeting and turbulence.

"Captain?" the lieutenant said, his brow crumpling. "Something about these sensor readings isn't right."

"Apart from the interference?"

"Yes, sir." The younger man gestured to the static-garbled tactical display. "Even through the charged atmospheric particles, we're already close enough to detect *some* sign of the rebel base. But I'm reading absolutely nothing. Not even a stray calorie of waste heat."

Picard pondered what that might mean. Then he glanced at his chronometer and decided to put the matter to one side for the moment. "Carry on, Mr. Hawk," he said, rising from his seat. *Best to let the lad do what I brought him along to do.*

Picard sat beside Batanides and Crusher. The admiral was massaging her temples.

"Admiral, perhaps you should remain aboard with Dr. Crusher," Picard said. "If you're not feeling up to this—"

Meeting his gaze, she cut him off. "Remember the time I came down with that Berengarian virus?"

He was glad they lacked the time to tell Crusher that story. During their Academy days, Batanides had been exposed to an alien enzyme that put her into a coma and nearly killed her. She was alive now thanks partly to her own innate ruggedness, and partly because Picard and

Zweller had secretly—and illegally—taken her to the remote planet Yrskatdon for the gene resequencing therapy that had ultimately saved her life.

He wondered: Was she trying to remind him that she was tough? Or that their current circumstances might force him once again to bend Starfleet regulations?

"How could I forget?" Picard said, nodding. If she could survive that, then a little queasiness wouldn't even slow her down. He could already see the color returning to her cheeks.

"How's the mission timetable?" Batanides said.

"We're locked on course for the coordinates we received from Corey. The shuttle should be over the base in . . ." Picard paused to consult his chronometer ". . . two minutes and five seconds. We'll have only a few moments to beam into the base before the *Kepler* flies out of transporter range. That will put us inside the base four and a half minutes before the forcefields in the detention area come down."

"If the forcefields come down," Crusher said grimly.

Picard ignored the doctor's comment. "After the beam-in, Mr. Hawk will circle around, pass back into transporter range, and retrieve everyone from the beam-up point."

His eyes on the instruments, Hawk said over his shoulder, "It'll be tricky, because I'll have to do the beam-outs a few at a time. I'll just have to keep circling over the base until I've recovered everyone." With a sheepish grin, he added: "Assuming that the Chiarosans don't shoot me down first."

"And also assuming," Crusher said, her gaze trained on Picard, "that this entire situation isn't a trap. It's still possible that Commander Zweller's message was a ruse created by the rebels."

"Or perhaps even by the Romulans," Picard said as he

rose and walked to the portside weapons locker. He quickly removed two tricorders, a pair of hand phasers, and a compression phaser rifle. "I'll grant that we may be walking into a trap. On the other hand, we can't accomplish anything by waiting. This is the best—and the *only*—lead we've got."

Batanides followed him and took possession of a tricorder and one of the hand phasers. After checking the charge on her weapon, she turned toward the cockpit. "Heads up, Mr. Hawk." She threw the phaser to him, hard.

Hawk swiveled his chair toward her and plucked the phaser out of the air as though it had been standing still. The admiral smiled. "Good reflexes, son. You'll be a real asset to the away team."

Picard frowned as he slung the rifle onto his back. "Admiral, I prefer to have Mr. Hawk piloting the shuttle. His reflexes will be put to better use here in case of a Chiarosan attack. I hadn't intended on leaving the doctor on board alone."

Crusher gave him a look of mock umbrage. "I'm capable of piloting a shuttle, Captain."

Batanides took the remaining phaser and tricorder out of Picard's hands. "She won't be alone. *You'll* be staying aboard with her."

Picard struggled, not altogether successfully, to control a volcanic surge of anger. "Damn it, Marta, I brought Mr. Hawk along specifically for his piloting skills—"

She interrupted him once again. "Skills that we'll need more urgently *after* we've rescued the hostages. You've certainly got more than enough flying expertise to keep things going until we get to that point. In the meantime, Hawk and I will assemble the prisoners at the prearranged beam-up coordinates."

"Riker and Troi are *my* officers. *I* should be going down there to rescue them."

"As the captain of the *Enterprise,* you're less expendable than Mr. Hawk." Batanides nodded toward the young officer. "No offense intended, Lieutenant."

"None taken, sir," Hawk said, wide-eyed. He was still seated in the cockpit.

"With all due respect, Admiral, you're beginning to sound like my first officer. *You* are the most senior officer here. And that makes *you* the least expendable of any of us."

Batanides walked to the aftmost section of the cabin and took her place on one of its two transporter pads. "This hellhole has taken too much away from me already. I'm not going to put another old friend at risk unnecessarily. And I'm *through* discussing it." She pointed at the pips on her collar for emphasis.

Picard silently bit the inside of his lip as he contemplated just how deep and wide her stubborn streak had grown since their Academy days.

"Then Godspeed," he said after a long moment.

"Beam-down window opening in thirty seconds," Hawk said, staring at a readout. The viewscreen still showed nothing but featureless darkness, punctuated by sporadic auroral light-flashes that made the barren land stand out in sharp, shadowed relief.

Hawk suddenly looked up from his console, a puzzled expression on his face.

"What is it?" Picard said.

"It's strange. I'm picking up tetryon emissions from somewhere. It's faint, but it's interfering with the transporter lock."

"Can you compensate?"

Hawk made several minute adjustments to his console. "There. Lock established. Fifteen seconds to beam-down window." Hawk then rose from his seat and shot a questioning glance in Picard's direction.

Picard unslung his rifle and handed it to Hawk, who walked over to the admiral's side. The captain sat behind the cockpit controls and methodically punched in the transporter commands. Then he turned his chair aftward.

"Marta, I will be very upset with you if you get your-self killed," Picard said.

She grinned as the pads energized. "Just drive carefully, Johnny. And don't forget to leave a light on for us." The beam brightened and the pair shimmered out of existence.

Crusher took the seat beside him. " 'Johnny?' " she said inquiringly.

An alarm klaxon sounded. He said nothing to the doc-tor; the wavering image on the tactical display now de-manded his full attention. At least four small vessels were approaching, coming from all directions.

And they were all closing on the *Kepler* very, very quickly.

Will Riker paced back and forth in the holding cell for what seemed like days. Asking the guard for the time had been an exercise in futility, akin to soliciting a charitable donation from a Ferengi DaiMon. The total absence of any sort of clock gave time an elastic, unreal quality.

"Will," Troi said. Though she was sitting on the cell's single cot in a contemplative-looking lotus position, she appeared to be having trouble concentrating.

Riker stopped in his tracks. "Sorry. I can't seem to stop pacing. And there's not much else to do."

Zweller, who was leaning insouciantly against one of the cell's stone walls, chuckled.

"Is something funny, Commander?" Riker said testily.

"You're wearing a groove. I hope you don't tip your hand so easily during those poker games the counselor was telling me about."

"This isn't a game. Remember, we have no way of knowing if your little stunt will work. Or exactly when it's supposed to happen."

Zweller stroked the white stubble on his chin. "I'll grant you the first point. But not the second. I suggest you be ready to move in exactly four minutes and forty-two seconds."

Riker's eyebrows rose skyward. Even Deanna looked surprised.

"Where have you been hiding your timepiece, Mr. Zweller?" Troi said.

The older man smiled enigmatically, gently tapping his skull with his index finger. Then he nodded toward the guard who was standing in the corridor, his back toward the cell. "Don't distract me. I'm counting down."

"In your head," Riker said, still incredulous.

"Yes. In my head."

"And what are we supposed to do at the end of your countdown?" Troi asked.

Riker grinned. "I can think of something."

He laced his fingers together and popped his knuckles loudly.

Hawk almost couldn't believe his good luck. Not only had he persuaded Captain Picard to bring him along on the mission, but he had also been allowed to participate in the ground rescue itself. He might never get a better opportunity to unravel the mystery surrounding the death of Aubin Tabor—and to learn what Section 31 really expected to accomplish by helping the Romulans take possession of Chiaros IV.

Hawk clutched the stock of the phaser rifle tightly as the *Kepler*'s transporter engulfed and disassembled him, bringing on a feeling of vertigo. He felt as though he was dropping over the edge of an endless, iridescent waterfall, tumbling an impossible distance. The sensation brought to mind Reg Barclay's tales of similar experiences, until he reminded himself that this was no ordinary beam-down; the heavily ionized Chiarosan atmosphere was probably complicating the transport process.

Suddenly, Hawk was whole once again. He found himself standing beside Admiral Batanides in a rough-hewn, curving stone corridor. The place appeared to have been excavated from the planet's very bedrock and was surprisingly well lit, thanks to row upon row of ceiling-mounted light panels. Hawk could hear distant shouts echoing up and down the hallway, though no one was visible besides themselves. For a moment he wished they had brought a larger contingent with them from the *Enterprise*. But if they had, there would have been little room aboard the *Kepler* for the rescuees.

He glanced at the chronometer on his wrist. If the team's assumptions had been correct—based upon Commander Zweller's brief subspace transmission—then the security forcefields in the detention area were due to fail in exactly four minutes and thirty-three seconds.

The admiral opened her tricorder and studied it for a few moments. Then she nodded, indicating that she had found her bearings—if, Hawk reflected again, Zweller's message and its coordinate data could be trusted.

Hawk took the point, staying several paces ahead of Batanides. Cautiously, the lieutenant peered around a corner. He heard the sound of rapidly approaching footfalls and saw a flurry of motion at one of the corridor's far ends. He ducked back the way he had come, flattening against one of the rough stone walls. The admiral did likewise. Scarcely daring to breathe, Hawk watched as a half-dozen very large Chiarosans, some armed with blades, others carrying disruptor-type weapons, and still others holding Starfleet-issue phasers, ran quickly past. Hawk was struck by how quiet and graceful such large beings could be.

What was their hurry? Were they being mobilized to attack the *Kepler?*

Peering around the corner once more, Hawk established that it was safe to move, at least for the moment. They crept forward cautiously. Two corridor-turnings later, they entered a chamber filled with what appeared to be security holding cells, none of which were occupied. Unfortunately, their entrance surprised a lone Chiarosan guard, who immediately drew a pair of serrated blades and was on top of Hawk almost before he realized what was happening. The lieutenant brought his phaser rifle upward just barely in time to ward off the soldier's initial blow. Sparks struck as the gleaming swords skipped off the phaser's tough duranium casing.

Then the Chiarosan stepped quickly backward; with an impossibly limber motion, he delivered a spinning kick to Hawk's shoulder, knocking him to the stone floor. The wind rushed from the lieutenant's lungs. His fall was considerably more painful than he expected, no doubt because of the planet's intense gravitational field. Compared to the point-three-eight Earth-normal gravity he'd grown up with in Bradbury City, the pull of Chiaros was downright brutal. Hawk rolled, hugging his rifle, barely avoiding being eviscerated by one of the guard's swords. A second blade sang past his ear and clanged deafeningly against the stone floor.

Compared to this guy, Ranul's holodeck pirates are pushovers.

But although the Chiarosan was strong and fast, Hawk wasn't out of moves just yet. Tripping the release on the rifle's strap, Hawk swept the weapon beneath the warrior's feet, bringing him to the ground with a heavy thump. Hawk rose, then slammed the rifle's stock up under the Chiarosan's jaw as the guard scrambled to recover his footing. Hawk hastened to deliver another smashing blow, stunning his adversary and knocking him down once more. But the guard didn't appear injured—he looked annoyed, and again rose to confront Hawk.

A phaser beam suddenly hit the Chiarosan squarely in the chest, instantly incinerating most of his body cavity. He was dead before his massive body struck the stone floor. The stench of scorched flesh permeated the corridor, making Hawk's gorge rise.

Incredulous, Hawk turned toward the admiral, whose phaser was still raised. At that moment, he couldn't help wondering how Section 31 could really be any worse than the Federation's so-called "legitimate" intelligence agency.

Hawk spoke haltingly as he recovered his breath. "Was . . . that . . . really . . . necessary?"

The admiral's eyes were steel. "Stunning these people only makes them mad," she said. "And I'm through wasting time." Calmly, she holstered her weapon and resumed making tricorder scans. "There are no lifesigns in this part of the detention area. They must have moved the prisoners."

Hawk's throat clenched involuntarily. "Or killed them."

Batanides adjusted the tricorder and her expression brightened. "No. I'm picking up human lifesigns, about a hundred meters that way." She gestured toward a "T" intersection about twenty meters down the corridor, and they began quietly walking in that direction. Hawk stayed in front, controlling his breathing, keeping his rifle at the ready.

"The tricorder says there's a Tellarite among the humans," she said.

"That would be the *Slayton*'s CMO," Hawk said, nodding. "Dr. Gomp."

"You know him?"

Hawk shook his head. "I took a look at the *Slayton*'s crew manifest last night."

"Sounds more like you memorized it."

He shrugged, unaccountably embarrassed. Though he rarely showed off his eidetic memory gratuitously, he couldn't deny that it often came in handy.

The admiral returned her attention to the tricorder, then suddenly stopped walking. Hawk followed suit when he turned and saw the look of alarm on her face.

"What's wrong?" Hawk said. He thought he could hear distant shouting.

"A whole bunch of Chiarosan life-form signatures are approaching, fast," she said. "And they're getting between us and the prisoners."

He gripped the phaser rifle tightly. "I guess we're not going to make that first rendezvous at the beam-up coordinates after all."

She tucked the tricorder away and took up her phaser. "Then we'll have to switch to Plan B," she said, gesturing toward his rifle. Its stock was slick with sweat. "Lieutenant, this time you'd better remember that that thing is not a club."

Then she bolted ahead of Hawk in the direction of the oncoming din. He was surprised at her speed, and sprinted to keep up.

* * *

Picard took the *Kepler* into a steep dive until the dark ground seemed to be getting close enough to touch. Then he barrel-rolled to gain some altitude, temporarily evading the pursuing Chiarosan vessels.

Crusher studied an intermittently functioning sensor display. "There are five of them now, as far as I can tell," she said gravely. "And none of them is answering my hails."

"Phasers are armed," Picard said. Such weapons were not ordinarily standard on most shuttlecraft, but it would have been sheer folly to embark on a mission like this without them.

"The shields are still off-line," Crusher warned.

"Fine. Then theirs probably aren't working either." He tried locking onto the nearest target, but the computer refused to accept the command. The atmospheric ionization was playing hell with the automatic phaser-lock.

Picard activated the manual targeting controls. Using the tactical screen, he displayed his manual-acquisition targets. A split-second later, a Chiarosan disruptor beam lanced out in their direction, barely missing the shuttle's unprotected hull.

Picard returned fire just as his target drifted out of his makeshift sights. A clean miss. A second ship's beam rocked the shuttle with a glancing blow. Luckily, the *Kepler*'s hull held together. But he knew their luck couldn't last.

The battle reminded Picard of an exercise he had conducted decades ago, at the Academy. The cadets had been expected to cope with glitches and malfunctions of all sorts; one such test had involved the unexpected failure of a simulated starship's computerized phaser target-lock. Picard had very quickly dispatched a pair of Tzenkethi raider ships using what Corey Zweller had admiringly called "dead reckoning." For weeks afterward—and for reasons he still couldn't fathom—Batanides had referred to him as "the Pinball Wizard."

Just as he had in that simulation, Picard allowed his instincts to take over. A Chiarosan ship dropped into the path of his drifting manual target-lock, and he fired at it. The bright orange beam contacted the unshielded alien ship squarely, blowing it apart. He swung the manual target-lock to his far right and just as quickly dispatched another before resuming his rolling, swooping evasive maneuvers. The three remaining Chiarosan ships continued to buzz about undeterred, trying to encircle him.

Picard glanced at Crusher, whose somber expression reminded him that this was no simulation. People were dead, by his hand—and it would never be a thing he would take pride in. Without speaking, he looped back toward the coordinates of the invisible rebel base, hoping for an opportunity to beam the captives aboard and outrun his pursuers.

But the three Chiarosan fighters were quickly gaining ground.

Will Riker watched as Zweller held up four fingers, then three, then two, then one.

A split-second later, the orange forcefield that barred the cell's only doorway crackled and vanished. The guard turned toward the silence and Riker leaped on the man, surprising him and knocking him to the stone floor. As they landed, Riker drove both of his knees into the Chiarosan's stomach, then rolled onto his shoulder and sprang back onto his feet. The guard was already getting up, but he was winded and startled. Riker knew that he would be dead very soon if he failed to press that very slim advantage.

One of the soldier's huge hands grasped a sword pommel just as Riker sent a flying kick toward the Chiarosan's head. Wincing as his bootheel connected sharply with the other man's skull, Riker almost fell over when he landed, his hip stitched with pain. The guard sprawled onto the floor heavily, and Riker landed a two-handed hammer-blow at the base of his skull.

The alien wheezed, then lay still.

A moment later, Troi and Zweller were standing in the corridor beside Riker as he panted with exertion. Ignoring the agony in his hip, Riker knelt beside the unconscious guard, taking his swords and removing a large, pistol-shaped beam-weapon from the Chiarosan's belt. He rose and handed one of the swords to Zweller, who hefted the weapon appraisingly. Riker gave the pistol to Troi.

"All right," Troi said, examining the weapon's controls. "We're out of our cell. What's our next move?"

"We find the rest of the hostages," Zweller said, pointing his sword down the stone corridor. "Then we fight our way to the hangar and take one of the rebels' flyers."

"Oh," Troi said laconically. "Is that all?"

Riker raised his sword before him, as though it were an anbo-jytsu staff. He was grateful for the chance to finally do something to end their confinement—even if it did seem to be a lost cause.

"If you've got a better plan, Deanna, I'm all ears."

Troi nodded, conceding his point. "Lead on, Commander," she said to Zweller, spinning her weapon by its trigger guard, in the manner of a gunfighter from the ancient American West.

As they made their way down the empty corridor, Riker could hear shouts and the sounds of a struggle. He saw Troi frowning at her pistol's electronic controls.

"What's wrong?" he said.

"I can't find the stun setting."

"Chiarosans don't believe in nonlethal weapons," Zweller said, then led them around a corner.

They entered a wide chamber that contained five empty holding cells. In front of the cells, four Starfleet officers—who had evidently also made a bid for freedom once the forcefields had dropped—were grappling hand-to-hand with a pair of hulking Chiarosans. An officer, a human male, lay on the stone floor, either dead or unconscious. One of the Chiarosans sent a human woman sprawling with a single backhanded slap.

The second guard raised a heavy sword and prepared to skewer a very angry Tellarite. Instead of fleeing the blow, the Tellarite leaped forward, sinking his tusklike teeth deeply into the soldier's bare forearm.

With surprising adroitness, Zweller hurled himself into the melee, striking from behind and hacking at the first guard's hamstrings. Roaring in pain, the Chiarosan fell to one impossibly flexible knee, twisting his torso almost backward to engage Zweller with two curved, scimitar-like blades. Riker rushed the second guard, parrying a downward sword-thrust aimed at the Tellarite's thick neck. The Chiarosan shrugged the Tellarite off of him, sending him flying, gobbets of gray flesh trailing through the air behind him. Seemingly unaware of his wound, the soldier turned toward Riker, a death's-head grin fixed upon his face. The guard rushed him, his blades twirling like the propellers of an ancient terrestrial aircraft.

Riker moved as fast as he could, sidestepping and parrying with his sword. But his hip, which was bone-bruised if not sprained, was slowing him. Sparks flew as metal hit metal with a deafening clangor. Something nicked Riker's scalp, and he felt a liquid warmth soaking into his beard and surging down his neck. The warrior paused, laughing in triumph.

"A little help here, Deanna!" Riker shouted.

The Chiarosan raised his blade, advancing with preternatural speed. Then his eyes went wide in shock and he flung his blades to the floor. Riker saw that the weapons had suddenly changed in color from silvery-gray to bright red. The blades of the guard Zweller had slashed struck the stone floor a moment later, and both warriors stopped moving, startled by their burned hands but bearing their pain stoically. For a moment, the room fell silent.

Troi stood a few meters away from the fracas, holding the pistol before her in a two-handed grip. "I won't be aiming at your weapons next time, gentlemen," she said icily. "Please don't force me to fire again."

It would have been easy for one or both of the guards to charge her, given their obvious strength and agility. But their muscles slackened and they backed away from her, apparently utterly convinced of her sincerity. Riker smirked, wondering for a moment if this was some new combat application of her empathic talents.

Zweller and one of the freed Starfleet officers—a man who wore a commander's pips—began helping the injured to their feet. Brushing blood away from his ear, Riker was relieved to note that no one appeared to have suffered any serious injuries.

Zweller and the Tellarite disarmed the guards and escorted them into one of the holding cells, whose forcefields by now had become functional again. Zweller then began distributing the remainder of the Chiarosans' weapons—swords, disruptors, and even a pair of Starfleet-issue phasers—among his crewmates.

"Commander Roget, one of those guards is cut up pretty badly," the Tellarite told his superior. "He needs medical attention."

"All right, Doctor," Roget said. "But make it fast."

Zweller spoke up. "Commander, the guard's pride is the only thing that got hurt."

"How would *you* know?" the Tellarite asked Zweller truculently. Riker assumed that the doctor was unaware of the commander's alliance with the rebels.

"We have to get out of sight," one of *Slayton*'s other officers said.

Roget looked convinced. Hefting a thick-bladed sword, he said, "Okay, then. We leave now."

"Exactly how are we supposed to get off this base?" snorted the Tellarite. His piglike eyes narrowed as his gaze fell on Riker and Troi. "And who are our new friends?"

Riker and Troi stepped forward and exchanged brief introductions with the *Slayton*'s officers.

Looking impatient, Zweller handed a newly confiscated particle weapon to Roget and gave a second one to Riker. "With all due respect, let's save the pleasantries for the debriefing. Right now, I need everybody to follow me to the hangar."

Roget turned toward the Tellarite. "Gomp, stay up front with Commander Zweller. If you smell anyone coming, give us a shout."

Gomp nodded, his porcine nose twitching as he sampled the dank subterranean air. Then he inhaled sharply and issued a very loud, very moist sneeze. Someone behind Riker said *"Gesundheit."*

Zweller and Gomp took the point, and Riker fell into step a few paces behind them, his disruptor pistol ready. Farther back, Troi helped support an injured but ambulatory woman—Xenoanthropologist Kurlan—while Tuohy, the planetary scientist, assisted Engineer Hearn, who was moving with a very noticeable limp. Roget watched for trouble from the rear.

"Hold it," Gomp hissed, his flat nose snuffling loudly. Everyone stopped. "I think I smell—"

About ten meters ahead, a broad intersection suddenly began filling up with Chiarosans, some carrying blades, others clutching disruptors and phasers.

Riker saw that Grelun was standing at the forefront, a curved sword in each of his massive hands. The scowl on the Chiarosan leader's dark, saturnine face seemed to lower the room's temperature by five full degrees.

"—trouble," Gomp finished, almost inaudibly.

The hull of the *Kepler* banged and shuddered. Picard half-expected to be blown out of the cockpit and into the ionized darkness, but the shuttle somehow remained in one piece.

The tactical display fluttered, but not because of the atmospheric static. The system itself had apparently taken damage and was beginning to fail. Despite that, he could still make out the intermittent image of three Chiarosan attack ships. The pursuing vessels continued firing while Picard coaxed the *Kepler* into evasive loops that threatened to tear the small craft apart.

"Why aren't we returning fire?" Crusher said, her voice carrying a carefully controlled edge of fear.

He had to shout to be heard over the roar of the turbulent atmosphere and the discharge of the Chiarosan weapons. "We can't spare the power. We need it for the transporter and the structural integrity field." If the latter system were to fail, the shuttle would quickly become thousands of dinnerplate-size pieces, spread across hundreds of square kilometers of the frigid Nightside.

"We're going to abandon ship?" Crusher asked.

"There's no other choice. We've taken too much damage to outrun our attackers. And we'll never reach orbit in this condition."

The doctor calmly eyed a readout on her console. "Jean-Luc, at these power levels, we'll never be able to transport together. Only one at a time."

Picard nodded curtly. "The rebel base is in transporter range again. Beam yourself down first. I'll join you as soon as I can. And no arguments."

Though Crusher looked unhappy about her orders, she began trying to lock the transporter onto a safe destination within the rebel compound. Suddenly, her fingers stopped moving on the instrument panel. Picard saw the frown that darkened her face.

"What's wrong?"

"It's those tetryon emissions again. I'm having trouble establishing a lock. I'm trying to compensate . . ."

Picard swiftly rolled and yawed the *Kepler* until the shuttle was headed directly for the nearest of their attackers. He felt the seat harness biting into him as gravity in the cockpit shifted, the force of acceleration threatening to overwhelm the inertial dampers. The distance between the two craft evaporated swiftly.

"There," Crusher said. "Ready for transport."

"Energize," Picard shouted. A moment later, he sat alone in the cockpit.

The ship he was approaching went into an evasive swoop, but Picard had no trouble staying on top of the other pilot. He stole a glance at the transporter's energy indicator; there still wasn't enough power in the unit for a beam-out, though the system's capacitors were slowly building up energy. If he could continue evading his opponents for perhaps another minute or two, he still had a chance to beam out to wherever Crusher had sent herself—but only if he avoided squandering the shuttle's limited energy on the phasers.

Fortunately, there was an alternative to the phasers. As

the shuttle came within meters of the nearest Chiarosan fighter, Picard touched a release toggle, then sent his vessel into a dive. The *Kepler* lurched slightly, and the light of a fiery explosion flooded the viewport.

At close quarters—and with no shields—a shuttlecraft log buoy made quite a projectile.

On the tactical display, only two hostile vessels remained. Both were maintaining the chase. Glancing at his console, Picard saw that the transporter was still steadily recharging. But it wasn't quite ready yet.

Then he checked the transporter lock, only to discover that it wasn't working properly.

Damn. Tetryons again.

Picard knew well that tetryon emissions were a by-product of certain Romulan technologies. If there was a "smoking gun" pointing to Romulan involvement with the Army of Light, then this was it. And the presence of Romulans—and their cloaking devices—would account for the rebel base's complete invisibility from the air.

Suddenly, one of the Chiarosan ships increased speed, approaching the *Kepler* on an intercept course. And there were no more log buoys left.

A green light winked on in the transporter-power display. Relieved, Picard quickly compensated for the tetryons and locked the transporter onto the same coordinates Crusher had used.

Then, as he attempted to energize the transporter, every system in the *Kepler*'s cockpit went dead and dark.

Lack of time had forced Crusher to lock the *Kepler*'s transporter into the most easily detectable tetryon-free area in the rebel base—which was, ironically, located at the center of a tetryon-rich area. *The eye of the storm,* she thought as the transporter beam began disassembling her, molecule by molecule.

When the transporter's shimmering light faded, Crusher found herself standing in a narrow, teal-colored chamber. A sign on one of the bulkheads bore several characters of angular, alien script.

In the center of the chamber, two men and a woman, all wearing gray uniforms, busied themselves around what appeared to be a partially disassembled warp core.

A Romulan *warp core,* Crusher thought, just as the woman turned toward her, a disruptor in her hand.

At least two dozen pairs of iridescent Chiarosan eyes stared balefully from across the wide, branching corridor. Riker seriously doubted that he and his companions could survive a firefight against so many determined opponents.

The troopers were holding their fire, apparently awaiting orders from Grelun, who stood in their front ranks. The Chiarosan leader seemed to be staring intently at Zweller.

Riker heard Zweller hissing at Gomp, the Tellarite. "I thought Tellarites had keen noses! How could so many of them slip right past you?"

Gomp snorted unhappily, wiping his snout with one of the sleeves of his soiled uniform. "I'm a doctor, not a tricorder. Besides," he snuffled, "I think I'm coming down with a cold."

"Disarm, or die," Grelun said.

Riker stepped forward, his weapon lowered in what he hoped the Chiarosans would see as a nonthreatening gesture. He stopped beside Zweller and Gomp.

"Grelun," Riker said calmly. "We have to talk."

Grelun sneered. "Falhain should never have trusted you Federation folk. Particularly *that* one." He twirled one of his blades, then aimed its point straight at Zweller. "The man who tried to betray us to Ruardh."

Riker heard surprised mutters among the *Slayton* survivors, which receded slowly after Roget gave a terse order for silence. All eyes were upon Zweller now, and none looked very friendly.

Apparently oblivious to everyone in the chamber except for Grelun, Zweller was still holding his particle weapon, his arms at his sides. In a steely voice, Zweller said, "Not true, Grelun. I could have done a lot more than just tamper with your communications and security systems. I could have sabotaged the cloaking devices that keep this place hidden from your enemies. But I *didn't* do that."

Cloaking devices. The words echoed in Riker's mind. *Looks like the Romulans have been stacking the deck, after all.* He saw from Troi's expression that she must have come to the same conclusion. *But what,* he wondered, *did the Romulans have to gain?*

Zweller continued: "And do you know why, Grelun? Because I believe in your cause. I want to help you stop the slaughter of your people."

Grelun appeared unmoved. "You outworlders and your schemes. You plot and you plan. You manipulate us as though we were but pieces in a game. And who suffers? Those who dwell in the provinces you conquer."

"We've never 'conquered' anyone, Grelun," Riker said. "And I would like a chance to prove it to you."

"How, human?" Grelun said.

"I offer you a neutral place to meet with us: aboard our starship, the *Enterprise.* There, you can learn more about our history."

Grelun laughed, then said, "The writing of history is ever the privilege of the conqueror. Life here was far better, far simpler, before outworlders came among us.

Then, only Ruardh and her death-dealing minions stood against us."

"What's really bothering you, Grelun?" Zweller said. "Are you regretting Falhain's decision to accept aid from the Romulans? Are you worried about what they'll expect in return after the Federation leaves?"

Zweller had evidently touched a nerve; Grelun was baring the razor-sharp points of his silvery teeth. One didn't need to be a Betazoid to divine his emotional state.

"Get down!" Troi yelled.

Grelun raised his swords high and shouted, "Kill them all!" At least two dozen Chiarosan rebels advanced, amid an ear-splitting, ululating cry that seemed to issue from a single gigantic throat. Gomp turned tail and ran as Riker and Zweller both made rolling dives to the stone floor, bringing their weapons up as they landed. Riker could already hear weapons discharges, even before Zweller began firing his disruptor at the oncoming soldiers.

Then Riker realized that he was hearing weapons fire coming from *behind* the charging Chiarosans. He noticed the distinctive whooshing sound of a Starfleet compression phaser rifle, a weapon he'd not seen in the hands of Grelun's troops.

The sound of phaser blasts grew louder and the Chiarosans' united charge became a disorganized scatter. Grelun, his bare forearms badly burned by energy fire, fell back into his men. Chiarosans had begun dropping to the floor.

Moments later, none of the rebels was standing. Miraculously, none of the Starfleet contingent appeared seriously hurt. Near the chamber's far wall, behind the stunned Chiarosans, stood Lieutenant Hawk, armed with a phaser rifle. Beside him was Admiral Batanides, who was holding a hand phaser.

Zweller smiled broadly as they approached. "Marta, I was expecting to see Johnny. What the hell are *you* doing here?"

Her face was set into hard lines. "Saving your ass yet again, apparently."

Riker noticed that something subtle had changed in the way the admiral carried herself. It was as though she had aged a decade since he'd seen her last on the *Enterprise.*

Zweller apparently sensed something, too. Anxiously, he asked, "How is Aubin?"

"Dead," she replied coldly, gripping her phaser hard. "And now really isn't the best time to discuss it, Corey."

"Admiral," Riker said, happy to interrupt. "Since you managed to get in here, I'm assuming you also have a way of getting everyone out."

"Right, Commander." To Hawk, she said, "Lieutenant, signal Captain Picard. Tell him we've got ten to beam up."

Hawk nodded. Tapping his combadge, he said, "Away team to *Kepler.*"

Riker was relieved to learn that Zweller's gambit had paid off. The captain had indeed brought a shuttlecraft into transporter range for a lightning rescue. Riker smiled at Troi, who grinned back, evidently thinking similar thoughts.

Then Riker looked again toward Hawk and realized that something wasn't right. The lieutenant was repeatedly tapping his combadge, which issued a burst of static before going silent.

Hawk's eyes locked with Riker's. "I can't raise the *Kepler.*"

Riker told himself that the shuttle's transmitter might simply have run afoul of the local weather patterns. But he knew that the combadge's silence might also indicate that something far more serious had happened. He felt a deep chill spreading in his gut.

"Damn!" Batanides said. "Keep trying. And let's find someplace to hide. The last thing we need now is to get captured by the Chiarosans. Or the Romulans."

"Admiral," Riker said. "Maybe the Romulans are exactly what we need."

Batanides seemed to grasp his meaning. "What's your plan, Commander?"

Hawk thought that the Chiarosans looked intimidating even when sprawled unconscious on the floor. He tried to ignore them as he adjusted his tricorder to scan for Romulan biosignatures. While Hawk worked, the admiral quickly brought Riker, Troi, and Commander Roget up-to-date, including some of the details surrounding Ambassador Tabor's death, Captain Picard's rescue mission, and the discovery of a Romulan cloaking field some five AUs south of the Chiaros system's orbital plane.

When Hawk idly mentioned that the energy field the *Enterprise* had encountered might have been partly responsible for the *Slayton*'s destruction, a collective gasp went up among five of the bedraggled former hostages. Zweller, however, stood apart from his crewmates, stony-faced. Hawk wondered: *Had the Section 31 agent known all along about the* Slayton*'s fate?*

"Oh, my God," Troi said, her dark eyes moistening as she appraised Zweller's colleagues. "No one's told them." Hawk's tricorder nearly slipped from his suddenly nerveless fingers when he realized what a bombshell he had dropped on these already-shaken people.

Admiral Batanides interrupted Hawk's unpleasant train of thought. "Are any more troops coming, Lieutenant?"

Hawk forced himself to concentrate on the business at

hand. He raised the tricorder again, watching as its indicators moved slowly across the readout panel. "No, sir," he said. "But there are definitely Romulan lifesigns here. It's hard to tell, scanning through all this rock, but there may be as many as half a dozen of them in various parts of the complex."

"Scan for tetryon particles," Riker said. Without hesitation, Hawk again adjusted the tricorder and resumed scanning.

"What good will *that* do?" barked Gomp.

"Romulan ships are powered by quantum singularities," Riker explained patiently, "that usually give off tetryon particles as a by-product."

"Got it," Hawk said, smiling triumphantly—the tricorder had indeed picked up the fingerprint of a Romulan quantum singularity drive. "And it's located exactly where Commander Zweller's message said the spacecraft hangars would be."

Hawk noticed then that all eyes were upon Commander Riker, who clutched a Chiarosan pistol in his right hand. Acutely aware that they were looking to him to tell them their next move, Riker turned a questioning look on the admiral. Batanides gave him a quick nod, effectively transferring command of the mission to him.

"Mr. Zweller, you'll lead us to the hangar," Riker began. "Deanna, I want you to keep trying to raise the *Kepler.* Mr. Roget, I'd like your people to bring Grelun along with us. Lieutenant Hawk will assist you."

As the counselor tried without success to contact the shuttlecraft, Hawk stowed the tricorder and walked toward the Chiarosan leader's supine form. Unconsciousness did little to soften Grelun's fierce visage; it occurred to Hawk that it would be very bad if he were to awaken unexpectedly. He began helping two of Roget's officers half-carry and half-drag the man, whose dead weight was akin to that of a small tree. The intensity of this planet's gravitational field wasn't making matters any easier.

As he strained, Hawk heard Troi raise an objection. "So now it's *our* turn to start taking hostages?"

"I prefer to think of him as a shield, Deanna," Riker temporized as the group began moving. "The Chiarosans might not fire on us while their leader's in harm's way."

Zweller shrugged and looked over his shoulder at Riker as he led the group along. "Then again, they might not let that stop them. They're desperate people, Commander."

And so are we, Hawk thought, his back and shoulder muscles afire as he continued to help move the insensate Chiarosan.

The three Romulan officers wasted no time confiscating Crusher's phaser and combadge. Crusher understood, too late, that she must have locked the *Kepler*'s transporter onto the engine room of a Romulan ship located somewhere within the Chiarosan rebel base. Romulan warp cores, after all, were known to scatter tetryon particles. In her haste, the "shadow" in the tetryon field, which had probably been created by the shielding of the warp core itself, must have looked like a safe refuge. But that knowledge could do her little good now.

As the seconds slowly ticked by, Crusher's apprehension grew. *Where is Jean-Luc?*

The female Romulan, who appeared to be in charge, herded the doctor into the corner of the room farthest from the warp core. The woman spoke tersely into a small communication device attached to her uniform.

"Centurion, this is T'Lei from the technical group. We have captured and disarmed a lone Starfleet officer in our engine room. I presume she is here to try to hijack our vessel."

"Detain her," replied a harried-sounding male voice. Crusher heard some sort of commotion going on in the background. The two male Romulan technicians, who had clearly heard the noises as well, looked nervously at one another.

But T'Lei never took her eyes off Crusher, and the weapon in the Romulan woman's hand never wavered.

"Centurion?" T'Lei said, tapping the transmitter on her tunic.

A moment later, the voice replied: "We have just been advised that the Starfleet prisoners have escaped. They have captured Grelun and are taking him in your direction. If they wish to leave the planet, they will have no choice other than to take your ship."

Crusher felt a surge of hope rise within her. But she didn't dare move.

"Surely Grelun's troops will neutralize them before they can attempt it," T'Lei said.

"No. They will stand down, to ensure their leader's safety. You and your men can better handle this situation using stealth. There are only ten escapees, after all. Expect them to arrive momentarily."

Crusher's heart abruptly sank. *They're going to walk right into an ambush.*

"Understood, Centurion," T'Lei said, signing off. The male technicians raised disruptor pistols of their own.

Wearing a viper's smile, T'Lei spoke directly to Crusher. "The ship's hatch is narrow, Human. Your friends must enter it single-file.

"Rest assured, we will be ready for them."

Jean-Luc, where the hell are you?

* * *

A moment after the *Kepler*'s instrument panel went dark, the emergency lighting kicked in, coloring the cockpit a dull red. Picard silently thanked whatever capricious fortune continued to keep the shuttle's structural integrity field functioning, though he knew it soon wouldn't matter. The two remaining Chiarosan fighter craft were still closing in, and he didn't even know for sure how close to the ground the shuttle had plunged.

Picard channeled every joule of emergency power to the transporter, taking care to leave the structural integrity field in place. Obediently, the transporter controls lit up. Fortunately, he still had a lock on Beverly's coordinates, and had stayed within nominal transporter range of them.

But he could also see that the transporter's power level had fallen far below safe operational levels. There was no power to spare anything else now, even life support. It was going to be close.

He checked the transporter's scanner, which again showed evidence of tetryons. Beverly had evidently beamed into a tetryon-free "shadow" located in the very heart of the most abundant tetryon activity in the rebel base.

Which told Picard what he could expect to find at the beam-down site: *Romulans*.

Picard left his flight seat long enough to grab a hand phaser from the weapons locker. He entered the "energize" command and shut off every other onboard system.

The hull creaked and groaned, and one of the braces let go with a loud snap. As the light from the transporter began cascading around him, something slammed very hard into the *Kepler*. His ears popped as the cabin's atmosphere vented into the chill Chiarosan night.

A gale-force, ionized wind ripped the shuttle's hull apart as though it were nothing more than an autumn leaf.

* * *

ANDY MANGELS & MICHAEL A. MARTIN

Hawk was relieved beyond words when Riker's appraisal of the Chiarosans turned out to be correct; when they'd seen their unconscious leader being spirited away by ten heavily armed Starfleet officers, the Chiarosans had made no move to bar their way to the hangar facility, nor did they pretend ignorance about the location of the Romulan vessel Hawk's tricorder had detected. After Zweller had made a rather emphatic inquiry into the matter—all the while pointing a beam weapon at the slumbering Grelun's skull—a Chiarosan technician sullenly punched an authorization code into a console, decloaking a small Romulan scout ship. The vessel's narrow hatchway now beckoned.

"Scan that ship for Romulans," Batanides ordered Hawk, who swiftly consulted his tricorder.

After a moment, Hawk shook his head. "I'm picking up too much tetryon activity. It's jamming my scans."

"Deanna?" Riker prompted.

Troi closed her eyes, reaching into the small Romulan vessel with her empathic senses. "All I'm picking up right now is a lot of emotional tension," Troi said. "As though several people were about to engage in combat."

"Or maybe preparing an ambush?" Zweller ventured.

"Maybe I should knock," Gomp said, apparently to no one.

Batanides raised her weapon, signaling an end to the debate. "We can't stay here, people. We've no choice but to chance it. Let's go." Riker nodded his acknowledgment and took the point, with Zweller and Roget immediately behind him.

Hawk tucked his tricorder away. Muscles straining, he resumed the not inconsiderable task of helping to drag Grelun forward as the group moved across the hangar floor toward the open hatch.

* * *

Picard shook off the slight dizziness he felt when the transporter released him. It had been close, but he was satisfied that he was in one piece.

Phaser drawn, he now stood in what appeared to be an engine room. To his right was what he recognized as a Romulan warp core—obviously the source of the tetryons the *Kepler*'s sensors had detected. Some five meters away, in a far corner to his left, stood Crusher, surrounded by a trio of armed Romulans, one of whom had just turned in his direction. The doctor saw him as well, and rolled lithely to the deck.

Using the warp core as cover, Picard opened fire.

Riker held his Chiarosan disruptor at eye level as he entered the hatch. He expected to be fired upon at any moment, and was mildly surprised when nothing of the kind happened. As the others followed, Riker led the way into the crew compartment.

It was empty.

Riker heard an electronic hum coming from the forward portion of the vessel. It sounded as though someone were in the process of activating the scout ship's instruments, perhaps even preparing the vessel for flight. His weapon ready, he moved toward the sound as Zweller, Roget, and Batanides covered his back. Cautiously, Riker stepped through an open hatch and into a small cockpit.

He was shocked to see Captain Picard and Dr. Crusher seated behind the instrument panel, evidently trying to make sense of the Romulan script on the control panels.

Picard looked up and smiled broadly. "What *kept* you, Number One?"

Lieutenant Hawk thought that fitting a Tellarite male, a half-Betazoid woman, eight assorted humans, and an insensate Chiarosan aboard such a small craft might be problematic, but it turned out that there was enough room, after all. But only barely. Hawk accompanied Batanides into the small cockpit, where the admiral had relieved Crusher to allow her to assist Riker, Troi, and Dr. Gomp in tending to a trio of unconscious Romulan technicians. For a moment, Hawk had wondered how much important information the Romulans might reveal—until he considered how crowded the vessel already was. There simply wasn't enough room to take the Romulans along.

The lieutenant was impressed by how well the admiral knew her way around Romulan instrumentation. It made sense, though; she *was* an intelligence officer, after all. Perhaps the study of things Romulan was her specialty. Hawk watched her carefully, memorizing each control she touched, each command sequence she entered.

As Picard and the admiral powered up the little vessel, the Chiarosans scrambled to open the hangar doors for them, apparently unwilling to engage in a game of "chicken," which would more than likely get their leader killed.

Hawk smiled triumphantly. "We're actually doing it. We're getting away."

"We haven't gotten away *yet*, Lieutenant," Picard said, still working busily alongside the admiral to get the ship moving.

Batanides nodded in agreement with the captain. "They can still chase us. Or even shoot us down, Grelun or no Grelun."

Seconds later, they were under way. The scout ship ascended quickly into the chill darkness of Nightside. Hawk continued observing and memorizing while the admiral coached Picard on the instrument panel.

"That blue rectangular touchpad beside your right hand should control the cloaking device. Activate it."

Picard complied, smiling ironically. "I suppose we're in violation of the Treaty of Algeron now, Admiral."

She chuckled gently. "I don't think the Romulan diplomatic corps will be in any position to complain about that, under the circumstances." Hawk was well aware that under the current Federation–Romulan treaties concerning Chiaros IV, neither side were permitted to conceal either personnel or equipment anywhere on the planet.

He wondered what other secrets the Romulans guarded—and if Zweller had any inkling of what those secrets might be.

The admiral frowned as she stared at a readout. "The cloak's not working."

Picard activated the comm system. "Picard to engine room."

"Hearn here, Captain," responded the chief engineer of the late starship *Slayton*.

"The cloaking device is not functioning, Mr. Hearn. We need to engage it immediately."

"Sorry, Captain, but Commander Roget and I have our hands full right now just keeping the engines operational. The Romulan techs had everything in pieces down here."

Hawk suddenly became aware of Zweller's presence behind him. "I know a thing or two about cloaking devices, Marta," the older man said.

"Then get below and get the damned thing working before they start chasing us."

Finally seeing an opportunity to speak with Zweller in relative privacy, Hawk turned toward him. "Need a hand, Commander?"

Zweller raised a curious eyebrow.

"I did some . . . extracurricular study on Romulan cloaking technology back at the Academy," Hawk offered. He looked toward Picard for permission.

"We've no shortage of qualified pilots up here, Lieutenant," the captain said from the front of the cockpit. Picard then turned his chair toward Zweller and regarded him coolly. "Commander?"

Zweller looked significantly at Picard and Batanides for a long moment. Hawk knew that something important was passing between these three people, though he wasn't sure exactly what it was. But it seemed clear they all shared some history together.

Zweller turned away from Picard and Batanides, and regarded Hawk with a shrug. "Why not?" he said, then began making his way aftward.

Hawk followed Zweller into the main crew compartment, past Troi and several members of the *Slayton*'s crew. They stepped over Grelun's unconscious form, which was splayed across the floor while Dr. Gomp and Counselor Troi watched over him; none of the seats aboard the vessel were designed to accommodate anyone so large. Nearby, Crusher tended to what appeared to be a superficial wound on Riker's scalp, and a nasty-looking burn on his shoulder. Then Hawk followed Zweller down a companionway ladder and into a cramped, equipment-filled lower compartment that reminded him of one of the horizontal Jefferies tubes aboard the *Enterprise*. Hawk could hear Roget and Hearn discussing their work on the engine core from around a corner junction.

Zweller removed an access panel just above the deck gridwork, revealing the cloaking device's winking, glowing interior. Hawk found a tool kit in an adjacent drawer and handed it to Zweller, who lay supine in order to reach the leads running from the device to the ship's main EPS lines.

After a few passes of an isodyne coupler, Zweller signaled to the cockpit that the cloak was operational. Then he rose, handed the tool kit to Hawk, and headed back toward the companionway ladder.

Hawk took a deep breath. *I may never have a better chance than right now.* He put a firm hand on Zweller's shoulder, stopping him in his tracks.

"I need to speak to you," Hawk said softly, not wanting to be overheard by Roget or Hearn. "About Section 31."

Zweller turned slowly around and regarded Hawk with a sober expression. "I'm afraid I don't have any idea what you're talking about, Lieutenant," he said in an admonishing tone, his gaze dilithium-hard.

Hawk stood his ground and stared right back at Zweller. "Ambassador Tabor told me about Thirty-One. He told me you're working for them, too. And he tried to convince me that *losing* Chiaros IV and the Geminus Gulf would be better for the Federation than winning them. He even tried to recruit me to help him accomplish that goal."

Zweller digested this in silence. He appeared to be a difficult man to catch by surprise. *But that must be part and parcel of the spy game,* Hawk thought.

Zweller spoke quietly after a long, introspective pause. "I suppose Tabor died before he could answer all of your . . . fundamental questions."

Hawk nodded. "And now that we know the Romulans are mixed up with the Army of Light, I have even more questions."

"So it appears you have a choice to make, Lieutenant. The same choice I had to make when I was around your age."

Hawk nodded slowly. "I either have to help you or stop you."

Zweller smiled. "You've got a third option, kid. You can back off. Pretend you don't know anything about Section 31. Believe me, that would be your safest option."

Hawk considered that for a moment, then dismissed it out of hand. If he'd been of a mind to play it safe, then he never would have gone against his father's wishes and entered Starfleet Academy. And he'd be on a safe, dull tenure-track in the antiquities department at some Martian university right now instead of piloting the Federation's flagship out at the boundaries of human experience.

"Ignoring what Tabor tried to do here would be the same as helping you, wouldn't it?" Hawk said. "No, I can't just pretend I'm not involved, Commander. I *am* involved. And I need to know what you and Tabor were really trying to do here, and why."

Zweller folded his arms across his chest and paused once again, evidently weighing options of his own. Finally, he said, "Let's strike a deal, then, son: I'll tell you whatever I think you need to know. But only *after* we get safely away from this hellhole.

"And assuming, of course, that both of us live that long."

And with that, Zweller crossed to the ladder and climbed out of sight, leaving Hawk alone, the coppery taste of fear in his mouth.

Chapter Nine

Koval strode into the control center of the warbird *Thrai Kaleh*, his thoughts dark. Speculations about the Empire's future had weighed heavily upon his mind of late. Despite the best efforts of the Tal Shiar's vice-chairman, Senator Vreenak, to negotiate a nonaggression pact with the sprawling Dominion, Koval found it difficult to believe that those shape-shifting Gamma Quadrant devils—and their unctuous Vorta middlemen—would honor any such agreement for long. For months now, a sense of urgency had been steadily growing within the Tal Shiar leader's gut, an almost desperate need to prove that the best days of the Praetor's venerable congeries of worlds had not already passed.

Of course, there were things to be thankful for, to be sure. Nine years previously, Tarod IX, a world just on the Federation's side of the *stelai ler'lloann*—the Outmarches, which the Federation called the Romulan Neutral Zone—had suffered a devastating attack by the rapacious Borg collective. Koval often wondered what would have happened had the conquest-driven cyborgs continued across the Neutral Zone toward the core of the Empire. Could Romulus itself have survived such an on-slaught? Would he have been forced to seek a long-term alliance with the Federation, whose continual, omnidi-rectional expansion many in the Empire regarded as a threat in and of itself?

If the Dominion behaves as treacherously as seems likely, Koval thought glumly, *then I may yet be forced to take just such an action.*

Fortunately, some of the reassurance Koval sought was now displayed upon the *Thrai Kaleh*'s central viewscreen. He looked upon a vast assemblage of spaceborne con-structs, a colossal loop of machinery, energy-collectors, and habitat modules that dwarfed even the largest warbirds of the Praetor's armadas. And in the ring's center lay a con-centration of unimaginably potent forces, a discovery that promised to revivify the Empire—and perhaps, one day, even to extend its reach to every quadrant of the galaxy.

Taking a seat in the command chair, Koval silently watched the coruscating energies in the screen's center for the better part of an hour, while junior officers busied themselves monitoring the banks of equipment. It was their responsibility to assist the energy station's technical crews in locating and dampening out all local subspace instabilities before irreparable harm could befall either the energy-extraction equipment or the power source's delicately balanced containment apparatus.

Koval was unpleasantly aware that the crew had failed to mask *all* evidence of the phenomenon's presence; the recent unwelcome intrusion of the first Federation star-ship into the cloaked zone had amply demonstrated those failures. In the aftermath, an overzealous warbird captain had overstepped his authority by destroying that

Federation vessel, forcing Koval to have him summarily executed. Now that the incident had attracted the attention of the Federation's flagship, Koval would countenance no further errors or unforeseen complications.

A hatchway opened and a distraught young decurion entered the control center, practically at a run. "Chairman Koval," he said breathlessly. "We've just received a stealth signal from the Chiarosan orbital comm tether. There has been an . . . incident on the planet."

Koval sighed. Why were so many junior officers averse to speaking plainly these days? "Specificity and brevity are among the cardinal virtues, Takal. Let me have both."

The younger man paused for a moment, composing his thoughts before continuing. "Somehow, the Starfleet detainees have escaped from the base on Chiaros IV. They've taken one of our small scout vessels off-planet."

Koval suppressed any outward show of surprise or anger, but he felt them both nonetheless. He quickly reassured himself: *Even though the Federation now surely knows of the covert Romulan presence on Chiaros IV, they still have virtually no chance of correctly assessing the Empire's larger agenda.*

By the time they do that, it will be far, far too late.

"What is the status of our people there?" Koval said evenly.

"The Starfleet prisoners evidently overpowered three of our technicians, Chairman, and forced them off the scout ship before using it to make their escape. The technicians were fortunate not to have been taken hostage."

Koval shook his head. "Not at all. There probably wasn't enough room on the scout ship to take anyone else aboard. What is the status of the rest of our personnel on the base?"

"There were no casualties, Chairman."

"Fortunate. Even with a memory scanner, I cannot debrief the dead. The rebel base is compromised, Decurion. Evacuate it at once. Instruct all personnel to withdraw to the secondary compound."

"Yes, Chairman."

"As soon as the evacuation is complete, you will purge the facility."

"It will be done, sir." The decurion saluted, touching his clenched fist to his chest. He turned swiftly and was gone.

Koval smiled to himself. Any scan of the base's remains would reveal the blast signatures of Starfleet quantum torpedoes—armaments that the Tal Shiar had acquired through third parties and then hidden beneath the Army of Light complex during its construction long ago. Thus, the Chiarosan electorate would have even further proof of Federation perfidy before voting on the question of Federation membership, just two short days from now.

By that time, Koval expected to have concluded his business with Commander Zweller as well. Zweller had aided the Chiarosan rebels to sway the election in favor of Romulus, just as he had promised to do. And despite Zweller's subsequent falling out with Grelun, a deal was still a deal. Spies had to be especially circumspect about honoring their under-the-table agreements. Or at least they had to *appear* to be. To do any less was simply bad business, and could invite unpredictable responses from one's adversaries.

Now that Zweller had escaped from the rebels, Koval fully expected to give the commander his just due: a list of Romulan agents working on Federation worlds. A list of probably-compromised intelligence officers who would shortly find themselves purged, their families vanished, their lands and properties confiscated. Section 31 would almost certainly execute the spy-purge themselves, thereby saving Koval and his bureau a great deal of trouble and expense. Quietly lauding himself for his own cleverness, Koval allowed his lips to torque into an—almost—perceptible smile.

But there would be plenty of time to consider such things after the Chiarosan referendum. In the meantime, much remained to be accomplished.

Koval rose from his seat and approached Subcenturion V'Hari, the young woman who was monitoring the helm console. Though her collar did not bear the bureau's insignia, she was, nevertheless, one of his most prized Tal Shiar staff officers, one of the many sets of clandestine eyes and ears he had positioned throughout the Praetor's fleet. She was someone to whom he could entrust a great deal of privileged information. Most important, she refrained from prying into anything he chose deliberately *not* to tell her.

The subcenturion snapped to attention. "Sir?"

"I must inspect the main energy facility and witness the next series of full-power tests," he said, nodding toward the image on the screen. "Send the technicians who came into contact with the Starfleet escapees to meet me there for their debriefings."

"It will be done, Mr. Chairman," she said crisply.

"I will return to the *Thrai Kaleh* within two days," he said, and then left the control center.

Two days, he thought. *At which time I will have a very important appointment to keep.*

Chapter Ten

As soon as the Romulan scout ship touched down in the *Enterprise*'s shuttlebay, Crusher had the still-slumbering Grelun and the surviving *Slayton* crew-members—including Corey Zweller—beamed directly to sickbay, where Dr. Anthony and Nurse Ogawa had been instructed to await their arrival. Leaving Riker in charge of securing the scout ship, Picard entered a tur-bolift, followed by Batanides. She was silent, almost brooding.

"Bridge," Picard said wearily. The car began moving smoothly upward.

"Johnny, what do you intend to do with Grelun after he wakes up?"

"I want to hear his side of the Chiarosan conflict," Picard said. "From what Riker, Troi, and Corey have already told us, Falhain's indictment against Ruardh's government may have real merit, after all."

"Too bad the rebels conveniently relieved Corey of his

tricorder before we could examine their alleged evidence," she said acidly.

"Do you think Grelun's people are fabricating the massacre stories? My first officer and counselor have made a pretty good case that they're not."

She sighed and seemed to let down her guard. "Since Aubin's death I'm really not sure *what* to believe."

"But you don't trust Grelun."

"In my field, trust has to be earned. And I have trouble trusting people who've just tried to kill me."

Picard nodded. "I understand that. And I also understand that they're desperate people."

"No doubt. But it still strikes me as strange that Grelun confiscated the evidence that might have convinced us that he's in the right and Ruardh's in the wrong."

Picard felt the car change direction. Now it was moving horizontally toward the center of the ship. "It's like you said, Marta. Trust has to be earned, and we have yet to earn Grelun's. He sees us as in league with his sworn enemies. And from his own people's point of view, we've just taken him hostage."

"Then we've got to send him back to Chiaros IV as soon as possible," she said. The turbolift shifted again, resuming its upward motion. "The longer he's with us, the more tensions will escalate on Chiaros IV. And going down there again to gather new evidence to prove who's in the right and who's in the wrong is just going to make us targets for both sides."

True, Picard thought. *Up to now, every one of our encounters with Chiarosans has led to violence.*

He looked her in the eye. "Believe me, I am excruciatingly aware of that." He hadn't been enthusiastic about Grelun's capture in the first place, though he had understood the necessity of it after Will and Batanides had explained it during the flight back to the *Enterprise.*

"Then you agree we've got to send him home," she said.

"Of course. Once Dr. Crusher has certified him fit to travel." *And after I speak with him. And Corey.*

The doors opened, and Picard and Batanides stepped together onto the bridge.

Data rose from the command chair, an urgent expression on his pallid face. "Captain, we have just detected an extremely unusual energy reading, centered on Chiaros IV's Nightside."

"What sort of reading?" Picard said.

"It is difficult to be certain, given the atmospheric turbulence and magnetic field-driven planetary radiation belts. But it appears that several Starfleet quantum torpedoes have just been detonated on the planet's surface."

Picard was taken aback. "That's impossible."

"We're receiving a hail, sir," Lieutenant Daniels said from one of the communications consoles. "It's coming from the communications tether orbiting Chiaros IV. It's First Protector Ruardh."

"On-screen, Lieutenant," Picard said coolly, standing very straight in the center of the bridge.

The Chiarosan leader sat behind an impressive desk that appeared to have been carved from a single block of wood. *An unabashed display of opulence,* Picard thought, on *a world with an ostensible lack of forested regions.* Beside Ruardh stood Senator Curince, elbows bent backward and hands behind her back. Both women wore solemn expressions.

Ruardh spoke first. "Captain, I have just been told of the explosion on Nightside."

"As have I, Madame Protector," Picard said.

"There are many on my world who would like to thank you for at last locating and destroying the Army of Light's principal military facility. Unfortunately, in the minds of many this development will also cast additional doubt upon the Federation's motives. You see, our traditionalists prefer field-of-honor combat to guerrilla warfare."

Picard shook his head. "Madame Protector, let me assure you that the Federation had *nothing whatsoever* to do with that."

"Please do not misunderstand me, Captain," Ruardh said, holding up one exquisitely articulated hand. "I applaud what has happened. Whoever is responsible, the Army of Light now lacks the limbs to hold its blades. If you are responsible, then you have earned my thanks."

"Madame Protector, the Federation does not try to curry favor with planetary governments by taking sides in internal disputes," Picard said emphatically, his tone deliberate and measured. "Nor do we engage in sneak attacks."

Curince displayed several rows of sharp, gleaming teeth. "Then we have an inconsistency. Ambassador T'Alik has informed me that the explosives used appear to be of Federation origin."

" 'Appear' is the operative word, Senator," Picard said. "It would not be the first time the Romulans have attempted to misdirect the blame for their own actions."

Ruardh looked puzzled. " 'Blame'? Why would they not wish to take the *credit* for themselves?"

"You said yourself that the attack on Grelun's base may actually compound the electorate's growing anti-Federation sentiment," Picard replied. "If your 'traditionalists' were to see the hand of the Romulans in this, then the referendum might turn out very differently. I think you may have answered your own question, Madame Protector."

Curince glared at him. "Perhaps," she said, then paused. "Speaking of Falhain's rebel successor, we have also been informed that he is now aboard your vessel."

Information which also no doubt came from T'Alik, Picard thought. He was convinced that the Romulan ambassador knew far more about her own government's covert activities on Chiaros IV than she was willing to admit.

Picard decided there was nothing to be gained by dissembling about the Chiarosan leader. "Grelun was seriously injured shortly before his base was destroyed," he said. "He's presently in our sickbay."

"I trust that his wounds were not mortal," Curince said, her voice flat.

"No, Senator. In fact, Dr. Crusher expects him to make a full recovery."

Ruardh looked disappointed to hear that. "Captain, you will turn him over to my military guard," she said in a low growl.

"I understand, Madame Protector. But first, I would like to know what will become of him."

Ruardh's eyes narrowed dangerously. "He will be dealt with as an enemy of the state according to Chiarosan law." She didn't need to tell them that meant a death sentence. "My government tried once already to reach out to Falhain and Grelun in friendship. You witnessed the results yourself."

Picard had been afraid she might say something like this, but he wasn't surprised. "I'm very sorry to hear that, Madame Protector," he said.

Curince tipped her head with evident curiosity. "Are you refusing our lawful request, Captain? Surely, that would not be consistent with the vaunted neutrality of your Federation."

"Let me assure you both, I have no intention of flouting your laws. However, my chief medical officer has yet to certify Grelun as ready to travel."

Ruardh nodded, a disconcerting smile on her face. "Your physician is wise, Captain. No one should be consigned to the flames while infirm. Death must be faced with strength."

"But please make no mistake, Captain," Curince said. "The vote will go badly for you. And if you try to take Grelun with you when you withdraw from our world, a great deal *more* will go badly for you."

At a gesture from Ruardh, the two Chiarosans vanished from the screen. An orbital vista of their storm-tossed homeworld replaced their images.

Batanides broke the silence that had fallen over the bridge. "You know I can't let you keep Grelun aboard the *Enterprise* in defiance of the Chiarosan government."

"The referendum is still two days away, Admiral. I have at least that long before it comes to that. But in the meantime, I can't simply hand him over to someone who feels entitled to summarily execute him."

"And what about *after* the referendum? If the Chiarosans throw us out, you won't have the legal authority to make that decision."

Picard was bitterly aware of that fact. But it changed nothing in his mind.

"You have the conn, Mr. Data," he said, and then stalked back into the turbolift, Batanides following close behind.

Standing beside Grelun's biobed, Crusher was methodically applying a dermal regenerator to wounds on the Chiarosan's forearms; the burns began to vanish almost immediately. Picard glanced at the biobed readouts. To his untrained eye, the Chiarosan's vital signs appeared strong.

A quartet of alert security personnel stood behind Crusher, watching vigilantly as she worked. Ensign Lynch, the head of the security detail, stared wide-eyed at the Chiarosan, obviously impressed.

"He must mass a quarter of a ton," Lynch said incredulously. "What I wouldn't give to see him in action."

Batanides scowled. "Ensign, you'd better pray that you never have to tangle with anything that big or mean outside of your daydreams."

Lynch reddened slightly, as though chastised. But he did not avert his gaze from the slumbering Chiarosan.

Picard glanced to the other side of the sickbay, where Dr. Anthony, Dr. Gomp, Nurse Ogawa, and a pair of orderlies were tending to the various bumps and bruises suffered by Counselor Troi, Lieutenant Hawk, and several members of the *Slayton* crew, none of whom appeared to be grievously injured. Liz Kurlan, the *Slayton*'s xenoanthropologist, still had a livid bruise across her forehead. Chief Engineer Hearn took a tentative step on a newly repaired knee.

Picard noticed that Zweller was conspicuously absent, as was Riker.

Picard tapped his combadge. "Computer, locate Commander Cortin Zweller."

"Commander Cortin Zweller is in the main shuttlebay," the computer responded.

During the flight back to the *Enterprise*, Riker had mentioned Zweller's propensity for cloak-and-dagger behavior. For a split second, he feared that Corey might be trying to flee the ship.

"Computer, is anyone with Commander Zweller?"

"Commander Zweller is with Commander Riker and Lieutenant Commander La Forge."

Batanides approached Picard and spoke quietly. "At least we know he's staying put. I think we ought to go to the shuttlebay and ask him for some details about what he saw down on Chiaros IV."

"I quite agree," Picard said quietly. "Then we can return to the problem of whether we can repatriate a guest whose government wants to murder him." He nodded toward Grelun.

Suddenly, the Chiarosan began to move, as though roused by the captain's words. His crystalline eyes fluttered open, darted quickly about the room, and locked with Picard's. One of his large, bronzed hands reached upward toward Crusher, who backed away as Lynch and the other security officers drew their phasers. The forcefield restraints crackled against Grelun's biceps and thighs, forcing him back against the table. He struggled again, this time throwing his body into the forcefield.

Through it all, his gaze never wavered from Picard's.

"He's going to kill himself if he keeps that up," Crusher said. Moving with a dancer's quickness, she emptied a hypospray into one of the Chiarosan's treelike calves.

As he began slipping back into unconsciousness, Grelun whispered three clearly-articulated syllables. From the shocked expressions on the other faces in the room, Picard knew instantly that he had heard the Chiarosan correctly, and that Batanides and Crusher had as well. No one else spoke for a long moment.

Finally, Batanides broke the silence. "Well, that certainly complicates things, Jean-Luc."

Picard nodded gently. "It changes everything." *But at least I'm no longer bound by law to hand this man over to his executioners, regardless of how the vote turns out.*

"News travels fast on Chiaros IV," Batanides said. "How do you think those people will react when they learn that a Starfleet captain has decided to harbor a known terrorist on the Federation's flagship?"

Picard's voice turned to sandpaper. "It won't be pretty. But my duty under both interstellar law and Starfleet regulations is clear. Grelun will receive Federation protection pending a full investigation of Falhain's allegations against Ruardh's government. Referendum or no referendum."

His options were sharply limited the moment the rebel leader had uttered a single word, the first he had spoken since coming aboard:

Asylum.

Chapter Eleven

Picard and Batanides entered the main shuttlebay, which currently held a pair of type-9 personnel shuttlecraft in the flight deck, though neither was powered up at the moment. No other officers were present on the deck, which was as Picard had expected; at Batanides's request, he had ordered the shuttlebay cleared. Apart from the two shuttles, the cavernous hangar was seemingly empty. Their footfalls reverberated loudly across the deck.

The Romulan scout ship was nowhere to be seen, which was also as Picard expected; it was cloaked, also at the admiral's request.

Picard deplored having to take these sorts of precautions, but he understood their occasional necessity. During the trip back to the *Enterprise,* Batanides had made it clear to Commander Roget that his officers weren't to speak to anyone about the scoutship. Given the fragile complexities of Chiarosan geopolitics, Picard thought her mandate for discretion was probably the wisest course. And despite his reticence about illegally operating a cloaking device, Picard nevertheless thought it prudent to give the Romulan vessel as low a profile as possible while it was aboard the *Enterprise.*

Picard tapped his combadge. "Number One, two to beam aboard the scoutship."

"Acknowledged, Captain," came the reply.

A moment later, Picard and Batanides stood in the small Romulan engine room, where Data, La Forge, and Zweller labored over a partially disassembled computer core. The three officers noted the presence of Picard and Batanides, but went back to their work after the captain made a subtle "as you were" gesture.

Riker, who was standing nearby, approached Picard and Batanides.

"Progress report, Number One," Picard said.

"First, we've managed to stop the flow of tetryons from the warp core."

"Good," Picard said. "Those emissions might have defeated the purpose of activating the cloaking device."

Batanides looked thoughtful. "This ship makes me wonder about something Ruardh said about the referendum."

"What do you mean?" Picard said.

"I mean that if the outcome really could hinge on our producing proof that the *Romulans* are really the ones who are up to no good here . . ." Batanides made a broad gesture encompassing the entire room, then said, ". . . well, what more proof do we need than this ship?"

Zweller approached, shaking his head. "If we try to use this ship to prove that the Romulans have been backing the rebels, I think it'll strike most Chiarosans as a bit too convenient."

"How so?" Batanides said.

"I took a moment to review the electoral poll data,"

Zweller said. "The Chiarosan electorate is a skeptical lot. Most of the voting populace thinks we're so desperate, that we'd say or do just about anything in order to win them over now."

"I'm inclined to agree," Picard said.

Batanides shook her head. "Very well. But I think you may be punting too early in the game."

"Admiral, I think we have to look at the big picture here very carefully," Picard said. "We mustn't forget that the election is only a small part of the Romulans' real agenda. I suspect that what they're really after remains hidden elsewhere in the Chiaros system."

"You mean behind the energy field," Riker said, as La Forge and Data set aside their task and approached.

"Exactly, Number One. We may have to accept that the referendum is already lost. Therefore that ship will provide a tactical advantage rather than a political one."

"You want to keep it in reserve," La Forge said, smiling. "A 'hole card.' "

"That's right," Picard said to the engineer. "And I want you and Data to find a way to play that card to our best advantage. We can use this ship to see what the Romulans are up to behind that energy barrier. And perhaps, if necessary, to put a stop to it."

Batanides didn't look entirely convinced. "If the referendum is already lost, then two days is all we have. That's pretty slim timing."

"We've done more with a great deal less," Picard said.

"I must point out," Data said, "that if we take the scoutship into the region the Romulans are concealing, we will not have the advantage of surprise. The Romulans are no doubt well aware that we have taken this craft. They are certain to be ready for us."

Picard smiled. "Well, I didn't say it would be *easy,* Mr. Data. Consider it a challenge."

"I do indeed, sir."

"We'll get right on it, Captain," La Forge said. "We can also modify another probe to look inside the energy screen, to get a better handle on what the scoutship's got in store for it."

Picard nodded his approval. "Make it so." Geordi and Data excused themselves and returned to their work.

Zweller remained behind, looking intrigued. "I'd like to know more about this energy field you keep referring to, Johnny," he said to Picard.

Picard studied his old Academy friend's eager expression. Ordinarily, his impulse would have been to tell him everything he knew. But during the flight back to the *Enterprise,* he had seen how Zweller's own colleagues had distrusted him. Riker, Troi, and Dr. Gomp had made him aware of their suspicions that Zweller had illegally aided the Chiarosan rebels; Gomp had even gone so far as to suggest that Zweller had prearranged their capture by the Army of Light.

Batanides was evidently having the same misgivings. "You'll be briefed in due course, Commander," she said coolly. "In the meantime, there are a few questions *we* need to ask *you.*"

Picard couldn't have agreed more.

Turning back toward Riker, he said, "Please ask Counselor Troi to come to my ready room, Number One. Immediately."

"What the hell kind of reunion is this anyway, Johnny?" Zweller said, looking surprised. "What exactly is going on here?"

"That's something I'd like to know as well." Picard

spread his hands across the ready-room desk and settled back in his chair. Batanides and Troi sat on the sofa on the other side of the small room. Both women were looking intently at Zweller, who stood with his arms at his sides, fists clenched.

"Your shipmates have leveled some very serious charges at you, Corey," Batanides said.

"Is this an interrogation, Marta?" Zweller said angrily.

Picard sighed. He would have thought that forty-plus years of starship duty might have mellowed his old friend's youthful hotheadedness.

"No one is interrogating you, Corey," Batanides said, leaving an unspoken but obvious *yet* hanging in the air.

"Nevertheless," Picard said, "these charges *are* serious, and must be answered. And there's also the matter of your DNA having been found on the combadges we recovered after the fight in Hagraté. The circumstantial evidence would suggest that it was *you* who removed those combadges from Commander Riker and Counselor Troi after they were struck unconscious in the melee."

"I noticed that Chiarosan disruptors can lock onto subspace signals," Zweller said, nodding. To Troi, he added, "Don't bother to *thank* me for saving your lives."

Picard considered that for a moment. "If that's so, then you certainly have earned *my* thanks. But Counselor Troi and Commander Riker have both told me that Grelun granted you privileges that he denied to his other prisoners. So I still must ask you: Did you supply arms or assistance to the Army of Light?"

Zweller pointed at Troi. "Why don't you get the answer from your Betazoid? You obviously don't have any faith that I'm going to tell you the truth, or else you wouldn't have sicced a telepath on me."

"I'm only half-Betazoid, Mr. Zweller," Troi said

calmly. "I can only pick up emotions, not specific thoughts."

"And what is it you're 'picking up' from me?"

"I sense mainly that you are a master of evasion. As well as a skilled manipulator of people. And of the truth."

"Come now, Counselor," Zweller said, his lips turning upward in an asymmetrical half-smile. "In my experience, that description could fit just about any front-line Starfleet officer who's managed to stay alive as long as I have. Present company excepted, of course."

Picard bridled at Zweller's verbal jab, but said nothing. There was no point in allowing his old friend to provoke him into losing control of the conversation. Batanides also allowed the comment to pass unanswered.

"Commander," Troi said, unflappably patient, "I've known ever since we were confined together that you've been concealing something significant. All I've ever sensed from you is a superficial emotional veneer, almost as though you were able to consciously block my empathic abilities."

Zweller adopted a sincere expression that belied his words. "Now that *would* be a remarkable talent. On the other hand, I may just be an extremely shallow person. Maybe there's nothing underneath that 'emotional veneer,' as you call it."

Or perhaps it conceals hidden compartments, Picard thought. *Like a smuggler's cargo hold.*

Turning toward Picard, Troi said, "I don't think I'm going to be of any help to you here, Captain. Perhaps it would be better if I started interviewing the other *Slayton* survivors instead."

"Very well," Picard said. "Make it so."

As Troi got up to leave the ready room, Zweller spoke

to her back. "Good idea, Counselor. I knew you'd get
around to helping those traumatized people eventually."

Troi paused in the open doorway for a moment as
though contemplating a rejoinder. Then, apparently realizing the futility of the gesture, she departed.

Picard was alone with his two oldest friends for the first
time in more than four decades. It struck him then just
how profoundly time could change a man. Yes, this Corey
Zweller was still a hothead, as he had been at Starfleet
Academy; but the loyal, to-Hell-and-back Cortin Zweller,
the comrade-at-arms who had fought the Nausicaans at
Bonestell so long ago, *that* Cortin Zweller had never made
such blatant stabs at a colleague's emotional buttons.

"Corey . . . did you give the rebels weapons?" Batanides said, beginning to lose her patience.

Zweller answered with exasperating serenity. "Don't
you think Grelun would have shown me a little more
gratitude if I had?"

"Not if he thought you were selling him out to Ruardh," Picard said.

Zweller sat down in one of the seats between the sofa
and Picard's desk. Focusing his gaze on the viewport, he
said, "Grelun suffers from a freedom fighter's paranoia.
When he caught me hacking into the rebel base's command systems, he naturally assumed the worst."

"And why were you doing that?" Batanides said.

"I was a prisoner, just like my crewmates. And a prisoner's first duty is to escape."

Batanides studied him with obvious skepticism.
"Some of your crewmates don't seem to believe that,
Corey. Dr. Gomp told me that you'd received special
treatment from your jailers all along."

"Must have been that vaunted 'mastery of manipula-
tion' the counselor says I excel in," Zweller said dismis-

sively. Turning toward Picard, he said, "C'mon, Johnny, don't tell me you've never charmed your way into an adversary's good graces before turning the tables on him."

Picard felt his own fund of patience beginning to run out. "Not by violating my oath as a Starfleet officer."

"If I *did* bend a regulation or two," Zweller said, "then you can rest assured that I did it in the service of a greater good."

"You mean the Army of Light's struggle against Ruardh's government," Batanides said.

"If you like," replied Zweller quietly, nodding slightly.

Batanides scowled. "I thought you said Grelun was an adversary."

"Sometimes it's hard to know exactly what that means, isn't it?" Zweller said tartly. "You won't find any angels on Chiaros IV, Marta. *Everyone's* hands get bloody in a civil war."

How ironic, Picard thought, *that Chiarosan blood is gray.*

He decided to try a placating tone. "Corey, please. You have to admit that you aren't being very forthcoming. You still haven't answered our primary question. For the sake of the friendship the three of us shared, I would have hoped that you'd——"

Zweller interrupted gently. "That's *exactly* why I can't tell you anything more, Johnny. If you keep probing into whatever I might or might not have done down there, you're only going to put yourselves in harm's way. Frankly, I'd prefer it if you didn't do that."

"Corey, that almost sounds like a threat," Picard said, taken aback.

Zweller shook his head, then paused to gather his

thoughts. "Could I speak absolutely candidly to both of you for a moment?" he said finally.

"That would be a nice change," Batanides said. She was not smiling.

"All you have is the hearsay of two of your officers and the word of an obstreperous Tellarite doctor against mine. You've got no proof of anything—even with an *empath* in the room! So if you're not prepared to arrest me and convene a general hearing, I respectfully suggest that you both let this matter lie."

Picard watched as Batanides silently fumed. He realized that Zweller had outmaneuvered them. For now.

"All right, Corey," Picard said at length. "I *will* put this matter aside. But only until Grelun or some of your colleagues from the *Slayton* can shed some more light onto it."

"Thank you," Zweller said, his emotions inaccessible.

"You are dismissed, Commander," Batanides said icily.

Pained that his old friend would not reach out to him, Picard watched in silence as Zweller exited the ready room.

Feeling weary, Zweller entered the quarters Riker had issued him. Picard's first officer had strongly suggested that he remain there pending the resolution of the political business on Chiaros IV. Noting that he didn't actually seem to be under arrest, Zweller decided he was too tired to argue the point tonight. He'd take the matter up directly with Johnny in the morning.

Ensconced in his quarters, Zweller contacted La Forge to request information about the huge volume of space the Romulans were apparently concealing. Though the engineer had seemed a bit overworked and harried, he had promptly uploaded the relevant observational data into Zweller's computer terminal. Though there was no conclusive information about what the Romulans were doing behind the vast invisibility screen they had constructed out in the Chiaros system's far reaches, they were clearly using it to hide an artificial construct of some sort.

Zweller waded through the data late into the ship's night, a worm of apprehension turning deep in his gut as he read. The *Slayton*'s crew had not detected the cloaking field before Zweller and his crewmates had taken the shuttlecraft *Archimedes* down to Chiaros IV.

If they had, Zweller thought as sleep finally began to take him, then Section 31 might never have struck its deal with Koval.

Picard was not surprised in the least to learn that Romulan Ambassador T'Alik wished to meet with him. What *did* surprise him was that the ambassador had waited an entire day to respond to his acquisition of the officially nonexistent Romulan scoutship.

It was shortly after 0800 when Batanides and Troi entered the ready room, where Picard was already seated behind his desk, sipping a cup of Earl Grey. Lieutenant Daniels signaled from the bridge that the Romulan delegation had been beamed aboard and was on its way.

Picard smiled over his teacup at the two women, who seated themselves on the ready-room couch.

"This should be good," Picard said, smiling mischievously for a moment before restoring the impassive demeanor of interstellar diplomacy. Troi and Batanides did likewise.

Moments later, a pair of security guards escorted T'Alik and her assistant, V'Riln, into Picard's ready room. Picard noted that V'Riln was the very same Romulan whose life he had saved during the armed contretemps in Hagraté. V'Riln nodded curtly to him, but there was no hint of gratitude in his eyes. *You're quite welcome,* the captain thought wryly.

Picard did not rise from his chair, nor did he offer T'Alik or V'Riln a place to sit. He knew there was nothing to be gained by making them unnecessarily comfortable.

"Madame Ambassador," Picard said simply.

"Captain," the Romulan responded, unsmiling.

"Allow me to introduce Vice-Admiral Batanides of Starfleet Intelligence. And you have already met my ship's counselor, Commander Troi."

T'Alik bowed her head in courtly fashion. "Admiral. Counselor."

V'Riln cast a sour glance at Troi. "I wish we had been advised of your intention to bring a Betazoid to this meeting, Captain. Perhaps we would have furnished a telepath of our own."

"Surely that would be unnecessary, Mr. V'Riln," Picard said, deliberately adopting the smile of a magnanimous host. "After all, what do either of us have to hide from each other?"

Troi's expression told Picard that she could probably spend several hours answering that single question. Batanides, for her part, seemed content to let Picard do all the talking. She sat in silence, watching the Romulans closely.

"Please allow me to come to the heart of the reason for this visit," T'Alik said.

"I would appreciate that, Ambassador," Picard said. "We only have one day left before the planetary referendum, so time is fleeting. And I suppose you've read the polls."

T'Alik almost smiled at that. "We are well-aware of the referendum's likely outcome. And frankly, I have come to ask you to concede those results sooner rather than later. After all, no purpose can be served by waiting until the bitter end."

"The writing, as you humans say, is on the wall," V'Riln said.

"Perhaps you're right," Picard said, smiling. He hoped to throw them off-balance. "It might do my crew some good to leave this dreary region a day or so early."

"That would be a great relief, Captain," Troi said, falling in step.

Picard smiled at the counselor, well aware that the relief Troi had just registered was not her own; T'Alik was evidently both surprised and pleased to hear that the *Enterprise* might be leaving early.

Perhaps she sees that as a sign that we won't embarrass her in front of the Chiarosans by unveiling the unauthorized ship we captured.

That was the moment when V'Riln floored him.

"The Tal Shiar has informed us that you still have the scoutship you used to escape from the Army of Light's Nightside compound," the Romulan assistant said in a matter-of-fact tone.

Picard did his best to hide his surprise. "I'm sure I don't know what you mean."

T'Alik did not appear fazed in the least by her assistant's revelation. Picard supposed that their presentation had been well-rehearsed for maximum emotional impact.

"No, Captain," the ambassador said with a faint smile. "I don't suppose that you do. But I must tell you that I am delighted to hear you say it."

"I'm sure if we *were* to discover any unauthorized Romulan vessels on Chiaros IV," Picard deadpanned, "it would greatly complicate your mission here."

"Indeed it would," T'Alik said.

Picard put on his most solicitous expression. "And it

would probably place you, personally, in an extremely awkward position."

"It would force the ambassador to protest the actions of her own government, Captain," V'Riln said haughtily.

T'Alik began to look ever-so-slightly uncomfortable. "In the event of any such discovery, Captain, I would likely have no choice other than to resign my post. As a fellow diplomat, I'm sure you can understand that I cannot be a party to a treaty violation, either official or otherwise."

Picard smiled broadly. "Madame Ambassador, as a fellow diplomat, I wouldn't dream of placing you in that position."

"I'm delighted that we understand each other so well, Captain," T'Alik said, bowing her head fractionally.

And with that, the Romulan diplomats said their short but polite farewells, then allowed the security officers to escort them out of the ready room.

"Well," Troi said. "Now we know that *they* know we have the scoutship."

"Data was right," Batanides said. "Whatever we decide to do with that ship, I suppose we can forget about having the element of surprise."

"I'd already accepted that as a given," Picard said, frowning. "But if there's a way around that problem, Geordi and Data will find it."

"For some reason, our continued presence is making the Romulans very nervous," Troi ventured.

Batanides nodded. "It can only have to do with whatever the Romulans are hiding behind their cloaking field."

Picard rose from behind his desk and walked over to the viewport. The darkness outside was punctuated by thousands of distant pinpoints of light.

For a long moment, he silently contemplated the loss of three wide, nominally empty sectors of space to the

Romulans. He found the notion unacceptable. He suddenly couldn't stomach the thought of losing *anything* to such Machiavellian schemers.

"I quite agree," Picard said with determination. "This has all gone on long enough. One way or another, we're going to find out what's behind that cloak."

Chapter Twelve

His eyes closed tightly, Chief Engineer Geordi La Forge sagged heavily against the side of the turbolift. "Bridge," he heard Data say.

Geordi opened his eyes as the car began moving. The android was staring at him, concern evident in his golden eyes. *Eyes as artificial as mine,* La Forge thought. It struck him as ironic that he could observe his friend's efforts to become human only by means of a synthetic sensory apparatus. At first glance, the engineer's ocular implants appeared to be perfectly ordinary, natural human eyes—until a close inspection revealed the intricate filigree of hair-thin circuit-patterns etched into their metallic-blue irises.

"Are you all right, Geordi?"

La Forge smiled weakly. "Never better, Data."

"I have noticed that, among humans, even the closest of friends will, on occasion, deliberately prevaricate to one another," Data said evenly. "I believe that your response constitutes what Commander Riker would almost certainly describe as a 'whopper.' "

La Forge nodded, sighed wearily, and massaged his temples. His head felt as though it were being squeezed in a colossal vise. According to Dr. Crusher, his headaches would cease once his nervous system had had a little more time to adjust to its new sensory inputs.

"Guilty, as charged, Data," La Forge said.

For most of the past two days, he and Data had worked alongside engineers Kehvan and Waltere Zydhek—the hulking brothers from Balduk—poring over the countless gigaquads of data contained in the captured Romulan scoutship's computer core, seeking two critical command pathways. The first was the electronic portal into whatever Romulan security systems might lay behind the cloaking field; the second was the precise cloaking-harmonic frequency needed to get a ship *inside* that field undetected.

He noticed that Data was still staring at him. "Did Dr. Crusher not caution you that sleep-deprivation might aggravate the temporary neurological discomfort your new sensory inputs are causing?"

Geordi nodded. "She did, Data. And if she asks me about it, I'll promise to sleep for an entire month. *After* we finish our job here."

As the turbolift sped forward and upward toward the bridge, Geordi considered the ramifications of the problems he and Data had just spent nearly thirty-six continuous hours trying to solve. Tracking down the correct lines of Romulan code among the quadrillions of irrelevant commands had been no simple undertaking, Data's prodigious computational power notwithstanding. The solution had remained stubbornly elusive for the first day, despite the endless specialized recursive "search" programs he and Data had devised for the purpose.

Geordi's first hurdle had been overcoming his astonishment over the tremendous storage capacity of the Romulan scoutship's computer core, and the extraordinarily complex information that filled it to overflowing. Such inelegant, convoluted programming techniques made no sense from an engineering perspective, and he had said as much to Cortin Zweller during the commander's brief visit to the shuttlebay.

Maybe you should stop thinking like an engineer, Zweller had said, chuckling as though La Forge's comment had been unbelievably naive. *Instead, why not try looking at it from the perspective of a Romulan Tal Shiar operative?*

The very mention of the Tal Shiar made Geordi's skin crawl. He remembered only too vividly how Romulan agents had manipulated him six years before, nearly turning him into an assassin.

But Zweller's remark had also given Geordi renewed hope that somewhere in the Romulan vessel's electronic labyrinth lay a definitive—if subtly hidden—solution to his problem. And sure enough, a few hours after he had put aside his engineer's tendency to seek out the shortest, simplest solutions, the relevant pieces of code had revealed themselves.

Geordi didn't notice that the turbolift had halted until its doors opened, interrupting his reverie. He and Data strode out onto the bridge, where the members of alpha-watch were at their customary places. Commander Zweller and Admiral Batanides stood in the center of the bridge, their eyes upon the forward viewscreen, which displayed a featureless region of space.

Their attentiveness told La Forge that there must be a great deal more on the screen than met the eye. "What exactly are we looking at?" he asked aloud.

"The sensors have picked up several small subspace

'hiccups' over the past few hours," Riker said. "And every one of these distortions has been localized within that region."

"Behind the cloaking field," Zweller added.

Picard regarded La Forge and Data. "Were you able to learn anything new from our first probe's scans?"

"No, sir," La Forge said. "Whatever's at the center of that effect is still invisible. But I believe I can get a second probe across the barrier intact, and bring in some clear images."

"Make it so," Picard said, nodding. La Forge and Data immediately busied themselves at the engineering consoles. Data loaded the correct cloaking-harmonic information into the probe's isolinear memory buffers while Geordi initiated the device's remote launching system.

The admiral shook her head, looking defeated. "I've really got to wonder how anything we might discover could possibly affect the Romulan takeover of the Geminus Gulf this late in the game."

"We should have an answer for you momentarily, Admiral," Data said. "The probe is away."

"Let's just hope that the Romulans haven't changed their cloaking-field frequencies," Zweller said.

La Forge's breath caught in his throat. The notion that all of his hard work might have been for naught was simply too much to contemplate right now.

"I do not believe that will be a problem," Data told Zweller. "The cloaked area is no doubt maintained by thousands, perhaps *hundreds* of thousands, of field generators. Adjusting the harmonics of the entire field would require making very precise changes to each component with utterly perfect synchronization. It is highly unlikely that the Romulans could accomplish this without momentarily lowering the cloaking field. So far, we have seen no evidence of this."

La Forge started breathing again. *Thank you, Data. I needed that.*

Everyone's eyes were riveted to the screen's tactical display as the probe rapidly approached the cloaking field's invisible perimeter—

—and then vanished into its imperceptible interior.

La Forge felt moistness on the back of his neck. Had this probe been silenced as easily as the last one? The moment of truth had arrived at last. "Any probe signals, Data?" he said.

"Negative," the android replied.

Damn! The harmonics must have been wrong after all—

"Correction," said Data. "I am now receiving narrow-band subspace telemetry. I do not believe the Romulans will be able to intercept it."

The engineer grinned broadly. *Bingo!*

"Put it on the screen," Picard said.

Lieutenant Hawk's fingers flew across his console in response. The image on the viewer abruptly changed, and La Forge heard sharp intakes of breath coming from points all over the bridge. A small, six-sided metallic shape with a hole through its center hung in the void, occupying the precise center of a spherically arranged network of even smaller orbiting platforms. Surrounding this was a second—and far larger—conglomeration of tiny pods of gleaming metal, an outer sphere composed of thousands of individual components, each separated from the next by several kilometers of empty space. Geordi had no doubt that this outermost layer made up the network of cloaking-field generators, which had kept this gigantic assemblage hidden until now.

"I want a better look at the object at the center," Picard said. "Maximum magnification, Mr. Hawk."

The view changed again, and the artifact in question

resolved itself into a complicated aggregation of asymmetrical spaceborne structures, clumped together in apparently slapdash fashion into an irregularly hexagonal torus. Geordi and Data exchanged surprised looks after seeing what lay at the object's open center. It raged at them from within an annular metal structure, which could not have measured more than a kilometer or two in diameter. There, in an extremely compact volume, blazed a primordial inferno—a barely constrained fury so intense that it might have been the cosmic forge in which the universe itself had been made.

"*Mon Dieu*," La Forge heard the captain say, apparently to no one in particular.

La Forge, Data, and stellar cartography specialist Ranul Keru stood on the raised central dais of the cavernous, three-story Stellar Cartography room. Captain Picard and all of the senior officers stood beside the dais, along with Batanides, Zweller, Commander Roget, and Lieutenant Hawk.

Picard gazed briefly at each of the three officers on the dais. "What definitive information can you tell us about the phenomenon out there?" The captain's voice echoed slightly in the oversize domed chamber.

"Based on our probe's sensor telemetry," the engineer said, "the object at the center of those cloaked structures is a subspace singularity."

"The first one, in fact, ever discovered," Keru said.

Batanides's eyebrows rose inquisitively. "Would you explain that a bit for the benefit of those of us who aren't physicists or engineers, Commander?"

"It'll be easier if we show you, Admiral," Keru said as he touched a control surface atop the dais' wide, swooping handrail. Everyone looked upward as an enormous holographic representation of the turbulent singularity—the roiling fireball at the center of the hexagonal Romulan array—suddenly appeared in midair, filling half of the map room's arch-ceilinged display space. As La Forge studied the spectacular image, he felt his fatigue draining away. Pure, adrenaline-fueled wonder took its place.

"What you are seeing," Data said, "is the singularity's event horizon, the boundary past which all infalling matter or energy—in this case, the solar wind from the Chiarosan star—becomes crushed to infinite density at the object's center. That region is invisible, since even light cannot escape it. The turbulent band of exterior material which you *can* see is located on the event horizon's periphery, where the object's powerful gravitational field is accelerating it into various forms of lethal hard radiation, such as delta particles and berthold rays."

La Forge saw Hawk and Keru exchange a worried glance. "How can a network of cloaking devices contain radiation as powerful as that?" Hawk said.

Keru shrugged, prompting La Forge to respond to Hawk's question. "It can't. The innermost sections of the Romulan facility seem to be doing that. The cloaking network's function is to keep the whole thing invisible and subspace-silent, along with a large volume of the surrounding space."

"In fact," Data said, "the entire apparatus may have been here for decades. Sensor telemetry shows that it orbits the Chiarosan star at a mean distance of about 800 million kilometers, about 650 million kilometers farther out, on average, than the orbit of Chiaros IV. Given the turbulent atmosphere on that planet, it is unlikely that the Chiarosans ever would have discovered it on their own."

"Strange," Batanides said blandly. "It looks like the

event horizon of a typical, garden-variety black hole to me. Albeit a bit more spectacular."

"It's very similar, Admiral, but there's one critical difference," La Forge said. "The object's singularity—that is, its point of infinite compression—lies in subspace instead of in normal space. For the moment, that's where most of its effects are confined."

"However," Data added, "local space–time curvature measurements show that the object's tremendous gravitational field has been steadily weakening the boundary between normal space and subspace, perhaps for billions of years."

"And now it finally has the potential to have serious effects on normal space," Keru added.

Zweller shook his head in apparent disbelief. "If this object has such a strong gravitational field, then why hasn't it affected the orbits of the planets in this system?"

"Good point," said the engineer. "My guess is that the object's gravitational influence is also largely confined to subspace. Along with most of its radiation output."

"That still doesn't explain why no Federation ship ever detected it earlier," said Crusher. "Say, from its subspace radio noise."

"The singularity's subspace emissions occur at much higher frequencies than those most starfaring cultures use for communications," Data explained. "Other normal-space phenomena, such as Chiaros IV's atmosphere and magnetosphere, generate far more noticeable interference in the communications bands."

"The Romulans obviously stumbled upon the phenomenon first," Picard said. "We've just come in a distant second."

"Or maybe third," Zweller said quietly. "The *Slayton* got here before the *Enterprise* did." To La Forge's broadband visual receptors, the man looked ashen, as though something had just gone radically awry with his cardiovascular system. But other than Counselor Troi—who was also gifted with unusual perceptions—no one else seemed to notice Zweller's apparent change of mood. Nevertheless, all eyes were now on Zweller, who had lapsed into silence.

It was Commander Roget who finally spoke up. "A couple of months before the *Slayton* entered the Geminus Gulf, the Argus Array picked up some unusual subspace distortion waves centered on this system. They were far too infrequent and intermittent to pin down to an exact epicenter."

"I am familiar with the Argus information," Data said with enthusiasm. "It is possible that the Romulans must periodically release some of their excess subspace energy into normal space, energy that manifests itself as subspace distortions."

"That might explain those subspace 'hiccups' we've been picking up over the past few hours," Riker said.

"And why the Romulan ambassador seemed so anxious for us to leave the area," Picard said. "Perhaps she knew that her countrymen were likely to spill some of their excess subspace energy today, and didn't want us nearby asking questions about it."

Roget shrugged. "It's also possible that the Romulans simply can't control the singularity as well as they think they can. There didn't seem to be any regular pattern to the distortions, after all. And the *Slayton* couldn't detect them at all—at least, not before she was destroyed."

"You think that the *Slayton* encountered the phenomenon after your shuttlecraft left for Chiaros IV," Troi said.

Roget nodded, his expression grim. "And I also think that those Romulan bastards destroyed her for getting too close to their secret energy project."

La Forge glanced once more at Zweller, noting that he was growing steadily paler in the infrared frequency band.

"The Romulans would certainly be highly motivated to keep this phenomenon under wraps until they've formally taken control of the Geminus Gulf," Picard said.

"And that motivation *would* seem to implicate them in the *Slayton*'s destruction," Data said. "They have found what may be the most powerful object ever discovered; as long as they can keep the bulk of the phenomenon's radiation and gravitational effects 'bottled' in subspace, so to speak, they will have access to virtually unlimited quantities of energy."

"And to think that all these years Starfleet believed that the Geminus Gulf was nothing but an empty desert," Batanides said, evidently to no one.

"Interestingly," Data said, "one of twentieth-century Earth's most desolate regions also held vast reserves of energy, in the form of petroleum. Wars over this substance were fought in the region known as the Middle East, where—"

"Thank you, Data," Picard interrupted, his brow wrinkled with concern. "But our primary concern is how to deal with the subspace singularity. First, I need to know if it poses any immediate danger, either to the *Enterprise* or to Chiaros IV."

Data nodded. "That is a distinct possibility, Captain, particularly if the inner containment facility were to suffer a catastrophic failure. The singularity itself appears to generate the very power that the Romulans are using to contain it. However, the malfunction of a critical component of their power grid could allow a great deal of radiation to escape. Far more than either the *Enterprise*'s shields or the planet's magnetic field could cope with."

"Or," La Forge added, "a containment breach could

allow a lot of gravitational energy to escape into normal space. A large enough graviton flux could create havoc in this system."

"Meaning what?" Picard said.

Keru coughed quietly before speaking. "Meaning that Chiaros IV could be thrown clear out into interstellar space. Or dropped straight into its sun. Or simply ripped to pieces."

"How could something that powerful have come into existence in the first place?" Troi said.

"No one knows for certain," Data said as he executed an extraordinarily human-looking shrug. "It is possible that only the primordial fireball from which all matter and energy originated could have created such a dense concentration of energy and mass."

"The Big Bang itself," Picard said, the awe in his voice unrestrained.

Crusher fidgeted. "This all sounds a little too huge to comprehend. What does all of this mean in practical terms?"

"That's a fair question, Doctor," La Forge said. "Theoretically, this subspace singularity has a gravitational potential millions of times more powerful than that of even the most massive black holes. We've known for a long time now that Romulan ships are powered by small artificial singularities. If the Romulans manage to harness this thing, it would yield trillions of times more energy than even their largest singularity-driven warp cores."

Batanides whistled quietly, obviously impressed. Picard, too, seemed to grasp the implications immediately. Zweller stood in brooding silence, his hands clasped behind his back.

"With a power source like that at their disposal," Picard said somberly, "the Romulans might be able to manage transwarp drive, like the Borg. Their ships could venture from Romulus to Earth in moments."

"And that's only the beginning," La Forge said. "With that much energy on tap, they could probably build and dismantle stable wormholes at will. They could send their troops anywhere in the galaxy—maybe anywhere in the *universe*—without even having to bother *building ships*. They'd make the ancient Iconians look like they were standing still." He paused while everyone in the room silently pondered the implications.

Finally, Riker ended the silence. "Well, now that we know *why* the Romulans want this system so badly, the next question is: What to do about it?"

"Agreed," said Picard. "Options?" The captain looked quickly at each person in the room. Another uncomfortable hush descended.

This time it was the admiral who broke the spell. "I'm inclined to agree with Commander Roget's interpretation of this thing," she said, massaging one of her temples. "The fact that this singularity is still belching fire and subspace distortions every so often tells us one thing loud and clear: The Romulans don't have complete control over it yet."

"That may be, Admiral," La Forge said. "Commander Data, Commander Keru, and I have been wondering all along if the Romulans haven't bitten off more than they can chew."

La Forge nodded to Keru, who activated another control on the railing. Instantly, a multilayered graph superimposed itself over the image of the subspace phenomenon, highlighting it with a series of colored bands.

Data spoke again. "The amber-colored areas show the pattern of gravimetric stresses that the singularity is bringing to bear on normal space. These stress-patterns seem to indicate that the Romulans are trying to maximize the phenomenon's energy output by keeping it balanced precisely between normal space and subspace."

"This is where things get very dicey," La Forge said. "If they've miscalculated the stress-points between normal space and subspace, then the singularity will rip into our universe directly through these stressed regions. It'll be like an iron anvil smashing through a rotting wooden floor."

"And what happens then?" Riker said, his blue eyes wide.

La Forge spread his hands and shrugged. "Worst case scenario? All of normal space gets sucked into subspace."

"Or perhaps vice versa," said Data, obviously intrigued with this line of speculation. "In fact, it is possible that all of space and subspace would be drawn *into* the singularity, precipitating a repeat of the Big Bang explosion itself. Such a phenomenon might even subsequently create an entirely new universe."

"After blowing this one to quarks first," Riker said dryly.

The admiral spoke up, getting everyone's attention. "Just before the first atomic bombs were tested on Earth back in the twentieth century, nobody was sure what the outcome would be. Some physicists worried that they might burn up every last oxygen molecule in the atmosphere in a single colossal, unstoppable firestorm. But they went ahead and detonated the first bomb anyway. The worst didn't happen. Luckily."

She looked gravely at every person standing in the cathedral-like room before continuing. "This time, we can't afford to be quite so . . . callous. Or allow the *Romulans* to be."

Picard stood by quietly as the singularity's image blazed overhead, eerily quiet. No one spoke for perhaps an entire minute as the captain ruminated, his expression unfathomable as he stared at the representation of the singularity. Finally, he looked away and regarded each and every face in the room once again, settling at last on La Forge and Data, who still stood on the dais beside Keru.

"If the Romulans were smart enough to beat us to discovering and harnessing this thing," Picard said, "then surely they've also anticipated the risks. They must have a plan to abort what they're doing. Some means of jettisoning the singularity permanently into subspace."

"That would be a rational contingency plan, Captain," Data said. "A successful abort, however, would involve causing a deliberate and extremely precise collapse of the Romulans' containment forcefields, while simultaneously sealing the breach between subspace and normal space. There would be no margin for error."

"If we could neutralize this new Romulan toy," Batanides said, "then losing the Geminus Gulf to them would be an acceptable price to pay."

"And it would also remove the Romulans' entire reason for coming here in the first place," Riker said, smiling slightly at the irony.

"Mr. Keru, please deactivate the image," Picard said, signaling that he had come to a decision. Keru touched a button and the singularity abruptly vanished.

Once again, the captain spoke toward the dais. "Mr. La Forge, Mr. Data, in just under four hours, the Chiarosan referendum will officially conclude. I expect that we won't be able to remain in this system for very long after that without seriously provoking the Romulans."

La Forge smiled. "Data and I already have a plan that we think we can pull off before the electoral deadline."

"I was hoping you'd say that," Picard said, a slow smile crossing his face. "What will you need?"

"The Romulan scoutship, Mr. Data, a good pilot, and a couple of hours of preparation time. That singularity ought to be back where it came from permanently by the time we get booted out of here."

"Hold it," Batanides said sharply. "You can't be planning to fly that scoutship into the lion's den, Mr. La Forge. The lion already has a pretty good idea that we're coming."

"Fortunately," Data said, "the element of surprise will be entirely irrelevant to our plan. We will need only to stay within the cloaking field long enough to establish a link between the Romulan security network and my own neural nets."

"With a little luck, the scoutship will be halfway back to the *Enterprise* before the Romulans even know what hit them," La Forge said.

Zweller was wearing a sour expression. "So *that's* your solution? *Destroy* the most potent source of power ever discovered?"

"I'm not thrilled about it, Commander," said the engineer. "But it seems like a better idea than giving the Romulans a chance to use it against *us*."

"Why are you so sure your plan is going to work, Commander La Forge?" Batanides said, sounding skeptical.

The engineer placed an arm about Data's shoulders, momentarily surprising him. "Because, Admiral, even the smartest Romulan can't think nearly as fast as the *Enterprise*'s second officer."

Data looked embarrassed. "Why . . . thank you, Geordi."

Picard smiled. "Then make it so, Mr. La Forge, Mr. Data. Mr. Hawk, I'd like to have you aboard that scoutship as well."

La Forge noticed a slight scowl forming on Keru's face, though the stellar cartographer said nothing. Hawk beamed, apparently not noticing Keru's reaction. "Captain, I'd be happy to volunteer. I'm looking forward to having a go at that scoutship's cockpit."

Picard dismissed his officers, and La Forge and Data were the first to leave the room, nearly at a run. With yet another inscrutable riddle before him, the engineer felt fairly abuzz with excitement. *Sleep is overrated anyway,* he thought, his agile mind already setting up several new equations as he entered the turbolift alongside his android friend.

The knowledge that the Romulans were now poised to take over—or perhaps even *annihilate*—the universe settled uneasily in Cortin Zweller's gut. Compared to the singularity, Koval's list of Romulan spies now seemed impossibly trivial.

Zweller now had to accept the bitter truth that he—and Section 31—had been duped. Taken in by a master deceiver, to be sure. But fooled nonetheless.

He mulled these self-recriminations over as he watched Lieutenant Hawk and most of the other officers file out of Stellar Cartography. He wondered if Hawk had said anything to Picard or Batanides about their conversation on the scoutship—and which way Hawk's loyalties would ultimately lead him.

Suddenly, Zweller noticed Counselor Troi's appraising stare. Hurriedly, he reinforced his mental shields. Had he allowed his regrets to compromise him?

Troi spoke briefly—too softly for Zweller to overhear—to both Picard and Batanides. A moment later, the captain approached Zweller, regarding him with a taut expression.

"Please wait for us in the aft observation lounge, Commander. I think there's still some unfinished business left over from our previous conversation."

Zweller's pulse thundered in his ears as he left the chamber, alone. He knew he had to be the principal topic of whatever conversation was now occurring in the room behind him.

He closed his eyes for a moment, and the flames of the singularity blazed behind his eyelids. *What a waste,* he thought, *to banish such a useful thing forever into subspace. There has to be a better alternative.*

He decided to speak to Lieutenant Hawk about that at the earliest opportunity.

Chapter Thirteen

"Are you sure of this, Counselor?" Picard asked, his voice booming across the nearly empty Stellar Cartography room.

"Not entirely, sir," Troi admitted. "The feelings I got during the meeting were so fleeting that I only have vague impressions." She hated sounding so equivocal, but she knew that evaluating the emotions of others was far from an exact science.

"Just because you sensed feelings of betrayal coming from Commander Zweller doesn't necessarily mean he's working with the enemy, Counselor," said Batanides, her expression showing slight annoyance.

"All the same, Marta, we both know that Corey's story hasn't been adding up." Picard splayed his fingers on the dais railing and stared down at them. "Was he working with Falhain's rebels or was he just playing along to find a way to free his fellow officers? Did he provide them with weapons? How much does he know about the Romulans' involvement in this sector? What isn't he telling us?"

"I'm afraid I can't be of much help, Captain," Troi said. "According to his records, Commander Zweller is a nontelepathic human, but he apparently knows how to erect mental shields."

"Maybe some people just don't like to have their minds probed without *permission*," Batanides said testily, crossing her arms. "In Starfleet Intelligence circles, it's not uncommon to protect oneself against Betazoids, Ullians, Vulcans, or other telepaths."

Troi knew that the admiral had been uncomfortable around her ever since her return; she assumed it was most likely because of what Batanides had learned about her lover and his possible provocative actions at the peace conference. The counselor momentarily considered confronting the senior officer with this observation, but decided against it. Best to let the matter drop.

"Sir, I still have more work to do helping the *Slayton* survivors. Is there anything else I can help with?"

Picard nodded to her, his eyes darting momentarily to Batanides. "No. Thank you, Deanna. I'll . . . *we'll* take your concerns under advisement."

With a curt nod, Troi backed away and stepped through the door and into the corridor. She scarcely needed her Betazoid abilities to interpret the admiral's hostile parting glare.

The doors to the aft observation lounge parted with a faint pneumatic hiss, and Picard strode in, the admiral at his side. Picard found Cortin Zweller standing in the dimly lit chamber, staring idly at the sparse starfield that lay beyond the *Enterprise*'s stern. Zweller turned desultorily toward him, and the captain stared at his friend for a moment, searching his eyes, looking for some sign that things were not as confused as he feared. But all he saw was a carefully blank countenance, a Vulcan-like mask that concealed all emotion.

The silence stretched uncomfortably. Picard sighed heavily. "We need to talk, Corey. Just you and me and Marta."

"Again? What about, exactly?"

"I think you know," said Picard. He sat behind the long, low table, and gestured for Zweller to take a seat across the table from him. Batanides sat beside Picard, her hands steepled under her chin as she studied each of her old friends in turn.

"There are still some troubling . . . inconsistencies in your accounts of your time on Chiaros IV," Picard said.

"Such as? Have you gotten new information from Grelun? Or has my esteemed colleague Dr. Gomp renewed his campaign of character assassination?"

Batanides spoke up then. "Grelun's not talking much. And none of your 'esteemed colleagues' seem to have a very high opinion of you right now."

Zweller snorted, but the admiral pressed on. "Everyone seems convinced that you worked closely with Falhain and Grelun both, aiding the Army of Light rebels in their fight against Ruardh."

"I've said as much. I freely admit that I helped them somewhat," Zweller said, leaning back in his chair. "The only way I was going to get my fellow crewmembers off that planet was to pretend to work with them until such time as I could seize an opening and escape."

"What lengths were you willing to go to before your attempted escape, Corey?" Batanides asked. "Did you provide them with the weaponry that they used in the attacks on the peace conference? Or the other attacks on

Ruardh's forces? And why did you aid them in kidnapping the *Enterprise* officers?"

"Whoa, slow down, Marta. One question at a time. They already had some weapons when I was captured—when *we* were captured. I assume they may have gotten them from the Romulans. It didn't seem particularly important where they got them at the time, just that they *had* them. And I did not participate directly in the melee at the peace conference—"

Picard was incredulous, and interrupted his friend. "Then how did you remove Riker's and Troi's combadges?"

Zweller's jaw clenched, almost imperceptibly, and he spoke again, his voice as carefully modulated as before. "I said that I did not participate *directly* in the melee. I was with Grelun's troops in an antechamber, trying to keep them calm while their leaders negotiated. I hoped that all of us from the *Slayton* would be released if the talks went well. When the fighting began—which, I might add, was *not* precipitated by any of Falhain's men—I bullied aside two of my guards to rescue Riker and Troi before they could be killed. I still don't know *who* started the attack, Jean-Luc. But I was trying to save your officers' lives!"

Batanides's voice was stony. "Why did you remove their combadges? You allowed them to be taken prisoner."

"It all happened very fast. I grabbed the combadges because I thought Ruardh's people were behind the attack. I already told you: They could have used the combadges as automatic target locks and killed Riker and Troi. You have to admit that the creation of Federation martyrs would have given Chiaros IV's pro-Federation faction a real boost."

Picard wasn't entirely convinced by the argument. But Zweller's easy facility for providing plausible-sounding answers impressed him. The captain leaned forward and pitched his voice low. "Corey, did you come to believe in Falhain's cause?"

"Do you mean did I think that Ruardh's regime was an oppressive, murderous, genocidal government that the Federation shouldn't ally itself with?" His eyes narrowed. "Yes."

Picard sat back in surprise as Zweller stood and began pacing. "I saw what they did to the Chiarosan villagers," the commander said. "So did Riker and Troi; they witnessed what was left of one settlement. They *told* you about it. There are only so many charred bodies of men, women, and children you can see—slaughtered for no reasons other than resource-greed and politics—before you begin to know that something is fundamentally wrong."

Zweller turned to look at Picard. "The Federation wasn't thorough in their investigation of this world before they began the process of acceptance, Johnny. They were more concerned with beating the Romulans to the punch. But they chose the wrong side this time. And not *everyone* at Starfleet disagrees with me."

He paused for a moment, and looked Batanides squarely in the eyes. "Not even everyone in Starfleet Intelligence."

"What?" The admiral stood, an expression of amazement on her face.

Zweller appeared unfazed. "You haven't asked me about the Romulans yet. Did I know that they were working with Falhain?"

Picard's mind raced as he tried to formulate a line of questioning for *this* new revelation. He went with the most obvious choice first: "*Did* you know about them?"

"Of course I did. Certain echelons of Starfleet knew about them. You'd have to be dense not to at least suspect it."

"There's a fine line between suspecting and knowing," Picard said harshly.

"You keep bringing Starfleet into it as if that justifies your actions," said Batanides. "I hate to be so blunt, Corey, but you're only a science officer. I think that Johnny, as a starship captain, or myself, as a vice-admiral in Intelligence, might have some better firsthand knowledge of Starfleet's intentions."

Zweller took a deep breath, closed his eyes, then opened them and spoke in a quick, precise cadence. "I was billeted to the *Slayton* to help facilitate my other assignment. My *real* assignment. That mission was to find out what was really happening on Chiaros IV, by any means necessary—including infiltrating the rebel factions—and to let the Federation know exactly who they were getting into bed with."

Batanides's eyes widened. "Your mission for *whom? What the hell are you talking about?"

"I'm not at liberty to discuss my orders, or exactly to whom I'm reporting," Zweller said coolly. "Let's just say that I've been working on behalf of an unspecified branch of Starfleet Intelligence, and leave it at that."

"So you've lied to us again," Picard added, feeling pained and more than a little angry. "Everything you've told us thus far is just another string of—"

Zweller interrupted. "I've told you what you needed to know, Jean-Luc. In fact, I've probably told you too much."

"Too much?" Picard said, his ire threatening to boil over. "Your ship was destroyed. Your people were taken captive, as were some of mine. I've narrowly escaped death twice, and Marta's fiancé was not so fortunate. The Chiarosans are voting right now to reject Federation membership, which will leave this entire sector at the mercy of the Romulans, who have just found a way to use this system to make their fleets unstoppable!" Picard paused, letting the enormity of his accusation sink in. Glaring, he continued. "I think you haven't told us nearly *enough*, Commander."

Zweller turned his back to his friends, and walked over to the viewing window, staring out at the sparse sea of stars floating in the blackness. Finally, he spoke. "None of this was supposed to happen. Certainly not the *Slayton*'s destruction or the ambassador's death. And *nobody* knew about the subspace singularity."

He paused and put one hand to the back of his neck, before speaking again. "As for the fate of Chiaros IV, I don't believe that its destiny has ever lain with the Federation. Ruardh's brutality would have been a black eye on the UFP's peaceful, smiling face. The planet was a write-off before you ever got here."

Batanides's tone was wrathful. "Are you saying that Aubin died for *nothing?*"

"No. I'm saying that a deal had already been brokered to hand Chiaros IV over to the Romulans. At the time, my superiors believed that the only result of Romulan annexation would be the loss of an expanse of space that perfectly defines the term 'void.' As I said, no one knew about the singularity."

Picard became aware that his mouth was hanging open in surprise. He shut it with an audible snap, then spoke again. "You said that these supposed higher-ups in Starfleet had made a deal. What were *we* allegedly getting in exchange for handing this system over to the Romulans?"

"The Romulan Tal Shiar was going to furnish a list of all Romulan intelligence operatives working inside the Federation. Prior to the discovery of the subspace singularity, it had looked like a pretty good deal." Zweller picked at a loose thread on his tunic, a mannerism so casual that the revelations he was sharing might have been something as innocuous as soufflé recipes. Picard wasn't sure what angered him the most, the secrets, the lies, or Zweller's cavalier attitude.

"I'm to meet with Tal Shiar Chairman Koval at a remote location in the Chiarosan asteroid belt immediately after the Romulans win the referendum," Zweller said. "There, he'll give me a data chip containing the list."

"In other words, you're betraying the Federation to the Romulans for a *chip?*" Batanides said, her voice taut.

Zweller's face and voice betrayed only a flicker of emotion as he leaned forward, hands on the table. "No, Marta. I'm acting on behalf of an agency whose highest priority is the Federation's security. As far as my superiors knew, my mission would have cost us little and benefited us *greatly.*"

"You know as well as I do that those Romulan agents are probably set to be purged anyhow," she replied. "And that there are probably innocents on that list who will be removed from their posts or charged with conspiracy so that the Romulans can replace them with their own people."

"I don't think that any Starfleet Intelligence operatives will be charging forward blindly to arrest and prosecute everyone on the list without first—"

"Enough!" Picard slammed both hands down on the table, scowling at his two oldest friends. He had a hard time swallowing everything Zweller had just told him; on the other hand, he certainly couldn't dismiss out of hand the commander's charges against Ruardh's government. Riker and Troi had corroborated that part of Zweller's story, after all.

The captain turned toward the admiral and spoke, his tone measured. "We must salvage as much of this situation as possible. I think it's clear now that Ruardh and her government have been concealing their ethnic cleansing pogroms from us all along. And now that the rebel headquarters have been destroyed—regardless of who is responsible—the people seem certain to reject Federation membership, and perhaps even Ruardh's continued rule. I'm afraid I must agree that the loss of Chiaros IV seems a foregone conclusion at this point."

He switched his gaze from Batanides to Zweller, and continued. "You've obfuscated the truth so much, Corey, that I almost don't know what to believe anymore. Except for this: Your exchange with the Romulans must go ahead as planned."

"*What?* Why?" Batanides appeared dumbfounded. Zweller looked surprised as well.

"Marta, if the Romulans are playing straight with Corey," Picard said, "then we'll at least get that list of spies. Corey's extralegal skulduggery and the loss of the *Slayton* won't have been entirely in vain." Picard observed Corey wince almost imperceptibly at the mention of his destroyed starship; he didn't need Troi's talents to notice Zweller's obvious burden of self-recrimination, deserved or not.

Picard looked at Batanides, who seemed to be weighing his words carefully. After a moment, she nodded and said, "I think you and I are finally on the same page, Johnny, though I have to confess to some surprise to hear you sanctioning a covert operation."

Picard's memory conjured images of his capture on the planet Celtris III four years ago, during a secret mission to find a Cardassian metagenic weapon; he fleetingly recalled the horrendous torments, both physical and psychological, he had endured at the hands of his inquisitor, Gul Madred.

"It wouldn't be the first time," Picard said, his throat suddenly dry.

Batanides shrugged. "Be that as it may, you left out an important detail."

"What's that?" Picard said, his brow wrinkling.

"I'm going with him," she replied.

Now it was Picard's turn to be surprised. "Actually, I was thinking that *I* should be the one to go, Marta."

"You're not an intelligence officer, Johnny," she said, a sly smile crinkling the corners of her mouth. "I am. And I outrank you, so please don't bother arguing."

"I suppose you are the best choice to . . . render aid to Mr. Zweller should he need it," Picard said, admitting defeat. *And to keep an eye on him in case he has any other tricks up his sleeve.* Picard knew that he didn't need to say that out loud; he assumed that both Batanides and Zweller were already thinking it as their reflections regarded each other appraisingly across the polished tabletop.

Breaking the silence, Picard said, "Still, I have to point out that there's some real danger here." Batanides flashed him a *no kidding?* look of mock surprise; he ignored it and continued. "While we're trying to neutralize the singularity, we'll stand a greater chance of success if we can divert the Romulans' attention elsewhere."

"Onto the two of us," Batanides said.

"In other words," Zweller said acerbically, "we're going to serve as a distraction."

Picard ignored the comment. "You'll be issued a shuttle so you can make your rendezvous at the appointed time."

The captain's combadge suddenly chirped, and Will Riker's voice issued from it. "Captain, I think we've finally got some good news. Geordi has worked out the details of his plan for dealing with the singularity."

And not a moment too soon, Picard thought. "Splendid, Number One. I'll join you on the bridge in a moment."

Rising from his chair, Picard took a last look at his

two friends and fleetingly saw them as they had once been—rousingly ebullient and slightly rebellious cadets.

How time and politics change us all.

"It is vitally important that you keep the Romulans occupied," he said, straightening his tunic as he prepared to exit the observation lounge. "And personally, for me . . . it's equally as important that *both* of you return from your appointment alive. We'll deal with these *other* matters . . . later."

If there is *a 'later' for the three of us,* Picard thought as he strode down the corridor.

The silence in the room was palpable after Picard departed. Batanides's thoughts were awhirl as she tried to make sense of the revelations to which she had just been made privy. She looked over at Zweller, who was now slumped in his chair, refusing to meet her gaze.

He spoke first. "I'm sorry, Marta. It wasn't my intention to have this all go south. I'd do anything to bring the crew of the *Slayton* back, and Aubin was—"

"Don't." Her voice was firm and unyielding. "Don't you dare bring Aubin into your—" And then it hit her. Troi's premonition of danger at the peace conference, when she had pushed Picard to safety. The emotion-amplifying chip and its contents, as described by the android. Some of the things Aubin had said and done on this mission. Before now, none of them had connected. Now, though she didn't want to think it, the words came into her head in a flood. *Aubin was Cory's partner in sabotaging the Chiarosan peace talks.*

Steeling her nerves, she began moving around the conference table toward Zweller. "He was working with you, wasn't he?" she asked.

Zweller looked up at her, a flicker of surprise in his

gaze. She was glad to see that for once in the last hour, she had been the one to surprise *him*. She continued: "He was part of your group. He didn't come here to promote peace, he came here to help end Ruardh's regime and lose the Geminus Gulf to the Romulans."

"He was doing what was *best* for the Federation, Marta. He was following his orders."

She began to turn, then brought her left hand up in a clenched fist. Her blow connected to Zweller's jaw with a crack, and he went cartwheeling backward, out of his chair.

Sprawling, the commander rubbed his jaw. "Ow," he said simply.

"Get up too soon and I'll knock you right back on your ass, Corey." Batanides massaged her fist a bit, and looked down at her friend. "How *should* I react? First I find out that one of my oldest friends has betrayed his ideals and is collaborating with the Romulans. And now I find out that the man I loved—who was slaughtered in the midst of a peace initiative—is just as much a traitor to everything I believe in!"

"I'm *not* a traitor, Marta," he said emphatically, holding his hands up, palms outward, as if to ward off any further blows. "And neither was Aubin. We were following orders from Starfleet, orders that worked to the benefit of the Federation."

"Oh, yes, I can see the big benefit. A starship and her crew destroyed. Countless Chiarosans dead. A famed ambassador murdered. The fleet's flagship about to be booted out of the system, unless, of course, we go to *war* over a rebel prisoner who has requested asylum. Have I *missed* any of your benefits?

"And who exactly was it who cut your cloak-and-dagger orders, Corey? I'm a flag officer in Starfleet Intelligence! Don't you think *I* would know about any clandestine deals with the Romulans?"

"You know as well as I do that there are branches of Starfleet that are more . . . covert than Intelligence."

Batanides seemed unconvinced. "Shadowy government bureaus may be all the rage for your buddies, the Romulans, or some of the other warlike cultures, but they haven't existed on Earth since the twenty-first century."

Zweller sighed, then stood, keeping a discreet distance from the admiral's striking range. "What do you want to hear, Marta? That you're *right?* That those in power have never seen a need to secretly bend the rules that they uphold in public? That even Starfleet Intelligence has never stepped over the line to protect the Federation from its enemies? What is it you want to hear?"

Squaring her shoulders, Batanides looked her compatriot in the eyes. She had to say the words out loud, though she feared even thinking them. For years she had heard the rumors of a shadowy group of operatives; now, she might have been in bed with them, literally and figuratively.

"Tell me there is no Section 31. Tell me that you're a rogue agent. Tell me that Aubin was an ambassador who was just trying to settle a civil war on behalf of the Federation's diplomatic corps."

In Zweller's eyes, Batanides saw sorrow, and perhaps a bit of pity. She knew then that her friend still loved her, and that his loyalties were conflicted.

But she also saw the cold, brutal truth: Section 31 was real, and Aubin Tabor had done its bidding.

He turned away from her, hands clasped behind his back, and stared out at the stars.

Batanides massaged her bruised hand, trying to calm herself, breathing as regularly as she could. A smoldering rage was building inside her. But what could she do about it?

Batanides turned her back on Zweller and started to go. Then she stopped at the door, and spoke to him once more over her shoulder. "I'm going to bring Section 31 *down*, Corey. For my memory of what Aubin was ... and for the man *you* used to be.

"And you have to decide whether or not you're going to stop me."

Chapter Fourteen

For a few moments after he returned to the bridge, Picard stood quietly beside one of the aft consoles as he surveyed his crew in action. Various officers were busily manning stations, scarcely pausing to note his presence. Riker sat confidently in the center seat as if he was born to it. Picard smiled to himself, taking quiet reassurance from the seamless performance of his crew. It was preferable by far to shouts of "Captain on the bridge!"

"Report, Number One," Picard said as he approached Riker.

"Geordi and Data are nearly finished loading their attack plan into the Romulan ship's computer core," Riker said as he rose from the chair. "And Lieutenant Hawk is getting her ready for launch."

Picard nodded. "Good. How soon can we get the mission under way?"

"No more than another thirty minutes. Maybe sooner."

Picard suddenly noticed how drawn and exhausted Troi looked. *Who counsels the counselor?* he thought.

"Have the survivors from the *Slayton* been keeping you busy, Counselor?"

Troi smiled gently. "They *have* required a lot of attention, Captain. But that's to be expected, considering the ordeal they've suffered. Apart from their suspicions about Commander Zweller, their morale is actually quite good. I'm really much more concerned about our other guest."

Picard understood immediately. "Grelun. Dr. Crusher tells me he's already made a complete recovery. Has he been causing any problems?"

"Not at all," Troi said, sounding surprised.

Riker grinned wryly. "I suppose it's a lot easier to be polite when no one's shooting at you."

"I'm certain it's only a temporary cease-fire, Will," Troi said. "First Protector Ruardh isn't about to simply leave him in our custody, political asylum or no. And she'd probably go apoplectic if she saw the VIP stateroom we issued him."

Riker shrugged. "Big people need big quarters."

"Do you think Ruardh would actually be foolish enough to attack the *Enterprise?*" Picard asked Troi.

"She's certainly angry enough, Captain. But I don't think she'll do anything overt until after the results of the referendum are officially announced."

"Grand," Picard said, shaking his head. Still, his determination to safeguard Grelun from his would-be executioners had not wavered. "So we have to neutralize the singularity *and* withdraw to a safe position, all within a couple of hundred minutes."

"At which time the Romulans will be within their rights to use force to get us out of the Geminus Gulf," Riker said.

Picard heard a pair of doors swish open behind him.

He turned and saw Admiral Batanides enter, to be followed moments later by Zweller. Picard had to fight back his surprise at the sight of the bruise on the commander's jawline. He and Batanides both wore somber expressions; Zweller looked for all the world like a cadet who had just been put on report for brawling.

Picard turned back toward Riker. "You have the conn, Number One. I'll be commanding the singularity mission myself."

Riker frowned. Picard didn't need Troi to read his first officer's intentions.

"No arguments this time, Will. Mr. Data and Mr. Hawk will be with me. This operation can be executed best by a small crew, and it's far too important for me to delegate."

"With all due respect," Riker said, "a crew of two seems a bit *too* small."

Suddenly, the ship lurched hard to starboard, forcing everyone to grab at chairs, railings, and consoles to avoid being flung violently about the bridge. An alarm klaxon shrilled as Zweller toppled hard against a console and Batanides fell onto her knees. The vibrations forced Troi out of her chair, unceremoniously depositing her onto her backside. Riker stumbled, then clutched at a console and struggled back to his feet.

Picard stood beside the command chair, grabbing its arms to steady himself. He experienced a fleeting instant of vertigo. Shaking his head to clear it, he wondered if Ruardh had chosen this moment to launch a surprise attack.

Then, almost as quickly as they had come, the vibrations ceased. A quick glance around the bridge revealed that no one was seriously hurt.

"Number One, what just happened to us?"

Holding tightly to his console, Riker said, "It was another subspace distortion-wave, Captain. Quite a bit stronger than the previous ones."

"What the hell are the Romulans up to?" Picard said, not expecting an answer. "Yellow alert. Status report, Lieutenant Daniels."

Staring at his readouts on the upper bridge, Daniels spoke breathlessly. "I'm getting reports of minor hull-breaches on decks eleven and twelve, Captain. Force-fields are up and damage-control crews are responding. It could have been a lot worse."

"What about the Chiarosans?" Picard said. "Can you tell if the planet was affected?"

"Apparently not, sir," Daniels said. "I'm monitoring their orbital communications tether now. It seems to be working, and I'm not picking up any emergency message traffic. The atmosphere and the planet's Nightside must have taken the brunt of the shock."

"I recommend we don't take the *Enterprise* any closer to the singularity than it already is," Riker said. "We can't predict when these subspace slippages will occur, and a ship this large is a sitting duck for spatial disruptions this intense."

"Won't our shields protect us?" Troi said.

Riker shook his head. "Subspace distortions alter the shape of space itself. The *Enterprise* occupies a pretty fair amount of that space. And she can't take this sort of punishment the way the planet can."

Batanides strode toward the turbolift, where Zweller awaited her with a sullen expression. She paused in the open doorway and turned to face the bridge. To Picard, she said, "Commander Zweller I and will be in the shuttlebay."

Picard nodded to her. "Everything is ready for you," Picard said simply, then watched as his two oldest friends entered the turbolift, headed to their rendezvous with Chairman Koval. Just before the doors hissed shut, Picard saw the thunderheads looming behind Batanides's gaze.

He was supremely thankful that he was not Cortin Zweller.

Thanks to the tireless efforts of Data and La Forge, the Romulan scoutship was ready for launch ten minutes ahead of schedule. The bridge crew had detected three more strong subspace distortion wave-fronts that followed no perceptible pattern. The Romulans were clearly stepping up their efforts. It could be that they were closer to harnessing the subspace singularity's colossal power than anyone had suspected.

But they might also be losing control of it, Picard thought. *No wonder they wanted us to clear out of here yesterday.*

The shuttlecraft *Herschel,* carrying Zweller and Batanides, had already departed when Picard entered the shuttlebay. Now that the damage had already been done to Federation–Chiarosan relations, Picard could only hope that his old comrades-at-arms could extract some useful information from the Romulans. And that they would survive the attempt.

Aboard the Romulan ship, Picard found Data seated directly behind the cockpit, where he had become part of an arcane and faintly disturbing tableau. The back of the android's head, including much of his hair, lay discarded on a nearby seat. The gleaming cortenide and duranium of his skull lay exposed, baring the busy polychromatic flashings of the positronic matrix that comprised his sentience. A flat, paper-thin cable ran from near the top of his head to an information access port in one of the bulkheads.

Picard realized he was staring when Data smiled up at him. "Please forgive my appearance, Captain. This direct interface will allow me to access the array's security grid a great deal faster than I could by entering commands through the consoles."

Picard had rarely seen Data in such a state of partial disassembly. The sight was a stark reminder of the huge gulf that still separated his inorganic friend from the humanity to which he aspired. Organic beings, Picard reflected, tended to take their basic bodily integrity as a *fait accompli.*

"Carry on, Mr. Data," Picard said as he made his way forward into the cockpit, where he took one of the two narrow seats. Lieutenant Hawk sat in the other, and was running a series of preflight checks.

During the flight from the rebel base, Picard had become quite familiar with the scoutship's many systems and instruments, despite the alien appearance of the icons in the cockpit's graphical interface. Still, he was glad to have Hawk at his side on this mission; the lieutenant was not only a fine pilot, but also an exceedingly quick study. Picard was well aware that Hawk had been watching the cockpit controls attentively during much of the voyage from Grelun's compound to the *Enterprise.*

Assuming that we get out of the current circumstances alive, Picard thought, *I expect you to go quite far, Mr. Hawk.*

"Captain, could I ask you a question?" Hawk said, setting his activities aside for a moment.

Picard could see that something was bothering the younger man. "Certainly, Lieutenant. What's on your mind?"

"Assuming we succeed ... what are the chances of anyone ever locating this subspace singularity again?"

"Commander La Forge is of the opinion that it won't be detectable again for centuries. If ever."

"I . . ." Hawk hesitated, then seemed to find the courage to go on. "Commander Zweller spoke with me shortly after the mission briefing."

Picard thought he knew where this was heading. "And he believes that we may be overreacting to the threat posed by the singularity."

"I think he may have a valid point," Hawk said. "May I speak freely, sir?"

"Of course."

"We're about to destroy this thing, for all intents and purposes. Doesn't that fly in the face of our overall mission of exploration? It might even be questionable under interstellar law."

"With the fate of the universe at stake, Lieutenant, I'd gladly face the consequences of my decision in a court of law," Picard said. A moment later, he added, "I take it Commander Zweller brought these matters to your attention as well."

"Yes, sir. He did."

"And are you *strongly* in agreement with him?"

Hawk looked uncomfortable. "I just thought . . . I think that the question needed to be raised. Once we do this, there's no turning back."

"You're right. There *is* no turning back." Picard sighed and looked through the scoutship's forward viewports through steepled fingers. "Lieutenant, I'm not insensitive to your concerns. I've wrestled with the same issues myself. This mission goes against all of my instincts as an explorer. If I thought there were any safe way to preserve this phenomenon for scientific study, I would. But I can't. The risk is simply too great."

"Still," Hawk said glumly. "If we could find *some* way

to save this thing, and harness its power for some peaceful purpose . . ." He trailed off into silence.

"Lieutenant, are you acquainted with the writings of Lord Acton?"

" 'Power tends to corrupt,' " Hawk quoted, nodding. " 'And absolute power corrupts absolutely.' " A smile slowly fanned across the younger man's lips.

"Strange," Picard said. "That old caveat always struck me as more chilling than humorous."

Hawk looked mildly embarrassed, and his smile abruptly vanished. "That isn't it, sir. It's just that . . ." he trailed off again.

Picard frowned. "Yes?"

"It's just that Commander Zweller told me that you'd probably quote Lord Acton to me if I spoke to you about this."

Picard's combadge overrode his tart response before he could deliver it. "Crusher to Captain Picard."

"Go ahead, Doctor."

"I just heard that you're planning to fly the mission yourself," the doctor said, her tone slightly chiding. "I'm not sure it's a good idea for you to enter the cloaking field. We don't know what effect it will have on your artificial heart."

"Doctor, what does the cloaking field have to do with my heart?"

"Cloaking devices tend to give off tetryon particles," Crusher said. "And that energy field is made up of literally thousands of cloaking devices."

"Then why wasn't I harmed by the tetryon emissions that led us to this scoutship?"

"The tetryon counts inside the cloaking field could be much higher," she countered. "You could be flying into a veritable *soup* of tetryons."

The only thing Picard disliked more than medical conversations like this one was having them in front of other members of his crew. "Damn it, Beverly, I'm not an invalid."

"Captain, do I have to remind you what happened at the Lenarian conference?" Crusher said, beginning to sound impatient.

He remembered all too well; the Lenarians had shut his heart down with a compressed tetryon beam. That incident had nearly cost him his life. But Picard knew that the stray tetryon output from any number of cloaking devices was a far cry from a weapon of that sort.

"Doctor, if you believe that I'm endangering my life unnecessarily, then I suggest you relieve me of duty."

"I wish I could. No one really knows for certain what the conditions will be like inside the cloaking field. But you need to know the risks."

Picard had never enjoyed being reminded that he owed his life to an artificial heart, and that was especially true now that Batanides and Zweller had come back into his life. After all, the only reason he now needed the synthetic organ was because the three of them had once lacked the simple common sense to demur from a fight against three bloodthirsty Nausicaans.

Picard spoke into his combadge, his manner somewhat gentler. "Objection noted. And if it's any consolation, Doctor, we won't need to stay behind the barrier for more than a few minutes at the most. Picard out."

Hawk quietly cleared his throat. "Everything's green to go, Captain."

"Then, I trust that means you've put your misgivings aside?"

"Truthfully?" Hawk said. "Not entirely. It still strikes me as a horrible waste. But we don't have a better option."

Picard appreciated Hawk's candor. "Then let's get under way," he said as he took control of the helm.

"Cloaking system still functioning properly," Hawk said, looking up from one of his indicator panels. No one would be able to observe the scoutship's departure from the *Enterprise.*

Picard brought the scoutship smoothly forward, guided her through the wide launch bay, and departed for the inky blackness beyond. The viewer now showed the livid red-and-ocher daylight side of Chiaros IV.

Seeing that their heading was already laid in, Picard instructed Hawk to engage the impulse engines at warp point-two. Crossing the approximately five AUs that separated Chiaros IV from the subspace singularity's cloaking field would be slow going at that speed—the journey would take about three hours—but pushing the scoutship's engines any harder would risk drawing unwanted Romulan attention. Even at this velocity, they would still reach the cloaking field a few minutes before the *Enterprise*'s departure deadline. And a few minutes ought to be all the time Data would require.

Hawk acknowledged Picard's order and adjusted the forward velocity to twenty percent that of light. Chiaros IV quickly turned away into the darkness and fell away into the infinite night of the Geminus Gulf. The commandeered vessel dove outward beneath the ecliptic, arcing headlong toward the singularity.

"Your captain's beverage is delightful," Grelun said to Riker and Troi. "The human Urlgray who devised it must surely be a god among men."

Sipping from a mug that looked absurdly tiny in his enormous hand, the Chiarosan sat shirtless at the edge of a bed that seemed scarcely capable of supporting his weight. Now that Will Riker was in close quarters with Grelun, he noticed that the rebel leader smelled faintly of freshly turned earth and lilacs. The aroma, as well as Grelun's fierce mien, reminded him absurdly of Worf.

But what struck Riker most was Grelun's astonishing recuperative powers. Less than three days after he had regained consciousness—and had refused further dermal regeneration treatments—Grelun's body bore not a trace of the severe disruptor burns he had sustained during the battle in the rebel compound. Even the coarse brown hair on his thick-thewed arms had grown back almost completely.

Riker was just as impressed by the huge Chiarosan's quiet dignity, as well as by the extreme delicacy with which he held his drinking vessel. Surely, he could have smashed it with a mere twitch of his fingers.

"I must thank you again for the hospitality that you and your captain have shown me," Grelun continued, setting the mug down on a bedside table. "These are splendid quarters, though I must confess that the floor serves me better as a sleeping place than does this child's cot."

The Chiarosan bared his razor-sharp metallic teeth as he finished this last utterance. Though Riker was reasonably certain the mannerism was the equivalent of a human smile, he was still glad that he had posted a pair of security guards, both armed with compression phaser rifles, just outside the cabin door.

"We wanted to make you as comfortable as possible," said Counselor Troi, who stood beside Riker. She appeared confident that the Chiarosan posed no danger. Still, Riker was uncomfortably aware that Grelun could easily snap her neck without even having to rise to his feet.

Grelun tipped his head in apparent perplexity. Riker wondered for a moment if the universal translator had malfunctioned. Or perhaps the Chiarosan tongue simply contained no word that corresponded to "comfort."

"No matter," Grelun said. "We have much larger problems, you and I. Your captain even now risks his life to expose the treachery of my predecessor's outworld allies." He practically spat this last word.

Riker tensed at Grelun's mention of Picard's secret incursion behind the Romulan cloaking field. Grelun was somehow aware of the mission, despite his not having been briefed about it.

Zweller, Riker thought sourly. *We should have arrested him as soon as he came aboard. Even now, he's trying to play both ends against the middle.*

"You disagreed with Falhain's decision to accept aid from the Romulans," Troi said to Grelun, her tone matter-of-fact. It was clear that she wasn't asking a question.

Grelun raised and lowered his shoulders in an elaborate triple-jointed shrug. "I did not want an alliance with *any* outworlders. But during Falhain's rule of the Army of Light, my opinion was neither day nor night, and was not sought. While my leader lived, it was my part to go where he led and do as he bid."

Grelun paused to raise his cup for another drink before continuing. "Falhain's untimely slaying changed this."

Riker hadn't seen exactly how Falhain had died during the skirmish in the Chiarosan capital; he'd already been knocked unconscious by the time the deed had been done. Not for the first time, it occurred to him that maybe Grelun *had* witnessed Falhain's death, or perhaps even arranged it. Could he somehow be concealing from Deanna his own complicity in the rebel chief's demise?

"Whatever you might think of us," Riker said carefully, "your people will be on their own against the

Romulans if the referendum forces the Federation to withdraw from your world."

"That is now spilled grain," Grelun said. "My people will fight *any* who seek to conquer us."

"You won't be able to direct a revolution from a Federation starbase," Riker pointed out. "That's where we'll have to take you next, if you're really serious about petitioning the Federation for political asylum."

Grelun straightened his back, looking both resigned and defiant. "Should you not worry instead about your more immediate problem? Ruardh will send her forces against this ship if you do not surrender me to her before you leave this system. She is implacable. She will not allow me to escape without a fight."

A look of deep understanding crossed Troi's face. "You want us to return you to your people. You want to continue leading the resistance against Ruardh's government."

"Of course I do," Grelun said, his eyes narrowing with menace, his voice an angry growl. The fur on his neck rose, like that of an agitated cat. "Do you think me a coward?"

"Of course not," Troi said calmly, standing her ground; it was unwise to show fear to a Chiarosan warrior. "I think of you as a leader in exile."

At that, the tension in Grelun's muscles relaxed visibly. Leaning forward, he said, "You could *end* my exile. You could return me to the hinterlands to which my people have withdrawn. From there, I could continue the fight."

"Are you telling us that your asylum request was just a *tactic?*" Riker said, his eyebrows ascending involuntarily.

Grelun folded his massive arms across his chest. "He who fights and retreats in the now may fight and win in the fullness of time."

Riker did not enjoy being manipulated. But he knew

that Grelun and his people had few alternatives to subterfuge. Having seen the carnage Ruardh's regime had inflicted upon the rebel tribes, Riker couldn't say he wouldn't make some of the same choices Grelun had.

But there were still rules that had to be observed.

"Are you withdrawing your asylum request, Grelun?" Riker said.

Grelun studied him, as though over a hand of five-card stud. "What would be the consequence of such an action?"

"We would be legally bound to turn you over to the Chiarosan authorities," Troi said sadly. Riker saw tears forming in her dark eyes; she, too, had seen the carnage.

Riker expected to see rage welling up in Grelun's visage. Instead, there was only sorrow there. "Even after I have shown you the villages of the slain? Even after *your own instruments* have recorded the ghosts of the slaughtered children?"

"Your people deprived us of the tricorder evidence we gathered in the village," Riker said. "Until both sides stop shooting long enough to let us gather *new* evidence, we have no objective way to back up your allegations against Ruardh. And no legal way to get around her extradition request."

The last thing Riker wanted was to condemn someone—anyone—to certain death. He hated the situation, and was frustrated with himself for his failure to find an honorable way out. But he knew that Deanna's analysis was correct: they had to either grant asylum to Grelun or else extradite him. It was a clear and apparently irresolvable conflict between law and morality. Still, Riker clung to the hope of finding an acceptable third alternative.

Data keeps saying that I rely on traditional problem-solving methods less than a quarter of the time, Riker thought. *Maybe now's the time for yet another unortho-dox solution.*

"Let's speak off the record, Grelun," he said aloud. "Starfleet officers are bound by laws that respect the sovereignty of democratically elected governments. Whether you intend to leave your world behind or not, if you withdraw your asylum claim we'll *have* to hand you over to Ruardh immediately. You'd be giving us no other choice."

Grelun sat in silence as he considered his scant alter-natives. "Then I shall *not* withdraw my request," he said finally. "But I *will* find the means to return to the Army of Light, and to lead my people to freedom."

Troi turned toward Riker, concern etched on her brow. "Can we still consider his asylum request, Will? He's just admitted that it was only a ruse."

"Maybe according to your empathic sense," Riker said. "But I'm not sure that's admissible in a Federation court. Besides . . . weren't we speaking off the record?"

Troi smiled, evidently satisfied with that.

"Tell me, Commander Riker: What will you do when Ruardh attacks?" Grelun said earnestly. "And she *will* at-tack, rest assured, probably within the hour. When that happens, will you raise arms against this 'sovereign gov-ernment' your laws respect so well?"

Riker wasn't sure what to say to that. After an awk-ward pause, he said, "I'm sure the captain will negotiate a resolution everyone can live with."

"If he survives his present undertaking," Grelun said earnestly.

"Jean-Luc Picard is an extremely resourceful man," Riker said. "And he has a pair of excellent officers at his side."

"Then I will pray that will be enough," Grelun said.

The voice of Lieutenant Daniels issued from Riker's combadge. "Bridge to Commander Riker."

"Go ahead, Lieutenant."

"You wanted to be alerted when the captain's scout-ship reached the edge of the Romulan cloaking field, sir. That's due to happen in a little under ten minutes."

"I'm on my way," Riker said, then excused himself.

Data sat motionless behind the scoutship's cockpit, his golden eyes unfocused. Interfaced directly with the ship's systems, the android consulted the sensors and confirmed that the cloaking field lay dead ahead. It was almost time to begin the mission's most critical phase.

He heard the captain speaking, his voice sounding as though it had traversed a great distance before reaching him. "Any sign we've been detected, Mr. Hawk?"

"Negative, Captain. Our cloaking frequency still matches the data we got from the telemetry probes. The maximum harmonic variances aren't even worth mentioning."

Picard sounded relieved to hear that. "Good. Mr. Data, it appears there's nothing standing in our craft's way. Let's hope that means there's nothing standing in *your* way, either."

Data paused to damp down the output from his emotion chip. Nervousness was an emotion he did not partic-ularly enjoy.

"Contact with the cloaking field in fifteen seconds," Hawk said. Data listened as the lieutenant began count-ing down. He recognized the slight quaver of apprehen-sion in the lieutenant's voice, and understood its source well enough. After all, if the Romulans had indeed somehow managed to rotate their cloaking-field harmon-ics at any time since the *Enterprise* had last probed the area, then the scoutship would immediately become conspicuous. A warbird could be upon them in moments, ending the mission ignominiously—and there would be no time for a second attempt.

Data's android perceptions were now attuned to an extremely minute resolution, which enabled him to notice the trillions of separate information cycles that occurred every second within his positronic brain. Each of those seconds seemed to last for hours, enabling Data to review most of the onboard library of Romulan literature, music, and drama in an eyeblink. Using an infinitesimal fraction of his positronic resources, Data listened as Hawk continued with his countdown, leaving protracted lacunae between each word.

"Four."

Data reiterated the mission plan two thousand and seventy-one times, while simultaneously reviewing the probability theory equations of Earth's Blaise Pascal as well as the collected sonnets of Phineas Tarbolde of the Canopus Planet.

"Three."

Data monitored and corrected an almost undetectable engine-output imbalance—which he attributed to the close proximity of the subspace singularity—and at the same time revisited Kurt Gödell's axiom negating the recursive validation of mathematical systems.

"Two."

He reviewed the mission plan several dozen times yet again while composing a complex contrapuntal string interlude based on large prime numbers and the mathematical constructs of Leonardo Fibonacci and Jean Baptiste Fourier. At the same moment, he extracted from the ship's computer core the rules to a multidimensional Romulan strategy game that was strongly reminiscent of the meditative Vulcan pastime known as *kal-toh*.

Stop fidgeting, Data told himself.

"One."

Just as the ship crossed the threshold, Data transmitted a simple handshake code to one of the buoys located on the Romulan array's periphery, then patiently awaited a response. After an eternity—which concluded in an almost negligible fraction of a second—the countersignal arrived. The buoy appeared to have accepted his credentials, recognizing him as a part of its own programming. His foot, as Geordi might have said, was in the door.

Data briefly permitted some real-time visual inputs to enter his accelerated consciousness. He watched as the Romulan array winked into existence on the forward viewer, along with the nearest few dozen of the outermost layer of buoys. From the array's still-distant center, the subspace singularity's accretion disk stared out like a baleful red eye. Though he was tempted to pause and continue admiring the vista before him, Data instead shut down his optical inputs and shunted those resources back toward his mission objectives. He resumed parsing time infinitesimally.

"I can see some of the nearer cloaking buoys," Picard said. "There must be thousands of them out there. It's extraordinary."

Data felt a stab of envy, since the sensory information he was receiving at the moment couldn't really be described as sight. For about a femtosecond, he longed to see everything the two humans in the cockpit were seeing. He wondered if the abstract polygonal shapes and solid geometrical forms now impinging on his consciousness resembled the universe as Geordi La Forge perceived it. He put the matter aside for later consideration.

Redoubling his concentration on the task at hand, Data extended a significant portion of his positronic matrix through the scoutship's communications system, across a frigid gulf of space, and back into the spaceborne cloaking buoy with which he was linked. He entered the labyrinth of hyperfast subspace channels and positronic pathways that connected the buoy to thousands of identical others. Dozens of blocks of angular Romulan text, each of them scrolling past at lightning speed, flickered almost tangibly before him, though he knew that their ideographic code was visible to no one else. He read them, digested them, analyzed them, and memorized them as though each byte were taking weeks to move through his quickened sensorium. Slowly, he channeled still more of his positronic resources through his subspace connection with the Romulan security network, bringing his artificial metabolism to a near standstill.

"Initiate Phase One, Mr. Data." Picard's voice was glacially slow, his words like millennia-old potsherds that required long and painstaking reassembly.

"Acknowledged," Data said, opening his aperture into the Romulan network ever wider. Now, forced to use a great deal more of his cognitive resources than before, Data put aside still more of his background activities, concentrating on the swiftly churning labyrinth of visual icons that crowded his subjective "sight." Still, it wasn't a severe challenge; all he had to do was repeat particular Romulan algorithms and follow specific electronic pathways he and Geordi had discovered during their lengthy analysis of the scout vessel's computer core. Still, the work took more and more of his attention, and Data felt an increasing sensation of something akin to kinesthesia. It was as though the torrent of information in which he now swam had palpable form, becoming an extension of his artificial body.

Disguising several of his own subroutines as maintenance programs, Data slipped into an information channel normally reserved for Romulan engineers and repair technicians. An agonizingly slow search—which lasted just short of half a second of objective time—deposited him inside yet another subsystem, this one designed to allow Romulan technical personnel to adjust the entire facility's cloaking-field harmonics. He immediately began making subtle alterations to the programming code contained on several of the array's most critical isolinear chips. At the same time, he altered the scoutship's cloaking frequency so that it would continue to blend in with that of the array.

Data's emotion chip surged with elation. If the ploy worked, then the defense systems would soon perceive the array's own structures as external invaders. Those circuits would almost instantly become overloaded with faulty information, freeing Data to use the principal maintenance channel to send the containment system an "abort" order—thus launching the Romulans' entire suite of failsafe programs, and thereby irretrievably banishing the singularity into subspace.

With Phase One of the mission completed, Data swam out of the information stream, forcing his cybernetic awareness to resume assimilating time scales meaningful to Captain Picard and Lieutenant Hawk.

"Have you noticed any Romulan security programs yet, Mr. Data?" Picard asked.

Data smiled triumphantly. "No, sir. And my alterations to the defense system are spreading throughout the network. It should be completely paralyzed in another four-point-three seconds."

"Excellent, Mr. Data. Begin Phase Two."

At once, Data resubmerged himself in the information stream, marshaling his consciousness into the maintenance channels. From this viewpoint, the flow of bytes through the adjacent security network had become a raging torrent, a storm-swollen river of multiplying, self-contradictory information that would surely overwhelm any conscious entity caught on its virtual shoals. Fortunately, the maintenance channels were relatively tranquil by comparison.

With a cybernetic whisper, Data loosed the "abort" command into the maintenance channel's information queue. He watched in contemplative silence as his handiwork propagated itself, copied and relayed through the entire network by dozens of buoys, then by hundreds. The "abort" protocol began working its way toward the singularity's containment facility, moving at first in a leisurely inward spiral, then taking on increasing urgency.

So far, Data thought, *so good.*

Then one of the buoys said: *No.* Immediately, two others rejected the "abort" order as well. An almost defiant refusal swiftly began escalating throughout the network. The inward spiral slowed, then stopped.

Then reversed.

<You do not belong here> declared an unseen presence from behind/above/below/between/within/without him.

"Uh-oh," Data said.

The warbird *Thrai Kaleh* lowered her cloak and approached a battered, lifeless asteroid orbiting at the fringes of the system. This far out, all the violence of the Chiarosan sun fit neatly into a deceptively placid pinprick of light.

Koval stood in the vessel's control center, observing the Federation shuttlecraft that was keeping station nearby. According to the sensors within the lumpen planetoid, the shuttle had come out of warp at the system's edge nearly three hours earlier. Koval had no doubt that

Commander Cortin Zweller was aboard the little craft—and that the Section 31 agent hoped to hold him to his part of their original bargain.

Koval had no objection to doing just that. After all, a list of soon-to-be-purged Tal Shiar operatives wasn't worth the smallest fraction of the Geminus Gulf's true value. And with the formal announcement of the Empire's acquisition of the entire region now only minutes away, Koval was more than happy to conclude his deal with his Federation counterpart; magnanimity after such a decisive victory cost very little.

Over his centurion's objections, Koval had himself and a pair of low-ranking Romulan soldiers beamed into the small habitat module built deep into the asteroid's nickel-iron interior. Moments later, Koval was standing in the cool confines of one of the Tal Shiar's small but richly-appointed safe-houses, his guards standing quietly alert behind him. At the opposite end of the chamber, Commander Zweller and a silver-haired woman in a Starfleet uniform shimmered into existence. Koval and Zweller briefly exchanged pleasantries, and Zweller introduced the woman as Marta, his assistant.

Silently noting the lieutenant's pips on the woman's collar, Koval nodded courteously to her. It took Koval a moment to place her face, but he quickly recognized her as an important admiral attached to Starfleet's principal intelligence-gathering bureau. *Batanide,* he thought. *Or is it Batanides?* Regardless, she was one of several Starfleet Intelligence operatives whose dossier was familiar to him. Koval surmised that she might not appreciate the extent of her notoriety, and that she had removed her true rank insignia in the hope of obscuring her identity and avoiding capture.

He turned his attention back to Zweller, and noticed a

slight discoloration along the side of the human's face. "Your escape from the rebels appears to have been rather more perilous than I thought, Commander," Koval said. "One would think your Federation doctors would have repaired your injuries days ago."

Zweller put a hand to the remnants of the bruise on his cheek, then smiled. "Oh, you mean *this*. It happened on the way out to the asteroid. It's an amusing story, really." He paused for a moment to look significantly at his 'assistant.' "I fell down. Marta, make a note to have that shuttle's artificial gravity generator checked as soon as we get back to the *Enterprise*."

"Yes, sir," the woman said, her tone almost surly.

Humans, Koval thought. *They say we are difficult to understand.*

The Romulan walked to a table in the center of the room and lifted a clear decanter in which a pale, aquamarine-colored liquid sloshed. He poured a small amount into three glasses, then raised one to his lips.

"To the future of the Geminus Gulf and the Chiaros system," Koval said before emptying his glass. He relished the burning sensation the pungent liqueur created as it went down.

Zweller picked up the other two glasses and handed one to the woman. "I can drink to that," he said, and downed the beverage without a moment's hesitation. Though the woman seemed a bit put off by the drink's piquant bouquet, she drank her portion as well, though not as quickly.

"It's been a good while since I've had nonreplicated *kali-fal*," Zweller said. Though he was smiling, his eyes were hard.

Regarding Zweller coolly, Koval segued straight into business. "You must be aware by now that the Federation's presence on Chiaros IV is at an end, Commander.

Most of the precincts have already reported their election results. Within perhaps ten of your minutes, First Protector Ruardh will formally announce her people's willing entry into the Empire."

"I suppose so," Zweller said, nodding slowly.

"Then perhaps we should finish our transaction as quickly as possible," the woman said evenly.

Koval held up his left hand, palm up, and one of the guards stepped forward and placed a slender data chip into it. Koval was about to present it to Zweller when the secure comm chip implanted into his jaw vibrated gently. Because the tiny speaker conducted sound through the bones of his skull, only he could hear Subcenturion V'Hari's urgent hail.

Go ahead, Thrai Kaleh, Koval subvocalized. Only the slight clenching and unclenching of his jaw muscles betrayed the fact that he was having a covert conversation.

"There's been an attempt to sabotage the Core, Chairman Koval," V'Hari said emotionlessly. "However, the security failsafe programs are already isolating and purging the intrusion."

Acknowledged, V'Hari. Keep me informed.

Koval studied Zweller and Batanides through narrowed eyes. He was well-aware of Ambassador T'Alik's failure to persuade Picard to make an early departure from the Geminus Gulf. He could only assume that this incursion on the Core was Captain Picard's doing. The scoutship that T'Alik had said Picard claimed to know nothing about—despite the fact that he'd used it to escape from the Army of Light compound—could have given the Starfleet captain some of the tools necessary to mount an effective assault on the Core.

But he knew it couldn't give him the capacity to defeat the *rokhelh,* the state-of-the-art artificial intelligence that patrolled the Core's every system. Nothing Koval had ever encountered could do that.

"Chairman Koval?" Zweller said, ending the protracted silence. "Are you all right?"

Koval still held the data chip tightly in his hand, and continued searching the humans' faces with his eyes. Their expressions betrayed nothing. Was Zweller involved in the sabotage as well? Or had Picard undertaken the attack entirely on his own initiative?

Deciding that the *rokhelh* would render those questions moot soon enough, Koval surrendered the data chip to Zweller, who responded by flashing a toothy smile.

"When you return to the *Enterprise*," Koval said quietly, "tell Captain Picard that he plays a very dangerous game. That is, if he survives his current endeavor."

Koval was pleased to see that Zweller's smile had faltered ever so slightly. *So he* does *know something*. Koval suppressed a triumphant grin.

Koval set his *kali-fal* glass down on the table, none too gently. "The Federation's welcome in the Geminus Gulf is now worn out," he said, freighting his words with menace. "And when Protector Ruardh makes the official declaration, you and every other human in this system would do well to be heading back toward Federation space very, very quickly."

268

Chapter Fifteen

<You do not belong here> the *rokhelh* repeated. Most of a millisecond passed in silence as it awaited greeting protocols from the Other. <Identify self, or face decompilation.>

The errant code-sequence did not respond in any intelligible fashion, nor did the *rokhelh* immediately recognize it. Perhaps this unknown Other was, like the *rokhelh* itself, another security subroutine, but one that had somehow become corrupted. Whatever the Other's identity, the *rokhelh* recognized it as the source of the failsafe shutdown command, the fatal disease that had nearly been loosed into the heart of the Apparatus.

The *rokhelh* probed tentatively at the intruding lines of code, gently insinuating its binary feelers below the Other's surface. More code lay beneath, and more still below that, a seemingly infinite regress of expanding fractal complexity. The *rokhelh* saw at once that the interloper was a sentient artificial intelligence—a complex, constructed entity like itself.

But unlike the *rokhelh,* this Other was crafted by alien, non-Romulan minds.

With a thought, the *rokhelh* raised the alarm, even as it sought to do to the Other what the Other had just tried to do to the Apparatus—to neutralize it by probing its manifold cybernetic pathways with a billion fractally-expanding tendrils.

A millisecond later, the *rokhelh*'s consciousness was deeply embedded within the Other's innumerable circuitry pathways.

Data sat silently in his seat, his body rigid.

"Data?" Picard said, swiveling in the cockpit to face the android. The last word he had heard the android utter had sounded like an uncharacteristic "Uh-oh."

Hawk took over the conn as Picard disengaged from the cockpit and made his way over to Data. Kneeling, the captain was met with a glassy stare. "Data? Mr. Data, report."

He snapped his fingers before his friend's dead, artificial eyes. Nothing.

Picard stood and turned back toward the cockpit. Hawk regarded him uneasily.

"Captain, shouldn't the singularity have started slipping back into subspace by now?"

Picard nodded. "Yes. *If* Commander Data succeeded in transmitting the abort command into the singularity's containment protocols."

But on the forward viewer, Picard could see that the inferno at the singularity's heart continued to blaze just as brightly as ever.

Merde, Picard thought, his heart sinking.

* * *

Data felt disembodied, a ghost floating in cybernetic freefall. And he noticed the disconcertingly near presence of *something*. It was asking him questions, but he was having difficulty parsing them. Then this Presence was suddenly all around him, engulfing him, holding him immobile. A moment later, it began probing at his thoughts—from the *inside*.

Fear emanated reflexively from Data's emotion chip, coursing through his consciousness as he realized that another entity—an artificial intellect not altogether unlike his own—was attempting to seize control of him. He was being overridden, hijacked as he once had been by the multiple personalities stored in the D'Arsay archive. With a tremendous effort of will, he shut his emotion chip down. This maneuver did nothing to halt the advance of the Presence as it invaded his positronic systems, nor did it allow him to assess the damage the alien entity might be causing to his hardwired subroutines. But with the emotion chip inactive, he had at least exchanged fear for clarity.

Data clung tenaciously to that clarity, aware that without it he and his shipmates might never make it back to the *Enterprise*.

While the *rokhelh* devoted much of its digital substance to probing and testing the Other's vulnerabilities, it traced the interloper's origination point to a subspace carrier-band being directed toward one of the Apparatus's most peripheral exterior nodes. Backtracing the signal turned out to be a very simple matter, requiring only patience.

This was where most of the Other's resources actually lay; not within the diaphanous binary circulatory system of the Apparatus itself, but aboard a nearby cloaked vessel. Lashed to a positronic physical substrate of cortenide and duranium.

271

The *rokhelh* traced the Other's linear datastream back through the cloaked ship's computer and into the Other's own small but highly organized internal positronic computational network. After pushing the Other back to its origin point—the location from which it had invaded the sanctity of the Apparatus—the *rokhelh* found that there was ample unused storage space within the Other's physical shell.

For the first time in its existence, the *rokhelh* had taken on a humanoid form.

The *rokhelh* opened its newly acquired optical receptors and raised a pale forelimb before them. It examined the appendage, turning it clumsily this way and that, noting the jointed digits, the skeletal structure, the soft epidermal covering. *How like my creators,* it thought, intrigued. *Yet how unlike.*

The *rokhelh* looked past the hand. A humanoid creature stood nearby, an intent expression upon its face. This being was also like, but unlike, the *rokhelh*'s creators. It appeared weak in some indefinable way. Perhaps this was because of its distinctive lack of hair, or maybe owing to its underdeveloped external auditory organs. Or perhaps because its lips were drawn upward in an expression that the *rokhelh*'s own creators very rarely displayed—a *smile.*

"Mr. Data, are you all right?" said the weak-looking, small-eared, smiling creature.

The *rokhelh* reached toward the creature with its newly appropriated hand.

And seized the creature's throat.

And *squeezed.*

And smiled back at the frail, hairless entity, whose own smile had already fled.

Picard sensed what was about to happen a split-second too late. The android's fingers had locked around his throat before he could back out of the way. He couldn't speak, couldn't breathe, couldn't budge the viselike grip by so much as a millimeter, though he was tugging at Data's hand with both of his own.

The universe swiftly shrank to the size of the white hand clutching at his throat. He heard Hawk calling to him as though from light-years away, an edge of fear in the younger man's voice. Less than a meter directly behind the crushing hand, Data smiled like a death's head, though his eyes resembled those of a child studying a bug in a jar.

Picard knew he couldn't last more than another few seconds—and that he had only one chance to seize control of the situation. Instead of struggling away from Data's grip, he lunged toward the android, throwing both arms around his shoulders.

Spots danced before Picard's eyes as his fingers groped for purchase behind Data's back. But it was no use. The "off" switch was beyond his reach. Data's grip was unbearable, relentless.

Abruptly, the android's rigid fingers stopped closing. Data ceased all movement, though he remained stiffly locked in a seated position. The cable that connected his exposed skull to the Romulan ship's systems still appeared intact.

A moment later, Picard became conscious that Hawk was beside him, helping him pry Data's stiff fingers from his throat.

"What's gotten into him?" Hawk said.

Picard drew in a great rush of air, coughed, and cleared his throat. When he spoke, his voice was raspy from his near-strangulation. "I think that's a very appropriately worded question, Lieutenant. I wish I knew the answer."

And I wish I knew what stopped *him,* Picard thought, uncomfortably aware that his own fingers had never made it all the way down to Data's hidden "off" switch. Whatever had immobilized Data, Picard knew that he'd had nothing to do with it.

Hawk asked him if he was all right, but Picard assured him that he hadn't been seriously injured and sent the lieutenant back to the helm. Then the captain kneeled behind the deactivated android. Drawing his hand phaser, he tentatively waved a hand before Data's vacant eyes. The android remained immobile and unresponsive.

"Data, are you all right?" he said. There was no response.

Picard turned toward the front of the cockpit, though he kept Data in the corner of his eye. He did not put the phaser away. "Mr. Hawk, has there been any change in the singularity's behavior?"

"No, sir. There's no longer any doubt about it—Data's abort command could not have gotten through."

"Something stopped it," Picard said. "Perhaps the same something that caused Data to attack me."

"The abort sequence should have taken only a couple of seconds to engage," Hawk said. "If it was going to happen, it would have by now."

"Agreed. And the longer we stay here, the greater the chance we'll be detected. We'll have to find another way to force the array into abort mode."

At that moment, the viewscreen suddenly displayed the image of a huge Romulan warbird. As it decloaked before them, it blotted out the fires of the subspace singularity like a planet eclipsing its sun.

A deep, cool voice issued from the scout's communications panel. "Scoutship *Chula*. This is Commander T'Veren of the warbird *Gal Gath'thong*. You will decloak immediately and explain your business here."

Hawk sounded as though he were fighting to keep his

voice calm. "Captain, if they know this ship by name, then they *already* know what our business is."

"And who's aboard this ship," Picard said soberly. "Drop the cloak, Lieutenant. Then stall."

"Stall, sir?"

"Send a 'technical trouble' signal. We need to buy ourselves some time."

Hawk complied, glancing at the sensor readouts. "More bad news, sir. They're powering up their disruptors. Should we withdraw?"

The captain brushed a palm across the thin sheen of sweat that had formed on his brow. "No, Mr. Hawk. We can't outrun them. So we'll have to . . . out-*think* them instead."

Hawk nodded, saucer-eyed. Though Picard kept his expression impassive, he could hear his own pulse roaring in his ears.

Without Data's help, thinking my way out of a Romulan target-lock isn't going to be easy.

Data floated in a formless, sensory-deprived void. With his emotion chip deactivated, the fact that he and the Presence were becoming inextricably linked was no reason for panic—though it *did* give him cause for real concern. It was a development that Data could not allow to continue without a fight.

I cannot permit you to appropriate my body, Data told the Presence, his voice a gossamer construct of electromagnetic impulses, rather than sounds.

<Your statement is meaningless,> the Presence said, its words issuing from the nothingness surrounding Data. <You cannot stop me. You are helpless.>

Data considered the alien machine-entity's words for nearly a millisecond. For the moment, he concluded that the Presence was correct. He was indeed helpless, at least so long as the artificial intelligence maintained control over many of his body's higher functions. But Data also knew that he might succeed in bypassing or disabling some of those functions—at least for a short while—if he proceeded very carefully, camouflaging his efforts with the background maintenance subroutines that were always running.

A picosecond later, it was done. Rivers of heuristic neural information re-routed themselves into Data's secondary and tertiary control nodes. He sensed immediately that the Presence was no longer controlling his limbs. But then, neither was he. He wondered how long it would take the Presence to regain the upper hand. At the rate the entity's consciousness was expanding and entwining through him, it would surely not be long.

Perhaps I cannot stop you, Data admitted. *But I can make an effort to understand you.*

<That will avail you nothing. I will rewrite your code and seize your body permanently. You will cease to be, as will your organic accomplices. You will understand nothing.>

But Data had already begun to understand something important. The Presence had revealed that it believed itself capable of manipulating his positronic pathways. The Presence believed it could address the world through Data's senses. It believed that it could run Data's body as though it were its own.

That told Data that the Presence was comprised of code that was not significantly different from his own. And it further told Data that if he could find some subsystem in his android body that the Presence had yet to subvert, there might yet be a way to defeat the invader.

Tentatively, careful to steer clear of the Presence's notice, Data probed at his own systems. Three-point-eight-six milliseconds later, he discovered a sliver of his own consciousness that the Presence had yet to wrest from him: a little-used backup diagnostic subroutine, a system designed for use when his primary, secondary, and tertiary self-repair subroutines were too damaged to function properly. It led to back entrances to all of his autonomic and higher functions. Unfortunately, he could sense that the ever-vigilant Presence lay just on the other side of each of those positronic apertures, ready to pounce.

Then he noticed that the Presence was conspicuously absent from one particular component—his emotion chip. Had the chip been engaged, Data would not have been able to conceal his surprise from the Presence. But even without recourse to the chip, Data could not help but wonder why the Presence had not taken such an obvious prize. Was the Presence laying a trap for him? He dismissed the idea, since the Presence clearly believed that he was already helpless.

Then Data considered another explanation: Perhaps the Presence did not understand the emotion chip's purpose. Maybe the Presence was utterly unacquainted with humanoid emotions, like an organic immune system that succumbs to viral infections to which it has had no previous exposure. Briefly recalling the emotion-broadcasting cranial implant Dr. Crusher had recovered from Ambassador Tabor's body, Data wondered if it might be possible to use his own emotion chip in a similar fashion.

As a weapon.

Perhaps you are correct, Data told the Presence. *I may be unable to either stop you or to understand you.*

(Very slowly, and at extremely low power, Data brought his emotion chip on-line.)

<I will overwrite you,> the Presence said. There was

no trace of emotion in its soundless voice, no gloating, no spite, no suspicion. Only a sober and single-minded sense of purpose. A sentient utility program, merely performing its function.

(Gently, Data absorbed some of the emotion chip's output, concentrating on one emotion only: Hope.)

Perhaps, Data said. He felt somehow stronger than before.

(Carefully, Data directed the remainder of the emotion chip's output away from himself in all directions, toward the ever-expanding virtual tendrils of the invader's consciousness.)

And perhaps not.

(Quickly, Data brought the chip's output up to its normal power level.)

<What are you doing?> queried the Presence. Its voice no longer seemed calm. It sounded confused. Adrift. As though it had just been roughly subjected to a traumatic sensory assault, something altogether alien to its previous experience. Like a congenitally blind human suddenly acquiring sight.

<What have you done?> the Presence asked, giving Data the impression of an escalating state of confusion.

Hope rose and surged through Data's disembodied being. *I invite you to make a determination of your own.*

Then, taking advantage of the Romulan AI's distraction, Data gathered every erg of will he could muster and reached past the Presence, moving his awareness back out into the Romulan array—only to find an impregnable wall of "antibody" programs marshaled against any attempt to retransmit the shutdown command to the singularity-containment field. Clearly, the Presence performed much of its "watchdog" work on a subsentient level. Worse, he could already sense the

Presence slowly rousing itself to pursue him, struggling to regain its cognitive equilibrium.

Data knew that he might not be able to evade the Presence for more than another few seconds—enough time, he hoped, to make contact with Captain Picard. Wrapping his emotion chip–generated hope around himself like a cloak, Data sprinted toward the command pathways that governed his speech subroutines and language protocols, trying to make an end run around the Presence.

"Captain? Lieutenant . . . Hawk?" With a start, Picard realized that Data was trying to speak. The voice was strained and almost inaudible; the android seemed barely able to move his jaw.

Picard moved immediately to Data's side. "Mr. Data, are you . . . functioning again?"

"Not . . . entirely, sir. I believe I am engaged . . . in a battle of wills . . . against an . . . artificial intelligence."

"Something you encountered inside the Romulan array," Picard said, his fingers unconsciously touching his own bruised throat. Data responded with a single robotic nod of the head. The cable that connected the android to the ship's computer swayed like a badly constructed suspension bridge. *A Romulan watchdog program,* Picard thought bitterly. *I should have anticipated that. Damn!*

Hawk called back from the front of the cockpit. "The warbird captain isn't buying my 'technical trouble' messages, Captain. He's locking his main disruptor bank on us."

"Evasive maneuvers, Lieutenant!" Picard shouted, holding onto the sides of Data's chair as the deck lurched. "Maximum impulse!"

Picard felt the scoutship shudder just before the inertial compensators leveled the deck out. The first salvo had evidently been a clean miss. Crouching beside Data, Picard said, "Can you try again to transmit the abort code?"

"Not . . . at present."

"Are you still connected to the Romulan array?"

"The subspace channel . . . remains open. . . . The other machine intellect . . . must maintain it . . . to continue . . . affecting my body . . . But it is keeping me . . . preoccupied."

A grim realization suddenly slapped Picard in the face: Because Data was still connected to the scoutship's computer, every one of the vessel's systems—including its deflector shields—was just as vulnerable to outside cybernetic assaults as Data was. Picard briefly considered disconnecting the cable linking the android to the vessel, then restrained himself. Not only was he unsure about what the interruption would do to Data's positronic matrix, he also didn't want to sacrifice what might well be their only chance to resend the abort command.

Picard spoke urgently to the android. "Mr. Data, whatever you do, you *must* keep this intelligence from invading the scoutship's systems."

The scoutship rocked, and a loud *bang!* reverberated through the crew cabin. Smoke and sparks flew from an instrument panel. Picard ignored it, counting on Hawk's piloting skills.

"I will . . . endeavor . . . to do so, sir," Data said.

"I certainly hope you can, Mr. Data. Otherwise, I might have to disconnect you suddenly . . ." He trailed off, certain that Data understood better than he the danger that eventuality might pose.

Data nodded stiffly. "Hope . . . is all . . . I have."

"Understood," Picard said. "Continue doing whatever you have to."

At that moment, Data lapsed into a disconcerting silence, and Picard moved forward to take the cockpit seat beside Hawk. The lieutenant's full attention was focused on his evasive flying. "Mr. Hawk, how thoroughly did Commander Data brief you on the Romulan command protocols he's been using?"

"He showed me the entire abort-command sequence," Hawk said, casting his wide eyes momentarily on Picard. He added sheepishly, "Once."

"Lieutenant, I think it's time to test that photographic memory I've read so much about in your service record."

"Captain, I could never enter the commands as quickly as Commander Data could."

"Then slow and steady will have to do," Picard said, smiling grimly as he took control of the helm. "The subspace uplink with the array should still be open. I'll hold the warbird off while you enter the commands."

At once, Hawk began manipulating the instrument panel, slowly at first, then accelerating to an almost inhuman speed. Though Picard gave most of his concentration over to the flight controls, he saved some for the forward viewer. It showed the maw of the approaching warbird's main disruptor bank, which was glowing like the core of a star.

<Cease whatever you are doing at once.>
The Presence caught up with Data at last—it felt as though years had passed since Data had first distracted it with his emotion chip—and restrained him again within its cybernetic tendrils. Data became aware that he had once more lost command of his speech functions. That revelation discouraged him.

Until he noted that the emotion chip remained firmly under his control. That told him that the Presence *still* did not understand what he was doing. Emotion chip–generated hope sang within him.

<Cease whatever you are doing at once,> the Presence repeated.

No, Data said simply.

But he quickly understood that resolve would be an insufficient weapon against this AI. Data could feel his internal clock slowing, his information cycles becoming slow, lethargic. His consciousness itself was beginning to diffuse, as though it were a small blob of ink spreading out across a vast, wine-dark sea.

<You will have no further opportunity to infect the Apparatus with aberrant code,> the Presence said confidently. <I will overwrite you now.>

Data knew all too well what the Presence meant. His positronic matrix would be wiped clean. His experiences and memories, his dreams and hopes, his friendships and loves would be reduced to a blank slate. He would be erased as though he had never been.

The Presence had obviously adapted to the output of his emotion chip. The only weapon he possessed had been neutralized. Despair threatened to overwhelm him. How easy it would be to simply let it happen, and accept the surcease of deactivation and nothingness.

No! Data shouted silently. He recalled his brief glimpse of the scoutship's interior. He remembered that a Romulan warbird was about to vaporize Captain Picard and Lieutenant Hawk.

Then, even as awareness began to flee him, hope arose within Data once again: He recalled that he had set the emotion chip's output at nowhere near its maximum gain. That told him that he still had a weapon. Gathering up his will, he let the chip's energies build, as though it were a phaser set on overload.

A cybernetic eternity later, he released the chip's greatly increased emotional output, letting it flood into the Romulan machine-entity's consciousness.

<No,> said the Presence. Data could feel it actively resisting him.

With all of his remaining will, he directed the totality of his anger, his fear, his frustration straight into the algorithm-creature's core. It was as though the Presence had been forced to drink from a fire hose. Teraquads of intense emotion rushed through the chip, sweeping the entity away before it had an opportunity to sever Data's subspace connection to the Romulan array. The death-scream of the Presence reverberated in Data's consciousness as the entity's code decompiled, corrupting itself in a spontaneous cascade effect.

Even as Data felt his adversary's passing, he wondered whether his triumph had cost him the use of his emotion chip. At that thought, hope fled from him, as did every other human emotion he had worked so hard to acquire for so many years. But with no emotions to distract him, Data had no trouble accepting that the loss was infinitely preferable to nonexistence.

And he had no trouble giving the plight of Picard and Hawk his full attention. Noticing that his cybernetic connection to the Romulan array remained intact, he sent a portion of his consciousness deeper inside it, ready to re-send the abort command—

—only to find the data channels still aswarm with "antibody" programs, the final nonsentient remnants of the Presence. Or perhaps they had arisen as a consequence of that entity's contact with him, like a cybernetic immune response.

Regardless, Data knew that he could never get the abort command past them, even if he were to perish in the attempt. He quietly backed away, all but disengaging entirely from the Romulan array. Despair stung him then—

—and struck a spark that glimmered into joy. Only a functioning emotion chip could have made either experience possible. As his maintenance subroutines reawakened and began purging his matrix of whatever remained of the Presence within him, Data rejoiced at having succeeded in hanging onto his hard-won humanity.

And, even as he struggled to regain control over his body's many subsystems, Data clung just as steadfastly to the hope of finding some other way to neutralize the Romulans' subspace singularity.

His hands a blur on the instrument panel, Hawk entered the final command sequence, then tried to get a fix on the subspace singularity with the sensors. *This has to work,* he thought.

No change.

Ten long seconds ticked by as Picard continued dodging the *Gal Gath'thong*'s relentless disruptor fusillades, while staying less than quarter of a kilometer from the warbird's bifurcated hull. At this range, it was relatively easy to foil the Romulans' target locks. But it was still a minor miracle that they had thus far avoided a mutually destructive collision.

Sooner or later, Hawk knew, their luck was going to run out.

Hawk examined the singularity once again on the passive sensor display. It seemed indestructible. He closed his eyes, feeling utterly defeated.

"Report, Lieutenant!" Picard barked.

"It . . . didn't work. I don't understand it. I must have mis-keyed one of the command pathways."

Hawk heard a voice behind him. "I do not believe that is so, Lieutenant."

"Data!" Hawk said, startled. He turned in his seat and saw that Data was now standing in the crew compartment. Except for the cable that connected his metallic skull to the bulkhead, he appeared none the worse for wear.

"Forgive me, Lieutenant. I did not mean to startle you."

"Data, what happened to the AI you were fighting?" Picard said as he rolled the scoutship past a disruptor tube an instant before it fired. Hawk noticed that the Captain's hand was on his phaser.

"It has been . . . neutralized. My internal housekeeping subroutines are purging its remaining code-structures from my physical matrix even now."

"Excellent. But can you get back inside the array?"

"Not in the same manner as before. I just checked the information channel through which I originally entered the array, and I have determined that it is now filled with electronic 'antibodies' designed to cancel out any recurrence of my original externally introduced abort-command sequence. It is the positronic equivalent of an inoculation against a viral infection. I am afraid that we must find another avenue of attack."

Picard finally seemed to be running out of patience. "Data, don't you understand? We don't have *time* to look for another avenue of attack!"

Attack. The notion struck Hawk like a clap of thunder. *Attack! That's the key.* "Maybe we already have one," he said.

"Let's hear it, Lieutenant," the captain prompted, still obviously intent on staying one step ahead of the Romulan guns. A disruptor salvo rocked them at that precise instant, and the scoutship's responses to Picard's piloting seemed to be growing sluggish. Heaven only knew how badly they'd been damaged.

Hawk took a deep breath, then plunged forward. "Data, if the array's own defenses were to malfunction and attack the singularity's containment facility, wouldn't that bring on an abort automatically? And send the singularity back into subspace immediately?"

"That *was* the scenario that I originally attempted to make the singularity's containment machinery believe," Data said calmly. "However, I would still have to transmit the abort order through command pathways from which we are now blocked."

"That's not what I mean," Hawk said, his words piling onto one another in his excitement. "What if the array's defenses really *did* start shooting at the singularity's containment field?"

The android nodded, evidently grasping the idea. "In that event, the Romulans' own failsafe programs should initiate an abort command on their own from within the singularity's subspace containment system. I would not need to send any such command myself."

"All right, gentlemen," Picard said, now clearly preoccupied with keeping the ship in one piece. "How might we accomplish that?"

"What about trying to alter the containment facility's sensor profile?" Hawk said hopefully. "We could make the singularity itself appear to be surrounded by a fleet of invading ships."

"And thus in danger of suffering a fatal containment breach," Picard added, nodding.

"Unfortunately," Data said, "The systems that govern sensor data are now closed to me as well."

Hawk's spirits flagged again when he heard this. Then he glanced at Picard, and saw a slow smile spreading across the captain's face.

"Maybe there's another way to go about Mr. Hawk's idea, Data." Picard then handed the conn back over to Hawk. Though the evasive flying kept him busy, the lieutenant listened carefully to the captain's words.

"Tell me about the cloaking-generator buoys, Data. How do they maintain such a perfect spherical formation? You'd think that the singularity's periodic releases of gravitational energy would disturb that pattern."

Data did not reply, leaving Hawk to assume that he was accessing information, either from the ship's computer or from elsewhere in the Romulan array. A moment later, Data broke the anxious silence.

"The cloaking buoys maintain their relative positions by means of a system of onboard station-keeping thrusters. Each thruster pack carries a large fuel supply, so that the buoys can hold their positions for years without requiring maintenance."

"And what would happen," Picard said, "if each and every one of those buoys were suddenly to point their main thrusters away from the singularity, and fire them all at full throttle?"

"In that scenario, Captain, there would be an equal and opposite reaction. The entire cloaking-buoy network would quickly collapse inward, simulating an attack on the singularity."

"Bringing about an automatic abort," Picard said.

Data sounded intrigued. "Perhaps I can gain access to the buoys' thruster command pathways through one of the multiple backup channels in the array's maintenance grid—"

Picard interrupted him. "Do whatever it takes, Data. And *hurry.*"

Data once again lapsed into silence as Hawk fought with the sluggish controls, bringing the scoutship tumbling past an active Romulan gunport just in time to avoid a direct hit. Hawk ardently hoped that Data's silence meant that the android had already begun moving those buoys.

A moment later, the scoutship shook as though something extremely heavy had struck it. An overhead conduit ruptured, fogging the crew cabin with gray, foul-smelling vapors. The collision alarm hadn't sounded, so Hawk assumed that the scout had taken a glancing blow from one of the warbird's secondary disruptor banks. A glance at the tactical display showed that the scout's engine core had taken a high-angle disruptor hit as well.

Before Hawk could relay this information to Picard, the captain cried out in pain and went sprawling from his seat onto the deck. He lay there, groaning and clutching at his chest.

Hawk understood the problem immediately. The damaged engine core must have emitted an acute radiation burst—the tetryons Dr. Crusher had been concerned about—causing some sort of malfunction in the captain's artificial heart. But Hawk couldn't afford to be distracted from his duties at the helm, not if any of them were to survive this mission. He had to hope that Data could tend to the captain's urgent medical needs.

A split-second later, a flash of light issued from behind the cockpit, filling the scoutship's interior with the acrid smell of ozone, burnt circuitry, and scorched artificial flesh. Glancing behind him, Hawk saw patterns of blue incandescence shooting through the cable that connected Data to the scout vessel's computer core. Saint Elmo's fire briefly crackled around the android's head. He convulsed briefly, then became as motionless as a statue, frozen in the act of rising to render aid to the captain.

Not good, Hawk thought as he returned his attention to the viewer. There, the coruscating inferno of the subspace singularity still burned, as brightly and defiantly as ever.

And the warbird *Gal Gath'thong* was coming about, like a hungry shark closing in for the kill.

Chapter Sixteen

In the central control room of the warbird *Gal Gath'thong*, Commander T'Veren kept a dispassionate eye on the scoutship that rolled and tumbled across his screen. Though his directive to destroy the small vessel had been authorized by no less a personage than Tal Shiar Chairman Koval himself, T'Veren remained curious about the motives of whoever was inside. By flying evasive patterns at close quarters with the *Gal Gath'thong*, the scout had so far managed to avoid being severely hit by the warbird's weapons.

The heavy brows of the young decurion behind the weapons console were knit together in frustration. It was apparent that she knew that the other vessel should have been dispatched minutes ago.

That pilot deserves credit for his courage and audacity, T'Veren thought, smiling at his gunner's obvious pique. *But even the most skilled flyer will eventually make a mistake.*

Suddenly, the weapons officer grinned triumphantly. On the screen, one of the scoutship's warp nacelles had taken a savage blow, and was spewing superheated plasma in every direction. A moment later, one of the secondary guns hit the scoutship yet again, pummeling it squarely amidships. The smaller vessel began to spin in an uncontrolled manner, the glow of its shields dimming steadily, then finally guttering out completely. Without having to be told, the helm officer minimized the danger of a collision by increasing the distance between the two ships.

T'Veren smiled. It wouldn't be long now. "Bring us about, helmsman," he said quietly. "Then finish them."

This can't be happening, Hawk thought as he watched the warbird make its slow, stately approach.

Peering across the darkened cockpit, he saw the captain's insensate form sprawled on the scoutship's deck. Behind the cockpit, Data appeared to be in much the same condition, though the android had remained eerily frozen in a half-standing position, his golden eyes wide but vacant, his positronic network still cabled to the ship's computer core. Deciding that there was nothing he could do for Data at the moment, Hawk returned his attentions to the flight console. From the dozens of flashing readouts and alarms vying for his attention, Hawk gathered that a warp-powered retreat was out of the question. *At least,* he thought, *the main controls seem to be working.*

Hawk spared a moment to kneel beside the captain, and felt for a pulse in his neck. He found one, though it was weak and thready. He wondered what would happen to the captain's artificial heart if he were to remain exposed to the damaged engine's tetryon emissions for much longer.

But that'll be moot in a couple of seconds, he thought, *if I don't do something about that warbird now.*

Seating himself in the pilot's chair, Hawk shut down the visual and audio alarms to help himself concentrate. One indicator, attached to the computer's memory buffer, continued flashing in an irregular pattern, and Hawk didn't want to waste any more time trying to shut it down; it was easy enough to ignore.

Almost at once, he thought of a way to address two of his most immediate problems. Recalling a command sequence that Admiral Batanides had shown him once offhandedly just before the raid on the rebel compound, Hawk armed the warp-core jettison system. Firing a thruster to reorient the ship, he engaged the core launcher.

The scoutship lurched as it loosed the core into space. Hawk watched the screen, which showed the scoutship's cylindrical, green warp core arcing quickly toward the approaching warbird. But moments before impact, the warbird's forward disruptor banks vaporized it. The small singularity that powered the core abruptly spent its energies in subspace. The warbird's paint didn't even appear to have been scratched.

Too bad. But at least the tetryon problem is solved.

Hawk watched as the warbird's forward guns began glowing a dull red as they began powering up for another salvo. Absurdly, Hawk found his attention wandering to the computer memory-buffer light, which persisted in its mindless, rhythmic flashing.

So this is it. I'll never see Ranul again.

Captain Picard groaned and began trying to sit up. Hawk went to his side. "Try not to move, sir."

"I'll take your medical opinion under advisement, Lieutenant," Picard said, pulling himself into the copilot's seat. Hawk offered him a steadying hand.

"Ship's status?" Picard said, looking Hawk in the eye.

"The warp drive is . . . gone. Completely," Hawk said,

with a touch of embarrassment. But now wasn't the time for overly detailed explanations; what's done is done. "We have only minimal impulse power and life-support. Shields are down as well."

"Then I gather that Data's attempt to move the cloaking buoys hasn't worked." The screen showed that in the depths of space beyond the rapidly closing warbird, the subspace singularity's hellish aspect remained unchanged.

Hawk swallowed hard as he watched the warbird grow larger on the screen. Seeing death make such a close approach lent an air of unreality to the entire situation. "I'm not even sure Data was able to transmit the signal before that last direct hit crippled him," he said.

Picard looked across Hawk's console at the one light that was flashing there. Reacting to the captain's quizzical expression, the lieutenant explained what it was, and that he couldn't shut it down.

Picard sat quietly staring at the light for several seconds as it pulsated. Long flashes alternated with shorter ones, though Hawk could discern no obvious pattern. "You're right, Mr. Hawk," Picard said finally. "Data *hasn't* sent his transmission. But he *has* managed to load it into the transmitter's memory buffer."

Hawk was puzzled. "How can you tell?"

"Because he just told me. Those flashes—it's an old-style radio code. Morse, I believe it was called. Data is saying 'transmit buffer data now.' "

Hawk's eyes grew wide as he grasped the idea. Data had assembled the command sequences necessary to move the cloaking-buoy network and thereby trigger the singularity abort—but his injuries had forced him to dump the command into the memory buffer before he'd been able to take it all the way through his subspace link to the Romulan array.

Hawk's hands moved quickly across the console. He sighed with relief when he determined that the subspace channel he needed was still open.

"Transmitting," Hawk said, slapping the final touch-pad with his palm.

"Forward disruptor tube is fully charged, Commander," said the *Gal Gath'thong*'s weapons officer. T'Veren watched with quiet anticipation as the young woman's hand approached the firing toggle.

From across the central control room, the grizzled operations centurion spoke up, the customary steadiness missing from his voice. "Commander, something is happening on the security network's outer periphery."

The weapons officer paused in mid-keystroke, and T'Veren's diagonal eyebrows went horizontal with puzzlement.

"Has the cloaking field malfunctioned?" T'Veren said.

"It appears to have gone into a maintenance shutdown mode, sir."

"What?" T'Veren roared in outrage. He knew this could only mean that the Apparatus that held the subspace singularity in check was now decloaked and visible. Such a thing should not have been allowed to happen—at least not prior to the Federation's legally binding withdrawal from the Geminus Gulf.

"The field-generation pods also seem to be . . . *moving,*" the decurion reported, sounding perplexed.

T'Veren struggled to keep his voice level. "Moving in what manner?"

"Inward, toward the Core's containment facility itself. They have remained in formation, and are on a fast approach vector, heading toward the defense-pod network."

"The defense pods are becoming active!" the helmsman said excitedly, the crippled scoutship now all but forgotten.

"Tactical!" T'Veren shouted. He wanted a clear picture of what happened as the middle-level defenses protected the Core from this apparent systems glitch.

On the screen, a tactical diagram appeared, showing the outer spherical array of cloaking generators as it swiftly contracted. Inside that sphere lay a second, stationary globe, composed of hundreds of small but heavily armed defense pods. T'Veren noted that the synchronized collapse of the outer sphere of cloaking generators was accelerating.

T'Veren watched in mute astonishment as the two spheres merged briefly; a moment later, the shrinking cloaking array had contracted so much that it slipped *inside* the stationary defense-pod network. The cloaking devices continued moving in formation, heading even faster toward the Core Containment Apparatus itself.

"Defense pods are turning inward and acquiring target locks," the centurion said breathlessly. "They are taking aim on the cloaking-field generators!"

T'Veren felt a rush of cold terror rush up his spine as he realized the full implications of what was happening.

"They're about to fire directly into the Core," he said, feeling utterly numb and helpless.

Hawk pointed the scoutship away from both the warbird and the singularity, pushing the single impulse engine to the limit. He was mildly surprised to note that the warbird was not in pursuit; in the condition the scout's propulsion system was in, they wouldn't have been at all difficult to overtake.

On the forward viewer, Hawk saw several of the cloaking buoys streak by the scoutship, looking like stars as seen from a vessel passing them at high warp.

"Let's have a look at Commander Data's handiwork, Mr. Hawk," Picard said. His voice was strong, though he looked pale and drawn; Hawk chalked it up to a lingering effect of whatever the engine core's tetryon burst had done to the captain's artificial heart.

Hawk switched the forward viewer to a reverse angle, displaying what now lay aft of the withdrawing scoutship. On the screen, dozens of vessels, most of them small scouts and shuttles, dived and swooped to evade salvos from the spherical formation of stationary weapons pods, which were unleashing uncounted fusillades of disruptor fire in the general direction of the singularity's containment equipment. At the facility's core, away from the worst of the fighting, the singularity's accretion disk glowed with a preternaturally angry brilliance, like some ancient war god enjoying blood sports being staged in its honor.

Hawk magnified the small image of the torus-shaped facility at the core of the cloaked zone—the heart of the array that kept the subspace singularity contained—and saw that the outer edge of the torus was under siege as well. Metal-eating molecular fires danced across several of its outermost structures.

Then the center of the torus gave off an expanding wave of energy, a deluge of iridescent brilliance that leaped outward in every direction. The phenomenon organized itself into a gigantic horizontal band, a vast and growing sapphire expanse that reminded Hawk of the tsunamis that sometimes struck Earth's coastlines. It brought to mind holographic re-creations he had seen of the first human-controlled thawings of the subsurface Martian aquifers, and the titanic explosion that had devastated the Klingon moon Praxis eighty years ago.

Hawk watched uneasily as the strange phenomenon seemed to grow steadily, though its initial burst of light appeared to be dissipating harmlessly. Still, the thing hadn't yet shown any sign of quietly disappearing.

"Sir, are you fairly confident that we were right about this?"

"How do you mean, Lieutenant?" Picard asked, his eyes barely open. The captain appeared to be in some pain.

"I mean our theory that a direct attack on the containment field would start an automatic abort and drop the singularity back into subspace," Hawk said quietly.

"Mr. Hawk, there have been many occasions when I have trusted my life, and even my ship, to my senior officers' expert judgment. This is simply another one of those times."

But how many times was the whole universe in danger of being sucked into subspace if they made a mistake? Hawk thought.

Suddenly, the center of the accretion disk started to form a depression, as though some invisible but heavy object had been set down upon it. With agonizing slowness, the edges of the disk began contracting toward the center. The effect gradually accelerated until the phenomenon resembled a crumpled piece of paper. Then it collapsed onto itself completely, abruptly becoming too small and dark for the viewscreen to resolve.

It was gone.

Picard looked up at the screen and smiled. Hawk shot a brief, sorrowful glance at the motionless Data, whose condition was impossible to diagnose at the moment. *I hope I'll get to thank you, my friend.*

Turning back to his instrument panel, Hawk grinned. "Looks like it worked. And their cloaking field is down as well."

"One of the Romulan Empire's most closely held secrets is now on display for the entire Chiarosan electorate to see."

"Maybe they'll petition Ruardh to hold a recall election over it," Hawk speculated.

Picard shook his head wearily. "First Protector Ruardh has her own difficulties with the Federation at the moment," he said, recalling the still-unresolved custody battle over Grelun. "And I wouldn't be surprised if there's not enough left of that singularity to prove that the Romulans were ever up to any mischief here in the first place."

Hawk realized that Picard was probably right. "The Tal Shiar would probably see to that," he said quietly.

The captain shot a stern glance at him, and for a moment Hawk feared that he had said too much. Had Picard begun to wonder how much Zweller had told him about Section 31's secret agenda in the Geminus Gulf?

Some spy I'd make, Hawk thought, chiding himself.

Whatever the captain's thoughts, all he said was, "Set a course for the *Enterprise,* Mr. Hawk. Best possible speed."

And then, to Hawk's shock and chagrin, the captain's expression suddenly went slack, and he fell face forward across the instrument panel.

Koval and his two guards sparkled into existence in the warbird *Thrai Kaleh*'s principal transporter room. A centurion awaited him there, a youthful but able officer whose name escaped Koval at the moment. It occurred to him that he had been having entirely too many memory lapses of late, and made a mental note to consult his physician about the problem at the first convenient opportunity.

The young centurion was out of breath, and looked nearly panic-stricken. Koval had never had much patience with useless emotional displays. "Out with it. What is wrong?"

"Chairman Koval, the subspace phenomenon . . . the containment facility . . ."

Koval grew uneasy. "Yes?"

"Sir, they are both *gone!*"

That can't be, Koval thought, shoving past the centurion and repeating the words in his mind like a mantra until he reached the central control room. The viewscreen there graphically confirmed the centurion's improbable story. Koval stood in the center of the chamber for the next several minutes, quietly contemplating his next move.

"The Federation vessel is obviously responsible," Subcenturion V'Hari said from behind one of the weapons consoles. "I respectfully suggest that we attack the *Enterprise* immediately."

Such an action struck Koval as perhaps futile and certainly counterproductive. To fight over a secret thing, even a secret *vanished* thing, was to admit that it had existed—and that it had been a threat to one's adversaries—in the first place. Another factor to consider was that the Chiarosans would probably soon learn of the singularity-containment facility, as well as the efforts of the Romulan Star Empire to conceal it from them. Who knew how these barbarians might react? The revelation of a hitherto covert Romulan military presence might make the Empire's newest protectorate almost impossible to control. Unless the Tal Shiar covered things up very carefully.

"No," Koval told his subordinate. "I have an alternate plan. Please contact First Protector Ruardh immediately."

Picard's eyes fluttered open, revealing the muted blues and grays of the *Enterprise*'s sickbay, which were broken up by the dull orange glow of an overhead sensor cluster. He looked down past his chin and saw that he was lying on his back, his chest covered by a clamshell-like piece of equipment which he recognized as a surgical support structure. A quartet of figures wearing scarlet masks and gowns worked with feverish efficiency over the device, performing intricate maneuvers, manipulating tricorders, fetching, using, then discarding various surgical and diagnostic instruments. Though his vision was distorted by the azure glow of a sterilizing medical forcefield, he quickly recognized the lead surgeon's flashing green eyes as those of Dr. Beverly Crusher.

"He's conscious, Dr. Crusher," said a member of the trauma team. Picard recognized the gruff voice of Dr. Gomp.

"Thank God," Crusher said quietly.

"No brain damage," someone else said. "I think we got to him in time."

"*Just* in time," Crusher responded. "Let's get him stabilized. Then I need to know the extent of the damage to his heart."

"Done," said Ogawa, who was staring intently at a medical tricorder. "The heart's bio-regulator looks to be completely fused, but it seems to be the only component that's suffered damage. I'm already downloading the replicator specifications for a replacement." Then she headed for one of the adjacent labs, the Tellarite physician accompanying her.

"Beverly," Picard said, his voice a parched croak. He was mildly surprised to find that he could speak at all.

"It looks like you beat the singularity after all, Jean-Luc. Despite having ignored your kindly doctor's advice." The surgical mask couldn't conceal her smile.

"How are Hawk and Data?"

"Hawk came through the mission just fine, though I think your injuries scared the hell out of him. Data was . . . shut off somehow. Geordi thinks he entered some sort of protective shutdown mode while linked to the scoutship's systems. But he also thinks he'll have him on his feet again in a few hours."

Picard nodded, relieved; he owed much to the two officers who had braved the singularity's dangers at his side. With the immediate peril behind him, he felt exhausted, and was sorely tempted to rest. But even though his throat felt as dry as the Chiarosan Dayside, there were still questions he needed to ask.

"The referendum?"

"From what Deanna told me, everything's over but the shouting down on Chiaros IV. The long and short of it is this: We'd better have our bags packed within the next twenty minutes. Or else."

Grelun, he thought with an inward groan. The matter of the rebel leader's asylum plea had yet to be resolved.

"Have Admiral Batanides and Commander Zweller returned to the ship?" Picard said as Nurse Ogawa returned, a small electronic device in her hand.

Crusher shook her head. "No. But I think their shuttle is due back any time now."

He silently cursed his immobility. He wanted to leap up and run to the shuttlebay, but he knew that this wasn't an option while his chest cavity was clamped open beneath the sterile surgical field. "I need to see them as soon as they're aboard. Particularly Commander Zweller."

"What you need," Crusher said sternly, "is to sit absolutely still for the next few minutes so I can repair the damage you did to your artificial heart."

Picard sighed with frustration, then relented. "Fine. But after that—"

"No promises," she said, interrupting him. It occurred to him that Crusher was probably the only person on the entire ship to whom he allowed that privilege. "After the operation, we'll see."

His dry throat made his next words come out in a sandpapery rasp. "Doctor, I'll be damned if I'm going to let you confine me to sickbay."

"I don't negotiate, Jean-Luc," she said, holding up a hypospray admonishingly. "Why are you in such a hurry, anyway?"

"Beverly, Corey Zweller and I once took a foolish risk by fighting a trio of very hostile Nausicaans. That's why there's an artificial heart in my chest today. Forty years later, Zweller is *still* running foolish risks. Only now, he's gambling with the lives of his colleagues. Whole sectors of space. An entire *civilization.* Had the Romulans succeeded in keeping that subspace singularity, his political games-manship might even have jeopardized the entire *universe.*

"But no more. It ends today. And I have to be in the shuttlebay when he arrives so I can tell him that."

Crusher looked at him for a moment before nodding her assent. "All right, Jean-Luc. I think I can have you good as new—and out of here—in maybe an hour."

He smiled gratefully. "Thank you, Bev—"

"If," she said, once again interrupting and pointing the hypospray at him, "you will promise to swear off taking any more foolish risks *yourself* for at least a week."

Picard managed a smile as Crusher gently applied the hypospray to his neck. "Cross my heart," he whispered, and then slept.

The shuttlecraft *Herschel* vaulted away from the Chiarosan asteroid. Zweller watched as the battered, rocky worldlet dwindled on the viewscreen. He sincerely hoped never to look upon its meteor-scarred face again.

The cockpit had been devoid of conversation during the minute or so since their departure from the planetoid. In fact, neither Zweller nor Batanides had uttered a word to each other since the meeting with Koval had concluded. Zweller supposed it was because neither of them was overly eager to contact the *Enterprise*—and to hear from Will Riker that the Romulans had killed their oldest friend.

As she adjusted the small spacecraft's course for its rendezvous with the *Enterprise,* the admiral broke the uncomfortable silence. "Was it worth it, Corey?"

The question struck Zweller as a peculiar *non sequitur.* "What do you mean?"

"I mean that the Romulans have what they wanted: the Geminus Gulf."

He was willing to concede that to her. Although the referendum votes would still be gathered for about the next five minutes, most of the voting districts had already reported their results. The few that had yet to transmit their tallies couldn't possibly alter the overall result—which was the official ouster of the Federation from the Chiaros system, and thereby from the entirety of the Geminus Gulf.

"The Romulans have what they *said* they wanted," Zweller said. "Who can ask for more?"

"And you have what *you* came here for: a list of Romulan spies for your dirty little rogue bureau. So, was all the blood that was spilled here worth it?"

He knew she was talking about Johnny as much as Tabor. Anger sparked within him, for both men had been *his* friends, too. "My 'dirty little rogue bureau' has saved the Federation more times than I can count."

She looked unconvinced. "How about a recent 'for instance'?"

"All right. Are you familiar with an intelligent, proto-warp-era carnivore species called the Nizak?"

"It's a big galaxy," she said, shaking her head. *"Should* I have heard of them?"

"I admit, they're probably obscure, even to most intelligence officers. But you'd remember them if you ever ran into them. Big, scaly, conquest-bent, and mean as all get out."

"That sounds like a fairly subjective appraisal."

"You might not think so if any friends of yours had ever been on their dinner menu. Their own history shows the Nizak to be conquerors and predators by nature. Our exosociology branch concluded a long time ago that the Nizak constitute a clear and present danger to over a dozen nearby Federation systems."

Her brow furrowed. "I thought you said these people were 'proto-warp-era.'"

"They are," Zweller said, a mischievous smile involuntarily creasing his face. "For the moment. Unfortunately for these fine folk, their most brilliant scientists and engineers can't seem to keep their prototype warp ships from blowing up on the launch pad."

She raised her eyebrows incredulously. "Section 31 is monkey-wrenching the Nizak's warp experiments. Trampling on the Prime Directive."

"That's one way of looking at it, I suppose," he said with a shrug. "But no one else from Starfleet can prove that without making extensive contact . . . and risking committing violations of the Prime Directive themselves."

A frosty expression clouded the admiral's features. "You're saying that Section 31 is in the business of . . . *neutralizing* entire civilizations?"

"We only do what's necessary to protect the Federation. No more, and no less."

"And exactly how far does 'what's necessary' go, Corey?"

"I'm not sure what you mean," Zweller lied.

Her eyes narrowed. "I mean this: Starfleet has encountered hundreds of intelligent species over the past couple of centuries. I can think of at least a few that haven't been heard from since shortly after we made first contact with them. Your bureau wouldn't have anything to do with that, would it?"

He looked away from her penetrating gaze and stared instead at the forward viewer. After a brief pause, he replied, "It's like I already said, Marta. We do whatever's necessary to fend off threats to the Federation. No more, and no less."

When he looked back toward her he saw that she was studying him grimly, her jaw clenching rhythmically. "What's *happened* to you, Corey? The Federation has *never* sanctioned these kinds of actions."

He'd heard this argument often, and had long since grown weary of hearing it. "Of course it doesn't, Marta. It *won't*. But the Federation exists in a universe that often means it harm. I know it's no fun facing that fact, but it's the cold, hard truth. Surely, as an intelligence operative, you understand *that*."

"Corey, I understand that without the rule of law, the universe is even more dangerous than any adversary even the most paranoid Section 31 agent could ever imagine."

She fell silent then, staring hard at him for what seemed like an eternity. Then he saw the anger in her eyes slowly draining away, to be replaced by something else entirely. Was it pity?

The thought rankled him. He glanced away from her under the pretext of monitoring the helm panel. A glance at the chronometer reminded him that he might as well call the *Enterprise*—and finally learn whatever fate had befallen Johnny's captured Romulan scoutship.

Batanides evidently had just had the same thought. "Do you think Jean-Luc made it?"

Zweller wanted to say something hopeful, though he

truly didn't feel that way. It wasn't that he lacked faith in Picard's abilities; it was simply that he knew very well that when Koval wanted someone dead, that was the way that person usually ended up.

"I suppose there's only one way to find out," he said, then touched a control, opening a channel to the *Enterprise*.

He was surprised and pleased to see Picard's face appear on the viewscreen. Zweller noted that his old classmate looked haggard and tired. He was dressed in a robe and appeared to be speaking to them from his quarters.

"You've looked better, Johnny," Batanides said, grinning slightly.

Picard smiled weakly in response. "A lingering aftereffect of winning a brawl against a subspace singularity. It'll pass. How did *your* mission go?"

Zweller held up the data chip, displaying it triumphantly. "The only downside, in case you haven't heard already, is that all Federation personnel are now considered *personae non grata* anywhere in the Geminus Gulf."

Picard hesitated for a moment before answering. "I'm already well aware of that," he said finally. "But I don't think the Romulans have any cause for celebration, either. Without the subspace singularity, they no longer have any rationale for being here."

As Picard signed off and the craft approached the aft shuttlebay, Zweller smiled. Everything was going to work out well after all—despite the fact that the singularity's destruction could be as big a loss to the Federation as it was to the Romulans. But with the singularity gone, the Romulans would probably abandon the Geminus Gulf of their own accord soon enough, and Section 31 would be waiting patiently. By that time, the Chiarosan people would surely see the Romulans for the devious manipulators they were, and would welcome the Federation with open, triple-jointed arms. A full investigation of Ruardh's pogroms would almost certainly result in her ouster, if that result wasn't imminent already. Peace might come to Chiaros IV at last.

Zweller leaned back in the copilot's seat, his fingers laced behind his head. Yes, everything was working out very well indeed.

Still, he avoided looking at Batanides for the rest of the flight.

As Batanides and Zweller stepped from the *Herschel* onto the *Enterprise*'s main shuttlebay, the admiral wasn't surprised to see Dr. Crusher and Captain Picard—the latter now dressed in a light-duty uniform—already waiting there to greet them. What the admiral *did* find surprising was the pair of brawny security guards who stepped forward, bracketing Zweller and taking him into custody.

"Thanks for saving me the trouble," Batanides said to Picard as she confiscated the data chip. Zweller seemed remarkably unconcerned about what was happening.

"If you're thinking of using the information on that chip against us, you might as well not bother," Zweller said as one of the guards manacled his wrists and the other scanned him for weapons, finding none. "I'm the only one aboard this ship who knows the encryption key."

Damn! she thought, gripping the data chip tightly. She knew that the xenocryptography specialists in Starfleet Intelligence could no doubt crack Corey's encryption key, given enough time. But by then, the data chip's contents would most likely be useless.

"I'm sorry I'm forced to do this, Corey," Picard said in staid tones. "But you have deliberately interfered with the internal affairs of a sovereign government. Your actions demand a trial before a general court martial, which you will face after we remand you into the custody of the nearest starbase."

"You're assuming, Johnny," Zweller said, his expression enigmatic, "that we won't have any unscheduled detours between here and there."

Batanides was once again struck by Zweller's unaccountable calm. What was he up to?

As the guards escorted Zweller away, Batanides listened to the sound of their bootheels reverberating across the cavernous shuttlebay. A deep chill slowly ascended the length of her spine as she contemplated Corey's words, and wondered just how long his rogue spy bureau's reach really was.

In the meantime, Picard and Dr. Crusher had walked a few paces away, apparently conferring privately about something urgent. The doctor seemed to be greatly concerned about the captain's health, and indeed, he appeared slightly unsteady on his feet. After a quick exchange of tense whispers, Crusher strode toward the exit and a careworn Picard returned to the admiral's side, a resolute expression on his face. Batanides couldn't help but notice that neither of them appeared satisfied with the outcome of their deliberations. She wondered why it was that ships' doctors always treated their captains as though they were delicate Barkonian glass sculptures.

Maybe it's because captains always seem to think they're made of neutronium.

Her rumination was interrupted by the sound of Will Riker's voice, which issued from Picard's combadge. "Riker to Picard."

"Go ahead, Number One," the captain said.

"Three small ships on approach from Chiaros IV, and Ruardh's flagship is among them."

"Ruardh was evidently quite serious when she demanded that we hand over Grelun," Picard said as he began walking quickly toward the corridor. Batanides fell into step beside him.

"It certainly looks that way, sir," Riker said. "They should be in weapons range in just under six minutes."

"We're on our way. Picard out."

After they entered a turbolift, Batanides realized that her old friend was staring inquisitively at her.

"Something on your mind, Johnny?"

"Probably the same thing that's on yours," he said, placing one hand against a wall to steady himself. "Given the distinct possibility that Ruardh may attack us, do you believe that I should surrender Grelun to her?"

She genuinely wasn't certain about that anymore. The Chiarosan people had been so thoroughly misled already by the machinations of both the Tal Shiar and Section 31 that almost any course of action now seemed hopelessly muddled. Despite the antipathy she had harbored toward the rebels in the immediate aftermath of the battle in Hagraté, she was no longer prepared to hold them entirely responsible for Aubin Tabor's death. It was now obvious to her that Chiaros IV's treacherous political landscape was no longer a clear-cut matter of interstellar law and Starfleet regulations.

"Cooperating with a legitimate, sovereign government is one thing," Batanides said. "But kowtowing to a Romulan puppet regime is quite another."

Picard nodded. "I agree completely."

"One other thing still concerns me, though," she said, leaning against her side of the turbolift as the illuminated deck-markers sped past.

"What's that?"

"I wonder just how far Ruardh is willing to go in order to capture Grelun."

"Let's hope we won't have to find out," Picard said gravely. "Because a war with Ruardh . . ." Though he left his words hanging in the air, his meaning was abundantly clear.

A war with Ruardh could escalate very quickly into a war with the Romulans, she thought, chilled to the marrow by the very notion.

Chapter Seventeen

Looking up from tactical, Lieutenant Daniels announced "Admiral on the bridge."

Riker, Troi, K'rs'lasel, and Rixa had all risen from their seats. As Picard followed Batanides out of the turbolift and onto the bridge, he was greeted by an unaccustomed sight. Grelun, who stood in the center of the room, favored the admiral and the captain with a quick nod, then returned to his visual inspection of the bridge, his crystalline eyes apparently drinking everything in.

"What is this man doing on the bridge?" Batanides said sternly. Picard gathered that she thought that a man whose people had just voluntarily entered the Romulan Star Empire ought not to have the run of the Federation's flagship. He had to concede that she had a point.

"I understand your apprehension, Admiral," Troi said in placating tones. "But I can assure you that Grelun poses no threat to us now."

"Nor have I been unsupervised," the Chiarosan said,

baring his razor teeth in a vaguely disquieting smile. Picard found Grelun's presence and bearing impressive, to say nothing of his immense size. He probably could have brushed the bridge's vaulted ceiling with his fingertips had he extended his arms fully above his head.

Picard turned toward Riker. "Have the Chiarosan ships contacted us yet, Number One?"

"No, sir. But I don't think it's any mystery why they're here."

Ruardh wants Grelun, and very badly, Picard thought. He reflected uncomfortably on Grelun's petition for political asylum, a request which he was bound morally, ethically, and legally to honor. Even if First Protector Ruardh—or her new Romulan masters—decided to play rough.

"Let's have a look at them, Mr. Daniels," Picard said, seating himself in his command chair. Three rather beat-up looking Chiarosan spacecraft, each of them about the size of a Starfleet runabout, appeared on the viewer. They were approaching the *Enterprise* at a leisurely pace, the nearest of them now lying some thirty thousand kilometers off the starship's port bow.

"Give me a tactical appraisal, Number One."

"Sensors show nothing but simple disruptors and low-powered deflector shields," Riker said as he took the seat to Picard's right. "They wouldn't stand a chance against us in a real firefight."

"They might not have to," Picard said soberly. "Especially if they're being backed up by a cloaked warbird."

"Hail them, Mr. Daniels," said Riker. A moment later, the image of the approaching Chiarosan ships was replaced by a pair of dour faces. One belonged to a Chiarosan female, whom Picard immediately recognized as Senator Curince. He had last seen her two days ago, when First Protector Ruardh had made her initial demand that Grelun be remanded to government custody. The other visage belonged to a young and supremely confident-looking Romulan. His gray uniform and the insignia on its collar testified that he held the rank of centurion.

Why bother keeping the Romulan diplomatic corps around when the military can simply take over? Picard thought, struggling to keep his expression carefully neutral. To Curince, he said, "It would seem that the balance of power has shifted somewhat today, Madame Senator."

She bared her teeth, perhaps in a smile, or perhaps not. "I shall not play games with you, Picard," she said, purring the words as if she were some great predatory cat. "Grelun must come with us."

"He has asked for political asylum," Picard said. "And until and unless he withdraws that request, he will have our protection. I cannot allow First Protector Ruardh to execute him."

The Romulan interposed himself into the conversation. "Ruardh undoubtedly *would* have him executed. However, Ruardh no longer enjoys the autonomy she once did."

Picard wasn't the least bit sorry to hear that. He smiled with grim amusement.

Curince addressed Grelun directly. "Where would you go if you could go anywhere you willed, Grelun? What would you do?"

Grelun's eyes narrowed in suspicion. "I would go back among my people," he said after a deliberate pause. "I would gather the Army of Light about me and strike like an avenging hammer at those who murder our children."

"In other words," the Romulan said, "you would bring order to what is now in terrible disarray. You ought to know that the Romulan Empire abhors disorder."

"I don't understand this," Riker said, frowning. "Are you saying that you *want* Grelun to go back to commanding a guerrilla army?"

"If a large asteroid were headed for your homeworld," the Romulan said, "would you want to splinter it into millions of small, uncontrollable missiles? Or would you instead seek to keep the object in one piece and modify its trajectory?"

Picard glanced inquisitively at Troi, who was standing on the bridge's port side. "He's telling the truth," she said. "The Romulans see the rebel movement as becoming far more dangerous in the absence of coherent leadership."

Almost inaudibly, Riker quoted, " 'Keep your friends close. But keep your enemies closer.' "

"Grelun," Curince said, her manner softer now. "Will you come with us?"

"I believe that it was the Romulans who destroyed the Army of Light's principal stronghold," Grelun growled. "They have given me little cause to trust them."

The Romulan spread his hands, no hint of confirmation or denial in his voice. *"Whoever* destroyed your base, did they not give your soldiers sufficient warning beforehand for a general evacuation? Come now, Grelun. You are well aware that trust has nothing whatsoever to do with any of this. You want to return to Chiaros IV. You can do so either as Ruardh's condemned prisoner . . . or you can allow the Empire to return you to your ragtag rebellion."

Grelun stood in silence for several minutes, staring down at the carpet. His impossibly limber fingers flexed unconsciously as he considered the centurion's offer. Finally, he drew a deep breath and said, "I will accompany you. Willingly."

Apparently satisfied, the Romulan signed off without another word.

The Chiarosan turned to face Picard and Riker. "This is the best solution, although I trust the Romulans little, and Ruardh's lapdogs less."

"You could stay with us," Riker offered.

"No. Your Federation's appetite for conquest and penchant for self-serving trickery makes you little different than the Romulans." He paused for a moment, before adding, "Were it not for the actions of several of your crew, my opinion of you would be lower still. But you have shown me respect and mercy, even in apparent defiance of your own Federation's directives."

Picard nodded slightly at the compliment as he stood and faced the Chiarosan. "Before you leave, Grelun, promise me one thing."

"You have restored my life to me, Picard. Ask, and if it is within my power, I will see it done."

"Find a way to bring an honorable peace to your world," Picard said. "Your people stand at the threshold of a new age in your history, and only one thing can hold you back—the fighting that you do amongst yourselves. You know that it cannot continue indefinitely. Sooner or later, both sides will have to learn to forgive the past, and then move forward if your people are ever to build a future."

And handing the First Protector her walking papers might be a good place to start, he thought.

"Your people haven't always made war on each other," Troi said gently to the Chiarosan. "Perhaps you can make such horrors a thing of the past."

Grelun did not move for several long seconds. Picard thought that he looked like a man who was being asked to cut off his own head. But the Chiarosan also appeared to realize that he had a great deal to think about.

"Perhaps," he said after a protracted silence. Turning

to face Picard, he said, "Perhaps, one day, peace *will* come to pass."

After Riker had escorted Grelun from the bridge, Picard sank back into his command chair and sighed wearily. "Take us back into Federation space as soon as the transporter room confirms Grelun's beam-out," he said to the conn officer. "Warp nine-point-two."

Even at that speed, Picard thought, *this part of the Geminus Gulf is still six days out of Federation space.*

Picard wondered how long it would be before the Romulans abandoned this place, once they determined that their precious subspace singularity was beyond recovery. And if the Chiarosans would then ask him to return—not to help mediate their internal conflicts, but to inaugurate their entry into the Federation as a peaceful, unified people.

Hawk saw the shape silhouetted in the bedroom doorway and recognized it as his partner. He heard a tentative voice, whispering, "Sean?"

"I'm awake, Ranul," he said, shifting backward to a seated position against the bed's pillows. "I've just been taking some quiet time."

The Trill sat down on the edge of the bed, tentatively. He had given Hawk his space during the last several days since their quarrel. Hawk knew it wasn't fair to keep Ranul at a distance, physically or emotionally. He leaned forward and enfolded Ranul in his arms. "I'm sorry," he whispered into his ear, feeling Keru's beard tickling his cheek.

After a few minutes went by, Hawk leaned back again, but he took Ranul's hand in his own.

"So, after saving the universe, defeating the Romulans, and escaping with all your limbs intact, what are you gonna do for an encore?" Ranul's voice took a slightly higher tone, and Hawk knew that his lover was smiling at him in the dark.

Hawk snorted a laugh, and squeezed Ranul's hand. *It's now or never,* he thought. As jocularly as he could, he said, "I dunno. I was thinking about joining a rogue intelligence organization within Starfleet that goes around the rules to accomplish its goals."

"What?" Even in the dim light, Hawk could sense the look of confusion on Ranul's face.

Sighing heavily, Hawk leaned forward again, coming closer to his partner. "You know all that stuff I was talking to you about before? The classified stuff?"

"Yeah."

"I need to make a decision about it."

"What do you mean?" Keru asked.

"This needs to stay between us for now, Ranul." Hawk saw Keru nod in the dark, and continued speaking. "I was approached by Ambassador Tabor to join a secret organization within Starfleet. They're like Starfleet Intelligence, but more proactive. They respond to threats against the Federation by any means necessary, even if it means going around every law we have, even the Prime Directive. If I'm to believe what Tabor told me—and what Commander Zweller said later—this group is responsible for saving a lot of lives, and for keeping a sometimes too-fragile peace when less decisive authorities refuse to act."

Ranul put his other hand on top of Hawk's. "Why do they want *you?* Would you have to . . . leave the *Enterprise?*"

"I think they want me because of my eidetic memory, but it could be because of my piloting skills, or something else entirely. And don't worry. Nobody has asked me to leave the *Enterprise.* I'm assuming that I would be their agent on this ship."

"A spy, in other words."

Hawk was uncomfortable, but he didn't sense that Ranul was prejudging him. "No . . . maybe. I think they feel that they need someone on this ship who can work for them—who is working *with* them. You know as well as I do that the *Enterprise* gets itself caught in the middle of a lot of turmoil. And those sorts of situations are their specialty."

"If this organization is so secret, and they want an 'agent' on board, how do we know there isn't one here already?"

Hawk thought for a moment. That hadn't occurred to him. "I guess we don't," he finally offered.

Keru opened his mouth to speak, then shut it again with a sigh. "You remember how I lost my family," he said at last.

Hawk nodded. Keru's father, stepmother, and teenage sister had been living in a settlement on Hakton VII, a planet in the Federation–Cardassian demilitarized zone. Then the Federation signed a treaty with Cardassia in 2370, effectively abandoning several Federation colonies to the Cardassian Union's tender mercies. Many settlers had refused to relocate, not wanting to leave their homes and lands behind. A few months later, the Keru family was among those reported killed during an unprovoked raid on the settlement, following reports of anti-Cardassian factions stockpiling weapons there.

Ranul continued speaking, his voice taking on a slightly bitter edge. "I think that the Federation was wrong in giving its citizens a choice between giving up their homes and accepting Cardassian rule. When they chose to stay, our government deserted those people, knowing that they probably wouldn't survive." He paused for a moment and ruffled the back of Hawk's hair. "I don't have to remind *you* what was lost in the conflict with Cardassia, Sean."

Logan, Hawk thought glumly. *And four other Acad-*

emy classmates. Gone forever because the Cardassians breached the warp core on the Barbados.

Hawk put his hand up to his partner's cheek, and felt a tear there. Ranul had been close to his family, and invoking their memories now must have struck him hard. But Hawk felt pain as well. Logan had been Hawk's *first* love, and if their assignments out of the Academy hadn't forced them apart—or if Logan had gotten his transfer before the destruction of the *Barbados*—they might still be together. And he never would have met Ranul.

So, perhaps some good has come from the pain? He had never considered it that way.

Ranul sniffed, and turned to look at Hawk. "Didn't you once tell me that some of your ancestors fought in the Martian Revolution?"

Hawk nodded and smiled. "Native Martians prefer to call it the War for Martian Independence. And yes, I'm descended from some of the freedom fighters. They were New Reformationists—religious pacifists—so they were among the last people to join in the war. A few of them even fought at Gundersdotter's Dome and helped turn the tide for Martian sovereignty."

"So, you know what *they* did," Ranul said. "They set aside their stated principles in order to achieve a higher goal. Mars gained its independence, even if blood was spilled on both sides."

"I'm not convinced that Section 31 is always working toward the higher goal though, Ranul." Hawk looked his lover in the eyes, dark pools on the shadowed face.

"I guess if I were in your situation, I'd ask myself where this organization stands on situations of ethics and morality and honor. And if what you feel about Starfleet and its ideals is compatible with that answer." Keru looked down, his voice barely louder than a whisper. "I know that *I* think the Federation made a mistake in the past. And that mistake cost me my family. Do I think that the Federation and Starfleet *always* make mistakes? No. Do I think Starfleet's leaders and officers are fallible? You bet I do."

He paused, and added, "But I've never worked under a leader who was acting against what he felt was ethical and honorable."

Hawk leaned forward, and hugged Ranul tightly again, less sure than ever which way to proceed.

The door opened in front of Hawk, and he stepped inside. The officer standing near the console toward the center of the room stiffened slightly, looking at him. Hawk handed him a padd. "I need to speak with Commander Zweller. Here's my authorization, from Commander Riker."

The guard studied the padd's screen for a moment, then gestured toward one of the recessed detention cells across the room. "He's over there. Are you going to be long? You want a chair?"

"No. Actually, I'd prefer to talk to Zweller inside, if you don't mind."

The guard raised an eyebrow, glanced down at the padd again, and nodded. "Okay. If that's what you want. I'll keep an eye out for trouble."

Hawk approached the detention cell and saw Zweller sitting against one wall, his face blank, his eyes closed, and his posture relaxed, as if he were meditating. The forcefield at the front of the cell sparked for a moment, and Hawk stepped through it. The slight crackle behind him meant that the field was back in place.

"Commander?" he asked quietly.

Without opening his eyes, Zweller responded, gesturing beside him on the bench. "Mr. Hawk. Won't you sit down? The view from here is astonishing." His lips moved into a slight smile.

Hawk sat. He was edgy enough because of the discussion he sought, and the spartan accommodations made him even more uncomfortable. "I needed to talk with you a bit more before making my decision," he said, his voice low.

"I trust you've already talked to some of my erstwhile shipmates about me," Zweller said.

Hawk nodded. Unfortunately, those conversations—none of which involved questions about Section 31—had told him little more than he already knew. To hear Roget and Dr. Gomp tell it, Zweller was clearly a traitor who ought to be clapped into irons and sent straight off to the Federation Penal Settlement in New Zealand. Other former *Slayton* officers, like Kurlan and Tuohy, tended toward maverick stances in their professions, and thus seemed more willing to give Zweller the benefit of the doubt.

Hawk knew that only Zweller could tell him what he really needed to know. After a moment's hesitation, he said, "Why did you . . . how . . ."

"How did I come to be involved with this group?" Zweller opened his eyes and stared calmly at Hawk. His gaze seemed almost fatherly, but Hawk didn't sense much warmth behind it. "It's a personal story which I do not care to share in detail. Suffice it to say that I was a part of a mission in which I was forced to question a decision made by my friend and commander. We had received two distress calls—from a Starfleet vessel and an alien craft—with only the time to answer one. If we aided the Starfleet ship, we would save the lives of less than a dozen fellow officers. If we aided the alien ship, we would not only save hundreds of lives, but we would also keep a set of experimental weapons from falling into the clutches of the Breen.

"The decision my commander was compelled to make—because of Starfleet rules and regulations—meant that we were to save the other Starfleet vessel," Zweller continued. "I disagreed. In the process of disabling some of the warp systems to force us to the aid of the aliens, I was caught by a senior engineer. Luckily, the woman who caught me was there to perform the same bit of 'mutiny' that I was engaged in. And she was the person who recruited me for the bureau."

"Did you succeed?"

Zweller nodded. "Oh, yes. The sentients survived because of our actions, and the weapons were kept from the Breen. And the Starfleet officers on the other vessel managed to escape before their ship was destroyed. No lives were lost. To date, there have been no negative repercussions from our operation."

At least none that you're aware of, Hawk thought. *Or seem to give a damn about.*

Hawk considered Zweller's story for another moment, his mind awhirl with unasked questions. "Don't you think that your actions in this bureau are a form of anarchy? You decide which Starfleet regulations you'll follow, and which ones you won't. What makes you any more legitimate than, say . . . the Maquis?"

Zweller allowed himself another small smile. "Many of the Maquis weren't even born when I became an agent. But when I was a whole lot younger, I asked myself similar questions. About law and virtue. I concluded that they aren't always the same thing. Earth's history is replete with secret government organizations, and there have always been anarchists who fear those organizations. Both essentially want what's best for themselves and their families—a lawful, orderly society, in which everyone can reach his potential, free of tyranny and oppression.

"But it's their methods that differ," Zweller continued. "In a democratic coalition—which is, after all, what the Federation is—the people elect representatives, who then decide on rules to govern the populace. That's a difficult enough task for humans to achieve on their own, Mr. Hawk, much less humans and Vulcans and Andorians and all the other species that coexist in the UFP. What's good for one world might not be good for another.

"Which is one of the justifications for the Prime Directive. At its base, our noninterference credo should conceivably allow every civilization to control its own destiny. But do we really follow that? Ever?"

Hawk looked at him, his eyebrows scrunched together quizzically. "What do you mean?"

"Every time one of our away teams beams down to the surface of a planet, we are interacting with the people there. We are changing their destiny. We are breaking the Prime Directive simply by being among them."

"I don't see what that has to do with anything," said Hawk.

"You asked me if we represented anarchy, and in one way, I would have to say, 'Yes.' Our very presence in other cultures introduces unpredictable elements that would not normally be there. But once we have made that intrusion, we have an obligation to be the best visitors we can be. Sometimes, that means that we *must* interfere, for the greater good. And here's the paradox: Those same Starfleet rules that allow us to interject ourselves into alien cultures also forbid us from deliberately helping or hurting them. They keep us from fixing mistakes that can boomerang on us later."

Hawk looked down at his hands, which were clasped in his lap. Zweller made sense, more so than he had during their earlier too-brief exchanges. He was more persuasive than even Tabor had been.

"You asked what made us different from the Maquis," said Zweller. "If you're speaking of pure idealism, there isn't much that's different. The passion and the drive for freedom are the same. And sometimes in the particulars of technique, we don't differ that greatly either. Sometimes, you do what you have to do, even if it gets ugly.

"But the major difference between them and us is that Section 31 exists *within* Starfleet. It knows the rules and follows them whenever possible, and when circumstances compel us to break those rules, we do it with the greater good of the entire Federation in mind."

"So you wouldn't fight for the same aims as the Maquis?" Hawk asked. "The Federation citizens that the Federation–Cardassian Treaty uprooted were no less important after the treaty than before."

"Those people *chose* to stay behind, knowing the likely consequences," said Zweller.

Hawk tried not to flinch, but he did nevertheless. Zweller saw it, and put his hand on Hawk's shoulder as he spoke again, more soothingly this time. "I'm not saying that those citizens deserved to be brutalized by the Cardassians. But the Maquis represent an instability in the power struggle, a violent and confrontational wild card. Instead of fighting head-on, and losing lives needlessly, Section 31 has worked to undermine Cardassia's hold on the disputed worlds from *within* the Cardassian government. You'd be amazed how much change you can effect simply by replacing a few strategically important guls and legates."

"You and Tabor were working to undermine the referendum so that the Chiarosans would vote against Federation membership on Chiaros IV. And ever since the escape on the scoutship, you've avoided telling me the truth as to why."

Zweller sighed. "It was concluded privately by many Starfleet higher-ups that Chiaros IV wasn't valuable enough—or politically stable enough—to fight over. Especially not when you consider what the Romulans offered us in exchange for our withdrawal from the system."

"Which was?"

"Extremely important information. Data about most of the Romulan spies working within the Federation and Starfleet."

Hawk was suddenly extremely uncomfortable with what he was hearing. "You came here to trade an entire star system—and its people—for some ephemeral information? You lost a ship, risked all of our lives—"

Zweller rose as he spoke, his tone more strident. "None of that was part of the plan! The *Slayton* was destroyed, apparently, because she stumbled onto the secret the Romulans were hiding." His voice softened. "I told you what my initial mission was. My own secondary objective was to help Falhain and his Army of Light in their struggle against Ruardh. Her regime is brutal by *any* society's standards. In my judgment, my aiding her opponents was compatible with Section 31's plan for Chiaros IV and the Geminus Gulf."

"But in doing so, you were helping the *Romulans!*"

Zweller smiled slightly. "Not exactly. Falhain's rebels were anti-Federation already, and weren't terribly open to persuasion. Most of them saw us as friends of their enemies, after all. At least until I aided them in their struggle for freedom. Given some time, though, more of them might have come around. Even the Chiarosan electorate might be friendlier to the Federation later on—especially once they've experienced a few years of Romulan oppression firsthand."

"That's an awfully big 'might be,' " Hawk said.

"Yes. More than likely they'll first begin to fight against the Romulans," Zweller said, sighing. "A long shot? Maybe. But they've been beating the odds just by evolving on that gods-forsaken planet. And perhaps having to face an enemy like the Romulans will do more to unite the squabbling Chiarosan tribes than their world's harsh environment ever did."

Hawk gathered his thoughts for a moment. "You know that if you and Tabor had succeeded in your mission *without* all these complications, the Romulans would have gained control of the Geminus Gulf *and* the singularity. So who would have been guilty of making a mistake then?"

"And if there *hadn't* been a singularity, I'd be getting pats on the back for the benefits my mission brought to the Federation." Zweller gave a slight smile, but ultimately looked uncomfortable.

"Nothing in the universe ever travels in a straight line, Mr. Hawk. Even planets move in ellipses. You can't predict exactly what's going to happen when you're on a mission. *Any* mission. All you can do is make the best decision you can with the facts you have on hand. It's always easy to criticize others' decisions after all the information has come to light . . . once you've learned what they *didn't* know at the time."

Hawk stood and looked at Zweller, considering the motives of the man who stood before him. Though he felt that the commander was telling him the truth, the situation still unsettled him greatly. He wasn't reassured by Zweller's circuitous thinking.

Hawk's eidetic memory brought Ranul's words flooding back to him: *I guess if I were in your situation, I'd ask myself where this organization stands on situations of ethics and morality and honor. And if what you feel about Starfleet and its ideals is compatible with that answer.*

His ancestors had put their lives—and they believed, their *souls*—on the line to fight for their homes, their world, and their freedom. The Maquis were doing the same.

But it seemed to Hawk that Section 31's only apparent guiding principle—to defend the Federation using any means the bureau's unaccountable minions deemed necessary—was flawed. Zweller had just talked about learning from what other decision-makers had done in the past. But without accountability, without laws, what *could* one really learn?

Hawk signaled for the guard to lower the forcefield, then turned toward Zweller. Hawk did not extend his hand. "You've given me a lot more to consider, Commander."

Zweller proffered his own hand, his expression friendly. "I hope you will consider *all* that I've said. You seem . . . unnerved by what I've told you."

Hawk shook Zweller's hand quickly and awkwardly, then turned to step out of the cell. "I'll consider everything before I make up my mind about joining the bureau."

But as the forcefield shimmered into place behind him, Hawk realized that he had already made his decision.

Anarchy was not the equal to ethics and morality and honor. No matter *what* its ultimate goals. Section 31 was asking too high a price.

After taking off his uniform jacket and tossing it on a chair, Picard was retrieving a fresh cup of Earl Grey tea from the replicator when the door chime to his quarters sounded. "Come," he said to the air, and the door opened. In the hallway stood an uncomfortable-looking Lieutenant Hawk.

"Come in, Lieutenant," Picard said, gesturing with his arm.

Hawk walked in, an awkward expression on his face. "I'm sorry to bother you in your quarters, sir."

"Nonsense," Picard said, sitting down on a nearby couch. Smiling, he gestured toward a chair. "If it weren't for you, I might not even *be* here. I think that entitles you to at least one interruption." He paused to blow on his tea to cool it as the younger man sat down. "What can I do for you, Sean?"

Hawk looked surprised that the captain had used his first name, but he still seemed to be preoccupied by something else. "Sir, I have something important to tell you. I'm not sure you'll like it. In fact, I'm *sure* you won't like it."

Picard leaned forward, his eyes narrowing. "What is it, Lieutenant?"

As Hawk spoke, Picard sipped his tea. "A few days ago, I was approached by Ambassador Tabor to join a secret organization within Starfleet. Commander Zweller is a part of it as well. It's called Section 31."

Chapter Eighteen

Half an hour had passed since Hawk had interrupted Picard's relaxation so completely. The young officer had been telling his captain as much as he could about the conversations he had shared with Tabor and Zweller, with Picard interrupting only to ask pointed questions.

Through his astonishment, Picard was again impressed by Hawk's memory, which allowed him to remember details about the meetings that others might have forgotten. But that admiration was pushed into the background as Picard learned whatever scraps and pieces that Hawk knew about the heretofore secret organization known as Section 31.

Of course, Hawk had no way of knowing that Batanides had already come to him first with her knowledge of the organization and her suspicions. But Hawk's account of his discussions with Tabor and Zweller forced Picard to wonder what more Batanides knew about the group than she had told him; she *was* in Starfleet Intelligence, after all. And yet, she had seemed so sincere in her surprise over Tabor's and Zweller's actions. And unlike the two men, Batanides had never tipped her emotional hand to Counselor Troi, nor had she roused the suspicion that she might somehow be blocking her thoughts, as Zweller had done.

The captain paced back and forth. Hawk had quit speaking a few minutes ago, and had the presence of mind to stay silent while Picard considered his options. Still, the young man looked at him expectantly, like a child anticipating a scolding.

"Why didn't you come to me with this sooner, Lieutenant?" Picard asked.

Hawk looked down at his feet. "I'm sorry, sir. The ambassador made such a point about this being a top-secret organization. I didn't want to betray that confidence. And I wasn't sure that you didn't already know about it. At *first,* anyhow. And things got so complicated so quickly. I didn't know who to talk to about it and—"

"Lieutenant, despite Ambassador Tabor's assertion that he was working for the Federation's greater good, did it ever occur to you that he might simply have been a traitor? And that Zweller might be one as well?" Picard was staring down at the junior officer. "What proof did you have that *either* of them was working in the best interests of the Federation or Starfleet? Especially given all the conflicts their actions have dragged us into?"

"I didn't have any proof," Hawk admitted quietly. "Except that nothing they said seemed wrong, exactly. They had a good answer for everything."

"Most traitors do. But rules exist for a reason, Lieutenant, as do chains of command. That's why—"

"At the risk of getting myself into further trouble, sir," Hawk said, interrupting, "one of the things they pointed out to me repeatedly was how often you and Commander Riker have both broken the rules in pursuit of the greater good." He gulped, his Adam's apple bobbing.

Picard raised an eyebrow and regarded the lieutenant in silence. He considered lecturing Hawk about the unique decision-making skills of senior officers, or discoursing on the sorts of extenuating circumstances that might motivate one to . . . *bend* a regulation now and then, when particularly hazardous situations demanded it. But he couldn't.

Because he realized that the lieutenant was absolutely right.

I do *sometimes take risks or bend the rules, and damn the admirals.* Surely, he *always* had good reasons to make those decisions. But one man's sound justification was another's bad excuse.

"Sir?" Hawk stood, looking directly into Picard's eyes. "For what it's worth, I *did* come forward, even if not right away. I suppose I hesitated because Ambassador Tabor had me nearly convinced that the ends can justify a Starfleet officer's means . . . *sometimes*. But after talking things over with Commander Zweller, it seemed to me that for Section 31, the ends *always* justify the means. And I decided then that certain lines should never be crossed."

Picard sighed, smiled slightly, and then clapped one hand on Hawk's shoulder. "That's an important lesson to learn, Lieutenant. And I appreciate your honesty about this matter . . . and your forthrightness about the example I set for you and the rest of the crew."

"What happens now?" Hawk asked, looking apprehensive.

"To Zweller and Section 31? That remains to be seen. You may have blown the lid off of a conspiracy that will rock Starfleet to its core."

Picard noticed then that Hawk's chin was trembling slightly. "You're concerned about how your *own* conduct in this matter will look in your service record. Is that it, Lieutenant?"

Hawk nodded, his jaw still shaking. "Yes, sir," he said quietly.

"I imagine it will go something like this," Picard said, his tone soothing. "A special commendation will be placed in your file, noting your meritorious actions during the Chiarosan crisis. And you'll fulfill your duties on the bridge at your next work shift, and the one after that."

Hawk relaxed visibly, but Picard wasn't finished. "At some point, you'll likely have to testify about Zweller's actions before a Starfleet Command tribunal. But I don't expect this to affect your career negatively in any way."

He held his hand out toward the young man. "You've exhibited honesty and bravery throughout this mission, Sean. You made the right choices. *All* of them. Continue to make them."

Relief showed on Hawk's face. "Thank you, Captain." They shook hands firmly, then disengaged.

On the table, Picard's combadge chirped, and Data's voice filtered out of it. The captain was relieved that his android friend had recovered so completely from the after-effects of the raid on the subspace singularity, and whatever injuries the Romulan security AI had inflicted upon him.

"Captain," Data said, "there is a Priority One message for you from Starfleet Command."

"I'll take it here, Mr. Data." He turned to Hawk with a slight smile. "We'll talk more about this later."

"Yes, sir," the lieutenant said, then strode swiftly to the door.

Picard had donned his jacket before sitting behind his desk. He touched a small contact and its small screen lit up. On it was Admiral Connaught Rossa, whom he hadn't heard from in years.

"Admiral Rossa. It's good to see you, sir. To what do I owe the pleasure?"

Rossa clearly wasn't in the mood for the usual pleasantries. "It's my understanding that you have detained a Commander Cortin Zweller for various actions concerning this sordid liaison between the Chiarosan rebels and the Romulans."

"Yes, sir. We are transporting him to Starbase 424, where he will be bound over for trial."

"That won't be necessary, Captain. Instead, you will rendezvous in four days with the *U.S.S. Tian An Men,* just as soon as the *Enterprise* is clear of Geminus Gulf space. The exact coordinates for this meeting will be transmitted to you shortly. You will transport Commander Zweller and *all* his personal effects—including computer files—to the *Tian An Men* at that point."

Picard was jarred. After an almost imperceptible pause, he said, "May I assume that Vice-Admiral Batanides from Starfleet Intelligence will accompany the commander?"

"No. But after the rendezvous, you may continue on your heading for Starbase 424. Admiral Batanides and the remaining *Slayton* survivors will be ferried from there to their next destinations."

"Admiral, I must tell you that there are some very . . . unusual aspects to the charges against Commander Zweller." Picard shifted uncomfortably in his seat.

"As I said, Captain, you will transfer all files about

this to the *Tian An Men*. This includes *all* log material. The matter will be *classified* until such time as we contact you again."

"I will gladly make myself and my officers available to testify at the court-martial proceedings and—"

Rossa seemed annoyed. "Captain, perhaps I'm not making myself clear enough. *We* will contact you when we *wish* to hear from you. It is doubtful that charges will be brought against the commander—"

This time it was Picard's turn to interrupt her. "What? He allied himself with anti-Federation forces, aided in the abduction and incarceration of fellow Starfleet officers, and conspired with the Romulans! And I'm certain that's only the tip of the iceberg!"

The admiral's voice was sharp. "I'm sure we'll be able to decide for ourselves the truth about Commander Zweller's actions. Certainly, he was instrumental in revealing the atrocious war crimes being committed by a potential ally to the Federation, the Chiarosan government."

"Admiral, there's a great deal more going on here than you think."

"Captain, I'll allow for some small amount of insubordination from you, given the lateness of the hour. But I trust I needn't remind you of Starfleet's chain of command." She straightened in her chair, extending one hand toward the panel on the desk in front of her. "You have your orders. They are not open to discussion."

The image of Rossa vanished, replaced by the seal of the Federation. Picard gritted his teeth, fuming.

He slammed his hand down onto the comm panel. "Picard to Batanides."

"Go ahead."

"Marta . . . We need to talk."

* * *

Standing beside Picard in the passageway outside the brig, Batanides could scarcely believe what she was hearing. But the way things had gone on this mission, nothing was a complete surprise to her anymore.

"I've got a bit more pull with the brass hats than most starship captains do, Johnny," she said, her voice lowered. "Rossa might outrank me, but I promise you—I won't let this rest."

"I didn't expect that you would, Marta. But at the moment, *my* hands are officially tied."

"I wouldn't have expected this of Rossa. She's been in Starfleet a long time." Batanides had worked under the admiral on several earlier occasions.

Picard exhaled, shrugging slightly. "Let's give her the benefit of the doubt. We don't know if she's a part of this organization, or one of the people who help hide its existence. Or if she's only following orders *she*'s been given by others."

"No, we don't know," Batanides conceded grumpily. She gestured to the door of the brig. "Shall we get this over with then?"

They entered the brig, and Picard told the guard to wait outside, just beyond the outer door, to give them some privacy. The captain accessed the controls from the guard's console, bringing the security forcefield down. He and Batanides then stepped to the entrance of Zweller's cell, staying just outside it.

Their old friend looked up, a half-smile on his face. "Johnny. Marta. Have you finally come to your senses and decided to let me out of here?"

Batanides glared at him, but it was Picard who spoke. "Why the skulduggery, Corey? And why don't the rules apply to you and your unit?"

"Oh, please, Johnny, let's not get into more endless

debates about following the rules. I'm not that much different from the two of you when it comes to defending the Federation. These philosophical arguments about who's right or wrong are getting old. You have your methods, and they generally work. But when they don't . . ." Zweller spread his hands in the air, as if allowing sand to slip between his fingers.

Batanides spoke up, her shoulders straightening. "Commander Zweller, you appear to have friends in high places. Captain Picard has been ordered to release you to another ship's custody four days from now, no questions asked. And Starfleet Command isn't exactly champing at the bit to haul you before a court-martial."

"Well, that's certainly good news, Marta," Zweller said, brightening further. He stood. "Being punished simply for doing the right thing wouldn't be quite fair, now would it?" He turned toward Picard. "So, am I free to go to my quarters?"

Picard gave Zweller a soulful look, then turned on his heel. "I think given the circumstances . . . I'd feel much safer if you stayed *here* until your transfer to the *Tian An Men*."

The captain withdrew to the security console, leaving Batanides alone with Zweller. They stood staring at each other. Batanides looked into the eyes of her friend, but couldn't find the man he used to be anywhere in them. All she saw was darkness.

He moved his hand as if to touch her on the shoulder. The forcefield crackled into place—she wondered if Jean-Luc had chosen that precise moment for effect—and Zweller withdrew before he could touch it. "Marta, I'm sorry that—"

"You may be free to go in a few days, Corey," she said,

interrupting, "but God help you if our paths *ever* cross again after that. Not even Section 31 is invulnerable."

She turned and walked away. Corey's organization had taken her fiancé from her, and then one of her oldest friends.

It had much to answer for.

Chapter Nineteen

Jean-Luc Picard was not one who brooded often—if he did, he wouldn't admit it to others—but today, his mood was as black as obsidian. After Hawk's confessional visit, Admiral Rossa's orders, and his brief confrontation with Zweller, sleep had been coming only fitfully. The stress and fatigue of the last several days—to say nothing of his brush with death on the subspace singularity mission—had taken their toll.

He had spent the morning organizing the files to be sent over to the *Tian An Men* along with Zweller, and classifying all the other relevant documents stored within the *Enterprise*'s computer banks. Although he could have assigned the task to Data and gotten it done more efficiently, he preferred to do it himself, though every deletion, transfer, or security classification chipped away at whatever good humor remained within him.

If only there had been some way to read the encrypted information on that Romulan data chip, Picard thought bitterly. *At least then, Marta and I would have been able to warn some of Section 31's next targets. Perhaps even set some traps.*

Riker had contacted him a short while ago, telling him that the *Tian An Men* was approaching. The time of the scheduled rendezvous was almost upon them.

Just minutes from now, Corey Zweller will be free. He cursed under his breath.

The ready-room door chimed quietly, then slid open. Vice-Admiral Batanides hesitated for a moment before stepping in. "Good morning, Jean-Luc," she said, moving over toward the replicator.

"Either you have some news of which I'm not yet aware, or you mean that rhetorically," he said, forcing a smile.

She ordered almond amaretto coffee with cream, and then turned toward him as a cup sparkled into existence in the replicator. "No. No good news. And the *Tian An Men* is almost within transporter range."

Picard regarded her for a moment, his hand to his chin. "Marta, I need to speak with you off the record. *Truly* off the record."

"Sure, Johnny," she said. She took a seat before the desk, her coffee cup in hand.

He sighed heavily. "I've been running this week's events over and over in my mind. I've been reading and rereading the logs. And I'm still tremendously uncomfortable with Admiral Rossa's orders." He looked her directly in the eyes. "There are a lot of unpleasant consequences associated with this mission that I can accept. I can accept that a sovereign people have elected to reject Federation membership. I can accept that the Romulans have gained three sectors of relatively worthless territory at our expense. I can even accept the fact that we never learned whether Falhain's assassination was the work of Section 31, the Romulans, Ruardh, or even Grelun himself.

"But I *cannot* accept the prospect of Corey Zweller leaving this ship a free man after what he's done."

She looked supremely concerned. "What are you telling me, Johnny?"

"I have *no intention* of simply turning Zweller over to the *Tian An Men*. It's clear that Section 31 has contrived a way to sweep his misdeeds under the rug, as well as any proof of the bureau's existence that we might furnish."

Batanides sipped her coffee, but said nothing, nor gave any hint of her feelings. Picard continued. "I'm planning on proceeding to Earth with Zweller aboard, where I will appeal directly to the Federation Council. Something must be done about Section 31."

She appeared to mull his words over for a moment, then set her cup down on Picard's desk. "That would be a huge mistake, Johnny. We're not talking about taking on a trio of drunken Nausicaans here, after all."

And we know how well that *little confrontation went,* Picard thought. Perhaps that was part of her point.

She resumed: "The stakes are too high, and I won't have you jeopardizing your career. Heaven knows how many officers have had their lives ruined by this agency—and how many more *might* be, given this supposed 'Romulan spy list'—but I won't allow *you* to be among them."

"Marta, this travesty *cannot* go unchallenged."

"And it won't. I warned Zweller last night that Section 31 isn't invulnerable." She recovered her cup, took a drink, then continued. "Perhaps it wasn't such a good idea for me to warn him, but I think it's safe to assume that he was already expecting one of us to go after him anyway."

Setting her cup down, she reached forward and put her

hand atop Picard's, on his desk. *"I'm* the one who should go after him, Johnny. I'll use whatever resources are available to me through my rank and position in Starfleet Intelligence. Resources that not even the captain of Starfleet's flagship has. And if it's within my power, Commander Roget and his crew—and everyone who died aboard the *Slayton*—will see Corey and his superiors brought to justice."

She paused for a moment, giving his hand a slight squeeze. "Believe me, we both want the same thing, but *you're* too high-profile. And if you go off half-cocked, you might throw away any chance we have of ever stopping Section 31. You could drive them even further underground."

Now it was her turn to look him squarely in the eyes, her gaze studying him. "You have to do what you've never been inclined to do: *nothing.* And, you're going have to trust me to handle things . . . quietly."

Picard looked down at her hand atop his, feeling their warmth. "I don't want anything to happen to you," he said quietly.

"What more could they do to me, Johnny?" She gave him a sad smile. "All I've got left to lose is my friendship with you. So I ask you: *Please* just walk away from this. Leave it to me."

Though Picard's emotions roiled like Chiaros IV's stormy atmosphere, he could not refute her logic. There simply weren't any good alternatives to her plan. "All right, Marta. I'll keep my mouth shut. And I'll stay out of your way while you gather enough evidence to expose the bureau."

Batanides grinned warmly. "I hope you won't stay *too* far out of my way, Johnny. I'd hate it if it took another life-and-death crisis to bring us back together."

The door chimed again. Batanides quickly removed her hand from Picard's, and sat back in her chair. "Come," Picard said, and Commander Riker stepped into the room a moment later.

"Captain, the *Tian An Men* is standing by. They're requesting that we beam Zweller over immediately, along with all information pertaining to our Geminus Gulf mission."

Picard looked up at Riker wearily, and handed him a padd. "Number One, I'd like you to go to the brig and supervise the commander's release. I . . . It's probably best that I don't see him again for a good long while."

"I understand, sir."

Looking into his trusted first officer's eyes, Picard knew that he *did* understand.

Sean Hawk and Ranul Keru rounded a corner in the corridor, and came face-to-face with a security contingent led by Commander Riker. Two burly security officers accompanied him, flanking Cortin Zweller, who was dressed in a fresh Starfleet uniform.

"Hello, sir," Hawk said to Riker, nervous.

"Lieutenant," Riker said. "Congratulations again on your derring-do in the Geminus Gulf. I'm sure Ranul is at least as happy as we are that you're back among us."

Keru grinned. "It wouldn't be much of an anniversary celebration without him."

Hawk smiled as well. To Riker, he said, "Thank you, sir."

"See you on the bridge, Lieutenant," Riker said, leading his party on in the direction of the transporter room.

As Zweller moved past Hawk, he stopped and grabbed the young man's arm lightly. Riker and the security officers stopped as well. "It looks as though you've made your choice," Zweller said, his voice low.

"It was the *only* choice I could make," Hawk replied, looking Zweller defiantly in the eyes.

Without another word, Zweller turned and followed Riker. Hawk watched him go, without a trace of regret.

Hawk looked over at Ranul, who smiled and playfully ruffled his hair as they continued down the corridor toward holodeck three. Swashbuckling combat against Bluebeard and his pirates—which he and Keru had postponed for several days now—awaited them. It would be a tame diversion compared to the events of the past week. They might even get to enjoy some time together on a sandy beach after defeating the enemy's galleon full of brigands.

We have all the time in the world together now, Hawk thought as the holodeck door beckoned.

Chapter Twenty

Romulus, Stardate 50454.1

Senator Pardek looked out from the cliffside veranda, his dark, deep-set eyes surveying the sun-dappled surface of the Apnex Sea, which lapped gently at the jagged rocks far, far below. A small flock of *mogai* wheeled lazily overhead in a muted gray sky. Beneath them, blood-green waters stretched placidly to the horizon, and lapped at a shoreline teeming with multicolored succulents. Pardek thought, as he often did when he came here, that this must surely be the most beautiful vista on all of Romulus, the jewel in the Romulan Star Empire's crown.

It was also possibly the safest place he could be. There were no air- or watercraft anywhere to be seen, thanks to the warning messages broadcast by his auto-mated security system. But Pardek also counted on the protection of his own flesh-and-blood security staff, an experienced cadre of loyal Romulan soldiers who were as accomplished in the art of repulsing unwanted visitors as they were at keeping out of sight when not needed. The villa was the one place to which he could retreat from the often vexing intrigues of the Senate and the incessant infighting of the Continuing Committee. Here, he could almost convince himself that the vast length and breadth of the Empire contained nothing that might serve to trouble him, from his principal home in the Krocton Segment to the most remote Neutral Zone outpost; that young upstarts in the Senate weren't constantly gunning for his position; that the Vulcan radical Spock wasn't still at large somewhere in the Empire, spreading the subversive doctrine of Romulan–Vulcan unification to ever-increasing numbers of willfully gullible souls.

And that headaches such as the Tal Shiar's fiasco in the Geminus Gulf were merely bad dreams from which he would awaken.

Pardek had already decided that he would remain at the villa until tomorrow morning. Then, the Continuing Committee would begin its probe into the fitness of Chairman Koval to continue leading the Tal Shiar. Only then, once Pardek was forced to return to the Senate chambers to take gavel in hand before the board of inquiry, would he pause to worry about the possible consequences of Koval's inquest.

At least, that was the plan.

Returning to the central courtyard, Pardek tried to banish all thought of Koval and the Tal Shiar by concentrating on his garden. Here were the finicky Terran roses he so valued for their sweet scent, there the fast-growing crystalline life-forms, which the Tzenkethi called *nirikeh;* their crystals twinkled, silver and emerald and violet in the subdued sunlight, seeming to grow before his eyes. He continued walking, passing under the fronds of the rippleberry tree the Dominion Vorta Weyoun had given him last month as part of a nonaggression-pact overture. *That* offer was going to require some serious thought and debate, Pardek told himself; he trusted the Vorta even less than he did the Tal Shiar.

Beyond the rippleberry tree lay the patch of ground he reserved his prized Edosian orchids. The pink-edged, yellow flowers, which now stood on knee-high stalks, required specially prepared soils and a great deal of attention. This particular variety had come into his possession many years ago, introduced to him by an unusually well-mannered and talkative Cardassian groundskeeper he had met at the Cardassian Embassy, a few weeks prior to Proconsul Merrok's tragic demise. The orchids had provided Pardek with an agreeable diversion from that unpleasant business—Merrok had been a personal friend, despite their many political differences—and the orchids' delicate blooms had delighted him ever since, despite the constant labor they demanded.

Perhaps, Pardek thought, kneeling beside the orchids to inspect them more closely, *they serve as a metaphor for politics.*

He rose and walked into the house's sunlit central atrium, where he watched as his daughter, Talkath, practiced her martial arts exercises. So intent was the nine-year-old on the slow, intricately flowing motions of her hands, elbows, and legs, that she did not seem to notice his presence. He smiled silently as he watched her executing her precisely timed movements, delivering slow-motion kicks and blows in a lethal yet exquisitely lovely ballet.

She was a beautiful girl, bright and strong, her movements well-coordinated. Since his wife's untimely death in a shuttle accident four years prior, Talkath was all he had. She was his future, his legacy, his very life. Nothing in all of the Empire was more important to him.

Pardek walked farther into the house, got a warm cup of *kali-fal* from the replicator, and took a seat in the breakfast nook. The ethereal strains of one of Frenchotte's oratorios gently wafted in from the atrium. From his vantage point in the kitchen, he could still watch his daughter without her noticing his presence.

"She's such a lovely child," said a voice from behind him.

Startled, Pardek splashed the pungent blue-green liquor down the front of his tunic. He stood, turning quickly toward the voice.

Tal Shiar Chairman Koval stood in the spacious kitchen, craning his head to look at Talkath.

"How did you get in here?" Pardek demanded, his heart in the grip of an icy fist. He pitched his voice low, not wishing to alarm his daughter. But a quick glance in her direction revealed that she had heard nothing.

"A Tal Shiar chairman would be most ineffective if he were unable to come and go as he pleased," Koval said enigmatically. "Besides, your villa's transporter scramblers appear to be last year's model."

"We shouldn't even be speaking, Chairman Koval," Pardek said, realizing that he was still holding his cup—and that his grip had grown nearly tight enough to shatter it. Pardek carefully set it down on the breakfast nook table before continuing. "The hearing about the Chiarosan debacle will be held tomorrow. Not before."

"And that is why I am here *today*, Senator. I am well aware that some on the Continuing Committee have characterized my efforts in the Geminus Gulf as a failure."

Pardek found himself stifling a sardonic laugh. "Hence my use of the word 'debacle,' Chairman. How *else* could one describe what happened in the Chiaros system?"

"The Praetor now controls three new sectors of previously nonaligned space," Koval said, apparently unfazed by Pardek's comment. "That, in itself, should be cause for celebration."

Pardek wasn't convinced. The cost had been too high. "Three sectors of *nothingness,* Chairman. And the information you traded to acquire them—"

"Consisted," Koval said, interrupting, "of the identities of Romulan operatives who were already scheduled for termination. In addition, the so-called 'spy-list' I sold to the Federation includes the names of several Starfleet officers who have not engaged in espionage on our behalf, but whose continued existence our Praetor regards as dangerous. These individuals will therefore, in the eyes of Federation authorities, be strongly suspected of treason. And new double agents are even now planting evidence against these individuals, while getting in line to occupy their soon-to-be-vacant positions."

While Koval spoke, Pardek studied his face. Was Koval's right eyelid drooping slightly? Lately there had been whispers in the Senate chambers that the Tal Shiar chairman was showing incipient signs of Tuvan syndrome. Pardek could only hope that this was so; the man had thus far proved immune to all other threats.

Whether ill or hale, however, Koval still both impressed and unnerved Pardek. The Tal Shiar leader seemed to have a contingency plan for every eventuality, a talent for survival not seen in the Empire since the halcyon days of the bird-of-prey commanders of two centuries past.

"So, some benefit may accrue to the Empire after all," Pardek said noncommittally.

Koval nodded. "I would regard your public recognition of those benefits as a boon to the Praetor, to the Empire . . . and to the Tal Shiar."

"The disappearance of a strategically invaluable subspace phenomenon notwithstanding," Pardek said coolly.

"That is a minor thing, in the overall tapestry of history," Koval said with a slight shrug. "Not nearly so important, really, as what is to come."

"And just what *is* to come, Mr. Chairman?"

Koval looked thoughtful. He paused for a protracted moment, as though deciding just how much it was safe to reveal. "War," he said finally. "War on such a scale that I doubt you can imagine. And with that war will no doubt come efforts on the part of some to make . . . questionable alliances."

"Efforts by *whom?*" Pardek said, frowning.

Koval brushed the question aside. "The Empire will need the guidance of a firm hand if it is to survive its immediate future. Therefore the Tal Shiar must not be compromised. *None* of us, Senator, can afford to relax our vigilance."

Smiling beneficently, Koval gestured toward Talkath. The girl was now sitting on the atrium floor and engaging in some stretching exercises. "She really is a lovely child, Senator. You would do well to do everything in your power to protect her from harm."

With that, Koval touched his right wrist with his left hand, and an almost-inaudible chiming sound gently suffused the room. As a shimmering curtain of energy enveloped the spymaster, Pardek surmised that he had activated a site-to-site transporter unit. In the span of a few heartbeats, the dreaded Tal Shiar Chairman was gone.

Alone in the breakfast nook, Pardek sank back into his chair and looked into the atrium at his daughter, who was still intent on her workout. She was so young and innocent, so blissfully unaware of the evil that men did so casually. Koval's meaning could not have been plainer: He wanted Pardek to understand that he could spirit her away as easily as he had broken the villa's security protocols. Pardek realized only then that his hands were shaking like the spindly legs of a newborn *set'leth*.

For Talkath truly *was* all he had. She represented the future, a future he was determined to safeguard, regardless of the cost. A future that meant far more to him than any cause, any law, any principle.

EPILOGUE

Mars, Stardate 50915.5

Jean-Luc Picard hadn't been to Mars for quite some time; usually, it was to visit the Utopia Planitia Fleet Yards, where his current starship's predecessor, the *Enterprise*-D, had been built. During his departures from the shipyards' orbiting drydocks and hangars, he had often glimpsed Cydonia, a region located in the windswept northern lowlands, the site of a pair of human settlements—as well as the alleged location of the infamous "Martian face" formation, according to the myths of centuries past.

Now, he was on his way to Bradbury City with Lieutenant Commander Ranul Keru, in a shuttlecraft. It had been three days since the *Enterprise-E* had returned to McKinley Station, following its excursion into Earth's past, where the crew had fought the Borg and helped Zefram Cochrane make humanity's first warp-powered flight. During his time on McKinley, Picard had met with engineers, dealt with the well-being of his surviving crewmembers, and spent an interminable amount of time being debriefed by Starfleet's higher echelons—both from Starfleet Command and Starfleet Intelligence. He had even had to endure a protracted grilling by a pair of officers from the Federation Department of Temporal Investigations. Picard understood that Agent Dulmer and his junior partner, Lucsly, had genuine concerns about the inadvertent creation of temporal anomalies; after all, such effects could be every bit as dangerous to history's fragile tapestry as an incursion by the Borg. Still, their painstaking, exacting lines of questioning had sometimes tempted him to lose his temper.

But for all of his frustrations and problems, Picard knew that his own agonies did not cut as deeply as those carried by Keru.

The shuttle flight had been awkward and uncomfortable, and though both men tried to discuss topics unrelated to the grim reality of Hawk's death, the lapses into silence came often. It was during one of those interludes when Keru spoke, his eyes on the red-and-ocher world before them on the viewscreen.

"I don't blame *you*, Captain." He hesitated, and added more softly, "Well, I'm trying not to."

"I can see where you might, Ranul," Picard said quietly. "I was responsible for the specific mission that cost Sean his life."

"He volunteered, though. It was his own choice. His last great adventure." Keru shifted in his seat, as if uncomfortable. "I'm not sure I want to face Commander Worf any time soon, however."

Picard had expected this. "You know that Worf only did what he had to do. If there had been any way—"

"But there *was* a way," Keru said, interrupting. "*You're* proof of that. They were able to recover you

ROGUE

after you were assimilated. And that was after quite some time. Hawk had just been . . . infected. He could have . . . he might have been *saved*."

Picard kept quiet. Any response he could give would only deepen the pain. He concentrated instead on the consoles, his fingers tapping in coordinates as Mars loomed larger in front of them.

"I've thought a lot about it the last few days . . . about leaving the *Enterprise*," Keru said. "On the one hand, I think it holds too many bad memories. I wonder how I'd respond to you. How I'd feel if Worf came back aboard. How I'll feel when I'm walking those corridors, entering the mess hall or holodecks, even our quarters. All those things will remind me of *him*. Of *losing* him."

"I'm sure that if Deanna were here, she'd probably counsel you that the pain will grow less every day," Picard said.

"Yeah, she said something similar to that, along with quite a bit of other . . . crap." Keru turned to look at Picard, his eyes wet with tears. "You know, when you've lost the person you love *most* in life, the pain doesn't *ever* feel like it's going to go away. It's *not* going to be *okay*. You're never going to hold them in your arms again, never going to laugh at their stupid jokes, never going to quarrel over something trivial . . . they're never . . . just never *there* again."

Picard felt his own eyes well up with tears as he regarded his officer, and found himself again unable to respond.

Keru sniffed, and wiped his eyes. "I know you've lost family, and officers who've served under you. We've *all* lost people in our lives. Death is *inevitable*. We're supposed to realize that, we're supposed to celebrate the lives of those we've lost, we're supposed to take comfort in some place beyond death—Heaven, *Sto-Vo-Kor*, Valhalla, whatever. But there's no comfort for those still alive other than their *own* continued existence. And I'd give up years of my life to have more time with Sean.

"I always dreamed I would find someone I could love as much as Sean. I've forgotten so *many* of my dreams in life, but he . . . he was real. And he was *mine*. And I was *his*."

Keru turned away from Picard, wiping at his cheek again. Picard closed his eyes for a moment, then opened them again and began procedures for entry into the Martian atmosphere.

Leaving the shuttle docked beside one of the peripheral pressure domes, Picard shouldered a small duffel bag, and he and Keru entered Bradbury City through a tube-shaped extrusion of the municipal forcefield. Mindful of their awkwardness in the low Martian gravity, the two men made their way through a series of airlocks and settlement streets before entering an area of the city that seemed older and more antiquated than anything else they had seen here thus far. Picard noticed several people using archaic technology, and the modern, redundant interplexed forcefields—through which the salmon-tinged sky could be seen—gave way to older atmospheric domes composed of semi-opaque nanoplastic membranes; Picard noted that these antique pressure domes were of the same design as those used by the first Martian settlers more than two centuries earlier.

Picard followed Keru, who knew his way quite well, no doubt from past visits. They eventually found themselves walking along a broad, pebbled walkway. As they moved forward, surrounding them from the sides and above was a trellis, entwined with brilliant blue and red vines and creepers. Multiple forms of flowering plants, their forms elongated by the light Martian gravity, peeked through in strategic places, purple and white and green splashes amongst the bright primary colors of the vines. The scent of growing things reminded Picard of his family's vineyards in Labarre, France, which his late brother Robert had tended for so many years.

Passing the trellis, Keru and Picard continued on the walkway as it wended through a lush green lawn, similar to those the captain was used to seeing on Earth. Ahead of them was a multilevel house with transparent-walled hothouses and attached arboretums. Picard saw more examples of lush plant life through the walls.

A stocky man with reddish, gray-streaked hair emerged from the greenhouse to their left, carrying a three-pronged digging device in one hand, and a well-worn leather bag in the other. He puttered for a little bit, adjusting something in the bag, then noticed the two men standing there.

"Ranul!" he said, dropping his bag to the ground. He trotted over and heartily shook the Trill's hand, then gathered him in for a hug. Breaking away, he turned to look at Picard.

"Rhyst, this is Captain Jean-Luc Picard," Keru said, gesturing toward his superior officer. "Captain Picard, this is Rhyst Hawk."

Picard noticed that the elder man's smile dimmed considerably, but the handshake was firm and polite. Rhyst had a strong grip, and Picard imagined him to be only a few years his senior. "Welcome to Mars, Captain Picard," he said.

"It's a pleasure to meet you, sir. I only wish I could visit under different circumstances."

"Yes, well, uh, come on up to the house," Rhyst said, looking distracted. "It can get a wee bit hot out here around the nurseries. I think we've got some cool juice of some sort to offer you."

Picard and Keru followed Rhyst inside. The interior of the house was decorated eclectically, with knickknacks

355

sharing wall space with shelves full of old books. While Rhyst went off to get the drinks, Picard perused one of the shelves. He was pleased to find volumes dating back to the 20th and 21st centuries—he saw works by Hesterman, Tormé, and Zabel. A leather-bound copy of *The Martian Chronicles* by Ray Bradbury—the colony's namesake—was displayed proudly beside a dog-eared biography of Lieutenant John Mark Kelly, the leader of an early ill-fated Mars mission. It was rare to find books this old now; the few paper products to survive the Third World War had long since deteriorated, and today's books were almost exclusively produced on padds.

"Here you are. Some fresh tangerine-moova juice," said Rhyst, appearing in the entryway and holding out two glasses of cool, pink liquid. A woman appeared in the doorway behind Rhyst, and—upon seeing Keru—let out a slight yelp and rushed to hug him.

Picard sipped the drink the older man had offered him, as Keru smoothed the hair of the woman who was now clutching him. Eventually, they broke away from each other, and Keru introduced Picard to Camille Hawk. She gestured toward the bookshelf.

"One of my weaknesses," she said, her eyes moist. "Old books."

"I was marveling at the collection," Picard said. "I have a few ancient books of my own, but I doubt I could even fill one of your shelves."

"Well, I'd always been told that you were quite the archaeologist," she responded, smiling slightly. "Each to their own form of preserving the past, eh?"

"Yes," he agreed, returning her smile.

Camille moved over to one bookshelf and opened a leather-bound volume she found there. She held it out to Picard. He saw that it was a 1911 copy of *Peter and*

Wendy by James M. Barrie, and remembered his own mother reading the story of Peter Pan to him when he was a child.

"This was one of Sean's favorite books growing up," Camille said. "Even before he read any of *my* books, he loved this one."

"I think that's where he got his love for pirate stories," said Keru.

Rhyst gestured toward another room. "Why don't we sit in the living room?"

They moved to the living room, which featured a Napoleonic decor. Camille made herself comfortable in an easy chair, while Picard and Rhyst sat on a low divan, and Keru in another nearby chair. Camille placed the old book on the coffee table, its pages open to an illustration of a lonely and wounded Peter Pan standing atop Marooner's Rock in the rising water. Picard read the quote beneath it: "To Die will be an Awfully Big Adventure."

I hope that's true, he thought.

Picard set the bag he'd been carrying onto the plushly carpeted floor, near his feet. His eyebrows scrunched together slightly as he composed himself to speak. He knew that nothing could take the pain out of his first words.

"I'm very sorry about Sean."

Rhyst put his drink down on the coffee table before him, and stared at Picard coolly. "Yes, well, we got a message to that effect from you, or from one of your assistants. Got one from Starfleet, too. And from Ranul, of course. It's been a difficult few days. Sean's brothers, Darey and Jason, are on their way back home to join us in a . . . celebration of Sean's life."

Camille leaned forward, looking at Picard. "Please don't think us insensitive or uncaring, Captain, but we've raised our sons to believe that life is to be lived and savored. It's uncertain when or how any of us may be lost to this life—and we simply don't *know* what lies in the next—so we have tried to instill in our boys the importance of joy and love, adventure and passion."

"You instilled those values well," Picard said.

"We heard yesterday from the *Yorktown*'s Captain Kentrav," Camille said. "He was Sean's first commanding officer. We've been touched by how Starfleet has reached out to us." She paused for a moment, looking at Keru, then Rhyst, then back at Picard. "Does this sort of . . . personal attention happen with *every* family that loses a son or daughter in Starfleet?"

"Unfortunately, no," said Picard, sighing. "Resources and assignments do not always allow for it."

"Then why are you here?" asked Rhyst.

Picard pulled up the bag from the floor and unfastened the opening. He retrieved several items from it, placing them on the table next to the book. "I wanted to bring you Sean's personal effects. Sometimes it takes months for this type of material to be sent back to the families."

Rhyst leaned forward, his eyes locking with Picard's. "But you could have sent it with Ranul. Why are *you* here?"

"I suppose I wanted to see where Sean had come from. What had shaped him before he entered Starfleet."

"I was never as supportive as I could have been of his choice to join Starfleet," said Rhyst. "I guess I always thought he did it just to escape the boredom of the Martian suburbs. All of the boys have had . . . wanderlust. But Sean was always a smart one—*uncannily* smart. Maybe Starfleet was a good fit."

"It was the *best* fit for him. He was an excellent officer," Picard said soberly.

"To tell you the truth, I've always resented Starfleet a bit. It's always been so Earth-driven. I'm a Martian, and

I've always felt as though Earth treated Mars as if it was just a province. My ancestors fought and died to be free of the Earth consortium, but what have we become since the War of Martian Independence? A garage for Earth's starships."

"Hmmm," Picard grunted, not sure how to respond.

For a moment, the four of them sat quietly. Finally, Keru broke the silence. "Camille, why don't we get something more to drink in the kitchen?"

Keru stood, holding his hand out to help the older woman up. She put her arm around his waist lovingly, and the two exited the room. Keru looked back once, catching Picard's eye, before they were out of sight.

He's going to leave the Enterprise, Picard thought. *Maybe not right away, but he* will *leave.* Picard couldn't say he blamed Keru for making that decision.

And then he was alone, with Rhyst.

Rhyst sniffed, and turned toward Picard. "Can you tell me what *good* came from Sean joining Starfleet?" He held up his hand, motioning Picard to be quiet for a moment. "I don't mean in the abstract. Starfleet has hundreds of thousands of cadets joining its ranks each year, thousands of officers, hundreds of captains. My son sacrificed his *life* for that organization. Why *him?* What did it accomplish?"

Picard took no offense at the older man's pointed questions. They were the same imponderables with which he himself had to grapple each and every time he lost a member of his crew.

"Your son was *not* just one of a thousand officers to me, sir. He was a valued member of my crew, and one whom I trusted with my life. And he accomplished some truly great things."

Picard hesitated for a moment. He knew he would have to edit any reference to Section 31 from the story he was about to tell. But Hawk's father deserved to hear about his son's finest hour: the mission in the Chiaros system.

"About six months ago, your son went above and beyond the call of duty to defend his ship, its crew, and his own principles. And he did it without a moment's hesitation or doubt . . ."

About the Authors

Andy Mangels is the author of the best-selling book *Star Wars: The Essential Guide to Characters*, as well as *Beyond Mulder & Scully: The Mysterious Characters of The X-Files* and *From Scream to Dawson's Creek: The Phenomenal Career of Kevin Williamson*. Mangels has written for *The Hollywood Reporter, The Advocate, Just Out, Cinescape, Gauntlet, SFX, Sci-Fi Universe, Outweek, Frontiers, Portland Mercury, Comics Buyer's Guide*, and scores of other entertainment and lifestyle magazines. He has also written licensed material based on properties from Lucasfilm, Paramount, New Line Cinema, Universal Studios, Warner Bros., Microsoft, Abrams-Gentile, and Platinum Studios. His comic-book work has been seen from DC Comics, Marvel Comics, Dark Horse, Wildstorm, Image, Innovation, WaRP Graphics, Topps, and others, and he was the editor of the award-winning *Gay Comics* anthology for eight years. In what little spare time he has, he likes to country dance and collect uniforms.

Michael A. Martin's short fiction has appeared in *The Magazine of Fantasy & Science Fiction*. He was the regular co-writer (with Andy Mangels) of Marvel Comics' monthly *Star Trek: Deep Space Nine* comic-book series, and co-wrote other *Star Trek* stories for Marvel and Wildstorm. From 1998 through 2000, Martin was one of the principal writers for Atlas Editions' *Star Trek Uni-*

verse subscription card series. Martin has also written for the British *Star Trek* monthly magazine, Grolier Books, and Platinum Studios. *Rogue* is the first *Star Trek* novel to bear his name. When not hunkered over a keyboard in his basement writing office, he reads voraciously, watches documentaries, and performs folk ballads for the amusement of his two-year-old son, James; Martin lives in Portland, Oregon with his wife, their aforementioned son, and too many computers.

Look for STAR TREK fiction from Pocket Books

Star Trek®: The Original Series

Star Trek: Deep Space Nine®

Star Trek®: New Frontier

Star Trek®: Invasion!

#1 • *First Strike* • Diane Carey
#2 • *The Soldiers of Fear* • Dean Wesley Smith & Kristine Kathryn Rusch
#3 • *Time's Enemy* • L.A. Graf
#4 • *The Final Fury* • Dafydd ab Hugh
Invasion! Omnibus • various

Star Trek®: Day of Honor

#1 • *Ancient Blood* • Diane Carey
#2 • *Armageddon Sky* • L.A. Graf
#3 • *Her Klingon Soul* • Michael Jan Friedman
#4 • *Treaty's Law* • Dean Wesley Smith & Kristine Kathryn Rusch
The Television Episode • Michael Jan Friedman
Day of Honor Omnibus • various

Star Trek®: The Captain's Table

#1 • *War Dragons* • L.A. Graf
#2 • *Dujonian's Hoard* • Michael Jan Friedman
#3 • *The Mist* • Dean Wesley Smith & Kristine Kathryn Rusch
#4 • *Fire Ship* • Diane Carey
#5 • *Once Burned* • Peter David
#6 • *Where Sea Meets Sky* • Jerry Oltion
The Captain's Table Omnibus • various

Star Trek®: The Dominion War

#1 • *Behind Enemy Lines* • John Vornholt
#2 • *Call to Arms...* • Diane Carey
#3 • *Tunnel Through the Stars* • John Vornholt
#4 • *...Sacrifice of Angels* • Diane Carey

Star Trek®: The Badlands

#1 • Susan Wright
#2 • Susan Wright

Star Trek®: Dark Passions

#1 • Susan Wright
#2 • Susan Wright

Star Trek®: Section 31

#1 • *Cloak* • S. D. Perry
#2 • *Rogue* • Andy Mangels and Michael A. Martin

Star Trek® Books available in Trade Paperback

Omnibus Editions
    Invasion! Omnibus • various
    Day of Honor Omnibus • various
    The Captain's Table Omnibus • various
    Star Trek: Odyssey • William Shatner with Judith and Garfield Reeves-
        Stevens

Other Books
    Legends of the Ferengi • Ira Steven Behr & Robert Hewitt Wolfe
    Strange New Worlds, vols. I, II, III, and IV • Dean Wesley Smith, ed.
    Adventures in Time and Space • Mary P. Taylor
    Captain Proton: Defender of the Earth • D.W. "Prof" Smith
    New Worlds, New Civilizations • Michael Jan Friedman
    The Lives of Dax • Marco Palmieri, ed.
    The Klingon Hamlet • Wil'yam Shex'pir
    Enterprise Logs • Carol Greenburg, ed.